PENGU

SOWING THE

Sowing the Seeds of Love

TARA HEAVEY

PENGUIN BOOKS

PENGUIN BOOKS

Published by the Penguin Group
Penguin Books Ltd, 80 Strand, London WC2R 0RL, England
Penguin Group (USA) Inc., 375 Hudson Street, New York, New York 10014, USA
Penguin Group (Canada), 90 Eglinton Avenue East, Suite 700, Toronto, Ontario, Canada M4P 2Y3
(a division of Pearson Penguin Canada Inc.)
Penguin Ireland, 25 St Stephen's Green, Dublin 2, Ireland (a division of Penguin Books Ltd)
Penguin Group (Australia), 250 Camberwell Road,
Camberwell, Victoria 3124, Australia (a division of Pearson Australia Group Pty Ltd)
Penguin Books India Pvt Ltd, 11 Community Centre, Panchsheel Park, New Delhi – 110 017, India
Penguin Group (NZ), 67 Apollo Drive, Rosedale, North Shore 0632, New Zealand
(a division of Pearson New Zealand Ltd)
Penguin Books (South Africa) (Pty) Ltd, 24 Sturdee Avenue, Rosebank, Johannesburg 2196, South Africa

Penguin Books Ltd, Registered Offices: 80 Strand, London WC2R 0RL, England

www.penguin.com

First published by Penguin Ireland 2009
Published in Penguin Books 2010

1

Copyright © Tara Heavey, 2009
All rights reserved

The moral right of the author has been asserted

Typeset by Palimpsest Book Production Limited, Grangemouth, Stirlingshire
Printed in England by Clays Ltd, St Ives plc

ISBN: 978–1–844–88207–6

www.greenpenguin.co.uk

Penguin Books is committed to a sustainable future
for our business, our readers and our planet.
The book in your hands is made from paper
certified by the Forest Stewardship Council.

For my parents

The Winter Garden

And the trees were so glad to have the children back again that they had covered themselves with blossoms, and were waving their arms gently above the children's heads. The birds were flying about and twittering with delight, and the flowers were looking up through the green grass and laughing.

Oscar Wilde, 'The Selfish Giant'

I've been here before in my dreams. This magical place, where the tunnels of roses go on and on. Every hue imaginable. Every scent known to humankind.

Reds. Deep and dark. Familiar to me as my own blood. I bow my head and steal the scent, bury my nose in the folds. I'm taken aback as my senses flood – the confectionery aroma, the cola cubes of my youth, crammed with sugar and nostalgia.

I move to the yellows. I cup one in my hands and the colours swirl and unfurl, capture and enrapture. Good enough to eat so I do, one petal at a time, the nectar of the gods.

Then I'm immersed in the pinks, the petals smooth and satiny. When I crowd into them the scent is less heady but sweeter, more innocent; it stays with me longer. I brush the petals with my fingertips. It's like touching the cheeks of a thousand babies. A bittersweet happiness wells up in me and I can't stop touching them.

The delicate, delectable whites, more subtle in fragrance but no less lovely. My beautiful flowery girls, which I can't quite reach because my vision is fading and blurring, crumbling as reality dawns. Real life blots out everything. I wake newly bereft.

I

It was a sunny Saturday morning of freedom. The sky shone ice blue. Liam skipped alongside Aoife, his entire body grinning up at her. She looked down at her son, crimson scarf wrapped several times around his scrawny little neck, and couldn't help but smile. It was that kind of day and Liam was that kind of boy. His childish antennae seemed to be tuning in to her new-found sense of optimism. It was good, this feeling. The first time she'd noticed it in she didn't know how long, certainly since moving to Dublin.

The upheaval had been tougher than she had anticipated or would ever admit. She put on the bright smile – the happy voice – when she spoke to her mother on the phone. But there were times when the isolation threatened to overwhelm her. It was as if she was looking at the world from behind glass.

Her neighbours seemed impossible to get to know. She barely saw them, barricaded as they all were behind their front doors. Maybe it was just the wrong time of year – late October – dark evenings, autumn electricity in the air.

But there was something different about today.

Today felt like hope.

'Here we are.' She stopped and dragged Liam to a halt beside her.

'This isn't the sweetshop.'

'It's a different type of sweetshop. A very special one.'

This pacified him and he allowed himself to be led into the shady interior. The lady behind the counter gave Aoife a nod of recognition and her heart rose even higher.

The shop was like something you might expect to find in the old town of Barcelona. The type of store you might stumble across by accident, having become lost down a series of narrow, winding streets. You may have missed it if you hadn't had to leap out of the path of a manic young Catalan on his moped. And *what* you would have missed. It certainly wasn't the type of place Aoife would have expected to find in the outskirts of the city centre. But each day she was discovering anew how much Dublin had changed since her childhood visits. How much of the heart had been ripped out of the city. Georgian buildings knocked down to make way for fast-food outlets and coffee-shop chains. Faceless plate glass where graceful archways and doorways had once stood.

Progress.

This, at least, was a positive change.

It was a treasure trove of goodies. They had gourmet sausages, artisan biscuits, organic salmon, farmyard cheeses, handcrafted chocolates, homemade preserves and luxury shortbread. Her mother would love an Irish porter cake. With some Irish breakfast tea in a presentation caddy. She herself wouldn't mind the strawberries in Belgian chocolate. She could feel her mouth starting to water.

And then there were the sweets. Jar upon jar and row upon row of nostalgia: gobstoppers, bonbons, apple sours, liquorice laces, chocolate mice, iced caramels, bullseyes, aniseed balls, flying saucers, pear drops, striped humbugs, butter humbugs, clove rocks . . . Only the candy cigarettes were missing. Presumably now illegal.

Liam's mouth was agape. 'Can I have whatever I like?'

'Tell me what you'd like first. You can have five things.'

'Only five! I want –'

'Do you want the sweets or not?'

'Yes, I do.' Liam clung to the back of Aoife's leg and twisted himself from one foot to the other. 'Those ones.' He pointed decisively at the chocolate mice.

'Just them? Nothing else?'

He nodded vigorously and held up his hand, fingers outstretched. 'Five.'

'Five what?'

'Five mouses.'

'Five mouses what?'

'Please.'

One other customer stood between them and the counter, an older woman, perhaps seventy. Aoife couldn't help noticing how well groomed she was. Such elegance. Such co-ordination. She looked down at her own navy fleece and jeans and felt ashamed. The woman was buying Earl Grey tea and fancy biscuits. How fitting. She examined the other's face in profile. Her skin was like rice paper but her jawline barely sagged. 'Well preserved' was how Aoife's father would have described her.

The woman completed her purchase and left the shop, whereupon the lady behind the counter turned her attention to Aoife. The look she gave her was mischievous. Like a kid with a secret. She leaned forward ever so slightly. 'You'd never guess she murdered her own husband.'

'Pardon?' Perhaps she'd misheard.

The woman inclined her head towards the door. 'Mrs Prendergast. You'd never guess.'

'You mean that old woman who was just in here?'

'That's the one.'

'You mean she was convicted and everything?'

'Well, no.' Here the story floundered. 'They never found the body. If you don't have a body you can't have a trial, apparently. But everyone around here knows she did it.'

'How do they know?'

'Well. There's that garden of hers for a start. Hasn't been touched since the day he disappeared forty years ago.'

Aoife laughed. 'I'd hardly call that proof.'

The other woman's face closed and Aoife regretted her words. She'd been enjoying the impromptu conversation.

'What can I get you?' The woman was suddenly businesslike.

'I'll have five chocolate mice, please. And two flying saucers for old times' sake.'

That night, Liam couldn't sleep, so she let him into her bed. She knew she shouldn't and that it was setting a bad precedent, but a large part of her didn't care. The part that was empty and lonely and homeless. She needed the closeness as much as he did.

Although there was an entire double bed in which to expand, his sleeping body invariably gravitated towards hers. She was lying on her back, staring into the dark, when –

'Mummy.'

She'd thought he was asleep. 'Yes, Liam.'

'If Daddy was still here, would I be allowed into your bed?'

'Of course you would. Don't you remember coming into bed with me and Daddy when you had a bad dream or when you were sick?'

'No.'

'Well, you did. All the time.'

'Oh.'

They were quiet for a while.

'Night-night, Mummy.'

'Night-night, Liam.'

A few breaths later he was asleep, his knees sticking into her lower back. As if he were trying to burrow back into her womb.

2

Monday morning, and a nine o'clock lecture. Not a good combination. As Aoife watched her students stroll casually into the lecture theatre at ten past the hour, yawning and scratching, she had to stifle the urge to yell. There was no point in starting without them and lecturing to an empty theatre. Having said that, when they arrived, they just sat there like a pack of zombies anyhow.

Irish people were late for everything, she knew that. It still infuriated her. Maybe she was just too English.

At last. A reasonable complement had arrived so she could start. She cleared her throat, hoping they'd shut up straight away. 'Right. Today, people, we're going to continue our discussion on the Romantic poets.' She sensed some of them zoning out already. 'John Keats. I'm sure many of you are familiar with his Odes.'

If they were, they were keeping it to themselves.

'"Ode to a Nightingale" and "Ode to a Grecian Urn" are the most famous, of course, but right now we're going to focus on "Ode to Psyche".'

They looked positively thrilled at the prospect.

'Can anyone tell me about the legend of Cupid and Psyche?' She gazed out at the sea of young faces. Some were studying the blank pages of their notebooks, lest she suddenly spring on them. Others, with whom her words had barely registered, stared blankly into space, their faces grey from too much alcohol and not enough sleep. 'Anyone?'

No one. She sighed.

'Venus, the goddess of love, becomes insanely jealous of this mortal woman called Psyche, who's rumoured to be better-looking than she is. So she asks her son, Cupid, to shoot Psyche with one of his golden arrows and cause her to fall in love with the vilest creature on earth. The trouble is, as soon as Cupid sets eyes on Psyche, he falls in love with her himself. So, he abducts her and keeps her imprisoned in his walled garden. Not that she minds all that much, seeing as how he's the best-looking winged man in mythology.'

This got a few appreciative smiles from some of the girls.

'The image of the walled garden is interesting, because right throughout the Victorian era – an era in which the legend of Cupid and Psyche was rehashed many times – it was used as a symbol of female sexuality.'

Some of the boys seemed amused – or was it bemused? – as she related this fact. As if she were far too old to be concerning herself with such matters. She supposed that, technically, she was old enough to be their mother – if she had given birth in her teens. Which was hard to wrap her head around, given that Liam was hardly more than a baby still.

A new sound was emanating from the back of the theatre, unmistakable in its rise and fall.

Someone had started to snore.

3

They were on another of their weekend expeditions, getting to know their new neighbourhood, when Aoife saw something she hadn't witnessed in all her time living in London.

'Mummy, what's that man doing to that lady?'

'Oh, Jesus Christ. Hey!' she yelled at the height of her voice, and started to run.

A woman was being dragged along the pavement by a younger man. More accurately, he was attempting to relieve her of her handbag and she was hanging on for dear life. The man, clearly startled by Aoife's intervention, let go of the bag and sprinted in the opposite direction. She reached the woman and crouched beside her. 'Are you all right?'

'Do I look all right?' She pulled herself up into a sitting position.

Aoife was as surprised by her response as she was by her upper-class English accent. And even more surprised to discover that she was the woman she'd seen the previous week in the Good Food Store. Mrs Prendergast, wasn't it? She held out her hand. The older woman ignored it and struggled to her feet, unaided but shaken.

'I'll take you home. Where do you live?'

'There's absolutely no need.'

'I insist.' Aoife took hold of Mrs Prendergast's elbow, but the latter gave her a look of such ferocity that she withdrew her hand immediately. No wonder her neighbours thought her capable of murder.

'I'm quite able to walk, thank you very much.'

'Okay. I'll ring the police, then.' Aoife reached for her mobile.

'You will not. I have no desire for a plethora of PC Plods to be trampling all over my carpets. I've got my bag and all my belongings. I just want to put the whole unpleasant business behind me. So, if you don't mind . . .'

'Actually, I do. I'm walking you home and that's the end of it.'

Aoife held her own as Mrs Prendergast attempted to stare her down, her eyes unnaturally bright. Eventually, she snorted and began to cross the street. Aoife followed a few paces behind, hand in hand with a wide-eyed Liam.

'Where are we going, Mummy?'

'We're walking this lady home.'

'Why?'

'To make sure she gets there safely.'

'Where does she live?'

'I don't know.'

'Will there be any little boys there?'

'I don't know, Liam. I shouldn't think so.'

'But why –'

'Here. Have a sweetie.'

Mrs Prendergast had turned into the driveway of an elegant old red-brick. A corner house.

Aoife hoisted Liam up the steps to the plum-coloured front door and stood behind the tall, slim, almost ramrod-straight figure. She imagined her collapsing the moment she was alone.

Mrs Prendergast stood inside the hall now, facing her. 'As you can see, I'm home in one piece.' She swallowed. 'Thank you.'

'You're welcome. Would you like me to call a doctor for you?'

'No, I would not. Now, goodbye.'

The door was already closing when Liam started to run on the spot. 'Pee-pee, Mummy. I need to do a pee-pee.'

Oh, crap. She looked at Mrs Prendergast. 'I don't suppose . . .'

Mrs Prendergast rolled her eyes theatrically and opened the door just wide enough for Liam to dart through.

She wasn't seriously going to leave Aoife standing there? Ungracious old cow.

'I strongly suggest you let me in too, unless you want piss all over your floor.'

Mrs Prendergast glared at her, then flung the door wide open.

'Thank you. Where . . . ?'

'Up the stairs and on your left.' Her voice was like fine bone china.

As Aoife ran up the stairs, two at a time, dragging Liam in her wake, she felt a pang of guilt. This poor lady had just been mugged and here she was being mean to her. But, by God, she was so antagonistic.

The interior of the house was beautiful, from the graceful curve of the mahogany banister to the jewelled patterns that the stained glass threw on the burnished wooden floor. Safely inside the bathroom, Aoife stared absently at the pure white blind as Liam tinkled into the toilet. She inched it away from the window and found, to her surprise, that she was looking down at the remnants of a walled garden, paths, now overgrown, around the edges and dissecting the centre in a criss-cross pattern, stunted old apple trees choking with ivy and a tumbledown archway. Aoife imagined it as it might have been in its heyday, swathed in rambling roses. Soft pink, she thought. And the body of Mr Prendergast reclining in his shallow grave . . .

'Mummy, I can't reach the towel.'

She handed it to him and replaced it when he'd finished, trying but failing to leave it exactly as they'd found it.

Mrs Prendergast was waiting for them by the front door. Quite pointedly, it had to be said. Aoife would have loved a good nose around. A door leading off the hallway stood ajar, offering a tantalizing view of a room crammed with antiques. But Mrs Prendergast wasn't offering any guided tours: instead, she was holding the door open, nice and wide.

'Thank you very much, Mrs Prendergast. We're sorry for troubling you. What do you say, Liam?'

'You've got a cut on your knee.' Liam looked up at Mrs Prendergast from his knee-high vantage-point. 'You should get your mummy to put a plaster on it.'

'Thank you, I will. Now if you don't mind . . .'

'Yes, of course. 'Bye now.'

The door had shut behind them before they'd even reached the top step.

They set off for home, but Aoife couldn't resist taking a closer look at the garden. Oblivious to Liam's complaints, she skirted the perimeter of the wall, which was almost a perfect square and enclosed about an acre of ground. Then she came across a wrought-iron gate, tall and forbidding, black paint flaking off in lumps. It was locked tight, of course. The padlock looked as if it had been designed to keep out a marauding army, the heavy chain wrapped around itself many times.

Regardless of passers-by, Aoife pressed her right cheek to the cold metal and swivelled her eyes as far left as they would go. She thought how comical she must look to anyone on the other side. But there was nobody on the other side. Nothing much, in fact, except dense undergrowth. And the wall, of course, which was an attractive reddish-brown, much of it scrambled with dark-green ivy. The two colours complemented one another strikingly well. As she peered inside, she was just able to detect a pattern in the planting, only discernible because the garden lay sleeping in its winter sparseness.

There were two lines of unruly shrubs, which met in the middle at a stagnant pond. At least, she presumed there was water, but so much duckweed grew on the surface that it looked solid green.

There was something magical – romantic – about the concept of a walled garden. Aoife had always loved them. But she hadn't expected to find one so close to her new Dublin home. Still intact, if a little ragged around the edges. Buried treasure. She felt as if she was the first person ever to see the garden. As in *really* see it. Or, at least, the first person in a very long time.

She went home. But the garden stayed with her.

Myrtle turned the key and the padlock fell into her hand. The gate, newly installed, opened in one easy, fluid motion. Delight surged through her as she entered the garden. Everywhere there was growth, tangled and haphazard. Where one woman might have seen disorder and chaos, she saw only possibility. She smiled and twirled and was at home.

4

It was a week later to the day, almost to the hour.

Mrs Prendergast's front garden was mainly gravel, bordered by a few well-spaced, orderly, low-maintenance shrubs. The appearance of the front of the house bore no relation to the wilderness at the back. A grand flight of sombre stone steps led up to the front door, which was imposing and swirled with stained glass.

Aoife was standing in front of it. Somehow her feet had led her to the top step where she stood, regarding the tarnished brass knocker. No bell. What had brought her to this point? This wasn't usual behaviour for her. Maybe it was because she was starting a new life. Possibilities had awoken within her.

'Can I knock, Mummy?'

She lifted Liam up and he rapped the brass against the wood. Nothing happened. After an appropriate interval, she told him to knock again.

Still nothing.

'Shall I try again, Mummy?'

'No. She can't be in. Let's go.'

Feeling foolish, she descended the steps, then crossed the gravel briskly, anxious now to get out of there and put the folly behind her, convinced that Mrs Prendergast was peering out of an upstairs window, mocking her.

But behind her the front door opened. Liam heard it too. 'Look, Mummy, she's in!'

Mrs Prendergast was gazing down at them, her demeanour more forbidding, even, than Aoife remembered. She was regretting this already. But she went back up the steps until she was standing, once again, at the entrance to the house. Mrs Prendergast raised an eyebrow quizzically. 'In need of my facilities again?'

Aoife smiled nervously. 'We came to see how you were.'

'Couldn't be better.'

An awkward silence ensued.

'Was that it?'

'Look, Mummy, a doggy.'

A wet muzzle pushed past Mrs Prendergast's legs, followed by a canine face, as friendly as its owner's was not. A rotund body, a frenetic tail. The pong of elderly female dog. A golden retriever. She smiled open-mouthedly at Liam, as at a long-lost friend, her breath coming in hot, pungent waves.

'What's its name?' Liam asked.

'Harriet.'

'Is it a boy doggy or a girl doggy?'

'A girl, of course. Harriet is a girl's name.'

Aoife looked sternly at Mrs Prendergast. How on earth was a four-year-old boy supposed to know that? But she checked herself. Now was not the time. Instead: 'Beautiful day, isn't it?'

'Hmph.' That was what it sounded like.

'Look, Mrs Prendergast, since you're obviously in no mood for a conversation, I'll come straight to the point.'

'So you do want something.'

'It's about your garden.'

'What about it?' Her bearing was rigid, her expression more guarded.

'It must be hard for you to manage such a large area by yourself.'

Mrs Prendergast stared at Aoife from beneath hooded lids, as if she were something she might like to squash.

'What I mean is, it could be so lovely.'

'What is your point, my dear?'

Aoife guessed that 'my dear' was ironic.

So preoccupied were the two women with one another that they didn't notice Liam and Harriet inching into the hall.

'I could help you with it.'

'No, thank you. Harriet!' Mrs Prendergast looked around for her dog.

'What I mean is, not just you and me doing a bit of weeding. We'd get a few people together to work on it.'

'What people?'

'I don't know yet. I was thinking I could advertise.'

'Absolutely not. Harriet!' Mrs Prendergast craned her neck past Aoife.

'I think they went that way.' Aoife indicated indoors. Mrs Prendergast turned and disappeared into a door leading off the hall. Aoife could hear Liam's high-pitched giggles coming from inside. Should she . . . ? She wasn't strictly invited – she wasn't invited at all – but if Mrs Prendergast wanted Liam out, well, Aoife was the woman for the job.

She stepped over the threshold and stood behind Mrs Prendergast at the entrance to the room.

Liam was hunkered on the floor beside Harriet, who was lying on her back, her nose stretched out to the ultimate. He was rubbing her belly while she rotated one of her back legs in the air as if riding half of an invisible bicycle. Aoife glanced at Mrs Prendergast. She didn't look as stern now. And they said never to work with children or animals.

'What's that smell?' Liam lifted his head and wrinkled his nose.

'Liam!' The mortification.

'Oh, that'll be Harriet. She farts a lot.'

Liam rolled around on the floor beside the dog, his little-boy laugh full-bodied, infectious. Mrs Prendergast's lips twitched at one corner. Aoife knew an opportunity when she saw one. 'I really wish you'd reconsider. It could be wonderful. Imagine the garden restored to its former glory. We could grow fruit, vegetables, herbs . . .'

'What is your name?'

'Pardon? Oh, my God, I'm so sorry. I'm Aoife. Aoife Madigan. And this is Liam.'

'You're English.' For once it wasn't an accusation.

'Yes, I am.'

'Where are you from?'

'London. As I –'

'Are you married?'

'Used to be. Are you?'

'Used to be. But I expect you know that already.'

Aoife felt herself blush, but Mrs Prendergast didn't appear to notice.

'Are you Church of England?'

'No, Catholic.'

'Oh. Pity. The Mothers' Union are always looking for new blood. Like a pack of vampires.'

'No, sorry.'

Sorry? Why was she apologizing for her religion?

'And I take it you have lots of gardening experience.'

'Oh, yes, lots.' Growing sunflowers in the garden in Upper Norwood when she was nine.

'Anyway, I'm selling it.'

'What?'

'The garden. I'm selling it for development.'

'You can't do that.'

'I beg your pardon?'

'I mean . . . I didn't mean . . .'

'I think you'll find I'm entitled to do whatever I like with my own property.'

'I know, I know. Of course you are. It just seems such a terrible shame. It could be so beautiful. I'm sure it was once.' She looked searchingly into Mrs Prendergast's face but found no response. Not even a flicker.

Aoife sighed. 'Come on, Liam.'

Liam righted himself. 'Please can me and my mummy have your garden?' he asked Mrs Prendergast. 'I want to grow her some flowers.'

The silence was as embarrassing as it was deafening.

'Let's go.' Aoife scooped up her son before he had a chance to say anything else and headed out of the front door. On the step, she turned to speak but the door was already closed. She felt heartbroken and didn't know why.

5

She tried to put it out of her mind because, really, what was the point?

Then one day, not so very long afterwards, she was in the Good Food Store, rooting around for something that would taste homemade but wasn't, when she felt a tap on her shoulder. She jumped. She didn't know enough people to expect a shoulder-tap. 'Oh. Hello, Mrs Prendergast.'

'You can have the garden.'

'What?'

'I said you can have the garden. Do what you like with it, I don't care. I'll still own it, of course.'

'Of course.'

'Just let me know when you intend to start.'

'I will. Thank you.'

The older woman nodded curtly and was gone.

Aoife floated home. It was only when she got back to her kitchen that she discovered she'd forgotten her groceries.

She had no idea why the garden meant so much to her, perhaps because it was a perfect reflection of herself, desolate, laid bare by a long, hard winter and years of neglect, pruned by harsh frosts, icy winds and months of darkness where once all was lush and green with growth and optimism. But still.

Still.

Just below the surface new life was waiting to push out of the darkness and into the light. Just as she had always known it to be, in a place deep inside that she'd forgotten. If she could only help it to grow again – well, it would be as if all things were possible.

So it was in this frame of mind that she set out one blowy morning in mid-December for the Good Food Store, clasping a stiff white piece of paper folded down the middle in one sharp crease. She was relieved to see a different woman behind the counter. Girl, really. She couldn't have been more than twenty. Slight with shoulder-length dark hair. The kind of girl who absorbed the light rather than reflected it. She seemed miserable for someone who spent her working day surrounded by such glorious produce but Aoife, of all people, shouldn't judge.

'Can I put a notice up?' Aoife gestured towards the board.

The girl took a break from staring into space. 'Go right ahead.' She went back to staring.

Aoife would have loved to know what she was looking at. She stole a thumb tack from a poster for Pilates and secured her own notice in as advantageous a position as possible. Then she stood back to read it for the fiftieth time that morning:

Local garden in urgent need of care and attention.
Community effort required.
All those interested, please bring your green fingers along
at 8.30 pm next Monday night, 16 December, to . . .

She supplied her address. She'd even drawn a few flowers in the top right-hand corner. What a plonker. Was she really going through with this? Yes, she was. She turned away before she changed her mind again. On to more mundane matters: dinner. She checked out the minuscule vegetable department. 'Do you have any green beans?' She almost felt bad for dragging the girl back to a reality in which she clearly did not want to exist.

'We can't get Irish green beans. They all seem to be from Kenya so we don't stock them any more.'

Aoife nodded and left the shop. She tugged her woollen hat further down around her ears, as if to contain all the thoughts that were colliding inside her head. So they couldn't get Irish-grown green beans. How interesting. She pulled on her gloves and stifled a small smile. If she didn't know better she'd think she was happy.

6

It was 8.31 p.m. on the evening of 16 December. So where were they, the milling throngs? Had all the cushion-plumping, crumb-sweeping, coffee-brewing, biscuit-buying and notice-tacking been to no avail? She'd even bought a few pot plants so that she looked the part.

The doorbell rang and her heart leaped. She rushed out of the kitchen, slowing as she neared the front door. Calm. She opened the door. A man.

'Hello.'

'Hello.' He doffed his hat, delighting and surprising her at the same time.

'Are you here about the garden?'

'I am.'

'Please come in.'

Someone. It was someone.

She stood aside to let him pass. He was shorter than her, neat and dapper, closely trimmed beard – dark, even though he must be over seventy.

He took off his pristine coat, his movements deft and quick, to reveal an immaculate grey pinstriped suit. She felt messy and ungainly beside him. Too much time concentrating on her house and not enough on her hair, which was in the same ponytail she'd gathered it into that morning. She had kidded herself that the loose strands were softening tendrils. In reality, they were just straggly bits. Taking his coat, she ushered him into the sitting room.

'You're the first to arrive.' She felt stupid and nervous, as always with small-talk. 'Would you like some coffee?'

'That would be lovely.'

She thought she detected the faintest trace of an accent. She busied herself in the kitchen with the kettle, transferring biscuits on to a plate, fumbling with the wrapper, fussing about with milk and a sugar bowl – something to rely on when the evening fanned out before her in all its uncertainty.

She carried everything into the sitting room on a large tray. The man stood up when she entered, took it from her and set it on the coffee-table.

'Thank you.'

'Uri.'

'Thank you, Uri. I'm Aoife. Sorry, I should have mentioned that before.'

The doorbell. Someone else! She ran out to open it.

Her eyes widened in surprise. It was the sad girl from the food store.

'Hello.'

'Hello.'

'Come in. Can I take your coat?' She led her into the sitting room. 'I'm Aoife.'

'Emily.' The girl half smiled.

'Coffee?'

'Yes, please.'

'Mummy.'

Oh, shit. Liam was still awake. Not only that, he was standing at the top of the stairs.

'Get back into bed.'

'Who is it?'

'Just someone to see Mummy.'

'Who?'

'Nobody you know. Now go back to sleep.'

'But I wasn't asleep.'

'Well, go to sleep now.'

'I'm hungwy.'

In desperation, she closed the sitting-room door on this popular ploy. Inside, Uri was pouring milk into Emily's coffee. They looked up at her expectantly. She smiled tightly and glanced at the clock. Eight forty-five. 'I suppose we'd better make a start.' She settled herself in an armchair. 'I can go over things again if someone else comes.'

No one else did. Apart from Liam, whom Aoife could hear descending the stairs step by step. It was only a matter of seconds before the door swung open and there he stood, resplendent in Spiderman pyjamas. His confidence deserted him as soon as his eyes alighted on the strangers and he ran to his mother and climbed on to her lap, wrapping his legs around her waist and burying his face in the soft, warm place where her neck met her shoulder. The irritation Aoife had anticipated didn't materialize. Instead, she felt the tension melt from her body.

'So. We have the opportunity to restore a walled garden,' she began.

'Really?' Uri sat forward, face intent.

'Yes. The owner has very kindly agreed to let us do what we like with it.'

'Where is this garden?'

'Close by. About five minutes' walk from here?'

'Have you had plans drawn up?'

'Um. No. Not yet. I was waiting to see if I could generate enough interest first.'

'Do you have photos?'

'No.'

'How big is it?'

'About an acre.'

'An acre in this part of the city! It's a wonder no one's built an apartment block on top of it.'

'Yes. The owner was thinking about selling it to a developer, but she seems to have had a change of heart.'

'What do you envisage for it?' Again, Uri asked the question. Emily had yet to speak.

'I see it as a community garden. Anyone who's interested can come and help. Try to restore it to its former glory. Flowers, vegetables, herbs, fruit trees.'

'We could grow figs – vines, even.' Uri was smiling broadly now.

'I suppose we might be able to get a greenhouse.'

He was looking at her carefully now, choosing his words. 'Well, as you know, the temperature in a walled garden is always several degrees higher than that of a normal garden so it should be possible to grow such fruit against the walls, where the heat is retained.'

Aoife nodded and looked at the carpet. She could feel herself blushing to her roots.

As you know.

She met Uri's eye briefly. He was still looking at her and she could have kicked herself for not having done more research. She of all people.

'Can we see it?' It was the first time Emily had spoken.

'The garden?'

'Yes.'

'Now?' She hadn't anticipated this.

Emily nodded.

'But it's dark.'

'I have a torch,' said Uri.

You would, thought Aoife, somewhat bitterly. Then she checked herself. She was damn lucky they had someone who knew what he was talking about. Because she clearly didn't.

'What if someone else shows up . . . ?' Her voice trailed off. Her two visitors glanced at the clock, then back at her. Nine o'clock. There was no need for them to say anything.

'What about Liam?'

'I can come too, Mummy.' Liam's words were moist against her throat.

Why not? she thought. He was wide awake anyway. 'Okay.'

'Yippee!' Liam climbed off her lap and ran out to the hall, presumably to get his boots.

She remembered something. 'But I don't have the key yet.'

'Can we ask the owner?' said Uri.

'I suppose we could. But I wouldn't like to disturb her. It's a bit late.'

'Of course. You're right. But is there a way to see in at all?'

'There's a gate we can look through.'

'Well, then.' He got up.

And they all put their coats on and went outside.

It felt weird, walking along with the two strangers, close in the darkness, Liam's hand clinging to hers. They crunched along the pavement, their breath solid and white in the winter air. They were silent mostly, Liam's intermittent questions easing the tension.

When they were almost there, Uri drew alongside her. 'Are you a gardener?' he asked.

The question she'd been dreading. 'No. I'm a lecturer.'

'In horticulture?'

'No. English.' She looked at him. His eyes were on the ground. 'Are you?'

'A gardener?'

'Yes.'

'No. Just a keen amateur. I'm a tailor by trade.'

'Oh.'

That would explain his immaculate appearance. Could he tell she'd bought her clothes ready made and off the peg in Dunnes Stores?

'Here we are.'

'Oh, I know this place,' said Emily.

They arrived at the gate and peered into the darkness. The nearest streetlight was quite a distance away. Then Uri switched on his torch and shone the powerful beam. They all pressed their faces up against the gate and followed the arc of light as it illuminated various parts of the garden. She watched them. They were suitably spellbound. Good.

'Can I have a go?'

Uri handed the torch to Liam, who swung the beam erratically around the whole neighbourhood.

'Well,' said Aoife, 'what do you think?'

'I'm in,' said Uri.

'Me too,' said Emily.

Good.

Good.

7

It was really happening. She was really going to do this, she and her army of two volunteers. Thus she found herself, for the third time, on Mrs Prendergast's doorstep, one drizzly morning in December. Her fingers had barely made contact with the brass knocker before the door opened.

'I was wondering when you'd turn up again.'

Charming.

'Good morning, Mrs Prendergast. I've come to let you know that I've decided to take you up on your offer. We'll be starting work on the garden directly after Christmas.'

'We?'

'Me and the other volunteers.'

'Will there be many?'

'Only a few at first.'

'All right, then.' She started to close the door.

'Mrs Prendergast?'

'What?'

'I'm going to need a key.'

She nodded and disappeared. Aoife could hear a drawer being opened and some rummaging. Mrs Prendergast returned with a massive, rusty object. 'Here we are. I dug it up in case you came back. It's for the padlock on the gate. I don't even know if it works any more.'

She handed it to Aoife, gave her a strange look, as if she couldn't work her out, then shut the door.

As Aoife went down the steps she could feel the joy soaring into her throat. She felt like singing. Bouncing along the pavement, she rounded the corner and headed for the gate. The key fitted. But that was as far as it went. She wriggled, she pushed, she twisted and she turned. Nothing. She cursed her weak, feminine hands. Michael could have opened it.

Angry with herself for the thought, she tried again, more forcefully this time, making grunts worthy of a Wimbledon champion. She was on the verge of giving up when she felt something give. A subtle twisting into place. She felt a kind of elation as the padlock came undone and fell into her palm. She unwrapped the chain – once, twice, three times. The gate emitted a creak worthy of a Hammer horror film. How long since it was last opened? She stepped quickly inside and secured it.

How quiet. How eerie. How suddenly cut off she felt from the outside world. The traffic whizzing past. The pedestrians rushing by. Here, all was still. Timeless. Untouched for nigh on forty years. She walked silently to the centre, feeling as if she'd suddenly become invisible. She bent and touched the duckweed on the pond. It separated to reveal dank, dark-green water beneath. You couldn't see the bottom. It was probably only a foot deep but to Aoife, in that moment, it could have gone on for ever. The ground was soft with rainfall and the air was still. The garden seemed to be breathing all around her, the plants silently growing.

She sank to her knees and started to cry.

Myrtle bowed her head and locked the gate. That was it for her. She would store the key somewhere obscure. She took one last look at the garden through the bars. But was she looking out or in? All she knew was that she wasn't going back.

8

Christmas was over, the less said about it the better. It was time to make a new start. Onwards and upwards in the garden.

Aoife had asked all her family for garden implements as presents, ignoring their comments and strange looks, which would have been decidedly more so had they known that she herself had only a yard with a few scattered pots. She had received a spade, a big fork, a trowel, a little fork, a thing for pruning low branches and another thing for lopping high branches. She'd been swotting too, having realized that an in-depth knowledge of the legend of Cupid and Psyche wasn't going to get her far in a real walled garden. Not that she had a hope of fooling Uri. She had a feeling she'd already been rumbled there.

That first morning they were both waiting for her at the gate. She saw them before they saw her. Uri had his hands dug deep inside his overcoat and his face pressed up against the wrought iron. It must have been freezing. Emily was staring into the middle distance, in what Aoife was beginning to think of as her habitual pose.

'Sorry I'm late. Liam wouldn't let me leave the crèche. He must have known something was up.' She reached them, breathless and pink-cheeked. The cold air was making her nose run and she wiped it surreptitiously with a ragged piece of toilet tissue. Uri smiled at her broadly and Emily gave her a little nod. She noticed they had tools with them too. All the better for digging.

She struggled a little less with the gate this time and they went into the garden. Emily walked a few paces and looked all around. Uri took himself off to explore the furthest reaches, bending and prodding and muttering to himself. Aoife gave them a few minutes to familiarize themselves, letting them wander back to her in their own time. Uri seemed excited, Emily expectant.

'Where do you want us to start?'

This was a critical moment for Aoife. Uri clearly knew far more about gardening than she did yet he was deferring to her. She wasn't sure how she would have handled it if he had tried to take over. She might have been half inclined to let him. But he hadn't. So . . .

'Well. The place is a bit of a mess, so the first thing that has to be done, I think, is to clear it.'

'I agree,' said Uri, nodding and smiling as if she'd said something really intelligent rather than blindingly obvious. 'Of course, it would have been better if we could have started the clearing in the autumn but not to worry.'

'Of course,' said Aoife, experiencing a surge of excitement. She'd learned that from the swotting. 'Now, we may find some plants that are salvageable, so be careful what you pull out.' She directed this comment at Emily who, for all she knew, was as clueless as herself. 'So,' she said, 'let's get gardening.'

Aoife, Emily and Uri spent three successive days pulling, yanking, chopping and hacking in the walled garden. On the second day there was light snow. Uri brought along a yard brush and beat it from the upper branches of the evergreens.

'But it looks so pretty up there,' said Aoife.

'It might damage the trees if we leave it.'

'Oh.'

'I've been thinking,' he said. 'We might be eligible for a grant.'

'Really?'

'If we billed it as a community project. It might help with the planting costs. Would you like me to look into it?'

'Yes, please!'

'In the meantime I can bring in plenty of cuttings.'

'That'd be great, Uri.'

It *was* great. *He* was great – with his ridiculous yet charming deference to her authority. If she hadn't had him helping her, she'd have been well and truly banjaxed. The reality was that stark. It was as if somebody had sent him – ordered him from some magic mail-order catalogue.

Liam came along with the snow, speeding up and down the partly cleared paths on his yellow tractor. Aoife hoped the others didn't mind his presence. They didn't appear to. She had noticed Emily watching him intently, but she didn't seem annoyed. Intrigued, rather. Uri told him stories. Long, convoluted tales, mostly involving dragons, with Liam invariably the hero of the piece. They didn't talk much, the three adults. There didn't seem any need to, apart from 'Pass the secateurs,' and suchlike. They settled into a silence that Aoife found oddly companionable, seeing as they hardly knew one another. It must have been something to do with their common cause.

On the third day – a Sunday – they agreed to stay on for the afternoon. Lunch consisted of goat's cheese and green tomato chutney on ciabatta, then organic apples, all washed down with sparkling elderflower cordial. This came courtesy of Emily, whose aunt happened to be the proprietor of the Good Food Store. Aoife brought hot tea in a flask and Uri supplied the cups. Liam had his first gobstopper, under the close supervision of his mother. He stuck his tongue out at intervals. 'What colour is it now?'

'Red,' said Aoife.

'Green,' said Uri.

'Blue,' said Emily.

It was late on Sunday afternoon and the light was failing.

'Shall we call it a day?' said Aoife.

'I think so,' said Uri.

They stood back to admire the progress that had been made. It was getting easier to discern the original shape of the garden.

'Of course,' Uri went on, 'we'll have our work cut out for us in the spring when the new growth starts. Keeping down the weeds.'

Aoife nodded solemnly, but inside she felt something close to jubilation. What did she care for a few weeds? Look at what they'd achieved in three days!

'Over here. Quick!' It was Emily. Shouting! Emily, who scarcely raised her voice above a whisper. The two rushed over, expecting a pruned finger at the very least. But when they got there Emily was crouched on the ground, her face shining, as if she'd had a vision. 'Look.'

Aoife and Uri peered at the small patch she had been clearing.

There, in the fading light, in all its smallness and whiteness, was a snowdrop.

9

Emily's future spread out before her like a vast expanse of Montana grassland. Endless. Limitless in its possibilities. She'd never been to Montana, although she had seen *The Horse Whisperer*. Nevertheless, this was the image she'd hugged to herself ever since she'd left home and started college.

Maybe it was because her family was so large, so overwhelming, and their home so small in comparison. Always having to share a room. Never being on your own. Which was why, growing up, she had learned how to spend so much time in the spacious, beautifully furnished room of her imagination. And why her current one-bedroomed flat, lit by one tiny window, was to her the glittering, multi-mirrored Palace of Versailles. She would lie on her bed in the morning, feeling the weight of the sun pressing on her eyelids, rendering everything blood-coloured. She would stretch out her bare toes and fling her arms back on either side of her head. She would imagine her dark hair fanned out on the white pillow and luxuriate in her aloneness, knowing what it was to be young and free with the space to grow into herself at last.

Emily knew she'd be lying to herself if she pretended she'd felt like this from her very first day of college. On the contrary, she'd been terrified. These city girls seemed so unbelievably sure of themselves. They made her feel like such a dork. It wasn't so much what they said or what they did, just the way they were. So to deal with this, Emily had adopted a kind of strategy. She'd lain low for a couple of weeks and studied them – how they moved, how they gesticulated, but mostly how they wore their clothes. By Monday of the third week she was ready. This was how she looked. Her haircut was gamine – dark and sleek. Then from the bottom up: nude Ugg boots, black diamond tights, denim miniskirt and short black leather jacket, cinched at the waist. Around her neck, in the manner of a tie, was a scarf she'd bought secondhand in Temple Bar. Her bag was vintage and so was her jewellery. She especially loved the chandelier earrings. They made her feel like Queen Nefertiti. She was confident she looked nothing like the farmer's daughter she was, and felt ready to insinuate herself into the company of her female classmates. During lectures, she would sit beside a likely-looking girl and one or other of them would strike up a conversation.

Her strategy worked. Before long she was in a magic circle of girls who, in their quest for individuality, wore identical clothes and held identical views. Part of her knew that this set-up was shallow, but so far nobody had noticed that she wasn't cool. Mission accomplished, as far as she was concerned.

The boys were another matter. They were everywhere, in every conceivable incarnation, their voices and laughter over-loud with exaggerated self-confidence. She was in awe. She felt like she had as a child when she'd fantasized about being locked in a sweetshop overnight, even though, so far, she hadn't so much as stolen a kiss. She didn't want to make a mistake and choose the wrong one. It was far too important a selection to make.

One night, some time around the beginning of her second term, she was sitting in the college bar. It was freezing outside and the bar held a welcome glow. She was surrounded by five or six of her gal-pals, chatting and texting and going out for a

Marlboro Light. A group of lads sat across the way, drinking pints of lager and pretending not to look at them.

One of the boys, Joe, noticed Emily before she noticed him. It was his friend Niall who brought her to his attention. He nudged Joe's arm. 'What do you think of her?'

'Which one?'

'Twelve o'clock. Dark hair, legs crossed.'

Joe stole a casual glance, then returned to his pint. 'Looks like a librarian.'

'Yeah, but a hot librarian. Like she'd whip off her glasses and do you across the desk.'

'She's not wearing glasses.'

'You know what I mean.'

'You've been watching too much porn.'

'No such thing as too much porn.'

Joe glanced at her again. She was nice. Small and dark and neat. Pretty in a quiet, not too obvious way. And she looked like she'd be a tough nut to crack. Which was always appealing.

'Want to meet her?'

'What? Just like that?'

'I know one of the friends. She was in my sister's class in school. They must be first years. Come on.'

And so it happened that the two boys traversed the great divide and introduced themselves. Joe sat as close to Emily as propriety allowed. 'Hi, I'm Joe.'

'Emily.'

'Lovely name.'

'Thanks.'

'Are you a first year, Emily?'

She nodded.

'What are you studying?'

36

'Pure English.'

Joe thought it fitting that she should be studying something pure. It suited her primness.

'I'm doing engineering. Third year.' He volunteered the information as he had judged, quite rightly, that she was unlikely to ask him for it. As it was, she just nodded. Other young men might have been put off by her reticence, but Joe, who was not in the least self-contained, was impressed by the quality in other people. Especially women.

'So. Do you drink here much?'

'Sometimes.'

'Why don't we meet up here Thursday night?' he suggested. 'Just you and me,' he added, lest there be any confusion.

Emily lowered her eyes and said nothing, which made Joe considerably keener.

'About eight.'

'Okay.'

'You will?'

'Yes.'

Joe beamed, and before long, he and Niall sidled back whence they had come.

Emily's friend Rebecca, the one who knew Niall's sister, slid over into the chair that Joe had just vacated. 'That looked very cosy.'

Emily grinned. She couldn't help herself. 'He asked me out.'

'What?'

'Keep your voice down – they're only over there.'

The two girls looked over at Joe and Niall, who had rejoined the rugby scrum of mates, all huddled together around their table.

'They're probably talking about you,' said Rebecca.

'Stop!'

'I'm only teasing. Where's he taking you?'

Emily's crest fell a little as it struck her that he hadn't asked her out for a fancy dinner. 'We're meeting here for a drink.' She could see that Rebecca was having the same thought.

'Oh, well, it's a start,' said her friend.

10

It was Thursday night and Emily was mid-conniption. Only twenty more minutes to go, she thought, peering into her bathroom mirror, her breath making little clouds on the glass. What if he stood her up? Her belly lurched. God, what would she do? To be stood up in the college bar of all places, in full view of people she might actually know. Even if the place was full of strangers, she'd still have to report back to the girls. Rebecca had made short shrift of letting all and sundry know about her 'date'. If, indeed, that was what it was. God, she didn't think she could handle the humiliation of being stood up.

She had to adopt a strategy. She'd bring a book. Someone had just lent her *The Unbearable Lightness of Being*. Better still, she'd arrive ten minutes late. If he wasn't there, she'd merely keep walking, as if she was just passing through, and nobody there would be any the wiser. Of course, this meant an extra ten minutes in which to lose her mind. How on earth was she to occupy herself? She tried to read, but the pages might as well have been blank. She jumped on to her bed and, in an effort to quell her churning stomach, bounced for a full minute. Then she got down and performed a handstand against the wall. Her giggles were muffled by the maroon fabric of her gypsy skirt, which covered her face and made her feel twelve again. Upside down. A different perspective on the world. And the last time tonight that her underwear would be exposed, of that she was determined. She stood upright, red-faced and breathless, and looked at the clock. The hands appeared to have ground to a halt.

But time hadn't stood still, despite appearances to the contrary. Because it was now ten past eight and she was walking into the college bar, head erect, shoulders back, heart in mouth. There he was! At least, she thought it was him. The boy had his back to her. He was leaning forward, his elbows on his knees, hands clasped loosely together. The hunched shoulders were wide and his build stocky. His black hair was tightly curled and cut close to his head. As she reached his side, she recognized the dark sideburns and noticed him checking his watch.

'Joe?'

'Emily.' He stood up, like a well-brought-up young man, and his smile only slightly betrayed his relief. He gestured to the seat across from him, whereupon Emily promptly sat down and crossed her legs neatly.

'You came,' said Joe.

'Yes, I did.'

'Can I get you a drink?'

'Bottle of Corona, please.'

Joe purchased the beers, set them down and grappled for something to say. 'So. Pure English. You must like to read.'

'I love books.'

'Any particular kind?'

'Anything and everything.'

She wasn't giving him much to go on but he ploughed on regardless. 'I like books too. Mainly thrillers. Dan Brown, John Grisham – that kind of thing.'

There was no response.

'Do you read thrillers?'

'Not really.'

'What, not at all? You must have read *The Da Vinci Code*, everyone's read that.'

'I've read that one, yes.'

'And what did you think?'

'That it was badly written.'

'Well, I liked it,' Joe finished weakly and tried another tack. 'How are you finding college life?'

'Okay. Yeah. I like it.'

'Do you live on campus?'

'No, I have a bedsit.'

Emily could almost see the thoughts running through Joe's head: country girl, doesn't live at home – a point in her favour, perhaps.

'Where is it you're from again?' he said.

'Kilkenny.'

'Oh, yeah.' Another dead end. Clearly Joe knew diddly-squat about the place.

Emily sat anxiously in her seat and watched him struggle. She didn't mean to be such hard work. What other people mistook for aloofness was in fact shyness. And although this impression could be handy at times, at others – such as now – it was a downright nuisance. She had to throw him a lifeline before they drowned in silence and awkwardness.

'What's your second name, Joe?'

He was Joseph Francis after his two grandfathers and he'd taken Luke for his confirmation after Skywalker.

She wondered briefly if he was thick, then instantly dismissed the idea. He couldn't be if he was studying engineering. He was probably a whiz at physics and maths and that sort of thing. Emily had been terrible at maths in school and therefore had great respect for those who were not.

'I mean your second name. Your surname.'

'Joe Devine.'

Joe tried not to imagine her imagining his name tacked to the end of hers. He knew what girls were like. 'And you?'

'Emily Harte.'

Joe held out his hand and grinned. 'Pleased to meet you, Emily Harte.'

Emily took his hand and shook. Their eyes locked and stayed that way, fingers and gazes intertwined for longer than either had intended. They broke away finally and each party took a nervous sip of their drink. But the ice was broken, contact had been made and they smiled.

Emily threw herself on to her bed and luxuriated in the night that had just been.

Emily Harte-Devine. Emily Devine-Harte. Oh, it was too good to be true. She wouldn't even have to change her name if she became a romantic novelist. Although no one would believe that such a name could be real. And she couldn't believe Joe was real. Joe Devine. Devine Joe. The Devine Mr J. She made a half-hearted attempt to check herself. She was aware of her tendency to imbue the boys she liked with romantic qualities they did not possess. To see past the spots to the Byron within. But she was confident she wasn't doing that now. She hadn't felt this way since – well – since ever.

Emily wondered if Joe was good marriage material.

In a bedsit not very far away, Joe lay on his bed and wondered what colour Emily's nipples were.

11

They'd been together for two whole weeks now. And how deeply in love certain parties had fallen. Emily would have had to be in a very honest mood to admit, not least to herself, that she was partly in love with the image she and Joe presented to the world – or to college life, at least. They looked so well together. He was exactly a head taller than her. Her head fitted exactly into the crook of his neck, should she be so inclined to place it there, which she often was. If he had any objections to her doing so, he never voiced them. For his part, she was exactly the right height for him to sling his arm around her shoulder in a casual yet possessive masculine gesture. And they could walk along in this pose quite comfortably together – he the leading man and she his lady – trying on their new adult roles for size and liking the fit. They each felt they complemented the other, right down to their colouring and the clothes they wore. Emily liked Joe's style, even if it was a bit rugger-bugger for her taste. And Joe liked Emily's arty look. He felt it lent them elegance as a couple, and him a touch of panache.

In other words, they were ideally suited.

So it was only a matter of time before, you know, they both felt ready to move the relationship to the next level. Certain parties were more ready than others.

Joe had done it lots of times. He hadn't told Emily this. He didn't have to – she felt the pressure of it. She never had: she hadn't told him but she felt he knew it just the same. How glad she was now that she had waited, until she was an age that many of her contemporaries considered geriatric. She could have chosen to get it over with years earlier, in a sticky, clumsy fumble. But instead she had this precious gift that she and Joe could unwrap together. The prospect thrilled her. It set all her senses jangling. She literally could not think of anything else. Her lectures went by in a wordy blur – even those given by the good tutors, the interesting ones, the leave-you-breathless ones. Her inability to concentrate was complete. Unless, of course, she was thinking about the dress she was going to wear on the night. The night in question being this Friday. Her designated deflowering night. It was unspoken between them but they both knew.

The dress was rainbow-coloured and gossamer light and made her feel as if she was wearing butterfly wings.

Something lurched inside Joe as he watched her walking towards him across the cobblestones. She was smiling shyly, looking beautiful. They didn't say anything as their hands connected, just gazed at each other deeply. Then Joe bent down and kissed her mouth. 'Let's go.'

They had booked a table at a nearby Chinese restaurant. A rare treat. They sat and looked at each other mostly. Emily ate almost nothing. Joe ate too much, wolfing his food so fast that he couldn't taste it. Sweat broke out on his forehead. He wiped it away with his napkin, embarrassed. He was meant to be the one in control tonight. The one who knew what he was doing. And there was Emily, sitting calmly opposite, staring at him with those eyes of hers. Under the table, he ran his hand up the back of her calf.

'Let's go,' he said again.

They had chosen her bedsit, her place, because it was neater, less smelly and had a greater variety of atmospheric candles.

Once they were inside, Emily found that she could barely look at Joe, let alone take off her clothes. So she let him do it for her. He undressed her slowly. Reverently. Emily held her arms out, feeling herself open, exposed. This is my body which I have given up for you.

When it was over, she lay on the bed, the sheet drawn up to her chin – underwhelmed by the physical sensation of what she'd just experienced but overwhelmed by the emotion she felt for Joe.

Joe took himself off to the bathroom. It was only then that he realized the condom had split. He toyed with the idea of telling her but decided against it. Why spoil the night? The chances of anything happening were minuscule. He flushed the evidence away, wishing he could join the lads in Doyles. But he supposed he'd better go and cuddle her for a bit. Wasn't that what all the birds wanted?

Emily felt a little odd. She put it down to stress. Joe-induced stress. Things hadn't been the same since their night together. It wasn't anything she could put her finger on, but she sensed his interest waning, which filled her with panic. She couldn't have him withdraw from her now. Not after she'd given herself to him, body and soul. Some of the other girls had noticed it too. She'd had to endure a few snide comments about how he never used to keep her waiting. Twenty minutes of torture under the all-seeing eye of the big blue clock. And she could see his mind wandering when she spoke to him, his eyes straying over her shoulder. She did most of the talking nowadays – always trying to engage his ever-elusive attention. She just couldn't understand it. She'd given him what he wanted, hadn't she?

* * *

The stress of it all was taking its toll, making her physically ill. The very sight of meat or fish made her want to vomit, not to mention the smell of it. Especially in the morning.

Especially in the morning.

Ding.

Emily went to the chemist.

How remarkable that the mere act of peeing on a piece of white plastic can alter the trajectory of your life for ever. The thin blue line that separates your old life from the new. A line that might as well have been a yawning chasm. As she stared at the definitive evidence of her condition, Emily felt as if she was falling into such an abyss. Maybe the toilet would just swallow her like a giant mouth.

Her mind couldn't wrap itself around the improbability of the situation she found herself in. Ohmigod. This isn't happening. Ohmigod. This isn't happening. He used a condom. It isn't happening. Ohmigod.

She took the second test and it told her the same unpalatable truth. Then she went back to the chemist and blew the rest of her weekly budget on a second pack. The third time wasn't a charm and neither was the fourth. She paced her bedsit like a big cat in a zoo, sinking on to her bed every now and then, burying her face in her pillow, wrapping herself in her duvet, only to get up and begin pacing again.

Eventually she broke the cycle and left her bedsit. There was only one person who could help her now and he was in the college bar, meeting his mates. She ran down the street, realizing too late that she should have brought her coat, hugging her arms across her chest. Then she stopped abruptly. What if she was hurting the baby by running? She had a terrifying premonition of how her life was going to be from now on. Always putting another person's needs before her own. She wasn't ready for that. She was only nineteen. She could scarcely look after herself.

She began running again and didn't stop until she reached the entrance to the bar. She was inside now and the music helped to mask the thudding in her head. She looked around wildly for Joe, oblivious to the strange looks she was receiving. At last she found him, not with his friends but sitting in a booth with Rebecca. Emily's friend. They looked very pally-wally, their heads huddled together, his arm resting across the back of her seat. Emily stood in front of them and stared at Rebecca stonily.

The other girl gave her an arch look. 'I'm going to the bar,' she said, slinking off.

Emily took her place, the wood still warm. Joe's body language alarmed her. He didn't even try to touch her. 'I have to talk to you,' she said.

'What is it?' His face, his tone, his manner – all wary.

She handed him the final test, discreetly, under the table.

He looked down in confusion. 'What's this?'

She said nothing.

'Is this what I think it is?'

She nodded.

'Oh, Jesus Christ.' He brought his hand up to his face and covered his eyes. It was only then that Emily started to cry. She buried her face in his neck, sobbing quietly. She waited a long time for him to gather her up in his arms. It never quite happened. Instead he patted her shoulder awkwardly. 'Don't worry. It'll be all right.'

Joe's version of all right and Emily's turned out to be two very different things. It was Emily's misfortune that she thought of Joe as her saviour.

They were sitting on a bench in St Stephen's Green the next day, staring blankly at the ducks. It was a beautiful setting. Leaves rustled gently above their heads. The water rippled. In the distance Emily could see drifts of golden daffodils interspersed with scarlet tulips. The sight salved her soul somewhat.

The purpose of this meeting was to discuss the position they found themselves in. That was what Joe had said. As if they were running a small corporation. Emily didn't know what to feel. Joe was still here. That was good. Vital. But where was the joy, the excitement one usually associated with new life? There was none. She understood this logically. But her heart . . .

It wasn't what she'd ever imagined for herself. She had vivid memories of her mother announcing her pregnancies with Emily's younger siblings. How happy they had all been. The sense of anticipation in the house.

None of this horrible numbness.

'Have you given any thought to what you're going to do?' said Joe, looking at his shoes.

'What do you mean "do"?'

It was already done.

'I mean, have you thought of all the options?' His voice was level but she sensed that anger wasn't far away.

'Such as?' She wouldn't give him the satisfaction of saying it for him.

'Come on, Emily. You know what I mean. There are clinics you can go to in England.'

She said nothing. Her face was impassive, but inside she was falling apart.

'It happened to Niall a couple of years back with a girl from home. She just took a flight over. She was home the next day. All over and done with.'

The silence screamed between them.

'Don't you want us?' She heard her voice, tiny and pathetic. She hated herself for saying it, knew it was the worst thing she could possibly have said, but still she couldn't help herself.

Joe sighed, exasperated, and closed his eyes. 'It's not that I don't want you. It's just . . . You must see, Emily, what a disaster this is. For both of us. Neither of us has finished college. I've got another year and a half to go. You've got three and a half, for fuck's sake. It's going to be years before either of us is earning halfway decent money. And what about this course you say means so much to you? How are you going to carry on your studies with a baby to look after?'

'There's a crèche on campus.'

He struck his forehead with the palm of his hand. 'What about the rest of the time?'

'We could manage, between the two of us.'

The words hung suspended in the air.

The two of us.

He tried a different tack, his voice newly reasonable. 'It's only early days. What are you. Six weeks? It's not even a baby yet. It's a pinprick.'

'It has a heartbeat.'

He looked at her properly for the first time. 'You're not going to do this, are you?'

49

'I won't have an abortion, no.'

'Give me one good reason why not.'

'You don't know much about my family, do you?'

'I know there's six of you.'

'Yes. Six kids. As in, good Catholic family. My father's a Eucharistic minister and my mother's always going on about family values and the right to life of the unborn, that kind of stuff.'

'Your family doesn't have to know a thing. And you don't even go to mass.'

'Not up here I don't. But that's not the point, Joe. They might not know but I would. I couldn't live with myself.'

'Jesus Christ, you'll be wanting us to get married next.' He looked at her in alarm. 'You don't want . . .'

'Of course not.'

'Thank fuck for that.'

Her heart plummeted. Now she knew where she stood. Her place in Joe's affections: Swampland.

He leaned forward on the bench, his elbows on his knees, his face in his hands.

'Would you not even consider it?'

She tried but failed to keep the tremor out of her voice. 'Joe. This is our baby. Part of you and me. I will not kill it.' Emily gazed straight ahead. She kept her eyes focused on a weeping willow. The irony wasn't lost on her as her vision blurred. 'Are you going to break up with me?'

Joe looked at her in despair. If only she wouldn't keep staring at him with those big weepy eyes of hers. He put his arms around her. 'Of course I'm not going to break up with you.'

Emily wept gratefully into his jumper.

For a while it wasn't too bad. She couldn't claim that Joe was as keen as he had been in those first few weeks, but he was turning up on time to meet her. And he showed concern when she was unwell – once even buying her a packet of gingernuts because he'd heard they were good for nausea. But every time she tried to talk about the baby, he fell silent. They'd agreed not to tell any of their college friends for the time being. Why add to the pressure? But when Emily was nearing sixteen weeks, her waistline disappearing, she felt it was time to bring up the thorny topic of their parents. She'd almost told her own mother twice, but courage had failed her at the critical moment. Her parents weren't much keener on pre-marital sex than they were on abortion. Quite frankly, she dreaded their reaction. But she couldn't hide it for ever.

She was going to have a baby. Her heart flooded with happiness at the thought. She really had amazed herself. In the beginning, the pregnancy had seemed such a tragedy, her career plans scuppered, her relationship with Joe threatened. But now they were going to be a family.

She announced her plans to Joe over coffee. They could go to his house and tell his parents this Friday night, then get the bus down to Kilkenny on Saturday morning to tell hers.

'Okay,' he said finally.

She smiled and squeezed his hand. It was all going to be 'official'.

So that Friday evening she dressed in her best clothes, not taking as much care as she usually did to hide her slight bump. She'd been dying to meet Joe's parents – to be introduced as 'the girlfriend'.

She arrived at their designated meeting place outside the library five minutes early, so she wasn't too concerned that he had yet to arrive. She watched college life whiz happily by, everyone in good form, preparing to go out for the start of the weekend. She didn't envy them. What she had was even better.

It wasn't until ten past that she started to worry. She texted Joe: 'Where are you?'

The response came about five minutes later. 'I'm sorry. I can't do this any more.'

Panicked, she rang his number but it went straight to voicemail. What did he mean? That he couldn't go through with telling his parents? Or that he couldn't go through with any of it? Ever again. She sat rigid for a couple of minutes, then got up and walked decisively to the public telephone. She bypassed the queue and headed for the directory suspended from the wall. D: Devine. There they were, Joseph and Patricia, at an address in Ranelagh. She walked quickly outside to College Green and hailed a taxi she couldn't afford. If Joe was too chickenshit to tell his parents, she'd have to do it for him. They had the right to know that they were going to be grandparents.

They were at the house already. She paid the taxi driver and got out. No point in asking him to wait. She sat on a wall opposite the house. Passers-by glanced at her curiously. She supposed she might look a bit unhinged. Someone turned a light on in a downstairs room. A woman in her fifties. She was tall with flicky, ash-blonde hair. Emily watched her as she picked up a newspaper, put on a pair of reading glasses and sat in an armchair beside the window. Her future mother-in-law. After a while, the woman got up again and drew the curtains. Emily saw her shadow sitting down. They had a nice garden, she thought dispassionately. She wondered if Joe's father was a keen gardener. Did his wife call him Joseph or Joe? She'd never know.

After about an hour, the owner of the wall on which she was sitting came out and stood in front of her. 'Can I help you?' she asked, her tone and expression lacking warmth.

'I was just leaving.' Emily got up. Her buttocks were ice-cold anyway.

The Spring Garden

Whoever loves and understands a garden will find contentment within.

Chinese proverb

13

Aoife was amazed at how satisfying it was, all that digging. Slicing through the earth with the blade of the spade. Feeling it give. Like sticking a fork into a moist piece of chocolate cake. And overturning the soil, all black and crumbly and teeming with earthworms. Worms that hadn't been disturbed for the best part of four decades – they and their great-grandworms before them. She felt guilty about them, but it was all for the greater good.

Like other activities you could carry out on autopilot, such as walking, driving and taking a shower, digging had an uncanny way of helping her sort out her problems without her consciously trying. She organized her life as she organized the piles of earth.

Uri came up behind her. 'It's coming on.'

She stopped digging and leaned on her spade, slightly puffed. 'It is, isn't it? I thought we'd start with a bed of nasturtiums, followed by a row of spuds along there, then carrots, Swiss chard, corn, turnips and finish up over there with the cornflowers.'

Uri nodded. Then he crouched and scooped up a handful of black earth, rubbing it through his fingers. 'This is good stuff. Very good stuff.'

'I know.' There was a time when Aoife would have considered an activity such as enthusiastic fondling of soil quite alarming. Now she understood. Something caught her eye. 'There she is again.'

Uri followed her line of sight towards an upper window

at the back of the house. He was just in time to discern the twitch of a curtain. 'Missed her again. What a shame she doesn't just come down and say hello.'

'Yes. Pity.' Privately, Aoife was quite pleased that she didn't have to deal with any interference from Mrs Prendergast.

She watched Uri as he returned to his apple trees, stopping now and then to tug at a weed, like a garden gnome come to life. The weeds were a problem that had only fully revealed itself come spring, one in particular, which Aoife had thought of as 'the pernicious weed' until Uri had told her it was called ground elder. It had taken over almost half the garden during the long years of neglect. The discussion about a chemical solution to the problem had been brief.

Aoife: 'We could always use weedkiller. Just this once.'

Emily: 'No.'

Uri: 'Absolutely not.'

Aoife: 'All right, then. Let's get weeding.'

She felt that they were winning the battle. Just about.

Aoife resumed digging. And then something wholly unexpected happened. There was a wooden door at the top end of the garden: none of them used it because it opened on to Mrs Prendergast's private garden. But this morning it opened. Enter Mrs Prendergast bearing a tray of tea things and a plate of posh biscuits. They stopped what they were doing and stared at her. Before anyone could approach she had put down the tray and exited the way she had come, closing the door behind her.

The three looked at each other and approached the tray cautiously, as if it had been left there by the fairies. It was laid out as if the Queen were coming to visit – delicate china cups and saucers and a doily on the plate. Uri laughed as he bit into a biscuit. He gestured to the teapot. 'Will you be mother?' he said to Emily.

*　*　*

Later that day, at going-home time, Aoife opened the wooden door and approached the back of the house. She knocked three times. When she got no response, she put the tray on the doorstep and walked away. She hesitated after the first few paces and turned. 'Thank you,' she called into the silence.

This pattern was repeated on every day they worked in the garden. At first, either Uri or Aoife would try and approach Mrs Prendergast to thank her or to engage her in conversation, but she was too quick for them. Sometimes they didn't even hear her. They would stumble across the tray at some point, the temperature of the tea indicating how long it had been there. Then, one day, the pattern was broken. Mrs Prendergast appeared at the door, earlier than usual, minus a tray. She was wearing a straw hat tied with a pink ribbon and worn brown leather gloves. In her right hand she carried secateurs, and in the left a wicker basket, such as one might use for gathering cut flowers. She brushed past Aoife. 'I'll do the roses,' she said. 'You're making a mess of them.'

Later that morning Aoife approached her. 'Hello, Mrs Prendergast. How are you keeping?'

'I've decided to put the garden on the market.'

'What?'

'I'm selling the garden.'

'But you can't!'

Mrs Prendergast turned abruptly and gave her a look designed to intimidate.

'I didn't . . . I mean . . . What about the roses? Why?'

'My son needs the money for a business venture.'

'But –'

'I'm afraid my decision is final.'

Aoife nodded weakly and withdrew. What was she going to do?

For three whole weeks she wrestled with her conscience. Should she tell the others? Frequently she woke at night in a sweat, the weight of not telling them pressing heavily on her chest. But she still had hope. She had to have hope. It must be a good thing, mustn't it, Mrs Prendergast working on the garden? Surely she'd be less inclined to destroy something she'd helped to create. And maybe nobody would want to buy a prime piece of development land so close to the city.

Her concern grew, as relentless as the pernicious weed and even harder to uproot. She bit her nails to the quick as she observed the first conversations between Uri and Mrs Prendergast. What were they talking about? She moved to work on a patch closer to where they stood, heads together. She heard snippets.

'David Austin roses . . . the best . . . richest colours . . . headiest fragrances . . . catalogue.' And was she hearing things or were they discussing tailoring as well? But why on earth not? They were two of the best-turned-out people she'd ever met. 'Pinking shears'. Or was that some gardening implement? She wasn't sure. And so far so good. Nothing about apartment blocks or developers. But she had to, had to, had to say something to Uri tonight. She owed it to him. And, besides, she was going to lose her mind if she kept quiet any longer.

They were packing up that evening. Emily had already left for her shift in the Good Food Store and Liam was playing quietly with his toy excavator in the newly dug herbaceous border. Her golden opportunity. Except it didn't feel golden. She approached Uri as he was putting away his tools meticulously in the little makeshift shed. 'I have something to tell you.'

'I already know. And, yes, you should have spoken to me about it.'

This unbalanced her. Were they talking about the same thing? She didn't want to put her foot in it. 'You mean . . . ?'

'Mrs Prendergast's plan to sell the land, yes.'

Aoife deflated. 'I'm sorry. You're right. I should have told you sooner. All the work you've done over the last couple of weeks.'

Uri stared at her for a few moments. 'It's all right.'

She stared back. 'But I more or less lied to you. What if it's concreted over by this time next year? It'll have been for nothing.'

Uri observed her closely, his body still, his face composed. 'But it might not be.' He picked up his bag and walked towards the gate. He turned just before he reached it. 'You still should have told me.'

They agreed to tell Emily together.

She was hunkered down in the earth, humming softly to herself as she worked it with her trowel. She jumped when Aoife spoke, as if she'd been caught doing something she shouldn't.

'Emily, can we have a word?'

'Of course.' She looked wary, as was her custom.

'I – we – have something to tell you. It's about the garden. Something I should have told you a while ago.'

Emily looked alarmed.

'You know how I said before that Mrs P agreed we could have the garden and do whatever we liked with it?'

Emily nodded.

'And you know she still owns it?'

'Yes.'

'Well, she's decided to sell.'

'Sell? I don't understand.'

'She's selling it for development.'

'When?'

'As soon as she can get a buyer.'

'What? But that could be tomorrow! Today!'

'Hopefully it'll take longer than that. Maybe even a year or more.'

Aoife looked on in dismay as the girl's face crumpled. Emily hid her elfin features in her delicate little hands and started to sob.

Uri and Aoife exchanged a look.

Aoife reached over and tried to take her wrist, but Emily jerked away, mumbling something incoherent.

'What?'

'How could you?'

Aoife thought she had never been on the receiving end of such a look – such an expression of hurt and betrayal. Maybe once. Her face burned with the intensity of her shame. 'I'm sorry,' she whispered. 'Really sorry.'

Uri approached Emily and put an arm around the girl's heaving shoulders. To Aoife's chagrin, she didn't try to shake him off. He uttered strange, foreign-sounding soothing noises, reminding Aoife that he was not from these shores any more than she was. Emily kept repeating the same thing over and over. Aoife strained to hear. Something about how they couldn't take this away from her too. Finally the heaving and the sobbing came to an end. But Aoife was not entirely off the hook.

'How long have you known?' asked Emily.

'Three weeks.'

'Three weeks! And you never said anything!'

'I'm sorry.'

'And you, how long have you known?' She looked imploringly at Uri, eyes wide, willing him not to have betrayed her too.

'I found out yesterday.'

Emily was clearly relieved that she had nothing to forgive him for. She swiped at her eyes with her knuckles. 'What are we going to do?'

'We'll continue to do what we've been doing,' said Uri.

'But Mrs Prendergast . . .'

'Don't you worry about Mrs Prendergast.'

'Why?' Aoife was suddenly interested. 'What are you going to do?'

'I'm not going to do anything. I won't have to. I'll let the garden do it.'

'Do what?'

'Work its magic.'

The two women stared at him. He laughed. 'Don't you know that gardens are magic?' He squeezed Emily's shoulder. 'Especially this one.'

The scene with Emily had floored Aoife. She had known all along how much the garden meant to her but she'd had no idea how much it meant to Emily. How it seemed to go to her very core. Aoife had never had any sort of personal conversation with the girl, sensing her desire to be left alone. Or had it just been fear on Aoife's part? If she tells me her stuff I'll have to tell her mine? Because when she thought about it, it really wasn't all that normal. A pretty, twenty-year-old girl practically dedicating her life to a garden. Why wasn't she out boozing and sleeping around? It was okay for Aoife. She was past it – not to mention a single parent. No one could expect her to have a life. But Emily? Aoife took a silent vow to keep more of an eye on her. She could hardly believe that two other people were as insanely obsessed with the garden as she was. This lost-cause underdog of a garden. Perhaps they were all as mad as each other.

She felt as light as helium for a few days, no longer weighed down by the burden of her guilty secret. But this feeling was to be short-lived.

14

Emily went home to her parents on the weekend that Joe abandoned her. But she didn't tell them about the baby. How could she? They looked at her with such pride: their eldest daughter, first in the family to go to college. She wore baggy jumpers, not knowing how long she'd be able to get away with it. She had her meals prepared for her, got her laundry done and let her mother wrap her love around her like an old patchwork quilt. She'd need it to sustain her through the coming weeks.

She took to waiting for Joe outside his lectures. He never showed. She saw Niall noticing her. At the end of day three he came over to her. 'If you're waiting for Joe, don't bother.'

'I'm entitled to wait for him if I want to.'

'You're not getting me. He's not here.'

'Where is he, then?'

'London.'

'What?'

'He left college. He won't be coming back.'

'What? But what about his exams?'

'He might repeat the third year. But he won't be back any time soon.'

Niall was accusing, aggressive as he addressed the little trollop who'd ruined Joe's life. He turned and walked back to his friends. Joe's friends. Did they all know?

She was halfway through her pregnancy now. Horror had given way to despondency. She went about her business, attending lectures, handing in essays, going home at weekends. It was characteristic of Emily that her bump was small and neat. It was still barely perceptible and easily hidden beneath loose-fitting clothes. Sometimes she felt as if she was holding it in by sheer act of will. Her mother commented once that she was very quiet. Emily brushed away her concern and the matter was dropped. She *was* quiet. That was what happened when you had a lot of thinking to do. But she reckoned she'd decided now. Arrived at a solution that would suit all parties. She'd done her research. She was confident that she'd selected the most reputable agency.

'You must be Emily.' The woman was holding out her hand. She was in her thirties. Smiley. Glasses and curly hair. Emily followed her into a small office. It was warm and feminine, designed to inspire security and confidence.

Once she'd made the decision, it wasn't so bad. In a funny way, she was able to pretend it wasn't happening. She began to socialize a little more. She studied for her exams and sat them. It was actually working out quite well. She'd elected to stay in Dublin for the summer and get a job – obviously not in her aunt's shop. Her parents would be disappointed that she wasn't spending the time at home but not half as disappointed as they'd be if they knew the truth. The baby was due at the end of September, so she could start the new college year as if nothing had happened. Then, next summer, she could go to the States, as she'd originally planned for this year. Visit Montana. Come back and eventually get her degree. Do an MA. Maybe even a PhD. Dr Emily Harte! Yes. Once again, her life was going perfectly to plan.

Emily had her first contraction in the supermarket, meandering down an aisle, her trolley full of ice cream. Braxton Hicks?

64

Another came. Maybe not. She abandoned the trolley beside the cereals and walked rapidly out of the sliding doors. She didn't think of it again until she was well into labour when she wondered had the ice cream melted. She stood outside and breathed in great big gulps of Dublin city air. Was this it or not? She still had a week to go. How could she tell if her labour was really starting? If only she had someone to ask. The truth was, she did. Plenty of people, in fact. She'd just chosen not to.

Her friends back home. She'd deliberately kept her distance since she'd found out about her pregnancy. They thought she'd gone all snobby on them since she'd moved to Dublin. Her classmates in college – she wasn't even sure if she could call them friends. And that, she supposed, was why she hadn't told them – absenting herself from college life towards the end, only attending vital lectures and tutorials, perpetually wrapped up in her multi-layers. If anyone suspected, nobody said. Her mother. God, no. Her aunts and cousins – they'd just tell her mother. Her sisters were too young and silly. No. The only people she spoke to about her pregnancy and the increasingly abstract concept of the baby were her doctor and the lady at the adoption agency. Emily had always been self-contained but now she was taking self-containment to a whole new level.

The truth was, she didn't want anyone talking her out of it.

Several contractions later she rang the hospital. The midwife on duty told her that, yes, she was probably in labour, but as it was her first baby, she most likely had hours, if not days, to go, and that she'd be better off staying at home and getting her hubby to run her a bath and make her a nice cup of tea. She stuck it out for another half-hour before she headed to the hospital. Let's get this over with.

She liked the midwife who examined her. Or maybe she just wanted to like her – she was desperate to latch on to anyone. And this woman was gentle. Soft, warm hands, quiet, measured movements.

'You're only one centimetre,' she was saying. 'You may as well go home. It'll be a long time yet.'

Please don't send me home.

The gentle one was leaving the room.

'Please don't send me home.'

The midwife came back and leaned over the bed, her hand clasping Emily's forearm. 'Are you on your own?'

Emily nodded, somehow unable to speak.

'Would you like me to call someone for you?'

Emily shook her head and bit her lip.

'Your mother? A sister? A friend?'

'I'm having the baby adopted. Nobody can know.'

The midwife squeezed Emily's arm. 'You can stay here as long as you like. You might get moved around a bit, though. Try and get some rest and I'll be back to check on you in a while.'

Emily sagged back into the bed. Thank you, God.

And, for the next twenty-four hours, that was the last thing she felt inclined to thank God for.

The pain was bad enough.

The terror of the unknown worse.

But the sense of aloneness. That's what unhinged her.

The gentle midwife was with her for the first half, holding her hand, massaging her shoulders and feet. The sense of betrayal she experienced when the woman's shift ended was enormous. But she had to pick up her children. She promised she'd call in the next day.

'Would you not give your mam a call?' was the last thing she said.

Emily shook her head, tears gathering momentum at the corners of her eyes. She couldn't. Not now. Not like this.

And as for Joe . . .

In her weaker moments, those moments of agony towards the end, her need of him was ferocious, as if he'd only just left her and the last few months of hardening her heart against him had never happened.

Her new midwife was briskly efficient and lacked the bedside manner of her colleague. In a funny way, this was an unexpected relief. Emily stopped being tearful and focused on the matter at hand. Let's get this done. And the woman was there when it was crucial. Push. Pant. Rest. Push again. Until at half past three that morning, Emily's baby was born. Six pounds, eleven ounces. They laid the baby on Emily's chest, inside her nightdress, where it lay snuffling and covered in sticky stuff. It only started to cry when they took it away to clean it up.

Later, when they were both sanitized and wheeled to the ward, Emily eased herself into a sitting position and reached for her mobile. She rang the last – the only – number she had for Joe Devine. The mobile number that had remained resolutely unanswered for a whole week after he'd left, before she'd given up trying to contact him. It went straight to voicemail. Her throat tightened at the sound of his voice. She waited for the beep. 'I thought you should know. You have a baby daughter.'

Then she switched off her phone, lay on her side and stared at her baby.

She looked just like her father.

Later that morning, Emily's daughter lay cradled in her arms as she fed her from a bottle. She was wrapped in a pink blanket that some nurse had given her and dressed in a borrowed Babygro and nappy. Emily hadn't thought of these things. She hadn't packed a bag. Why should she when it wasn't really happening? It had been more than an hour since she'd rung the woman from the adoption agency. The foster-family should have been here by now.

She heard footsteps coming towards her bed and saw a shadow behind her curtain – she hadn't wanted to talk to the other mothers.

It was the gentle midwife. She approached Emily's bed cautiously. 'They're here.'

Emily nodded.

'Do you want to meet them?'

She shook her head.

'I'll just give you a minute.' She went back out and Emily could hear her footsteps receding.

For a long time she looked down at the baby, who had finished feeding and was now sleeping, her tiny face puckered and closed. Emily brushed her daughter's cheek with the back of her finger. Then she bent low and breathed in the scent that emanated from her head. As she heard more footsteps approaching, she stuck out the tip of her tongue and licked her baby's temple.

The midwife came through the curtain. 'Ready?' She held out her arms. Emily handed her the baby, who squealed in protest.

Then they were gone. Footsteps receding again. Voices. Gone.

Emily sat there for a while. Then she lay down and faced the wall.

Her breasts ached, her stitches stung.

And in her heart there was a hollow place where the baby had been.

15

The next time Mrs Prendergast emerged from her little wooden door, she was accompanied not by a tray or a trowel but by a tall, dark-haired man in his forties. His bearing was so princely, his carriage so erect, that he could have been none other than Mrs Prendergast's son. Mother and son stood talking together for some minutes, just inside the door. Eventually they came over to Aoife, Mrs Prendergast a few paces ahead.

Aoife laid down her hoe and rubbed the worst of the muck off her hands on to the arse of her jeans. Nobody would be looking there anyway. She was touched by the pride and pleasure in the old woman's eyes as she introduced the visitor. 'Aoife Madigan, this is my son, Lance Prendergast.'

Lance stepped forward and held out his hand. 'How do you do, Aoife?'

Aoife shook it, no doubt leaving behind an earthy residue, which he had the good manners to ignore. His hand was cool and firm, his smile unwavering and his eyes direct. Shit. He was even quite good-looking, if you liked that kind of thing. He was dressed, very snazzily, in a dark suit, very much the businessman.

'My mother told me about the Trojan work you three have been doing on the garden, so I decided I'd have to come and see for myself.'

'Oh. Well. That's . . . kind of you.'

'What is it you're doing here exactly?' He pointed to the ground beneath them.

'I'm planting seed potatoes. Should have a crop some time in July.'

He was looking hard at her, as if trying to evaluate something. 'Excellent. My mother tells me she's been promised all the fresh fruit and veg she can eat.'

'That's right.'

He smiled at his mother and she beamed back. Aoife was quite taken aback. She had never seen Mrs Prendergast beam before – hadn't thought she had it in her. Even Liam, the most regular beneficiary of her smiles, never got the full-wattage treatment. Would Aoife be like that when Liam was older? Who was she kidding? She was like that now.

'I'll be looking forward to some spectacular dinners this summer, then,' Lance was saying. They all laughed politely.

'There's someone else I must introduce you to. Mr Rosenberg!'

Uri didn't hear her call, so Mrs Prendergast went towards the far corner of the garden where he was labouring, leaving Aoife and Lance alone. He drew a step closer, so that he was standing squarely in front of her. It was quite intimidating – he was so tall and smart.

'What the hell do you think you're doing?' he said.

'I beg your pardon?' Aoife genuinely thought she'd misheard. He was still smiling at her, but the words coming out of his mouth didn't match his expression. Until she looked into his eyes.

'I said, what the hell do you think you're doing, taking advantage of a helpless old lady like this?'

Helpless old lady? Aoife almost laughed when she realized he was referring to Mrs Prendergast. 'I can assure you I'm doing no such thing.'

'You know full well that my mother has all but agreed to sell this land. I'll not have a bunch of . . .' he searched for an appropriate phrase '. . . hippie misfits mess it up for her.'

She nearly laughed again. 'Hippie misfits'. Was that the best he could come up with? But she didn't laugh, because something in his eyes was really quite horrible.

He continued: 'We – she stands to make a lot of money out of this transaction. I'm sure you wouldn't like to stand in the way of a comfortable retirement for her.'

Or a whopping great inheritance for you, thought Aoife. 'Of course not,' she said, forcing herself to hold his eye.

'Lance, come and meet Mr Rosenberg.'

With one more warning look Lance turned away from her, baring his teeth at Uri, whom she heard admiring his suit.

The son wanted the garden sold.

The mother adored the son.

They were toast.

Later, after he'd gone, Mrs Prendergast came back out in her gardening gear. She stood beside Aoife as she pulled on her gloves. 'My goodness, that weed really does get everywhere, doesn't it?'

Aoife straightened and looked at her suspiciously. Could Mrs Prendergast actually be making conversation?

'You know he's single,' she went on.

'Who?'

'Lance. He's single.'

'Oh. Really.'

'Yes. He's handsome, isn't he?' She had a faraway look in her eye.

'Um, yes. Very.'

Mrs Prendergast smiled, then regarded Aoife critically. 'You know, dear, you might be quite pretty if you made a little effort.' And off she went to tend her roses.

16

Aoife gazed into her palm. She was holding a handful of possibilities. Myriad microcosms of worlds. Worlds she could so easily let slip through her fingers. Tomato seeds. Dozens of them. Each one capable of great things. But not one capable of becoming anything other than a tomato plant. Not a carrot or a courgette or a cauliflower. Just as she was incapable of growing into anything other than Aoife Madigan.

It was early in the morning. Ridiculously so. Not even half past seven. She'd come to the garden because Liam was on a sleepover – his first – with a little boy he'd got to know at the crèche. The other child's mother had offered to take them both there this morning. Such a sensible idea. Now it took every ounce of will-power Aoife had to stop herself going over to their house right now and hugging the breath out of her son. She hadn't been able to sleep without his knees sticking into the small of her back, and with no lecture to give until eleven and no little boy to prepare for the day, she felt utterly redundant. Which was why she had come to the garden. At least here she could do something useful. She could plant things that would grow into food.

She knelt on the earth that spring morning and slowly, painstakingly, following to the letter the instructions on the back of the seed packet, sowed her tomatoes in cute little seed trays. It was too early in the year to trust them to the soil. Then she sowed lettuce. She imagined the rows and rows of succulent green plants they were to become, like something out of *Peter Rabbit*.

She wasn't alone. A robin was perched in the uppermost branches of the tallest, oldest, most gnarled apple tree, singing his beautiful song. Aoife felt blessed, as if the song was for her ears alone. A private recital.

'Won't you promise to eat any slugs that come near my lettuces?' she said to him. He continued to trill. She smiled and returned to her task.

She must have spent a full hour sifting the soil with a giant sieve, discarding stones and roots, hair dusted with misty rain, overcoming her fear of spiders, when a thought came unbidden: all she needed was a man to steal up behind her and kiss the nape of her neck, where the soft downiness of her hair met the cool creaminess of her skin. The thought startled her and she shivered. She swung around. 'Michael?'

But no one was there. Nothing, in fact, but the brute force of her loneliness.

Uri arrived at nine o'clock, as expected. He was semi-retired and dedicated most of his mornings to the garden. But today he wasn't alone. He had with him a younger man, in his mid- to late-thirties, judging by the web of lines around his eyes. 'This is Seth, my son. Seth, this is Aoife.'

'Hi.'

'Hello.'

'Seth is a gardener. He'd like to help.'

'Really?' A gardener! Uri had never said. He'd mentioned his sons – he had two – but a gardener . . .

'That's if it's okay with you.'

'Of course it is,' Aoife said quickly. 'Absolutely. I mean, when can you start?'

He smiled and held out his hands. 'Right now?'

She never would have pegged him as Uri's son. He must favour his mother, she thought. He was taller than his father but by no means gigantic. His hair was brown, greying at the temples, and she couldn't tell what colour his eyes were because they were screwed up against the sun. His skin had the weatherbeaten texture of someone who spent a lot of time outdoors and his arms were freckled, like speckled birds' eggs.

'You do know that the future of the garden is very grim, don't you?'

'I know. But I don't see any fat ladies singing just yet.'

'No.' She laughed. Funny.

'So, Aoife, what can I do for you?'

The answers crowded inside her head. 'Well, no one's gone near the pond yet. You could give that a go.'

'Right you are.'

She watched him walk away, his jaunty steps, as though he had a spring in him. 'Why didn't you tell me your son was a gardener?' she asked Uri.

'He's had a rough time of it lately. I wanted to wait. I didn't want to put him under any pressure.'

They watched Seth work, straight into it already, his movements fluid, very unlike how Aoife imagined her own movements to be – awkward and stuttering. Amateurish. He'd be such a help. And he might even have a few spare plants knocking around.

Later that night, after Liam had gone to bed and before she climbed into a well-deserved bath, Aoife did something she hadn't done for a while. She looked at herself in the mirror. *Really* looked. Peered. Examined. Things had certainly changed since the last time she'd studied herself and she got quite a shock. Her hair, with its silver roots and faded, coloured ends, resembled an Ice Pop with part of the juice sucked out of it. God, she'd really let herself go. She'd never

74

thought that her appearance mattered that much to her, but now, staring at her haggard reflection, at this woman old beyond her thirty-five years, she cared. What had happened to the laid-back, smiling girl Michael had fallen in love with and married? She could remember a time when the only thing that ever got her down was gravity. Now look at her! All dragged down and dishevelled. It was time to drag herself back up again. She owed it to Liam and she owed it to herself.

17

The for-sale sign was up now. They tried their hardest to ignore it, but it still cast its long shadow over the garden. March came in like a lion and went out like a lamb. The gales blew the sign down. They all cheered. The onset of April's showers cooled them, enchanted them, soaked them to the skin.

Liam had his own patch now – sunflowers. He watered them diligently every day with his Winnie-the-Pooh watering-can. He was in a state of high excitement over the introduction of fish into the pond. Seth had brought along some tiddlers one Saturday morning, allowed them to rest for a while, their plastic bags floating as they became acclimatized to their new home, then released them. This morning he had brought another tiddler with him – his four-year-old daughter, Kathy. She was two months younger than Liam and a head taller. And, Aoife discovered as she lifted the little girl up into the arms of the apple tree, at least a tonne heavier.

'I thought they could play together,' said Seth. 'Keep each other out of trouble. You don't mind, do you?'

'Why should I?'

'You just seem surprised.'

'Only because I didn't know you had a daughter.'

'Well, I do.'

'So I see.' She smiled at him and he averted his eyes.

'Are you using those loppers, Aoife?'

'No. Work away.'

He had this way of saying her name. Other Irish people

had it too. In England, once people had come to terms with its strangeness, they pronounced it 'Eefa'. Flat. But here, the pronunciation was softer. As if every vowel mattered.

Coming across other Aoifes had been a novelty. As a child, she had despised her name. Nobody could spell it, nobody could pronounce it and it marked her out as different. But as she became older, it made her special. Unique. Until she had come to Ireland where she was one of many. She had felt quite put out at all those other women stealing her name.

'I like your hair,' said Emily, wandering by with a wheelbarrow.

'Thanks.'

They smiled at each other. They'd been having the odd conversation of late, mainly about books, and Aoife felt she was making progress. Emily still wore her sadness like a cloak, but sometimes you could find an opening. She watched her trundle the wheelbarrow along the path. Then her heart caught. 'Liam!' She began to run. 'Liam!' she screamed. 'Get down!'

The others stopped what they were doing and stared, first at her and then at Liam – hanging upside down by his knees from a branch of the apple tree. She reached him. 'Jesus Christ, come here!' She dragged him off the branch, turned him the right way up and hugged him. 'You're all right, you're all right,' she muttered over and over again, kissing the top of his head repeatedly.

'Ow. You're hurting me.' Liam squirmed.

She released him reluctantly.

'What's wrong? What happened?'

'We were only pretending to be bats, Daddy,' said Kathy, giving Aoife a resentful look.

They were all gathered around now, staring at her. She realized, with embarrassment, that she'd overreacted. 'Sorry, everyone, it was nothing. I just got a fright, that's all. I thought he was going to fall.'

They murmured and returned to their tasks. Mentally Aoife kicked herself. Just when she'd thought she was getting back to normal something like this happened to remind her that she was still mad, after all.

That Saturday afternoon was magical. The sun shone magnificently. It was the first day they'd been able to wear T-shirts – apart from Mrs Prendergast who wore a white broderie-anglaise short-sleeved blouse. The robin had found a mate and they'd decided to build a nest. When they didn't have twigs in their beaks, they sang their heads off. Seth had introduced some frogspawn into the pond earlier that spring and the water was alive with tadpoles. Liam and Kathy were forever capturing them in jam jars and peering at them, willing their little froggy legs to appear. Harriet, the fat, old retriever, snuffled around, wagging her geriatric tail, eventually flopping down in a panting heap on the newly planted herbs.

Some days they drew quite a crowd, passers-by staring in at the gate pausing in their rush-hour rush. Occasionally somebody would call one of them over and ask what they were doing.

Defying logic?

They had a definite plan now and the planting was gathering momentum. Each gardener had his or her own tasks and they had divided the garden into four quadrants: the kitchen garden, the rose garden, the orchard and what they called the secret garden, because Emily wouldn't tell them what she was doing in it. At first Aoife thought it was a cottage garden, but there seemed to be more to it than that. Seth cared for the pond and was, as he said, a general dogsbody. He was also in charge of wheelbarrow rides. Liam and Kathy would get in and he would zoom up and down the paths, making racing-car noises, swerving just in time to avoid trees and pretending to tip them into the pond. The children would giggle wildly. It made Aoife's heart ache to see how much her son loved the male attention.

Mrs Prendergast was less impressed with the great wheelbarrow races. '*Must* you make that infernal racket?'

'Why don't you hop in yourself, Mrs P, give it a lash?'

Seth tilted the barrow towards her. She gave him a withering look – she didn't have much time for him. Aoife imagined she thought him uncouth.

Aoife was mainly in charge of the kitchen garden, although 'in charge' wasn't the right way to put it. The arrangement was more relaxed than that. But she spent more time there than anyone else did. There was something about growing food that appealed to the practical side of her nature. What could be more fundamental to life? She liked to feel she wasn't squandering her time. Of course she made mistakes constantly, not having done it before. Take the tomatoes. She was only transplanting them from the seed trays to their little pots now. She knew she'd left it too late and that they'd be lagging behind, as she pressed down the compost with her bare fingers and sprayed the roots. 'Grow, little ones, grow,' she whispered, then looked around furtively to make sure that no one had heard her. She had made a start on the green beans too, erecting cane pyramids, anticipating their little orange flowers. Kneeling in the mud, she felt a ridiculous level of contentment. She didn't hear Emily come up behind her.

'I'm ready now.'

Aoife jumped. 'Emily, I didn't see you there.' Had she heard her talking to the plants?

'I'm ready to tell you now.'

'What. You mean . . . ?'

'To tell you what I've been planning for my part of the garden.'

'Oh.' Aoife scrambled to her feet. 'Let's go.'

'I didn't want to say anything before because I wasn't sure how it was going to work out.'

'That's okay.' She searched the girl's face. She'd never seen her so animated.

'Anyway, what I was hoping to make was a sensory garden.' She seemed to be seeking Aoife's approval.

'Go on.'

'Imagine a garden that was a total feast for the senses. You enter here, honeysuckle on one side, jasmine on the other. I was going to ask Seth to help me put up a pergola.'

She looked at Aoife, who nodded at her to continue.

'We could put a little swing seat underneath. A person could sit there and just absorb the fragrance. Then I want to put a pebble path here. You walk along barefoot first thing in the morning. It's a reflexology thing. At the end of the path there's a bubble fountain – the soothing sound of water. I'm going to hang wind chimes from the branch of that tree and I'll plant some tall, ornamental grasses to the right. The breeze will rustle them. And colour. I want lots of colour.'

Aoife said nothing as she watched Emily's hand movements become more expansive.

'A green area – like the green room in a theatre. Lots of lovely, relaxing foliage. Then pink – to relieve tension – a blossoming cherry, I think. Crimsons and golds and coppers to raise energy levels. Think daffodils and tulips in the spring. Wallflowers! Maybe Liam could plant me a row of sunflowers. And then we have to have some herbs.' She was gabbling now. 'Lavender lining that path – French lavender. It has a better fragrance than English. No offence.'

'None taken.'

'And I want to place troughs of herbs on either side of a bench right there.' She looked at Aoife expectantly.

'Is that it?'

'Oh, and fairy-lights around the pergola beams. I'll hang coloured lanterns from the bushes and plant a camomile lawn. That's it. For now. What do you think?'

'What do I think?'

'Yes.'

'I think you're either a madwoman or a genius.'

She saw doubt cloud the girl's features and amended her words quickly. 'What I really mean is I think you're inspired. A true artist.'

'Really?' Her cheeks bloomed.

'Yes, really. Only, Emily, you know as well as I do that the garden probably isn't –'

'Don't say it!' Emily held up a hand as if warding off a curse, startling Aoife with the ferocity of her emotion. 'I can't bear to think about it. The garden deserves . . .' she searched for the right words '. . . one last hurrah. And we're the ones who have to give it to her.'

Aoife liked that. A 'last hurrah'. Yes, why not? Why the hell not? 'Okay, Emily. Do your worst.'

Seth was putting up an archway for Mrs Prendergast's roses. She was supervising, with much derision. 'Not like that. Look at it, for God's sake. It's all lopsided.'

'Do you want to have a go?'

'Don't be ridiculous. Not with my arthritis.'

'Well, would you mind letting me get on with it, then?'

'What? And let you mess it up?'

'Hi there.' Aoife joined them.

'Great. Another woman to tell me what to do.' But when he looked at her, his eyes were smiling. She couldn't get a handle on his eyes. The colour, that was. They seemed to change in accordance with the landscape. Today they mirrored the sky in their blueness.

Mrs Prendergast sighed theatrically. 'I could murder a cup of tea.'

'Would you like me to –'

'No, thank you, Aoife.' Mrs Prendergast still didn't allow any of them into her home. They had to use the toilet in the Good Food Store, apart from Liam and Kathy who were allowed to go in the nettles, tinkling and squatting accordingly. 'I suppose *you* want a mug of that revolting coffee,' she said to Seth.

'That'd be marvellous, Mrs P.'

'Stop calling me that.'

'Well, if you insist on not telling me your name . . .'

Mrs Prendergast snorted as she walked off to prepare their elevenses.

'She loves me really.' Seth grinned.

'You know, I'm beginning to think she does. She just hasn't realized it yet.'

He recommended hammering the archway into place, Aoife handing him nails at intervals, working in silence. She was reminded again of how much she enjoyed his presence in the garden. Just to watch the way he carried out his tasks. To be with him. After a time, she sat on the ground, her arms wrapped around her knees. She wanted to know more about him.

'Kathy seems a very well-adjusted little girl.'

Instinctively Seth looked across at his daughter, who appeared to be teaching Liam how to make daisy chains. She took the lead in most of their games. 'She's great.'

'She's a credit to you and her mother.'

He shrugged. 'Thanks. She's a tough little thing, really. She's been through a lot.'

'Like what?' Aoife instantly wished she could take it back. She didn't know how far she could push it. Seth seemed such an odd mixture of confidence and reticence. He was standing upright now, his hands on his hips. He looked at Aoife as if he was working out whether or not he could trust her.

'You know her mother and I are separated?'

'No, I didn't. I thought . . . well, no, I didn't know.'

There was a silence. Seth appeared to be examining the mud on his boots.

'Does she see her mother?'

'Oh, yes. God, yes. She spends part of the week with her and part of it with me. It's just a bit confusing for Kathy at the moment.'

'Is there another –'

'Tea, everybody!'

18

It was quite a burden being an Irish teenager called Seth Rosenberg in the 1980s. He kind of stood out among the Seamus Brennans and the Paddy Moloneys. But his bald penis gave him rarity value in his twenties.

Seth liked girls and they liked him. He didn't know why this should be so, but he was glad it was. He had been accused more than once of having 'a way with the laydeez'. He didn't know about that. All Seth knew was that he was himself and that seemed to work. His sense of security came from several sources, not least his parents' unshakeable, immovable, unstoppable love for him. His mother adored her two boys with every ounce of her considerable being. Although Seth knew that it was him she loved best. Maybe his brother felt that too. It was a thought that had only occurred to him of late – as had many other previously unthought-of thoughts. He supposed that was what happened when your world got turned on its head.

His relationship with his father had been more turbulent. While his mother's love was pure indulgence, Uri's love was born of discipline – he was determined that his sons would make something of themselves. Although as it became obvious that Seth would never travel down an academic route, he had had the wisdom to let him go his own way, serving his apprenticeship as a gardener and eventually building up his own successful landscaping business.

Growing up, Seth had found his father's dark moods oppressive and had had to get away from him. Neither broody nor introspective himself, he couldn't handle either trait in another.

And he didn't want to think about it.

But as he'd got older, he'd deepened in understanding and his impatience with his father's faith had matured into respect.

So. His parents' love. His innate likeability. His popularity with women. The knowledge he'd had since boyhood that he wanted to work with plants. The successful realization of his ambition. It could have been said that Seth had led a charmed life. Of course he'd had his bad days. But, really, they were few and far between.

Seth was twenty-nine when he met Megan. He fell hard – harder than he would have thought possible. He'd assumed he'd been in love before but now he understood that he'd only ever been in lust. He'd said, 'I love you,' several times. He hadn't meant to lie to those women, but the moment he met Megan, he knew he'd been lying all along. She was pure, golden, unadulterated gorgeousness. She bowled him over.

The night they met had seemed inauspicious enough. He'd been in the pub with the lads. She was the friend of a friend of somebody's girlfriend. The link was tenuous, but enough to merit an introduction. He'd wanted to say something to make her laugh but he'd sat there like a fool. She had been kind, bailing him out, asking him questions about himself until he'd regained the power of speech. But he'd never really recovered. Not from Megan.

They'd got married almost two years to the day after their first meeting. As he watched her walk up the aisle towards him, he felt as if his heart was going to explode.

Had it all been a lie?

* * *

'It's so nice living with your best friend,' said Megan. She was sitting up in bed, propped up against Seth's pillow and her own. They weren't long back from their honeymoon – one of their first weekends of married life. She was watching Seth as he shaved in the en-suite. He stopped scraping the white foam off his jawline with his new razor and gazed back at the reflection in the mirror. She looked so incredibly contented. He padded out to her, fresh from his shower, white towel draped around his waist, and stood over her, dripping foam. 'Am I your best friend?' he asked.

'You know you are.' She patted the space beside her and he sat down on the edge of the bed.

'You're my best friend too and I love living with you,' he said.

She smiled at him and he admired her adorable dimples.

'God, you're gorgeous,' he said, reaching to stroke her cheek. She leaned her face into his palm. He still couldn't believe at times that he was permitted to touch her. But he was. He even had the papers to prove it. He wiped the rest of his shaving foam off with the edge of his towel and bent to kiss her mouth, softly at first. Then he cupped her face with his hands and kissed her deeply. He opened his eyes just in time to see her look of panic. And even if he hadn't seen it, he'd felt her pull back. 'What's wrong?'

'Nothing.'

'Don't you want . . . ?'

'It's not that. It's just that I've planned a special breakfast for you.'

'We can have it later.'

'I'm starving.' She flung back the covers and sprang out of bed. He watched as she put on her dressing-gown and drew the belt tight around her waist. 'I'm making bacon and scrambled eggs. Your favourite. And freshly squeezed orange juice.'

'Sounds great.'

She kissed his cheek and he listened to her dainty clop-clopping down the stairs. She was right. They were best friends.

Except he already had a best friend. His name was Barry and he'd known him since he was six. But he didn't want to have sex with Barry. He wanted to have sex with his wife. But he was beginning to form the distinct impression that his wife didn't want to have sex with him.

They'd abstained before marriage. He felt stupid admitting it now. It had been her idea. 'Imagine how special our wedding night will be,' she'd said.

And he had gone along with it. Because he would have done anything for Megan to keep her happy. To keep her. But the wedding night had come and gone and he had yet to see a marked change in her response. Sure, they did it sometimes, but he always had to initiate it and, hard as he tried, he could never shake the feeling that she was just letting him do things to her. It didn't feel as if they were doing it together. Making love. He would have laughed once at this phrase, but now he understood. He loved her. She loved him. What was the problem?

A couple of months into their marriage, he decided to broach the subject. They were in bed. Seth was lying on his side, propped up on his elbow, his head resting in his palm. Megan was sitting bolt upright as he ran his fingers delicately up and down her forearm. She looked almost virginal in her white nightgown. 'Is something wrong, Meg?'

She looked surprised. 'Wrong? No. What do you mean?'

'You never seem to want to have sex.' He tried carefully to read the expression on her face. Uncomfortable, maybe. As if she wished he wouldn't bring up such a distasteful matter.

'We do have sex.'

'Yes, but not very often. And I feel like I'm – I don't know – forcing you or something.'

'That's just silly.'

'Maybe it is. But that's the way I feel.'

Neither said anything for a while. He noticed she'd pulled her arm away. 'Don't you fancy me any more?' He hated himself for saying it, feeling pathetic and unmanly.

Megan rolled her eyes. 'Of course I do.' She sounded almost angry. Her tone, her body language screamed, 'Go away.'

'Did something happen to you?'

'What do you mean?'

'When you were younger, did something traumatic happen to you? Did someone hurt you?'

'Oh, don't be so ridiculous, Seth. You're blowing this way out of proportion.'

Was he? He couldn't tell. 'Am I?'

'Yes, you are. Look. As a man, your libido is stronger than mine, that's all. You naturally want it more than I do. It's perfectly normal. Probably all husbands feel the same way.'

Did they? Perhaps. He allowed himself to be soothed, wanting to believe it, although a niggle of doubt remained.

'Now, come here and give me a cuddle.' She pulled him close to her so that his head was resting on her chest. More cuddling. 'Do you realize how lucky we are, Seth, to have each other? I don't know any other girls who get on so well with their husbands or boyfriends. I mean, we do everything together.'

It was true. They did. Except . . .

'And there's no one else I'd rather spend my time with.'

'Me neither.' It was true. There wasn't.

'So let's just appreciate what we have.' She stroked his hair.

She was right as usual. Seth lay there and did his best to feel appreciative. Although mostly he just felt horny.

Then, the following month, something happened that changed things drastically. They were eating out one night, on the occasion of Megan's twenty-ninth birthday. Seth had ordered champagne. He watched his wife as she sparkled across the table. They were waiting for their dessert to arrive when she covered his hand with her own. He felt a surge of happiness at her touch. 'Seth,' she said. 'I've been doing a lot of thinking lately.'

'Oh, yeah. About what?'

'Well, I think it might be time,' she paused to take a sip of champagne, 'for us to try for a baby.'

'What?' Seth was astonished. He hadn't seen that one coming.

'A baby, Seth. You heard what I said. What do you think?' Her voice was gentle but her eyes were full of concern.

'Jesus, Megan! Of all the things to spring on me!'

'You can't be that surprised. We've talked about it before. You said you wanted kids.'

'I do, I do. Some day. Not right away.'

'Why not?'

'We're barely married. We still have loads of things to get for the house –'

'You think furniture's more important than a family?'

'No! No, of course not. I didn't mean that. I just mean – what's the big rush all of a sudden?'

'It's not a "big rush".'

He was pissing her off. He could tell.

'I suppose it's because I'm twenty-nine now. It's made me think. I can see thirty looming. The younger a woman has her babies, the better it is for her physically.'

Babies! They had gone from baby to babies in under a minute. How many sprogs did the woman want?

'I just don't see the point in waiting,' she continued. 'We have each other, we're married, we have our house. We're both bringing in an income.'

She was making perfect sense, of course. As usual. He smiled at her and covered her small, perfect, feminine hand with his big calloused one. 'I suppose I was hoping to keep you to myself for as long as possible.'

Megan smiled, sensing victory. 'You'll still have me,' she said. 'I'm not going anywhere.'

'When do you want to start trying?'

'Tonight if you like.'

That sealed the deal.

From that night on, everything became wonderful and rose-coloured in Seth's world. The one thing that had been missing from his life, he now had. The sight of his wife bouncing up and down on top of him, milky breasts jiggling, hair flying, became a common occurrence. He couldn't get enough of her. He felt as if he'd struck gold. At last he had a willing participant. When she wasn't having sex with him, she was reading books about fertility, most favourable positions, foods to eat. She even had him taking zinc tablets, one a day, every morning with his breakfast. She made him laugh, supervising him like a hospital matron. He wasn't allowed to carry his mobile in his front pocket any more. And he was under strict instructions not to put his laptop on his lap. Something about heating up the testicles. He was glad enough to go along with it all, just as he always did everything in his power to make Megan happy.

His best mate pulled him up on it. They were having a drink one night, in what used to be their local. Seth had just told Barry – still a bachelor and proud of it – that they were trying for a baby. 'So you could be looking at a daddy before long.'

'Is that really what you want?'

'Of course it's what I want.'

'Who came up with the idea?'

'Well – Megan, I suppose.'

'Ah, yes. What Megan wants, Megan gets.'

'What the fuck is that supposed to mean?'

'Nothing, nothing. I didn't mean anything.' Barry held up his hands defensively.

Seth took a gulp of his pint. 'Look, you're not even married. You don't know what you're talking about.'

'True. You're absolutely right. What do I know about having a wife?'

'Exactly. Fuck all.'

'I'm just looking out for you, that's all. Making sure it's what you want too.'

'It is.'

'Well, then, I'm happy for you.'

'Thanks.'

'You're welcome.'

They dropped the matter and spent the rest of the night discussing the Premiership. Neither wanted to jeopardize their friendship.

But the conversation had made Seth think. He spoke to his brother, Aaron. They were in their parents' house, fixing a leak under the kitchen sink. 'What do you think of Megan?' he said suddenly, as if he was trying to catch his brother off-guard.

His brother looked at him through the U-bend, puzzled. 'What do I think of her?'

'Yes.'

'What are you asking me that for?'

'Just answer the question.'

His brother considered it for a few moments. 'Well, she's a fine-looking bird and she makes a mean shepherd's pie.'

Seth laughed, comforted by his brother's lack of depth. But he knew it would be a cop-out to end the investigation there. He should take it to a higher court. To the people who loved him best in the world.

He didn't ask his mother. He was pretty sure he already had a handle on her feelings for Megan. She liked her as well as she could like any woman who had taken Seth away from her. He believed she thought Megan pretty, intelligent and personable – decent daughter-in-law material if one had to have such a creature in one's life. This was what he believed. He lacked the courage to put it to the test. So he asked his father.

He and Uri were clearing up together after one of his mother's delectable roasts. It was just the two of them. 'Da, can I ask you something?'

'Of course.'

'What do you think – I mean *really* think – of Megan?'

His father looked at him for a very long time. Then he spoke. 'I believe you are very much in love with her.'

Seth nodded. He wouldn't have expected anything less from the Zen master. Uri had hit the nail on the head. It didn't matter what anybody else thought of her. He loved Megan and that was the beginning and the end of it. The alpha and the omega. It was irrelevant now anyway, because after three months, during which time Seth had watched his wife's jiggling turn from enthusiastic to desperate, Megan had succeeded in becoming pregnant. *They* were pregnant – as she was prone to say, making him cringe.

He didn't know how he felt about it, really. He knew she was thrilled and he knew that they had stopped doing the wild thing. She didn't want to hurt the baby. Truth be told, he couldn't relate to the thing that was growing inside his wife's belly. She still looked the same to him. Apart from a funny look around her eyes at times.

Megan threw herself into 'their' pregnancy with much gusto. And Seth went along with it. Painting the nursery. Putting up a jungle-animal frieze and hanging a matching mobile over the cot. They went on shopping trips to Mothercare and bought tiny white Babygros and hats – they reminded him of miniature skullcaps. And then there were the interminable conversations about names. She never tired of that one.

In time, the pregnancy started to show. Megan had already bought a lifetime's supply of maternity clothes. Seth kept waiting for the baby to feel more real to him, but it never happened. He did, however, like to look at his pregnant wife, thinking her incredibly voluptuous, with her full breasts resting neatly on her swollen belly. He dutifully held his hand on her bump every time she alerted him to a kick – and tried hard not to think, So what? What she was feeling was clearly more profound than what he was feeling. But the days turned into weeks turned into months. Until the unbelievable became inevitable and his wife was full-term. As in, he could become a father at any second. And still the enormity of it escaped him.

Then one day he was out on a job. He'd just returned to his jeep, having spent the morning planting a grove of native trees, when his mobile rang. It was his brother, Aaron. 'Where the hell have you been?'

'Nowhere. Here. What's wrong?'

'Your wife's gone into labour. We've been trying to contact you for the last two hours. You'd better get to the hospital pretty sharpish if you know what's good for you.'

'Is she okay?'

'Far as I know.' Aaron laughed. 'You'd better hurry.'

Seth cut Aaron off only to discover he had fifteen missed calls and eight messages on his phone. He didn't stop to check them, just hot-rodded it to the hospital.

When Megan saw him she yelled, 'Where were you?' then

dissolved into tears. 'Seth.' She held out her arms. 'I'm so scared.'

'It's okay, love. I'm here now.' He felt a greater bond with his wife at that moment than he had in the past nine months.

Over the next few hours it seemed to Seth that some primeval creature, its face contorted with pain, had taken over his wife's body. All he could do was watch.

Their daughter was born a few minutes after midnight, a swirl of black hair on her pointed little head. Seth had never seen or felt anything like it. She was real at last, this child of his.

'What'll we call her?' murmured Megan.

'After what you've been through, you should choose.'

'I want to call her Kathy.'

'Kathy it is.'

'Do you like it?'

'I love it.'

'I love you, Seth.'

'I love you too, Megan.'

She moved out of their bedroom shortly after her return from the hospital. It was so Seth could get some sleep, what with the baby crying all night. She didn't want him to fall asleep at the wheel and crash the jeep. He was grateful for this as Kathy did cry a lot, but he missed his wife's presence in their bed. Looking back, he was too overwhelmed at the time with new fatherhood to give it much thought. Who was this tiny blob who had taken over his entire existence? The red-faced, screaming despot who, for some unfathomable reason, he loved to distraction. Everyone said she was the spit of him. He couldn't see it. To him she was oddly like Uri. This minute bundle of femininity reminded him of a bearded old man. He hoped she'd grow out of it – he knew she would: she'd grow up to be the most beautiful woman ever to walk the planet. Apart from her mother.

A year passed, and Seth was still sleeping alone. It couldn't be the crying any more because Kathy had stopped. And she'd dropped her night-time feed.

It was breakfast time. Kathy was in her high chair. Megan was feeding her baby gloop. Seth stood at the counter with his mug of coffee. 'When are you moving back in, Meg?'

The spoon of gloop hung suspended in mid-air. Kathy's mouth gaped open like a baby bird's.

'Moving back in where?'

'You know where. Into our bedroom.'

Megan sighed. 'Aren't we fine the way we are?'

'No, Megan, I don't think we are. I want you to move back in.'

'But, Seth, darling, you snore.' She laughed prettily.

'I'll buy you a set of ear-plugs.' Seth was grim.

Kathy began to protest and Megan shovelled the food into her mouth. 'Look, Seth, I've been giving this some thought and I think it would be best if we could –'

'If we could what?'

'If we could – well – live like brother and sister.'

Seth felt something dangerous well up inside him.

'I mean,' Megan continued, sounding ever more confident, 'essentially that's what we've been doing for the past year and it's worked out pretty well, don't you think?'

Seth could contain himself no longer. 'I don't want a fucking sister,' he roared. 'I want a wife. You're supposed to be my fucking wife.'

There was a terrible silence in the kitchen. The two women in Seth's life stared at him in horror. Then they began to cry, first Megan, her face crumpling, then Kathy, wailing inconsolably. Seth lifted his daughter out of her high chair, sickened that he'd frightened her to tears. 'It's okay, it's okay,' he murmured, over and over, stroking her hair and kissing her forehead. 'It's okay.'

When the child finally calmed down, he handed her back to her mother. 'I won't be home tonight,' was all he said.

That night Seth got well and truly bladdered. He met up with Barry and the lads and fooled himself that it was just like old times. Most of his friends were unmarried. No wives, no kids, no responsibilities. After the pub, they got the Dart into town and went to a club. Once inside, Seth felt like a fish out of water so he drank like a fish. To forget about that and to forget about everything. A girl came up to him. She had over-processed hair and a strong Dublin accent. She was forward, tarty. The exact opposite to Megan. Seth went back to her flat and shagged her brains out.

He woke the next morning feeling sicker than he ever remembered feeling. The girl was in the shower. At least, the other side of the rumpled bed was empty and he could hear water running somewhere close by. He pulled on his clothes and left the flat, shutting the door quietly, wanting to put the whole sordid business behind him. He was in a part of town he didn't recognize. He caught a glimpse of his reflection in a shop window. He didn't recognize that either. He looked rough. He hailed a taxi and got the hell out of Dodge.

Once home, and miraculously still in possession of his keys, he let himself in and walked straight up the stairs. He knew Megan was at home because her car was parked outside, but he didn't look for her. He dragged his clothes off and left them in a heap on the bedroom floor. Then he stepped into the shower and attempted to wash away the excesses of the night. Feeling marginally better, he grabbed a towel and walked back into the bedroom. Megan was sitting on the bed, looking at him coldly.

He stood directly in front of her, towelling himself viciously, almost taunting her with his naked body.

'Where were you last night?'

'I told you I wouldn't be home.'

'I asked you a question, Seth.'

He took a step closer to her, bearing down now. 'You want to know where I was last night?' he hissed. 'Fucking some tart. That's where.'

Megan's lower lip trembled. Seth threw his towel on to the bed and began tugging out drawers, looking for clean clothes.

'How could you do that?' She was openly sobbing now.

'It was easy.'

Something had shifted. She was crying and he didn't even care. He had reduced his beloved wife to tears yet he didn't give a shit. What kind of cold bastard was he? Later there would be guilt, self-hatred and shame. But for now . . . Perhaps he was still drunk. He was fully dressed. 'I'm going to work.'

'What? Now? Just like that? You can't –'

But he was already gone.

On his way out of the house, he heard a noise coming from the sitting room. He paused and looked in at the door. Kathy was in her playpen, gurgling at her teddy bears. She saw Seth and her face broke into smiles. She held up her arms to him. He went inside and picked her up, hugging her fiercely until she squealed. He lifted her away and looked into her face. She was rubbing the side of her cheek, which was red. He automatically touched his own with his fingertips. Rough and unshaven. He'd given his little girl razor burn. He hugged her again, more carefully this time. 'That's the last time I'll ever hurt you, Kathy.'

Then he began to cry.

19

Subtle changes were taking place in the neighbourhood. There was a conspicuous lack of litter on the streets surrounding the garden, and the saplings that the corporation planted along the roadside, routinely snapped every couple of months by the local yobbos, had remained intact. The gardeners became accustomed to faces pressed against the wrought-iron gate, as if their owners were starved of beauty. Aoife tried to convince Mrs Prendergast to leave the gate open, but she wouldn't hear of it.

Subtle changes were taking place in the garden too, and not just to the plants. Walls within the walled garden were crumbling, between those who worked there and around some of their hearts.

Seth was helping Aoife plant out her tomatoes. It was a glorious May morning as they knelt together before the south-facing wall. Mrs Prendergast floated by, carrying her new secateurs with the flowered handle. 'You're planting them out too early.'

Seth looked up at her. 'Do you think so, Mrs P?'

'Yes. We may have more frost.'

'I don't think so.'

'I think we will.'

'I think we won't.'

'Have it your way.'

'I will.'

Mrs Prendergast stalked off, her expression thunderous.

'Why do you always have to antagonize her?'

'Because it's fun.'

Aoife laughed. 'You obviously haven't heard the rumours about her.'

'What rumours?'

She lowered her voice. 'That she murdered her husband and buried him in the garden.'

'This garden?'

'Yes.'

'Is that why she won't let us dig by the back wall?'

'Could be.'

They resumed working the soil.

'It wouldn't surprise me. I'd say the old targer has it in her all right. She frightens the shite out of me.'

'She's just an old woman.'

'All women are terrifying. Didn't you know?' Seth grinned at her. 'Hand me the first plant, would you?'

Aoife turned it upside down above her palm and shook the tender little plant free. It came loose in a shower of compost. She paused to examine the intricate root system, like delicate white threads, only alive. She felt as if she was looking into the plant's soul – staring at its innards. Learning its secrets. She almost felt she should ask its permission first.

'I *am* waiting.'

'Sorry.' She handed the plant to Seth, who settled it into its new home – the hole he'd prepared for it – and firmed the soil around it. They both knelt back and admired it.

'Do you want to do the next one?'

'Yes, please.' Aoife began to dig.

'You know,' said Seth, 'it wouldn't surprise me if she'd started the rumour herself.'

'Mrs Prendergast?'

'Yeah.'

'Why would she do that?'

'To frighten little children.'

'But she's great with children.'

'So are you.'

Aoife, embarrassed, paused momentarily in her work. 'I'm not that great.'

'You are. It must be hard bringing up Liam on your own. His father –'

'Mummy, you said I could water the 'matoes.' The little boy charged over with his Winnie-the-Pooh watering can, bored in the absence of Kathy, who was with her mother.

'Course you can. We haven't planted them all yet.'

He plonked himself on Aoife's lap and she wrapped her arms around him like a seatbelt. 'I can finish up here, Seth. I'm sure you have other stuff you want to be getting on with.'

'Right, then.' He stood up and wiped his hands on his jeans. 'Catch you later.'

She hoped she hadn't hurt his feelings but she just wasn't ready.

20

The thing that really got to Seth was that, to the outside world, it looked as if they had everything. He was handsome. She was pretty. He had his own thriving business. She was the attentive mother, famed for her superb cooking. They had a lovely home, with a garden people crossed the road especially to see. And the most beautiful baby girl anyone had ever set their eyes on. Yet behind closed doors they had nothing – except Kathy. She was everything they amounted to now and the only reason Seth stayed.

He didn't have any more one-night stands. The level of his self-disgust was already at an all-time high and he didn't need to add to it. Since that night, he and Megan had settled into an uneasy truce. They each did their own thing mostly. If friends invited them for dinner, they went, and when they'd gone everybody commented on what a lovely couple they were. The pretence made him despair. It also made him wonder how many other people were living a lie – cosied up in their sham marriages.

In truth, Seth was at a loss. He didn't know what to do, and for the moment it was easiest to go along with the charade. He was petrified by the thought of losing his daughter. No court was going to take a one-year-old away from her mother. He'd have to move into some grotty bedsit, unable to hold his little girl first thing in the morning and bathe her last thing at night. The idea gave him such a pain in his chest that he avoided thinking about it. Instead he sat and drank his beer in front of the telly while Megan trotted off to the gym. She said she wanted to lose the baby weight. He couldn't tell if she had or not because he made a point of not looking at her. His life became work and Kathy, Kathy and work. And it continued that way for a whole year.

He sensed a change in Megan. She breezed in and out of the house, her demeanour airy, her conversation light. She chatted to him as if they were friends. And she started giggling again – the girlish giggle he used to love. Now it annoyed the fuck out of him. What business did she have being happy when she'd made his life a bloody misery? He suspected she was having an affair. Though why he should care what she did was beyond him. But he was damned if she was going to start a new life while he was still stuck in the old one. He appraised her. She certainly looked well. She'd got her figure back, restored her tiny waist. And she'd done something to her hair – got yellow stripes in it. It was blonder. And, of course, when a person was happy, they looked better.

'What's his name?'

It was dinner-time and they were all in the kitchen. Seth sat at the table, playing with his mashed potato. Megan suspended her search for ketchup in the upper press. 'What did you say?'

'I asked you what his name was.'

She laughed without humour. 'That's what I thought you said. Who are you referring to exactly?'

'I don't know. You tell me.' He sat back in his chair and folded his arms, staring at his wife while his dinner congealed.

She shook her head and looked away. 'You think I have another man.'

'Well – don't you?'

They watched their daughter as she transferred sticky

handfuls of potato from her bowl to the floor, delighted with the splatting noise it made.

'I can assure you, Seth, that the last thing I want in my life is another man.'

'Well, what are you so goddamn happy about all the time?'

'I've just got my life back, that's all.'

He examined Megan's face. Was it true? He couldn't tell. On the one hand, it wasn't as if he could accuse her of being a nymphomaniac. On the other, it didn't quite ring true. No person could be so transformed just by 'getting their life back'.

So he transformed himself – into a suspicious, paranoid obsessive. He began watching her, analysing everything she said. He even checked her bedside drawers when she was out. He didn't know what he was looking for. Wasn't it the wife who was supposed to behave like this? And then one day he followed her. No sooner had she pulled out of the driveway than he leaped into his jeep and sped after her, just catching a glimpse of her car turning right at the end of the road. She'd dropped Kathy down to her mother's earlier so she'd be free to meet whoever. And he could have sworn she was wearing lipstick. He wove in and out of the traffic in an effort to keep up with her. She was going at some speed. Couldn't wait to get to *him*, he thought bitterly. Then Megan indicated and Seth indicated too, and they both pulled into the local Spar. Seth parked at a discreet distance from his wife's car and craned his neck. He could see her selecting items and bringing them up to the cash desk. Probably condoms. And whipped cream.

He slid down in his seat as she emerged. He tried to see what she'd bought. It looked like a newspaper and a sliced pan, but she could have other items concealed under the newspaper. She tore off again and he was right behind her, just two cars between them. He'd get her now. But – what was she doing? She was heading home. Shit. He waited five minutes before entering the front door himself. She looked up as he walked into the sitting room. 'I didn't know you were going out.' Her voice was mild.

'I just went to buy a lotto ticket. There's a rollover tonight. Big jackpot.'

She laughed. 'I just did the same thing. I was afraid I'd be too late. The draw's on in a minute. Want to watch it together?'

'No, thanks.'

He turned and walked out to the hall. He stood there for a few moments with his hands in his pockets. What a plank. It was time he copped himself on.

So he did. Normal life was resumed. He couldn't claim to be happy but he was pretty much coasting in neutral, finding his joy in his daughter and his plants.

Then one day he forgot his phone. He was expecting an important call at midday so he had no option but to go home and get it. He could see it with his mind's eye on the cabinet beside his bed. When he got home, Megan's car was parked outside the house. This was strange because she normally worked on Tuesday mornings, ever since she'd gone back to her job part time. There was another car outside the house too. One he didn't recognize. Maybe somebody was visiting the neighbours.

He let himself into the house and bounded up the stairs two at a time. All was quiet. His bedroom door was ajar. He pushed it open. His phone was on his bedside cabinet, as he'd remembered. But he didn't see it. Instead he saw Megan, lying in the bed they hadn't shared for more than two years. She was naked from the waist up. A sheet covered her bottom half, but he presumed she was naked from the waist down too. One milky, pink-tipped breast was exposed. The other was covered with the sleeping head of a dark-haired woman. The woman was beautiful in repose, long, curly hair and a generous bosom. Megan was awake, looking at him levelly. Without a word, she extricated herself ever so gently from the other woman's embrace. The woman murmured and shifted her position but remained asleep. Megan put on a robe – Seth's, because it was his room – and, still wordless, walked past him on to the landing and closed the bedroom door carefully.

She went downstairs and he followed her to the kitchen where she filled the kettle. 'Coffee?'

He didn't reply. Just slid into the nearest chair and, elbows resting heavily on the table, held his head in his hands. 'How long?'

'Siobhan and I got together about five months ago.'

Siobhan. So that was the other man's name.

'No. How long have you known?'

Seth watched Megan as she shovelled three times the usual amount of sugar into his mug and stirred it vigorously. She placed it in front of him and he followed the foam as it swirled on top of the dark brown liquid. He knew he wouldn't be able to touch it. Megan sat opposite him and they faced one another. Her expression was completely without artifice, so much so that he hardly recognized her. He knew that he was going to get the truth and the prospect terrified him. 'Something happened when I was pregnant with Kathy. Something to do with carrying a girl. I can't really explain it.'

'Try.'

'It was like . . . I don't know. I just realized I needed to be with a woman. To share my life with one. And that I couldn't be with a man any more. Seth, don't look at me like that, please.'

'What do you expect?'

She swallowed and raked her hands through her hair. He thought she looked ashamed. Good.

'I was afraid to do anything about it at the time. We'd just had Kathy and I was all over the place. I suppose part of me hoped it would go away. Although I knew it wouldn't. So I just tried to get along with life the best I could. Then Kathy got older and a bit easier, and I started to get out and about and feel better about myself. I met Siobhan at the gym and . . .' her voice got smaller '. . . we made a connection.'

Seth winced.

'We were just friends at first. For ages that's all it was. Then this one time – well, I'm sure you don't want to know the details. I'm sorry, Seth. I was building up to tell you.'

'You should have told me the second you knew.'

'I know, I know. You're right. I should have told you a long time ago.'

'You let me waste the last two – more – years on you, when all the time you knew you could never –' He broke off and stood up. He walked around the kitchen table, put his hands into his pockets and stared out of the window at his much-admired garden. He supposed he'd have to leave it now. 'And the whole time you never loved me.' He hated how choked he sounded.

'Oh, Seth, that's not true.' Megan got up and stood behind him. 'I did love you.'

'No, you didn't. How could you? Not properly.'

'I loved you as much as it was possible for me to love any man, Seth. How could I not love you?'

'Spare me.'

'It's true. I thought I was in love. I didn't know any better. I guess I thought everyone felt the way I did.'

'What? Fancied women?'

'I wasn't going around fancying women all the time. I had the odd feeling every now and then but I thought it was normal. You hear about women having lesbian fantasies and I assumed that was all it was. I had boyfriends, growing up. You weren't the first man I'd been with. And it was different with you, Seth. I thought I'd found – my soul-mate, I suppose.'

'So did I.'

The silence hung in the air between them and buzzed in Seth's ears. He longed to put on the radio so that some inane talk show would block it out. Outside, the morning was clouding over, and he felt that nothing in his life was ever going to be right again.

'I'm sorry,' said Megan. 'I really and truly am. For everything I've put you through and for being too much of a coward to tell you before.'

'I'm sorry too – that the last five years of my life have been a joke. A lie. A big fucking waste of my time.' He could feel the anger building now. 'Tell me, Megan, were you just using me for the sperm? Is that what it was? You decided you wanted a baby and I had the one thing you couldn't get from a woman. You used me, was that it?'

'No – it wasn't like that at all. And can you please keep your voice down?'

'Don't tell me what to do, you lying bitch.'

'Don't call me that.'

'I can call you whatever the hell I like.' He was shouting now. 'Sneaking around behind my back. Having your affair.'

'I wasn't the only one.'

'That was one night, Megan. One lousy night out of years of – nothing. Nothing!'

'Are you all right, Meg?'

Neither had noticed Siobhan opening the kitchen door.

107

They swung around now to look at her, framed in the doorway, fully dressed.

'I'm fine, Siobhan.'

'Oh, Siobhan, is it? I didn't recognize you with your clothes on. I'm Seth, Megan's husband. Or is that "Meg" to you? Come on in and join the party. Oh, I forgot. You already had a party. In my bed.'

'You'd better go, love.'

Love.

'Yes. Even better idea. Why don't you go? Get the hell out of my home and don't come back.' Seth started to advance towards Siobhan, his eyes blazing.

Megan held on to him, one hand on his chest, as Siobhan retreated. 'Stop it, Seth.'

He heard the front door being opened. 'Nice tits, by the way,' he shouted.

The front door slammed.

Seth slumped into a kitchen chair before his legs buckled. He folded his arms on the table and rested his head on them. Neither said anything for quite a while. Then: 'Can I get you anything?' she said.

With great difficulty, he lifted his head. 'How about the last five years back?' He groaned. 'What a waste.'

'Don't say that. We have Kathy, don't we?'

Yes, there was always Kathy. Fear overtook him. 'You're not taking her away from me. She's all I've got.' Tears stung the back of his eyes and he covered them with his hand.

His wife sat down beside him and laid her hand on his shoulder. When he didn't shrug her off, she squeezed it gently. It was the tenderest touch he'd felt in years. 'I'd never do that to you, Seth. Never.'

* * *

108

As it turned out, Seth didn't have to move out of the family home: Megan moved in with Siobhan. True to her word, she agreed to a joint custody arrangement. Maybe she was afraid of losing Kathy too. Luckily, Kathy was too young to understand what was going on and, to everyone's relief, adapted beautifully to her new living arrangements. Which was more than could be said for Seth.

The house felt over-large and echoey when Kathy wasn't around. And although he'd barely admit it to himself, he missed Megan too. He would have sold up and moved out but he didn't want to cause his daughter further disruption. Besides, the house wasn't just his to sell. He spent as little time there as possible, and when Kathy was with her mother, he sat anaesthetized with booze in front of the telly – unless he was in the pub – eyes bloodshot, cheeks unshaven, well on the way to developing a beer gut.

A lot of the time he didn't bother going to bed. He'd fall asleep in front of the box and wake up with a crick in his neck some time in the early hours, a mad infomercial blaring at him. He'd turn down the volume, rest his head on a cushion and cover himself with his jacket. He'd wake up in the morning, judge the time by the brightness in the sky, and turn the volume back up. Then he'd have his coffee and, if he was feeling up to it, a vitamin pill. Sometimes he'd shower, sometimes he wouldn't. Sometimes he changed his clothes and sometimes he wore the same outfit three days in a row. He couldn't even consider another woman. He felt so completely emasculated that he doubted he'd ever be able to get it up again. He went to work, thanking his lucky stars that he didn't have a boss, because if he had, he would have been well and truly sacked.

Then his mother died – and it was as if someone had pulled a cosmic rug out from under him. Let's all laugh as Seth falls flat on his back again. Let's see if he can get up this time.

But Seth made it. Just about. He, his father and his brother united in their grief, making each other strong. And life went on. The legal separation came through. And Seth started to shave again and change his underwear on a more regular basis. And then one day his father rang him up and told him about this garden.

21

All month long they came, the men in suits, the speculators. They paced around the garden, incongruous in their formal garb. Sometimes they came in twos and threes, but often alone. Sometimes one would inadvertently step on a plant. 'Sorry,' they would say. So you should be. The odd time, one might even enquire about the garden – about the work they were doing. 'Such a shame,' they might say, as they walked away, pressing down the newly dug topsoil with their shiny shoes. 'Well, don't build on it then,' Aoife would scream silently in her head. But never out loud. Because she was used to keeping things in.

Emily was accustomed to keeping things in too. But even she couldn't do it any longer. She appeared one morning looking as if she'd been in a fight. Hay fever? But as the morning wore on, it became evident that there was more to it than that. Emily cried silently as she worked the same piece of earth over and over again, her tears dampening the soil. She had wiped her face so many times that it was mud-streaked. Uri and Aoife exchanged a concerned glance.

'Should we do something?'

'Ask her what's wrong. She talks to you,' said Uri.

So, Aoife approached Emily. Hesitantly, not wanting to frighten or upset her even more. She came up behind her and laid a hand gently on her arm. 'Emily?'

Emily turned and buried her face in Aoife's shoulder, sobbing openly. Aoife put her arms around her and they sank to the ground. Everyone else pretended not to notice, while

Aoife absorbed Emily's pain, feeling oddly privileged to be chosen. The sobs became less frequent and eventually Emily lifted her head, rooted around in her pocket for a tissue and blew her nose. Aoife thought she'd never seen anyone look so forlorn. She tucked a stray strand of hair behind Emily's ear. 'What is it, Emily? What happened to you?'

There was a long silence – so long that Aoife didn't think she was going to get an answer.

'I had a baby.'

Aoife was taken aback. She hadn't expected this – she'd guessed Emily had been dumped. She collected herself. 'When was this?'

'Eight months ago.' Emily sniffed. 'She's eight months old.'

'A little girl.'

Emily nodded.

'Where is she?' For one terrible second, Aoife feared that Emily was going to tell her she'd left the newborn baby in a skip.

'I put her up for adoption. She's been with a foster-family. But –' fresh tears were starting to flow '– they've found a family for her. They want me to go in and sign the consent papers.'

Emily began to sob again. Oh, God. Aoife searched her pockets frantically for something resembling a tissue. Emily's had disintegrated into a sodden ribbon. Not that she seemed to care: she was oblivious to everyone and everything. 'Hush now. It's okay. Everything's going to be okay.' Aoife rubbed Emily's arm, uncomfortable with this very public show of emotion, but mostly just desperately sorry for the girl. She waited until Emily had calmed down a little before she said, 'And the baby's still with foster-parents? She hasn't gone to a family yet?'

'No.'

'Are you going to sign the papers?'

'I don't know. I can't decide.'

'Surely the adoption people provide some sort of counselling?'

'They do. I still can't decide. I mean, how could I look after a baby? I've got no boyfriend, no money, no job. I'm not even close to finishing my degree.'

'What about your family?'

'They're really religious. They wouldn't understand.'

'You mean they don't even know?'

Emily shook her head.

'You never told them?'

'No.'

'Did you tell anyone?'

'You're the first. Apart from the woman in the adoption agency and the father.'

'And I take it —'

'He didn't want to know.'

'Oh, Emily.' Aoife drew her close, trying but failing to imagine what it must have been like for her.

They stayed like that for a while. Emily, her wet face buried in Aoife's neck, didn't notice Mrs Prendergast tiptoe over and place a mug of tea on the ground in front of her. Aoife and the older woman looked at each other. Then Aoife nodded and Mrs Prendergast tiptoed away.

'Here,' Aoife said, after a while. 'Your tea's getting cold.'

'Where did it come from?'

'The fairies left it.'

Emily picked up the mug with frail-looking hands, and sipped.

'Better?'

'A little.'

'You might not be giving your family enough credit.'

Emily shrugged.

'How do you get on with your mother?'

'Okay. Well, I suppose.'

'There you go. She might surprise you. But she can't help if she doesn't even know.'

Emily showed no reaction.

'And how do you feel about the baby?' Aoife looked searchingly into Emily's pink, swollen face.

'I don't know. I just don't know.' She gnawed at her fingernails.

Aoife took a deep breath. 'I have something to tell you,' she said. 'It might help you decide.'

22

The first time I gave my little girl chocolate, she laughed out loud. I'd made her mouth happy. It was a chocolate button on her first birthday. Her dad caught it all on the camcorder – he the Hollywood dad, we the Hollywood family. I've watched it so many times I know it by heart. But I've never managed to catch the deceit in my eyes. Michael never caught it either. Even though I was in the thick of it.

We were as entranced as she was, as the chocolate melted on her tongue, then stuck to the roof of her mouth. As her mouth filled with goo, her huge blue eyes filled with surprise, then delight.

'She's just like her mother,' said Michael, still filming.

I wasn't sure if he was referring to her looks or her new-found love of chocolate because she resembled me closely in both respects. It was gratifying at last to have a child like me. Liam was so unlike me he might have fallen from the clouds. Which didn't diminish my love for him. He was my firstborn, my finest achievement thus far in life. He'd stopped growing in the womb and had had to be cut out of me early so I was overprotective of him right from the start. It meant he was always small for his age. Some would say puny, I would say delicate. I had worried he'd be jealous of the new baby, having had the dubious benefit of my fierce attention all his young life but he seemed thrilled with her, and laughed with us at her reaction to the chocolate button before demanding one for himself.

'Come on, Liam, give us a smile.' Michael trained the camera on him.

'Cheese,' said Liam, the chocolate making brown lines between his teeth.

'How old is Katie today?'

'One.' Liam held up a finger.

'And what do we have to say to her?'

'Happy birthday, Katie.' He started to clap and Katie copied him.

Michael and I looked fondly at one another. Our clever, beautiful children. Then he laid down the camera and walked over to me. He put his arms around me and spoke into my neck. 'I love you, Aoife.'

I closed my eyes. 'I love you too.' It wasn't a lie. I remember that moment exactly, even though it wasn't recorded. The feel of his arms supporting me, his breath against my skin. The mixture of happiness and guilt. I had everything in that moment. Absolutely everything. Except I was such a stupid fool I didn't even know it. Always wanting more. Forever yearning for something I didn't have. Later I blamed myself for my ingratitude: if you're not sufficiently grateful, we'll take it all away.

How can I describe Michael? He was always Michael to me, although his friends called him Mick. Only his mother and I used his full name. We knew it suited him best. He worked as a quantity surveyor. In all our years together, I never fully understood what he did.

The first thing people noticed about him was his hair: red. He hated it – declared himself a lifelong victim of 'gingerism'. I loved it. Its silkiness, its floppiness. I think I nearly convinced him to love it too.

We met at this really naff party in Camden Town. I – unbeknown to myself – was meant for the host. I can't even remember his name now. Michael had been earmarked for the flatmate's sister, an unfortunate girl who got so inebriated that it took two men to carry her to bed. She's probably a respectable married lady now, who would cringe at the memory.

Michael was sitting opposite me. His sobriety marked him out. He sat back in his chair and sipped his wine slowly, casually surveying the chaos surrounding him. I was doing much the same at the other side of the kitchen table. Although part of me wanted to get roaring drunk, my desire to impress Michael stopped me.

'What's your name?' he asked. It wasn't the type of party at which formal introductions had been made.

'Aoife,' I said, waiting for the puzzled look, the furrowed brow, the request to repeat myself. To spell it out.

'That's beautiful,' was all he said.

I was sold.

He must have felt the same because, less than an hour later, the room having descended into drink-sodden chaos, he looked at his watch and then pointedly at me. 'Let's get out of here.'

They never even saw us leave.

We escaped together, the night blessedly cool and high after the claustrophobia of the flat, our laughter soaring into the starry sky, where it remained suspended on the air currents. Sometimes I imagine it's up there still.

We went to an all-night café and talked all night. His name was Michael O'Brien and he was London Irish too. His parents were from Mayo and he'd spent many a rainy summer there. We compared tales of Irish grandmothers and laughed uproariously.

'Mine says feck.'

'Mine too!'

'Does she get up at six every morning to bake sodabread?'

'I think she buys it in Londis.'

'Oh.' Slight disappointment. 'Mine told me she cuts the cross on the top to let the fairies out. For years I believed her.'

'Mine's called Kathleen.'

'Mine too!'

'They can't all be called Kathleen.'

'No, some are called Mary.'

It made it easy to agree on our daughter's name when the time came.

The London child of Irish immigrants, I had never considered myself English. My Irish cousins had never considered me Irish. In their eyes, I was the plastic Paddy. I preferred to think of myself as a rare hybrid.

I had spent all of my summer holidays at the home of my Dublin grandparents, marvelling anew each year at their strange vernacular. The delicious shock the first time my devout granny – holy water font in the front porch – said 'feck'. The pure joy of it! Had I misheard? Trying the word in London on my schoolmates. Being made to stand in the corner.

The memories were visceral, as if they'd seeped into my cells. Even now, on certain mornings in late June, I was back in my parents' Ford Cortina, being driven on empty back roads from the ferry to my grandparents' house. Birdsong and hedgerows. Then the joy of arrival. Grandparents spilling out of the house to meet us, down the front steps, through the roses, the snapdragons, the Michaelmas daisies. My grandfather and his pipe. Mellow Virginia. For years after his departure, the scent lingered in the drawer beside his chair. My granny. Hair newly coloured and permed. Tattooing our cheeks with her red, heart-shaped kisses. We would run up the path, lured by the smell of Irish rashers and sausages split up the middle. Sodabread and black and white puddings. The white spread thick and smooth on the bread. The black, made of pig's blood, spurned for reasons of morality and disgust. Then, later, the potato cakes sizzling, salty butter melting. The tea brack at tea-time. The aunties dropping in. Benny Hill on the telly. Photos of grandchildren on every surface. Love.

My grandparents were gone now. My grandfather had died when I was nineteen, my grandmother a few years previously. The house had been sold and the memories divvied up. I had received a battered gold locket that I lost intermittently, only to find with great joy every time.

When I first moved to Ireland, I used to drive by their house, tripping myself up on my own nostalgia. I'd had to stop. Too much pathos can drag at the soul.

Michael and I compared notes for what seemed like hours: the lurid colour photo of John Paul II in the hall, the Sacred Heart in the kitchen, its fake red candle perpetually aglow – all the babies named and blessed, including the ones who'd died at birth. Jesus offering his heart to share. Our grandmothers offering their limitless love – we didn't say that but it was tacitly acknowledged. It made Michael seem dear to me already. Familiar and safe. Like family.

He proved himself later that night when he escorted me to the front door of my block of flats. 'Which is yours?'

'See that window up there?' I pointed to a pane on the third floor.

'When you're in, turn on the light, look down and wave at me. I'll be waiting.'

'For what?'

'To make sure you got in safe.'

I gave him a quick, shy kiss on the cheek and ran inside, not waiting for the lift, taking the stairs two steps at a time, wings on my heels. I got in and turned on the light. Breathless, I went to the window. There he was. A lone figure in a dark coat. He waved and I thought I saw him smile. He walked away and I watched his glorious red hair glint as he passed beneath a streetlight.

That was it, really. We hardly spent a night apart until the one before our wedding two years later, the two Kathleens crying copiously in the church. I had no doubts. If Michael had them, he hid them well. I loved my gingerbread man and he loved me. And we lived in our gingerbread house. Because that was what it felt like – as if we were playing at being grown-ups. I thought I'd feel the same when our first baby was born – that we'd be playing at being mummies and daddies. But the advent of Liam catapulted us into adulthood and, suddenly, life wasn't a game any more. It was very real, very serious. What if something happened to him? Suddenly we were gambling on a planet that didn't always seem such a good bet. We started to row, nothing serious – only bickering – but the halcyon days were over. Reality had bitten us and life would never be the same again.

I didn't regret motherhood, not for one second. But I did regret failing to appreciate my freedom when I'd had it. I realized with a jolt that my ambitious travel plans had been curtailed. That I no longer had just myself and Michael to think about. Simple things, like taking my time in the shower, spending precious minutes slathering myself with body butter afterwards, were now distant memories. My grey hairs multiplied through stress and lack of care, and the tiny lines on my face multiplied through lack of sleep. I no longer cleansed, toned and moisturized. I was lucky if I managed to pass a baby wipe across my face at night before I fell into bed like a stone. Although these were only little things, they made me feel less human, less of a person and a woman. I was now 'mother' and all other aspects of my identity were secondary. As for Michael, I believe he felt as though he was stuck in a job he wasn't too crazy about. As far as our relationship was concerned, we couldn't – wouldn't – take the pressures out on Liam so we took them out on each other. It sometimes felt as though we were rivals rather than batting for the same team.

'You go up to him. I'm knackered.'

'And I'm not? I've been working all day.'

'Oh, and I haven't, I suppose.'

'I didn't say that.'

'You implied it.'

'Don't be so bloody sensitive.'

'I'm not being sensitive. You're being inconsiderate.'

'I went up last time.'

'And I went up twice before that.'

And so on.

It was a competition: who was the tiredest.

Nevertheless, we took another gamble on the planet and on ourselves, and shortly before Liam's second birthday Katie was born. Again my love for her was overwhelming, but different. With Liam, the funny little person with body parts I didn't possess, I had been excited but fearful, setting out on the strange odyssey of motherhood. With Katie, I was already home. She was a perfect fit inside my heart. I understood her tiny woman's brain. She loved the things I loved: her brother and her daddy.

Michael and I grew to inhabit our roles and, for a time, we grew in the same direction. Looking back, he kept on shooting upwards. It was me who veered off course.

I'd known Peter for years – since I'd started work at the college. He lectured in physics. I'd always liked the way his mind worked, so different from mine. But that had been it. He was friends with Michael too. We went to each other's houses for dinner and stuck together at boring work functions. They had a son who was slightly older than Liam and the two boys would play together. Peter's wife, Lara – a home-economics teacher – crocheted Katie the most beautiful blanket when she was born. I used it on her cot at first. Later, I would shove it at the back of the airing cupboard so I didn't have to look at it.

I went back to work when Katie turned six months, weepy at her easy withdrawal from my breast. I settled into my coffee-break routine, a group of us huddled around our habitual table with the wonky legs in the canteen. Peter was always there.

'Would you like more milk, Aoife?'

He was always solicitous. At first I thought it was because I'd had a baby, but it continued. One day, seemingly out of nowhere, it dawned on me that his eyes always sought mine when we were in a group. It was my opinion he looked for. My approval. As if I was special to him. It made me think.

It had been years since I'd fancied another man. Michael had been enough for me since the night we'd met. Of course, I still noticed a good-looking male on the street or the screen, but in a dispassionate way, as if I was admiring a work of art. And I suppose I'd always thought of Peter as handsome in that same, dispassionate way. It had never occurred to me to imagine what it would be like to be with him.

Looking back, I don't know if I can put it down to anything more exalted than boredom. My life, my identity, had become so subsumed into motherhood, so taken up with the humdrum details of my family's existence, that something in me yearned for escape. To become the heroine of my own romantic novel – the more Mills & Boon the better. Instead of trying to fix what I already had – which wasn't even that badly broken, just a few hairline cracks – I looked for something new and whole. In a way, I was being lazy. Another unthinking participant in our disposable, throwaway society. My marriage just needed a little recycling. And my children were far too precious for me even to contemplate throwing away their happiness and security.

It was a day like any other. Unremarkable weather. Drizzly. I had seen Michael that morning, of course: we had moved around each other, not saying much. This wasn't significant, just a usual workaday morning, people rushing to get ready. He had kissed me on the way out, on the cheek, mouth full of toast, leaving a residue of crumbs. I wiped them away.

I dropped the children at the childminder's, Liam battling against the constraints of his car seat, me against the traffic. Sheila was in her fifties and had raised a family of her own. My children adored her, which made me illogically resentful, for which I chided myself every morning. It was my choice to go back to work. Choice: the curse of the modern woman. Liam ran straight through the door the second it was opened.

'Look at my new twuck, Sheila.' He held up his latest toy for inspection.

'Oh, that's lovely, dear.'

Katie was almost leaping out of my arms in her eagerness to get to the other woman. For God's sake! She'd only known Sheila for three months.

'I'll see you later,' I said.

'See you later, dear. Liam, come and give your mummy a goodbye kiss.'

But Liam had already been swallowed into the dark interior of the house.

'Oh, it's fine. Don't bother him. I'm late anyway. 'Bye, Katie.'

I kissed my daughter's satin cheek and got back into the car.

I pulled away, with the image of Sheila trying unsuccessfully to get her to wave at me in my rear-view mirror. I asked myself for the millionth time if I was doing the right thing. The right thing. What was that? I supposed I was lucky I didn't have children who clung to me, wailing inconsolably whenever I tried to leave them. I switched on the radio and my thoughts were subsumed in the traffic.

By the time I got to the college, I was more than ready for coffee so I went straight to the canteen and who should be there but . . .

I was immediately self-conscious. How ridiculous after all this time. 'Is this seat taken?'

Peter smiled and gestured to the chair opposite him.

'You're in early,' I said, striving for normality.

'Papers to mark.'

It was hardly a romantic setting – the college canteen, sipping from polystyrene cups – so why did I feel like I was on a date? I wished I could shake this infernal crush. It was ludicrous even to suspect that he was feeling anything even remotely similar. I was projecting my feelings on to him, something I used to do all the time with men before Michael – always with disastrous results. It was quite distressing to learn that I hadn't progressed romantically beyond the mental age of nineteen. Had my third-level education, my marriage, my career not taught me anything? Apparently not. The sophistication I'd thought I'd developed was nothing more than the most fragile of veneers.

'How's Lara?' When in doubt, mention the wife. It proves you have no designs on him.

'Okay, I think. Haven't seen much of her lately.'

What does that mean? That you're not getting on? Doesn't your wife understand you? 'How come?'

He shrugged. 'Both just busy, I guess.'

How was it that I'd never before noticed the shape of his mouth? The unabashed sensuality of the upper lip, the squared-off curve of the lower. I tried not to stare. I took a sip of coffee and winced as it burned my mouth.

'Are you okay?'

'It's just hot.'

'Here. Have some of this.'

He leaned over and pressed his glass of water to my lips. I took a gulp, annoyed at how refreshing it felt. He took the glass away and a dribble of water ran down my chin. Embarrassed, I wiped it away with my sleeve, eyes lowered, rattled by the strange intimacy of it all. I got up. 'I'd better go.' Pushing my chair away awkwardly behind me, I gathered up my papers and walked past him towards the door.

He stood up and grabbed my arm. 'I'll see you later?'

I was completely taken aback. I felt my colour deepen, his fingers sinking into my flesh, his eyes boring into mine. 'I'll be around at lunchtime.'

He nodded and released me, and I walked out of the canteen on legs that seemed to belong to another woman, my head and heart full of confusion.

That night I snapped at Michael, even though he'd done nothing. And when he came to bed, I pretended to be asleep.

I was just playing, really, trying to make life a little less boring. Trying to feel alive, for God's sake.

That weekend we visited a garden. The whole family. I consider it my last pure weekend, the memory of which was to burn like a beacon in darker times. The sun shone in reality and even brighter in memory. In reality, I'm sure that clouds, occasionally and momentarily, blotted it out. In memory, there were none. In reality, I had a sore back, from lugging around Liam and picking up Katie, as she tripped over her newly found feet. Of course, Daddy could do this too, but so often, it was me they called: Mummy, the centre of their tiny universe. In memory, my back is pain free. I experience no tiredness as I lift my children into the air and swing them around. They squeal with delight and the afternoon resonates with their laughter. Bees buzz, birds trill, butterflies flutter by. The scent of sunblock, our picnic lunch. Pâté and Bakewell tart for Michael and me. Cocktail sausages and puréed fruit for the children. Warm, fizzy 7 Up in plastic cups. Katie fell over herself to get to the flowers. Liam ran manically around the borders. Michael and I revelled in the magic.

'It doesn't get much better than this.' He was lying on the chequered blanket, propped up on one elbow, legs crossed at the ankles, a supremely contented expression on his face.

'No, it doesn't,' I concurred, meaning every word. I lay on my back and shielded my eyes with my arm, blocking out the light but not the heat. It was impossible not to feel relaxed under the benign force of the sun.

I felt Michael move closer to me and anticipated his touch. Welcomed it. He whispered into my ear and his breath tickled. 'I love being here with you,' he said.

'I love being here with you too.'

'You know you're the centre of my universe, don't you?'

'Am I?'

'You know you are.'

I did.

'I don't know what I'd do without you, Aoife.'

'You won't have to do without me.'

'Promise?'

'Of course I promise. What is this, Michael? This isn't like you.'

'You've just seemed so distant lately. Like you're here but not here.'

I was shocked that he'd noticed. I'd thought I'd hidden it so well. Locked in my private fantasy world, locking him out. Telling myself that thoughts couldn't possibly affect him. But they had. The evidence was breathing in my very own ear.

The guilt was immediate and heavy, my enjoyment of the day eliminated. I propped myself up on my elbow and looked him in the eye. 'I'm sorry if I've seemed preoccupied lately. I promise I'll change.'

I meant it too. What need had I for a sordid, tawdry affair when I had all this? This perfect love. This perfect family. I vowed there and then to stay away from Peter, to make sure we were never alone, keep temptation at arm's length – not a hair's breadth away as it had been last week. Only a madwoman would jeopardize all this – all the gifts I had in my life. This goodness.

Michael did a quick check to see where the children were and whether anyone else was close by. Satisfied, he cupped my breast with his hand and kissed my lips. I giggled against his mouth. As it was in the beginning.

But I couldn't help it. It was like I was two different people living two different lives. In one, I was the devoted wife and mother, and in the other, the traitorous whore. Which was how I thought of myself at some moments, even though I hadn't done anything. But I knew what my intentions were – and they weren't good – every time I saw Peter. The thought of a different pair of hands on my naked skin was so unutterably exciting that I couldn't let it go. I did send him packing once: he came all the way to my front door when he knew Michael and the children were out – they were with his wife and child at the Fun Factory.

I opened the door and he stood there, looking at me. What had remained unspoken had become undeniable – through eye contact and body language. Through something strange and indefinable in the ether between us. The air we jointly breathed had become soup-like and vaguely tangible. It seemed incredible to me that nobody else was conscious of it. I stepped back and he came into the hall. I was still in my dressing-gown, luxuriating in having a rare morning to myself. I crossed my arms over my chest, acutely aware that beneath my dressing-gown I was wearing a flimsy nightie and no underwear. I couldn't speak. I felt absolute terror. Like that time on the motorway when I was convinced a lorry was going to plough into me. Yet it was only Peter standing in front of me. Peter my friend. Peter who, for some strange reason, had become the most attractive man in the universe. When I wasn't with him, I could deny it, discount it, but when I was in his presence, I felt myself drawn towards him, as if by an irresistible force. Again, I resisted. He took a step closer. I took one back.

'This is a surprise. I'm not even dressed.'

I'd deny what was happening with normal talk. Again, he wouldn't speak. Speak, goddammit. Help me break the spell. I was genuinely scared. I turned and went into the kitchen, heading for my trusty kettle and switching it on. 'Tea or coffee?'

'Aoife . . .' He came up to me and stroked the side of my arm with his familiar but unfamiliar hand. His face was close to mine now, his eyes imploring, pleading.

I shook him off. 'On second thoughts, I don't have time for tea. I think you'd better leave.'

He drew back and stared at me for a few interminable seconds. 'Is that what you want?'

'Yes.' I wouldn't look at him.

He left silently. I barely heard the click of the front door.

I don't know why I refused him that time. Maybe the venue was wrong: my home – photos of my babies on the wall. Maybe the knowledge that our spouses and children were out innocently together. Perhaps simply that I hadn't yet brushed my teeth. I'd like to think it was moral strength but I was soon to learn that that was weak indeed. When he left that morning, I felt so bereft. It was over. I had nothing left but banal reality. I didn't want it. Next time I went to him.

Fearing it was too late, I arrived at his office that Monday. A soft knock on the door.

'Come in.'

He looked amazed. I was the last person he'd expected to see. I stood for a long while, my hand stuck to the door handle, eyes lowered. When at last I looked up at him he was staring at me. He dropped his pen on his desk and pushed back his chair. I sat on his lap, avoiding his eyes, closing mine, focusing on his lips, covering them with my kisses, his cheeks and his forehead, finally knowing what it felt like, my questions answered. His taste, so different. It was magical, ecstatic. Like the first time ever. We smothered each other with ourselves. Entered each other. It was urgent and vital – and somehow inevitable. Maybe if one of us had had the willpower . . . but neither of us did. In the moment, I was exultant. Ten seconds later I was remorseful, guilt-ridden, devastated. I gathered myself up and made to leave.

'Don't go, Aoife. Stay and talk.'

'I don't want to talk. I have to go.'

'But –'

'I have to.'

I was never going back. Except I was.

*   *   *

I thought my guilt was at its pinnacle. I had no idea. That evening I went home and threw myself into my role as earth-mother and hearth-goddess with greater gusto than ever before. I collected the children and talked to them animatedly all the way home. When we got in, I didn't begin picking up the morning's detritus as I normally did. Instead – and this was revolutionary – I played with them. To hell with the house. I got down on my hands and knees and I played with all my might. I agreed to every one of Liam's requests. He lit up as I moved cars up and down endless ramps, drove trains backwards and forwards along infinite tracks, and picked up imaginary loads with pint-sized diggers. For Katie, I did whooshing in the air. Up over my head and down between my legs. Up and down. Again and again. She tired of the game before I did. Maybe there was a touch of mania about it all, but my children didn't seem to care. They revelled in the attention.

Once I'd given them their tea, I set to work on Michael's favourite dinner: steak fried with mushrooms and onions and homemade chips.

'What's all this?' He came through the kitchen door, his face showing delight – he'd smelled the steak out in the hall.

'I thought you deserved a treat.'

He put his arms around me and I allowed myself to be kissed.

'How lucky am I?' he said.

I hugged him tight and closed my eyes tighter.

'To come home to a wife like you, to food like this. Two beautiful children. I don't deserve it.'

No, you don't, I thought.

'Does this mean I'm on a promise?'

He smiled at me with such warmth, his eyes full of love.

'Might do.'

While he read Liam his bedtime story, I jumped into the shower and scrubbed myself furiously – especially the important bits. He was already in bed, waiting for me, when I came out.

'You don't have to wash on my account.'

'I know. I was feeling grimy.'

He turned the sheet down. 'Come on in.'

The phone rang.

'I'll just get that.' I rushed to pick it up. 'Hello?'

'Aoife.'

My heart pounded and my mouth dried. I could hear him breathing rhythmically, like waves crashing against the shoreline.

'I'm sorry. You have the wrong number.' I put the phone back in its cradle.

'Good,' said Michael. 'Now come to bed.'

I got into bed with my husband and put out. At least, half of me did. Good Aoife. Bad Aoife was very far away indeed.

Perhaps I could be like a Frenchwoman. I could take a lover between eating *salade* and smoking Gauloises. That's assuming real-life Frenchwomen actually did such things outside the genre of *film noir*. Occasionally I would attempt to justify my actions. But my excuses were paltry and pathetic and did nothing to convince me. I couldn't just blame my bad self. It was my whole self – and my whole self was wrong. I did my best to keep away from Peter after that first time in his office but, unfortunately, he didn't try to keep away from me. His marriage was, I think, in a genuinely bad place at the time. He might have felt he had nothing to lose but I had everything. I was the truly stupid one. But I thought I was in love – although I loved Michael too. It was all so confusing.

Maybe I just loved Michael as a best friend but was 'in love' with Peter. If only a woman could have two husbands. If only Michael would have an affair too, then I wouldn't have to be the baddie any more. If only he'd run off with Lara all our problems would be solved. But he wasn't going to do either because he loved me. Properly 'in-loved' me. It was exquisite torture. How could I be so happy yet so unhappy at the same time? Happy to the power of infinity when I was in bed with Peter, and miserable as soon as my conscience got the better of me.

Peter and I knew we couldn't go on like that indefinitely, but we avoided talking about the future, hoping, I think, that events would overtake us and that we'd be spared making any horrible definitive decisions.

It was an evening like any other. Dinner had been eaten and the dishes cleared away. Liam was tucked up in bed, *Thomas the Tank Engine* stories read to his satisfaction. Katie was restless, fretting and fussing. She was unhappy in my arms and unhappy out of them. I rocked her to no avail and fancied that she was absorbing my own agitated state. Michael and I were knackered and she was knackered, but she wouldn't sleep.

'Maybe it's her teeth.' I tried the Teetha, I tried the Calpol. I considered downing the bottle myself. Frustrated, I handed her to Michael. 'Here. You take her.'

'What can I do?'

'I don't know. Go out for a drive or something. It might knock her out.'

When Katie was younger, the rhythmic rocking of the car used to lull her to sleep. It was worth a try.

'Okay.' Michael grabbed his keys and a blanket for her. 'I'll give it a go. See you in a few minutes.'

Except I didn't see him in a few minutes.

My husband and daughter went out for a drive and never came back.

And, just like that, my family was halved.

23

Emily had stopped crying. Aoife had started, then stopped. They were silent for quite a while. Until Aoife spoke: 'A truck ploughed into them. The driver had a heart-attack at the wheel.'

'I'm so sorry, Aoife. I had no clue.'

Aoife shrugged. 'I told you for a reason. And I wouldn't have told you if I didn't think I knew what you were already thinking.' She looked at Emily seriously. 'I've lost my baby for ever. But you have a chance to get yours back.'

The Summer Garden

A sensitive plant in a garden grew,
And the young winds fed it with silver dew,
And it opened its fan-like leaves to the light.
And closed them beneath the kisses of night.

Percy Bysshe Shelley,
'The Sensitive Plant'

24

Uri could barely keep up with his lawns. Every week he was out there with his mower. Mrs Prendergast's roses were clusters of light-filled beauty, among which she floated in a selection of floral dresses, trailing her hands dreamily against the delicate petals – taking full credit for their glory even though Seth had put up the trellises, had kept down the weeds and fed them well-rotted manure – much to Mrs Prendergast's disgust.

'Must you?' she said. 'It stinks to high heaven.'

'Look. Do you want them to grow or don't you?'

'There's no need to take that tone.'

'If you want roses, you gotta have shit.'

'Honestly!'

But he didn't say a word now, surprising Aoife as he let Mrs Prendergast take the credit. Although, on second thoughts, she wasn't surprised. There was a new atmosphere in the garden – of joy. A sense of hard work paying off. In such a beautiful, life-affirming setting, it was virtually impossible to be anything but entirely pleasant to every other soul. It hadn't always felt this way – not to Aoife. There had been times when she'd felt that nothing was happening, that the earth was intent on retaining all her secrets. The morning she had arrived to find her *Peter Rabbit* lettuces devoured by slugs. The times she had knelt on the earth and willed her veggies on. 'Grow, goddammit,' she would hiss, peering into the furrows for signs of green. She agonized over everything – every blade of grass. The tomatoes weren't ripening quickly enough and she feared that there wasn't enough sunshine left in the season to redden them. As for the apple trees – a very poor showing considering all the pruning that had gone into them.

'We have an apple tree at home,' said Emily, 'an ancient thing, and she produces an incredible crop every second year.'

Maybe that was it. This wasn't their year.

On one such day Uri approached her, her anxiety visible to the naked eye as she peered into the soil. He bent low over her – she could almost feel his beard brushing her cheek – and murmured, 'Each blade of grass has its angel that bends over it and whispers, "Grow, grow."'

Aoife looked up into his face.

'It's not all about you, you know,' he said quietly, then smiled and walked away.

Aoife felt her arrogance. She straightened up and relaxed her shoulders, experiencing a new lightness. It wasn't all up to her, thank God. And she felt that with a new humility – quicker than she would have imagined.

'I'm a bit concerned about my potatoes. Would you have a look at them, please, Seth?' she asked one day.

'Sure. What's the problem?'

'Look at the leaves. They've gone yellow and withered. I'm afraid it might be blight.'

'Hmm.' He bent over and examined a leaf. 'I think you may be right.'

'Oh, no. What are we going to do?'

'There's only one thing for it.'

'What?'

'We're going to have to emigrate to America.'

'Seth!'

He laughed. 'When the leaves turn yellow like that, it means it's time to dig them up.'

'What? The spuds? You mean they're ready for eating?'

'No, for juggling.'

'Stop it!'

'Here,' he said, handing her a spade. 'It's only right that you should do the honours.'

She hesitated.

'Go on,' he urged.

She took it from him, feeling a ridiculous level of excitement and anticipation. They were spuds, for God's sake. She sliced the blade into the earth beside the plant closest to her, then stepped down hard on it. The soil gave way easily. She bent low over it and tugged the plant with both hands. She felt it give and pulled it out. Nothing but a compact little network of roots. She looked at Seth in dismay.

'That doesn't mean anything,' he said. 'Look in the ground.'

Aoife hunkered down and sifted through the soil with her fingers. She couldn't believe it. Nestled in the soil, for all the world like precious jewels, were three potatoes. 'They're pink!' she said, holding one up for inspection.

'They are.'

'Incredible.' She brushed away the earth with her thumb. 'They look just like something you'd get in a shop.'

Seth laughed. 'What were you expecting?'

'I don't know. I just didn't think that they'd be so – perfect.'

She had an overwhelming urge to ask Seth if he'd bought them in a supermarket the night before and buried them especially for her to find, like a bizarre adult Easter-egg hunt.

She rifled around and found three more. Then she dug up another plant. Then another. It was almost addictive, the thrill so unexpected. It made everything worth while – the impossible seem possible. It was the proof that everyday miracles could occur.

25

Michael was killed instantly. I like to think he felt nothing. I don't like to think of the terror he must have experienced as he saw the truck skidding towards him, out of control, on the wrong side of the road. The driver's heart-attack was fatal for everyone. Katie died in the ambulance on the way to the hospital, her little heart fluttering in her chest like a butterfly. Then still. Alone in the ambulance with no mummy. Not even her daddy's inert, smashed-up body, which stayed behind in the tangled metal that had been a Ford Focus, waiting to be cut out by the firemen. I like to think she was already gone, that only the mechanics of her body were still ticking over. That she was with the two other Kathleens, who'd finally got to hold and cradle their posthumous great-grandchild. Because she needed someone to look after her.

I didn't think I'd ever get through the pain. It immobilized me. Crushed me. I couldn't believe it at first – couldn't take it in. How could they be with me at one minute and at the next obliterated? Where was my Michael – the essence of him? His soul. And my baby. All the potential locked inside that chubby little body, where had it gone? It couldn't have vanished just like that. Yet it was nowhere to be found.

The morning of the funeral had an air of unreality about it. I wasn't in my own body. I didn't want to be. I was only aware of Liam's small hand, a permanent fixture in mine. He wouldn't let go and I wouldn't have let him. But I could scarcely look at his white, pinched face, permanently upturned towards my own. His large, questioning eyes. When I saw the tiny white coffin I lost all reason and my mother took charge of him. I held Katie on my lap one last time on the way to the graveyard. No need to worry about car seats any more. Hers hadn't saved her anyway. I believe what I did was keen – loud, open-mouthed wailing while I rocked over the body of my dead child. It was unbearable. Indescribable. I wanted to throw myself into the grave and be buried with her and Michael. I thought I'd die anyway, from the grief. Nobody could feel what I was feeling and keep on living. Nor would they want to.

All the arms that encircled me, the arms of the living. All the voices that said sorry, the voices of the living. It was all a blur of black and flesh and tears. My family rallied around me, a human shield, as did Michael's. Would they have been so understanding if they had known the truth?

Peter didn't attend the funeral, but Lara did. She embraced me fiercely, not attempting to disguise the rivulets of tears flowing freely down her cheeks. I presumed that Peter had elected to stay at home and mind their son. I was grateful for his absence.

He rang me two days later. 'Aoife.'

'Hello, Peter.'

'I don't know what to say. I'm so sorry.'

'Thank you.'

'How's Liam?'

'Coping, I think.'

'That's good.'

There was a brief silence.

'Do you want me to come over?'

'No.'

'Are you sure?'

'Yes.'

Silence again.

'What happens now?'

'You go and be with your wife.'

I heard his sharp intake of breath.

'Is that what you want?'

'Yes.'

'For ever?'

'For ever.'

'I'll call you again in a few –'

'Don't.'

'But just as a friend.'

'No. I don't want that. I need you to respect my wishes. Please, Peter.'

'Okay.'

'Goodbye, Peter.'

'' Bye, Aoife.'

I was letting him off the hook.

And that was the last time I ever spoke to him. It was the last time I ever saw him too. He and Lara moved away shortly after that, out of London to the countryside, to make a new start. Lara sent me a beautiful card around that time. I have it somewhere still. I wondered if what had happened to my family had made them value their own all the more.

I didn't miss Peter. Not once. Events had thrown everything into a stark perspective. What I'd had with him meant nothing. It had been meaningless lust. A petty excitement. A sordid betrayal. I couldn't understand how I'd been so blind, so deluded. My emotions were not to be trusted. I – clearly – was not to be trusted.

I missed Michael like a hollow ache that wouldn't go away. Our bed was cold and empty and huge. I'd spent the last couple of months of our life together trying to escape his embraces. Thank God he'd never found out why. Did he know now? Up in heaven looking down?

'Forgive me, Michael,' I whispered, over and over. But I didn't think I'd ever be able to forgive myself. I knew I was being punished for my betrayal. I hadn't valued them enough so they'd been taken away from me. My Michael and my Katie. My baby girl. When I wasn't in our bed, wrapped in Michael's dressing-gown, I was in Katie's room, on the floor in front of her chest of drawers as if it were a shrine. I would take out her tiny pink clothes and smell them. Then I'd fold them and refold them, rearrange them until they were perfection. I'd always loved to see them lined up in neat rows. I spent hours doing that. When I'd finished, I'd start all over again. It may have been meaningless, but so was life. And it gave me comfort. Afterwards, I'd curl up into a ball on the floor beside her cot and fall asleep.

I slept a lot in those first few weeks. I think it was the drugs the doctors had given me. Or maybe I just didn't want to be conscious. My mother took over Liam. I was useless to anyone – so much so that eventually she had to say something.

She called around one day to find me on the couch wearing Michael's socks and dressing-gown, a cup of cold tea in my hand, staring blankly at the blank TV screen. 'Why don't you come back with me, love?'

'I'm okay here, Mum.'

'But you need to be with people.'

'I'd rather be on my own.'

My mother knelt in front of me and forced me to look her in the eye. 'Listen to me, Aoife. I know you're feeling – just awful. I know your heart has been broken. God knows, we're all shattered. I remember how I felt when your dad died, and I know that this is much, much worse. But, my darling, it's not all about you. If it was I'd say, "Fine, wallow in your misery for as long as you need to." But you have a little boy to think of. Your son. Liam needs you. He's missing his mummy desperately and there's only so much I can say or do. It's you he needs. You have to pull yourself together for him, love. I know it feels impossible but you have to try.'

The tears were back, pouring down my face as usual. Hadn't I cried enough already? No wonder I was dehydrated, my skin desiccated. I nodded and blew my nose. 'Okay.'

'Okay, you will? You'll come home with me?'

'Yes.'

'Good girl. Jump into the shower first. You'll feel the better for it.'

But I was in no condition for jumping into anything. Instead, my mother helped me up the stairs, linking me all the way. Then she turned on the shower and, encountering some resistance, removed Michael's robe.

'Now,' she said, 'will you be okay from here on in?'

I nodded.

'Good girl. See you in a few minutes. I'm going down to make a fresh pot of tea.'

My mother shut the door behind her and I removed my pyjamas. It was like shedding a second skin, I'd been wearing them so long. I looked down at my body. My skin seemed grey, tired-looking. I was skinnier than I remembered. I seemed to have shrunk. Maybe I could disappear altogether.

I stood under the hot jets and willed them to wash it all away.

I did feel slightly better once I was clean and wearing different clothes. Immediately I felt worse for feeling better. What right had I to feel anything but despair? My husband and child were dead and it was all my fault. If I hadn't sent them out on the roads in the dark . . . If I hadn't submitted to my lust . . . If I had been a better mother, a better wife, a better person . . . It was the downward spiral that kept on spiralling downwards.

Downstairs, I allowed my mother to fill me with hot, sweet tea.

'That's better,' she said, stroking my damp hair.

She drove me to her home, a few miles away. I kept thinking that every car was going to career into us. I half wished they would.

Liam was sitting on the floor in the middle of the sitting room, surrounded by miniature diggers – consolation toys. Everything leaped when he saw me – his body, his expression, his heart. He ran towards me and I knelt on the floor and opened my arms to him.

'Mummy!' He flung his around my neck and clung on for dear life. 'I yuv you, Mummy.'

'I love you too, Liam.'

It was a minute before I tried to extricate myself, but he clung even tighter. 'Don't go, Mummy.'

'I won't, darling. I won't.'

The first anniversary was brutal. But the day after I felt a kind of relief. At least I'd no longer be thinking 'this time last year'.

When I saw a girl-toddler on the street, I averted my eyes.

Liam became my everything. The whole universe focused into his dear little face. He was the reason I ate, slept, lived.

The house was mine now. Michael's death had cancelled out the mortgage. It was cold comfort. For a long while I was just existing, putting one foot in front of the other, putting each day behind me with relief that I was a little bit further away from the source of my pain. But I had to think of our future. Liam would be school age soon. Did I want to carry on living here?

One night I had a dream. It was a dream like no other I'd

had before or since. A perfect record of a conversation I'd once had with Michael. I dreamed about him often, but this dream was so vivid, so real, that I woke up newly bereft, the feeling so strong that he was with me still. I could almost smell the coffee he was making in the kitchen, could almost hear the shower as he stood under its jets. But the house echoed with nothingness. And that was when I knew I had to leave.

He was never coming back.

The memory was this. It was mid-morning on a Saturday. The sun shone through the window as we sat at the kitchen table, the morning papers spread out in front of us, the children playing at our feet.

'You know,' said Michael, suddenly putting down the part of the paper he'd been reading, 'we should move to Ireland.'

'What?'

'It's the perfect time to do it. The economy there is strong. I'd get a job no problem.'

'What about my job?'

'You'd get one too. It might take you a little longer.'

'But I like the job I have.' Peter was there.

'The kids could start school in Ireland. Just think, they'd have Irish accents.'

We smiled at the thought.

'Are you serious about this?' I asked.

'Yes. Why not?'

'It's a really big step.'

'I know. But what have we got to lose? It'd be a better quality of life for us. Just think about it.'

I hadn't really thought about it, my mind taken up with other matters at the time. But I thought about it now, sitting in my empty bed, enveloped by the warm feelings the dream had engendered. Why not? There was nothing for me here.

Well, that wasn't strictly true. There was my mother, Liam's nana, who'd been such a support in the last year or so. But I was stronger now. And she could visit. Dublin was only a short plane ride away. Because it was always Dublin for me. That was my home from home. And it would make Michael happy, I smiled to myself, his son growing up to be an Irishman. A proper Paddy, not a plastic one like me and his father. It was settled then. That was what we'd do. For better or worse.

26

It didn't take Emily long to make up her mind. Not after she'd heard Aoife's story. Or, at least, the parts Aoife had deemed fit for her young ears.

She rang the woman in the adoption agency later that afternoon, sitting on the swing seat in her sensory garden, the beginnings of honeysuckle to her left, the stirrings of jasmine to her right. She rocked herself gently as she held the phone to her ear, one leg tucked under her, boots kicked off. 'Hello. Can I speak to Stephanie, please?'

'Certainly. Can I say who's calling?'

'Emily Harte.'

'Hold the line, please.'

The seconds ticked slowly by as Emily rocked to and fro, waiting for the opportunity to transform her future.

'Emily, Stephanie here.'

'Hi, Stephanie.'

There was a short silence during which each waited for the other to make the first move. Stephanie broke it. She was used to awkward pauses: they were part of her daily round. 'Are you calling to make an appointment to sign the consent papers, Emily?'

Emily noted the professional compassion in the other woman's tone and was grateful for it. 'I've changed my mind,' she said, feeling as if her heart was going to jump right out of her mouth and land on the ground in front of her. She pictured it coming to rest on the camomile lawn.

'About what exactly?' Stephanie's voice was cautious.

'I want to keep my baby.' Emily was exultant, the adrenalin racing around her body and forcing her to her feet. She began to pace as Stephanie breathed at the other end of the phone.

'Are you quite sure about this, Emily?'

'I'm one hundred per cent certain.'

'You don't need more time?'

'No. I've had enough time. Too much.'

'Okay, then. I'll put arrangements in place.'

'What does that mean?'

'That I'll organize a handover for a few days' time.'

'You mean I can have my baby back?'

'Of course you can have your baby back. She's still your baby.'

She was her baby. Her baby.

My baby.

Once the phone call was over, Emily was beside herself. 'Oh, my God, oh, my God.' She was still pacing, holding her face in her hands. She had to see someone, tell someone, touch someone. She ran out to the main part of the garden. Aoife wasn't there. She'd gone to give a lecture. Seth wasn't there. He was out working on a proper job. Uri was nowhere to be found. But Mrs Prendergast was walking slowly up to her house, oblivious to everything around her. Emily ran to her. 'Mrs Prendergast!'

Mrs Prendergast stopped and turned, startled. Emily sensed that she'd thought herself alone in the garden. She reached her and flung her arms around the older woman's neck, startling her even further. She squeezed her, then let her go, amazed at how fragile she had felt. How vulnerable. She drew back and looked at Mrs Prendergast as if for the first time, a woman she'd always viewed as formidable rather than frail. Mrs Prendergast's face was uncertain, her cheeks slightly flushed. 'What is it, my dear?'

'I'm getting my baby back. They're giving her back to me.'

'Your baby?' Now Mrs Prendergast was staring at her as if she had two heads.

'Yes. She's mine. My baby.' Emily started to cry. Big, fat, happy tears, completely devoid of shame.

The older woman was still staring at her, in amazement now, but with a strange expression in her eyes that Emily was too preoccupied to register. 'That's wonderful, my dear. I'm very pleased for you.'

'Thank you.' Emily laughed through her tears, like a summer shower, and hugged Mrs Prendergast again.

'Can I get you anything? Do you want to come into the house and sit down?'

'No, thanks. I'd better get home and start organizing myself.' Emily moved towards the gate, half walking, half running. ''Bye, Mrs Prendergast.'

'Goodbye, my dear.'

Mrs Prendergast watched Emily until she was really alone in the garden. Then she wrapped her shawl tight around her shoulders, hugging herself, even though the day was warm. She was no longer ramrod straight: with no one to watch her, she was a tiny figure passing beneath the shade of the ancient apple trees, back into the house that had sheltered her secrets for most of her adult life.

The handover was organized for Friday morning. Emily arrived ten minutes early and Stephanie drove her to the foster-family's home. Emily was ready. At least, she thought she was. The house wasn't at all what she'd been expecting, although she hadn't known that she'd been expecting anything. It was small and neat and modest. Emily realized she was put out that they hadn't placed her daughter in something more palatial. Her next thought was that it was a damn sight more than she could offer. Oh, God.

The car drew to a halt and it was time to get out. Incredibly, her legs were still functioning and she accompanied Stephanie to the front door. They rang the bell and waited. A man of about sixty answered. He nodded at Stephanie, clearly recognizing her, and stood aside to let them enter. He stared at Emily, averting his gaze when she caught him. They were ushered into a living room, where a woman sat in the centre of a couch, an infant in her arms. She looked more grandmother than mother. This surprised Emily, but she didn't dwell on it as she was far too busy staring at her daughter. Everyone whispered in deference to the sleeping child.

'You must be Emily,' said the woman.

Emily nodded.

'I'm Marie. Why don't you sit down beside us?'

Emily perched on the edge of the couch, her eyes fixed on the baby's face.

'I'd have known you anywhere,' said Marie. 'She's the image of you.'

'Is she?' Emily allowed herself a smile. Was that true? She couldn't see it. But she recognized her daughter, or felt she did.

'Wouldn't you like to hold her?'

'Won't she wake?'

'Here. Sit back.'

Emily eased herself into the couch and accepted the warm, floppy weight of her child. The baby stirred but remained sleeping. The minutes passed. 'Have you done this before?' asked Emily.

'Thirty-nine times now, including this little one,' said Marie, 'and each time it's like giving up one of my own.'

Emily looked at her properly for the first time. 'I'm sorry.'

The woman touched her arm. 'Don't be. I'm happy for you both. Very happy.'

'Are you ready?' said Stephanie, gently.

Emily nodded and eased herself up off the couch.

'Here are all her things.' Marie handed an oversized bag to Stephanie while she addressed Emily. 'You've got nappies, wipes, Babygros and other clothes, the little teddy she sleeps with and a bottle for later.'

'Thank you.'

'You're more than welcome. Take good care of each other.'

'We will. I'll send you photos, let you know how she's getting on.'

'Will you?'

'Of course.'

'I'd really love that.' Marie planted a swift kiss on the baby's forehead and turned away.

Emily stepped out of the house, feeling as if she were stealing her own baby.

Of course, the baby woke up and started to scream as soon as they attempted to strap her into her car seat. Emily sat in the back beside her and held a bottle to her lips. It kind of worked.

'I'll take you home,' Stephanie said.

'Would you mind bringing me somewhere else instead?'

Stephanie helped Emily lug the buggy out of the boot and assemble it on the footpath, then click the car seat into the frame. There was so much to know, and that was even before you got to the baby.

Although the day was balmy, Emily placed a blanket over

the now sleeping form of her daughter. Then she let herself in through the wrought-iron gate, newly painted by Uri – who was the first person to see her.

He approached her, smiling. 'We were wondering where you'd got to. Doing a little babysitting?'

'You could say that.'

Uri peered into the buggy. 'Where did this little one come from, then?'

'Me.'

'Pardon?'

'She came from me, Uri. This is my daughter.'

Uri looked from Emily to the baby and back again. 'Really?'

'Yes.'

She could see the questions passing across Uri's face but he contained them. Instead he stepped up to Emily, held her by the upper arms and kissed her on each cheek. '*Mazel tov.*'

Emily felt close to tears.

Then Aoife came rushing over and she *was* in tears. 'Emily! You're here. You're both here.' She leaned into the buggy. 'Oh, she's so like you, and I'm not just saying that.' Then she embraced Emily with abandon, rocking her back and forth in her arms, both of them laughing through their tears.

Seth and Mrs Prendergast approached with some caution. They stared at the baby, then at Emily.

'Is she yours?' Seth said eventually.

'She is.'

'Congratulations.'

'Thanks.'

'What's her name?' said Mrs Prendergast, unable to resist reaching out and touching the child's cheek with her dry fingers.

'Rose,' said Emily, looking down at her daughter. 'Her name's Rose.'

Mrs Prendergast nodded, then turned and walked away.

Aoife insisted that Rose and Emily stay with her for that first night. She didn't have to do much persuading. Rose screamed well into the early hours, waking even Liam. He snuggled into his mother's warmth, half asleep. 'Has Katie come back to us, Mama?'

Aoife hugged him close. 'Go to sleep, my darling.'

The next day, Aoife drove mother and daughter to Kilkenny.

'What time are they expecting you?' They were almost there.

'They're not.'

'What?'

'I didn't tell them I was coming.'

'Why not?'

'I wanted to surprise them.'

Aoife had a horrible thought as she glanced at Emily's impassive profile. 'You did tell them about Rose?'

'Not yet.'

'What?'

Luckily, there was a layby coming up for Aoife to skid into. 'Jesus Christ, Emily. What were you thinking?'

'I couldn't bring myself to tell them over the phone. And, besides, they're less likely to reject her if they see her in the flesh. I mean, she's beautiful, isn't she?'

'Of course she's beautiful. But, Emily, you should have told me they didn't know. What do I do when we get there? Do I come inside the house or do I just drop you off? Or do I wait outside in the car in case –'

'In case they kick me out.'

'Well, I wasn't going to put it like that. But — You don't think they will, do you?'

'I don't know. I hope not.'

'So do I.'

They sat quietly for a while, staring out of the windscreen, lorries whizzing by at intervals and shaking the car.

'Will you come in with me?'

'I don't see how I have any choice.'

'I'm sorry, Aoife. I didn't mean for you to feel emotionally blackmailed.'

'It's not that. I just need to pee. Really badly. And it's all your fault for making that tea before we left.'

It was a traditional farmhouse. Nothing cute about it, just functional. Some effort had been made — rambling roses up the side wall — and it was neat. But it was what it was.

They arrived close to lunchtime and, to Aoife's untrained eye, it seemed that no one was around. But, said Emily, given the location and the time, that was impossible. She removed the sleeping Rose, complete with car seat, and carried her into the house. Aoife followed close behind.

The large kitchen was empty but showed signs of life — pots bubbling and steaming on an old Aga. Emily placed Rose and her car seat carefully in a vacant corner, facing the wall. Footsteps approached from the hall and the two women looked at one another. A third entered, an overflowing laundry basket under one oxter. She looked just like Emily, only her colours were less vivid. She stopped dead. 'Emily!' Her face creased into a smile. 'This is a lovely surprise. What are you doing here?' She put the basket on the massive kitchen table and hugged her daughter.

'Hiya, Mammy.' Aoife watched Emily sink into her mother as if she was afraid it was to be for the last time.

Mrs Harte met Aoife's eye over her daughter's shoulder. 'Hello.'

Aoife nodded. Emily disengaged herself. 'Mammy, this is Aoife, a good friend of mine. She drove me down. Aoife started the whole garden thing – remember I was telling you?'

'Oh, yes. It's very nice to meet you. I'm Emily's mother, in case you hadn't guessed. Why don't you sit down and take the weight off?'

Aoife took a chair. 'Nice to meet you, Mrs Harte.'

'Oh, none of that. Call me Bridget.'

Aoife was amazed at how young she was – no more than mid-forties – and realized how inaccurate her vision of Emily's mother had been. She was only about a decade older than herself.

Rose chose this exact moment to whimper. It was a delicious sound – not ready to wake up yet, just settling back into her dreams. Three sets of eyes swung towards the car seat in the corner.

'You have a baby!' exclaimed Bridget, rushing over to examine her. 'Ah, would you look at her. How old?' She addressed Aoife.

'Um. Eight months, but –'

'Eight months. What a gorgeous age. What's her name?'

'Rose,' said Emily. 'Mammy, you have the wrong end of the stick.'

Bridget looked up at her daughter in confusion. 'What do you mean?'

Aoife watched Emily draw herself up to her full height. 'She's mine.'

Understanding and denial fought for dominance on Mrs Harte's face. 'What are you talking about?'

'The baby. She's mine.'

Aoife was sure the clock hadn't been ticking as loudly in

the seconds beforehand. But now it was all she could hear, as if it signalled the imminent detonation of a bomb.

She and Emily watched as Bridget's complexion turned from cream to pink to puce.

'Mammy, are you all right?'

Bridget was holding on to the side of a dresser as if to support herself. Wordlessly, Aoife got up, took her free arm, walked her to a chair and sat her down. Then she searched for a kettle and switched it on.

'Mammy, say something.'

Bridget was gripping the side of the table. The table that had been scarred by a thousand coffee cups. She appeared to be whispering something to herself.

'What did you say?'

'I don't understand.' Bridget turned to her daughter, her face now a somewhat normal colour. 'How could you possibly have a baby?'

'Well, I did it the old-fashioned way. It wasn't a virgin birth, if that's what you mean.' Emily's words were defiant, but Aoife noticed that she kept her eyes lowered.

'No. I mean she's eight months old. Where has she been all this time?'

Emily sighed and sat down heavily in the chair beside her mother. 'She was in a foster-home. I was going to have her adopted but I couldn't go through with it.'

'But your pregnancy . . .' Bridget was shaking her head slowly.

'I was small. I wore baggy clothes. And then when I was heavily pregnant I just didn't come home. Remember last summer when you were put out that I wasn't here for the weekends?'

Bridget nodded as if in a trance. Then, all of a sudden, she seemed to come to. 'Who's the father?'

'A boy in college. He's not important. He didn't want to know.'

'So you had the baby – you had Rose. In hospital?'

'I had her in hospital, yes.'

'Who was with you?'

'No one.'

The words reverberated around the kitchen as their impact resonated with all three women. Bridget's face crumpled. 'Why didn't you tell me?'

'I didn't think you'd understand.'

As both women began to cry, Aoife slipped out of the kitchen and closed the door quietly behind her. She found herself in a long hallway with a porch at the end. There, a boy – around eight or nine – was in the process of kicking off a pair of mucky shoes and simultaneously shrugging a schoolbag off his back.

'Hello,' said Aoife, walking towards him.

'Well.'

She assumed that 'well' passed for 'hello' in these parts. 'I take it you're Emily's brother.'

He nodded briefly. 'Who are you?'

'I'm Aoife, a friend of Emily's.'

He nodded, apparently uninterested, and walked past her towards the kitchen door.

'I wouldn't go in there if I were you.'

'Why not?'

'Because Emily and your mother need some privacy.'

'But I came home for me dinner.'

'Just give them five minutes. Go and watch some cartoons or something.'

The boy eyed her resentfully. 'What are you doing here anyway?'

'Actually, I was looking for a toilet.'

27

They didn't see Emily for the rest of the summer. She was on maternity leave. At first it was strange without her. But the others grew to fill in the gap. There were reminders of her everywhere, in the purple spikes of lavender – French, not English – and when a breeze or a childish hand jangled the wind chimes. In the evenings Aoife would sit beside Emily's night-scented stock like a woman intoxicated. Sometimes Seth would be with her and they would talk until late, the children playing around them, well past their bedtime. It was only a matter of time before they asked the questions that remained an unspoken barrier between them.

Aoife went first. She had faced more in life and was less fearful. It was like a confession box, that clump of night-scented stock. 'Do you see much of your wife, Seth?'

'Every time I pick Kathy up or drop her off.'

'Of course. What's that like?'

'All right. It was weird at first but we're used to it now.'

'Is she in another relationship?'

'Yes.'

'That must be strange. Knowing that Kathy has another father figure in her life.'

'Mother figure.'

'Pardon?'

Seth turned so that he was looking at her. She could see his eyes clearly now. Hazel flecked with blue and green.

'She has another mother figure. Megan left me for a woman.'

Several heartbeats were missed. 'Really?'

'Yes, really.'

'That must have been tough.'

He shrugged and looked down at his feet.

'Did you feel – I don't know – emasculated or something?'

'If you mean did I feel like she'd cut off my balls then the answer is yes.'

'Ouch.'

'Ouch is right. It didn't help that she was so open about it. She still lives in the same neighbourhood and doesn't try to hide it. I'm not saying she should or anything but it would be easier for me if everyone didn't know. Can you imagine the lads down the pub? It doesn't really go with my macho image.'

'No, I don't suppose it does.'

They were both quiet for a while.

'Have they grown back, then?'

'What?'

'Your balls.'

He laughed – she liked making him laugh. 'I almost have a full set.' He looked at her. 'Your turn.'

'What?'

'You know. You got my sordid details. Now you tell me yours.'

He was smiling but his eyes were serious. Had he been as curious about her as she had been about him? It took her a while to speak.

'My husband died,' she said eventually. 'A little over two years ago.'

'I'm sorry.'

'Did you already know?'

'How would I?'

'I told Emily a while back. I wasn't sure if she'd said anything to anyone.'

'Not to me she didn't. Although I did wonder why Liam didn't seem to have anything to do with his father.'

She nodded.

'How did he die?'

'Car accident.'

'Jesus. That must have been terrible. For you and for Liam.'

They watched Liam and Kathy race his extensive collection of tractors up and down the path, their commentary enthusiastic and bizarre.

'I sent him out.'

'How do you mean?'

She breathed deeply. 'We had a little girl too. Katie. She was one. She couldn't get to sleep that night so I suggested he bring her out for a drive.'

Aoife felt Seth's hand enclosing hers, his skin rough.

For a long time, neither of them said anything. Then: 'What was she like? Katie.'

Aoife smiled, her eyes filling with tears. 'Oh, you know. She was a one-year-old girl. She was gorgeous. Always smiling. Massive blue eyes, reddish-gold hair – her daddy was a redhead. Chubby little arms and legs. You just wanted to eat her. She'd just learned to walk. She was delighted with herself, toddling around, pulling the house apart. She was just – brilliant.'

'I'm so, so sorry, Aoife.'

She nodded in acknowledgement and they sat there for ages, watching the children, laughing intermittently at their antics, Aoife's hand in Seth's.

'Almost the worst thing has been the guilt,' said Aoife at last, staring straight ahead.

'It wasn't your fault – when I think of the amount of times I drove Kathy around when she was a baby, trying to get her to sleep.'

'It's not just that.'

'What is it, then?'

Aoife didn't know why she was telling him this. She was just struck by the urge to be absolutely honest. 'I was having a – a kind of an affair when they died.'

'Oh.'

'It was stupid. I thought it was serious but it wasn't. Michael had to die to make me realize how little it meant.' She looked at Seth to gauge his reaction, but he was consulting his shoes. She thought she sensed a withdrawal of sympathy, but perhaps that was her guilty conscience. 'The one good thing was that he never found out about it.'

'That you know of.'

'What?'

'As far as you know he never found out about it.'

'I would have known.'

'Not necessarily.'

Seth was sitting forward now, looking away from her. At some point he had withdrawn his hand.

'What's that supposed to mean?'

'It's like when Megan – my ex – started to see Siobhan, her girlfriend. I suspected for months before I actually found out about it.'

'Thanks, Seth.'

'I'm just being honest.'

'Don't you think I feel bad enough as it is? I know what I did was wrong. Unforgivable, even. But, believe me, I've paid a price for it. Jesus Christ.' She stood up, angry now.

'Where are you going?'

'Liam! Packing-up time.'

She looked back at Seth to find he was staring at her, his expression hard. She knew why: she'd disappointed him. She'd failed to live up to the image he'd had of her in his head. Well, fuck him. She'd never told him to put her on a pedestal.

She gathered up Liam's belongings and turned to him again. He was stony-faced. 'Do you know what it took for me to confide in you?' she said, struggling to keep the tremor out of her voice. 'I never thought you'd throw it back in my face. You might have thought better of me, but I thought better of you too, Seth.'

She turned and walked away from him, muttering, 'Arsehole,' under her breath, just loudly enough for him to hear.

The garden was by now producing far too much fruit and vegetables for the gardeners alone to consume. An emergency meeting was called. This consisted of Aoife, Uri, Seth and Mrs Prendergast standing in a rough circle, leaning on forks and spades.

'We have to decide what to do with the leftover veggies. We can't let them go to waste.'

'No. Absolutely not,' said Uri.

'We could have a harvest festival,' said Seth.

'Don't be ridiculous,' said Mrs Prendergast. 'It's far too early in the year for that.'

'But we have the produce now.'

'A harvest festival isn't held until the autumn.'

'We'll call it something different, then.'

'A harvest festival is a good idea. Maybe we can plan one for a couple of months down the line. But, in the meantime, I have another proposal.'

They all looked at Aoife expectantly.

'How about seeing if the Good Food Store would sell it for us? I'm sure Emily's aunt would agree. She's very accommodating and they have a little fruit-and-veg section already. What do you think?'

'It's worth a try,' said Mrs Prendergast.

'It's an excellent idea,' said Uri.

'What would we do with the profit?' asked Seth. 'There's hardly any point in ploughing it back into the garden.'

He found himself at the receiving end of three dirty looks.

'What?' He held up his hands. 'Well, there isn't, is there?'

Aoife, who still wasn't really talking to him, addressed him coolly: 'We can decide what to do with any profit we make at a later date. Let's just see if she'll agree to it first. Uri, will you come with me? Mrs Prendergast, I think I'm right in saying you don't get on with her particularly well, and Seth would just annoy her.'

'How would I annoy her?'

'You're just annoying.'

'Thanks.'

'Of course I'll come with you,' said Uri.

They spent the rest of the morning putting together a selection of their finest produce. When it was assembled, Aoife and Uri carried the box to the shop. As luck would have it, Emily's aunt, her father's sister-in-law, happened to be behind the counter when they called. 'Ah, Aoife, what can I do for you today?'

Among the Hartes, Aoife was widely credited with getting Emily back on the straight and narrow. This was a card she was prepared to play if she had to.

She plonked the box on the counter in front of her. 'It's more a question of what we can do for you.'

'Is that so?'

'Yes, it is. You do know Uri – Mr Rosenberg?'

'Of course. Morning, Mr Rosenberg.'

'Good morning, Mrs Harte.'

'What I have in this box is an example of the food we've been producing in the community garden – you know, Mrs Prendergast's old walled garden.'

'I do indeed.'

'We were wondering if you'd be interested in selling it for us.'

The woman looked as if she needed convincing.

'A percentage of the profit to go to the shop, of course,' said Uri.

'Of course,' echoed Aoife. 'And you can't get fresher fruit and veg than this. Hand-picked in the last hour. Local produce grown by local people. It fits in with the ethos of the shop: food for the community grown by the community, no air miles, no pesticides . . .' She trailed off, looking to see if her words were having any impact.

'I'll tell you what,' said Mrs Harte. 'I'll give this lot a try, and if it sells, I'll take some more off your hands.'

It was all sold by that evening. They were in business.

Aoife arrived in the garden first thing and carried out her usual tour of inspection. She'd had a heavy week in college and hadn't visited for days. She was heading towards the runner beans when she spotted it: one perfect, plump, shiny, voluptuous tomato. Bright red. Tomato red, even. She caressed it gently, loath to disturb such perfection. It looked so delicious. Nobody would know . . .

'Hi there.'

She jumped. It was Seth. 'What are you doing here?'

'Same as you.'

'You gave me a fright.'

'Why? What are you up to?'

'Nothing.'

She had quickly withdrawn her hand from the tomato, but she hadn't been quick enough in averting her gaze. Seth leaned over to the plant. 'Is it – A tomato. Brilliant.' He rubbed it between his thumb and forefinger. 'Aoife Madigan, you weren't thinking of eating it, were you?'

'Of course not.'

'Are you sure?' He was mocking her now.

Aoife felt herself redden. Tomato red?

'Something, something, something . . . money can't buy except true love – oh, you know the song, home-grown tomatoes.'

He delivered this in the most appalling southern American accent, pronouncing 'tomatoes' the American way.

'What?'

'It's a song. Guy Clark, I think. Country and western.'

Aoife laughed in spite of herself. 'I like it. Only please don't say it in that terrible accent.'

Seth laughed too, evidently relieved that she was talking to him. 'Do you think it's true?' he said.

'I don't know.'

'Why don't you give it a try?' He took a step closer to her.

'What do you mean?'

'Try it.' He touched the plant.

'Oh, the tomato.'

'What did you think I meant?'

'Nothing. I can't eat it.'

'Why not? That's what it's for.'

'But it's not mine to eat. It belongs to everybody.'

'There'll be other tomatoes. You started this thing. It seems only fair that you should get the first taste.'

'You think so?'

'Go on.'

Aoife gripped the tomato, prepared to give it a good tug, but it fell into her hand as if it had been waiting for her. She looked at Seth again. He nodded and smiled. Then she bit deep into the tender flesh, the unimaginable sweetness bursting on to her tongue. 'Mm.' She closed her eyes.

Seth laughed.

'Here.' She held it up to his mouth.

Seth, his eyes not leaving hers, held Aoife's hand as he bit into the tomato. He continued to hold her hand long after he'd finished chewing. 'I'm sorry, Aoife. You were right. I am an arsehole and I apologize.'

'I'm sorry too.'

'Yoo-hoo!' It was Mrs Prendergast. Seth withdrew his hand and the two stepped away from one another.

They were digging a new flowerbed, Seth and Aoife. Except Aoife felt as if she was just making up the numbers, Seth being able to dig three times faster and deeper than she was, no matter how hard she worked. Liam and Kathy were helping too, Kathy with her pink Barbie spade. Since she'd met Kathy, Aoife had discovered that they made a Barbie just-about-everything. The child had Barbie wellies and a pink Barbie bicycle. Liam was using his favourite yellow digger, scooping up minute particles of earth and moving them a few centimetres. If it wasn't for Seth, they'd have been digging until Christmas.

It was pleasant, satisfying work, despite or perhaps because of the hard physical labour involved. The children nattered aimlessly and asked all sorts of irrelevant questions. Such as:

'Aoife?'

'Yes, Kathy.'

'Are you going to be my new mammy?'

The rhythm of Seth's digging was disturbed for a barely discernible nano-second. Aoife didn't dare look at him. 'Why are you asking me that?'

'Because I already have two mammies and if I had you as well I'd have three.'

'Well, I think two mammies are plenty for any girl. And I'm already Liam's mammy. I'm pretty busy doing that.'

'You're not Liam's mammy. You're his mummy.'

'That's very true.'

'Well, if you're not going to be my mammy, why were you holding my daddy's hand the other day?'

Silence. Aoife could feel her face growing hot.

'Kathy, leave Aoife alone now. She's trying to work.'

'But I want to know why she was holding your hand.' Kathy's voice became whiny.

'Your daddy was holding my hand to make me feel better because I was sad.'

'Why were you sad?'

'I can't remember. But I'm better now.'

'Were you sad that Liam's daddy has gone away?'

Seth and Aoife glanced at each other. Aoife thought he looked as alarmed as she felt. 'Did you tell her?' she asked him.

'No! It must have been Liam.'

'My daddy's up in heaven with Holy God and all the angels,' announced Liam. 'And Katie's with him and she has wings too.'

'Where's heaven, Daddy?'

'It's a very long way away from here.'

'Like Bray?'

'A bit like Bray, yes.'

'Can we go there tomorrow after playschool?'

'No, Kathy. It's a really, *really* long way away.'

'We can get the bus.'

'No, Kathy.'

'Oh, why not? It's not fair.' She started to bash the earth with her Barbie spade.

'I know. Who'd like some chocolate?'

'Me!'

'Me!'

Aoife delved into the pocket of her fleece for the few squares of Dairy Milk she hoped she hadn't eaten already. No, they were still there. 'Here we go.'

'Yippee!'

'Yippee!'

She glanced at Seth. He wasn't looking at her but was instead focusing hard on pulling up a stubborn root. She recommenced digging, concentrating on the far end of the bed, hitherto unworked. The spade hit something hard. Must be a rock, and a big one at that, judging by the feel of it. She attempted to go around it, digging elsewhere, but kept reconnecting with it.

'You got something there?' Seth was behind her.

'Yes. I can't shift it.'

'Here. Let me have a go.'

Seth sliced into the earth she'd been digging and came up against the same hard object. 'I don't think that's a rock.'

Aoife grabbed at his sleeve, her eyes wide. 'You don't think it's – a bone, do you?' She looked around for Mrs Prendergast.

'I wouldn't say so.' He laughed. 'You don't seriously believe that story, do you?'

'I don't know. No. Of course not.'

'She may be a mad old trout but she's not a murderer.'

'She might have been driven to it.'

'How?'

'He might have been an annoying bastard.'

Seth laughed. 'Here. I'll prove it to you. It's not bone, it's metal.'

He was digging again, frenziedly now, then tugging at something with his hands. He lifted the object out of the soil. It was an old, square, rusty metal box. Liam and Kathy had finished their chocolate.

'What is it, Daddy?'

'It's a box.'

'What kind of box?'

'I don't know, Kathy.'

'Open it!' The children jumped up and down, excited.

'It's not mine to open,' said Seth. 'It might belong to Mrs Prendergast. We'll have to ask her first.'

Gathering Uri as they went, they trooped *en masse* to the back door of Mrs Prendergast's house and knocked. They heard her advancing steps.

'His teeth might be in there,' whispered Seth, as the door was opening, leaving Aoife to bite down on her giggles.

'Mrs P.' He held out the box with outstretched hands. 'Look what we found. Does it mean anything to you?'

Mrs Prendergast wore an unfamiliar expression on her face. She took the box out of Seth's hands and walked back into her house. The adults looked at one another. Uri nodded and they followed her into her hallowed living quarters.

The back door led them into a kind of coats-and-mucky-boots area, which opened into the kitchen. Seated at the surprisingly rustic table was Lance, Mrs Prendergast's son, a half-drunk mug of coffee in front of him. He was slumped in his shirtsleeves, tie loosened. He straightened as they entered, his expression shifting from tired to surprised to wary.

'Lance, look at this. Do you remember?'

She proffered the box and Lance took it out of her hands to examine it. Aoife could see now that it was an old biscuit tin, badly rusted, Jacobs USA. Recognition brought her whizzing back to her childhood in her grandmother's Dublin home at Christmas time. *Oliver Twist* on the telly and a brown-grey furry toy rabbit called Strawberry on her lap – her favourite present of that year.

'Have a biscuit, Aoife love.'

She'd selected a fluorescent pink wafer sandwich, her grandmother smiling at her indulgently. Aoife was suddenly nostalgic for the Irish food of her childhood: Galtee and Calvita cheese, Tayto crisps, Lemon's sweets, Kimberley, Mikado and coconut-cream biscuits. All of them you could probably still get, although she hadn't tasted most for years. She resolved to remedy that as soon as possible. Could you still get USA biscuits?

Lance and his mother were searching each other's faces.

'The time capsule,' said Lance. Then he laughed and attempted to prise it open.

'What's a time capsule?' said Liam.

Aoife scooped him up and held him to her. 'It's when you put some things in a box and bury them for somebody else to find years later. You put things in the box to show the person who finds it what life was like when you buried it. Sometimes it might not be found for hundreds of years. But this one wouldn't be that old.'

'How old is it?'

'Let's see,' said Lance, who had opened the box and was unfolding a newspaper. It was slightly damp and some of the pages were stuck together. Aoife took a step closer to peer at the date on the front of the *Irish Times*. As she leaned in, she breathed in the mustiness of the last forty-odd years and the scent transported her instantly to her childhood again.

When she was a little kid, her family used to take weekend breaks at Eastbourne, in a caravan belonging to friends of her parents. Each time they opened the caravan anew, months of mustiness would invade their collective nostrils. It was a scent peculiar and exotic to Aoife, and exactly the same as that which was now emanating from the newspaper. She had only experienced it one other time and that was when she purchased a secondhand book from a little shop in Notting Hill. She'd opened it and, *whoosh*, she was back in the caravan, six years old again. She looked into her son's four-year-old face. Would this moment become a memory for him?

Lance was reading out headlines from the paper. They all crowded around and peered in. It did occur to Aoife that perhaps they should give him and his mother some privacy but, quite frankly, she was too nosy. And Liam would have a fit if she took him away now. In any case, the Prendergasts had buried it with the intention of somebody else finding it, so it couldn't be that private. And, besides, nobody else looked as if they had any intention of budging.

It appeared, from the headlines, that not much had changed in the intervening years, which was either comforting or depressing, depending on how you looked at it.

'What else is in there?' said Kathy, standing on tiptoe, tense with impatience. Lance folded the newspaper and put it to one side. He delved into the box and pulled out a clear plastic package.

'Money.' He emptied out coins representative of every denomination and an old pound note.

'What else?' said Kathy, unimpressed.

Mrs Prendergast reached down and took out what appeared to be an old photograph. She stared at it for a good two minutes before handing it silently to Uri, who was standing beside her. After several seconds, his face broke into a smile. 'The apple trees.'

They all crowded around him, except Mrs Prendergast who sat, her face mask-like.

Trust Uri to notice the apple trees. Aoife had barely registered them, recognizable as they were, although less gnarled and more tender. Instead, she was focusing on the three people standing in front of them, smiling for the camera and squinting into the sun. A young boy – Lance presumably – dark-haired and skinny, wearing sixties-style shorts and a plaster on each bony knee. Standing behind him, a protective hand on his shoulder, was none other than a young Mrs Prendergast. It had to be her – the same narrow figure, the tiny waist. But her bearing was less stiff, as was her hair, pale gold and wavy, tied into a ponytail that cascaded over her left shoulder.

'Kathy, look at Mrs P,' said Seth. 'Wasn't she a fine thing?'

'That's not Mrs Prendergast,' said Kathy, her tone full of derision.

'Yes, it is.'

'Then why does she look so different?'

'It was taken a long time ago.'

Aoife could see that Seth was regretting bringing the matter up. But she was far too interested in the photo to pay much heed. The third figure was a man. He stood a little apart from the others, presumably his wife and son. He was large, attractive, muscular – his face and smile not unlike Lance's. His hands were on his hips and his shirtsleeves were rolled up. The famous Mr Prendergast.

'Is that your father?' Uri asked Lance.

'Yes.' Lance sat down again, his face closed.

'Look, roses!' Aoife's attention was momentarily distracted by a cloud of pale pink to the left of the photo. It was tremendously exciting to see this picture of how the garden had once been, if only in part.

One last thing remained in the box. Lance took it out now. He handed it to his mother and she turned it over in her hands, smoothing its face with her fingers. 'Do you remember this, Lance?' She was smiling now.

'Vaguely.'

It was a ceramic angel, faded and old, like something you might put on a Christmas tree. It was blue and white.

'Your father brought it back from Amsterdam.'

'It's a fairy,' said Kathy.

'Actually, no, Kathy, it's an angel,' said Uri.

'I didn't know you Jews believed in angels.'

It wasn't what Lance said so much as the way he said it. Indefinable. Yet unmistakable. The way he spat out the word instantaneously transformed the atmosphere in the room from wonder to hostility. Aoife felt as if she'd been slapped in the face. She could only imagine how Uri and Seth felt. It was horrible. With great dignity, Uri placed the photo on the table. 'You'd be surprised at what us Jews believe in.' He walked out of the kitchen, out of the house and into the garden. The silence in the kitchen grew. Aoife could feel something mounting in Seth beside her. She willed him not to say anything, not to thump Lance. He didn't. Instead, he glared at the man, then followed his father out to the garden.

Aoife was left in the kitchen with Lance, Mrs Prendergast and the two children, who were examining the angel minutely.

'How could you, Lance?' Mrs Prendergast turned to her son.

This time they needed their privacy.

'Come on, kids. It's nearly lunchtime. Let's go and get something to eat.'

'I'm not hungry.'

'Me neither.'

'I've got treats.'

'Yippee!'

'What are they?'

'Come outside and I'll show you.'

They left mother and son to discuss whatever they had to discuss.

Aoife hated the way the garden felt that afternoon – Seth and Uri so quiet. As if the very air itself had been tainted. She wanted to say something but they seemed so unapproachable, each man working in his own space. It was so awful, though, that she had to do something. She eventually went over to Seth, who had finished digging the bed. He was loading his wheelbarrow with an assortment of rocks.

'Hi, Seth.'

'Aoife.' He continued loading the rocks.

'How are you?'

'Grand.'

'Are you sure?'

'Why wouldn't I be?' He stopped what he was doing and looked at her, his hands on his hips.

'It's just that I thought, you know, what happened inside . . .'

'I wouldn't let an ignorant prick like him get to me.'

Except it was clear that he had.

She let the silence settle between them for a while. Then: 'It must have been strange for you, growing up Jewish in Dublin.'

'Not really. Most of the time it made no difference at all. I barely thought about it until my bar mitzvah.'

'So you had that, then?'

'Oh, yes.'

'And were you . . . ?'

'Yes, Aoife, I am circumcised.'

She gave an embarrassed laugh. 'I suppose everyone wants to know that.'

'Pretty much.'

'You must get sick of people asking.'

'Depends on who's doing the asking.'

He smiled at her then. Right into the pit of her stomach.

'What was Uri like when you were growing up?'

'He was pretty strict. A lot stricter than he is with Kathy. He wanted me and Aaron to "make something of ourselves".'

'Well, he got his wish.'

Seth smiled again and cast his eyes down, almost bashfully. 'Ah, you know. We had our moments. Mostly when I was a teenager. Didn't want to go to synagogue. Wouldn't study. Gave back cheek. The usual pain-in-the-arse stuff.'

'You? A pain in the arse? I don't believe it.'

'Yeah, well, it's true.'

'And how do you feel about it now? The religious side of things.'

'Well, it doesn't do all that much for me, but it means a lot to him. So I respect that. Respect him. More than anyone else, really. He's been through a lot, my da. And he's come out of it one of the best people I know. If I can be half the man he is, half the father to Kathy that he was to me and Aaron, well, I'll be doing pretty well.'

Seth, who seemed to have lost himself in this reverie, came back sharply into focus. 'Anyway, what are we doing standing around here, woman? There's work to be done.' He handed her a spade. 'Get digging.' He walked away then – to fetch a bag of compost, or so he said.

Aoife watched him go. A thought came unbidden: I could love this man.

She was momentarily distracted by the sight of Mrs Prendergast coming across the garden. She didn't look at Aoife but headed straight for Uri. He stopped what he was doing and turned to face her. Mrs Prendergast spoke earnestly to him, beseechingly, her body tense and bent slightly forward, her arms crossed tightly over her chest. When she'd finished, Uri looked at her for a few long seconds. Then he embraced her warmly and the two linked arms and walked towards the house, disappearing together through the wooden door.

'Did you see that?' said Seth, coming to stand by her side.

'I did.'

'What do you reckon it was all about?'

'She was probably apologizing for Lance.'

'She shouldn't have to.'

'Well. Maybe she wanted to. Unless . . .'

'What?'

'There could be more to it.'

'Like what?'

'Maybe you're getting a new mammy.'

They both laughed and everything felt okay again. At least to Seth. To Aoife, it was as if the entire universe had been flipped on its head.

28

It was so odd. So unfathomable to her. That moment in time when everything switched. The inner shift in consciousness that altered her world. One minute Seth was a friend, objectively attractive, undeniably useful, mildly annoying, and now she was thinking about him every second of the day. Obsessing about him. Could he tell? Could he feel the desire radiating off her in waves? Her wanton want?

Was it just like Peter all over again? Nature, her body, her emotions tricking her when ultimately all was an illusion? A house of cards that would come tumbling down in the face of reality?

She didn't know. She tried to ignore it and took refuge in what she did know. The garden.

It was mid-July and this was what the garden looked like. Four quadrants. The kitchen garden – tomatoes, lettuce, runner beans, spuds, Swiss chard, courgettes, cabbages and carrots. Aoife was particularly entranced by the carrots. You could see their broad orange tops poking up through the soil, as if somebody had bought them in a shop and shoved them whole into the ground. She was insanely proud of all her vegetables and privately thought them even more beautiful than the riotous flowers in Emily's sensory garden, although she had to admit that the girl had performed quite a task. None of her colours clashed, even where you might have expected them to do so. Shaggy yellow daisies alongside violet allium. Bright orange lilies against deep blue delphiniums. Who would have thought?

It was like a grand experiment to prove that everything in nature worked in harmony.

Mrs Prendergast's roses were like something out of a dream – tunnels of archways and trellises. Uri's fan-shaped fig tree dominated the back wall of the orchard. The apple trees sported their little green orbs, and there were alpine strawberries, rows of them, raspberry canes, gooseberry bushes, cultivated brambles. The dividing herbaceous border grew high and powerful. The pond teemed with life. Everywhere there were patches of glory, yet the garden, still in its infancy as gardens went, had yet to obtain an all-important unity. A vital maturity. All the elements hadn't quite come together, although they were working on it, nature and the gardeners, in their divine collaboration. All it would take was time. Time they didn't have. Because one day it happened.

It was a Saturday morning.

'What's he doing to the sign, Mummy?'

A man, presumably from the estate agent's, was up a ladder hammering the words 'Sale Agreed' across the for-sale sign. Aoife stood stock still.

'What is it, Mummy?'

'Nothing.' She was grateful he couldn't yet read.

Aoife walked rapidly over to the man, sorely tempted to kick the ladder out from under him. 'What do you think you're doing?'

'My job,' he said mildly, jumping lightly to the ground and lifting up the ladder as if it were made of air. He walked away from her, whistling maddeningly. She experienced an irrational surge of anger towards him, which the logical side of her brain knew was misdirected. But she had to direct it somewhere, because it was about to consume her. She entered the garden. Seth stood in the centre, in front of the pond, gazing up at the sign.

She went up to him, her new-found feelings for him pushed aside. 'You've seen it, then.'

'Yeah.'

'What are we going to do?'

'What can we do?'

'Try and talk her out of it. Convince her not to sell.'

'But she's already accepted an offer.'

'But the sale hasn't gone through yet.'

'Aoife . . .'

'We can't just give up.'

He didn't say anything, just looked at her calmly. She found this even more infuriating than the estate agent's whistling. 'Seth, don't tell me you're going to stand by and let this happen.'

'Aoife, you always knew it would one day. We all did.'

'I know. But I always held out a little bit of hope. Didn't you?'

'Not really, no.'

'Then why did you help us?'

'Maybe I have a weakness for a lost cause.'

'This is not a lost cause. Don't you dare call this garden a lost cause.' She could hear her voice rising dangerously high. A few seconds more and she'd be out of control.

'Calm down, Aoife.'

'Don't tell me to calm down. Patronizing git!' Seth looked taken aback. Then he laughed, angering Aoife even more. 'How dare you laugh at me?'

'I'm not laughing at you, Aoife. I know you're upset but it's happened. You have to let it go.'

'Let it go? How can I do that? How can you?'

'We have no choice.'

'There's always a choice. Always something you can do. I'll set up a petition. We can go door to door. I'm sure local people will support the garden.'

'But it's private land.'

'Why are you being so negative?'

'I'm not. I'm being realistic.'

'I can't just do nothing. Can't you see that? I can't let this all have been for nothing.' Her voice cracked.

Seth took her shoulders and turned her to face the garden. 'It hasn't been for nothing,' he said. 'Never say that. Just look at what you've achieved. Look at it. You've created something out of nothing. This beautiful garden out of a . . . wilderness. Never say that it's been for nothing, Aoife. It's incredible, what you've done. You're nothing short of a goddess.' He squeezed her shoulders. 'A green goddess.'

She could feel his breath on the side of her face, the warmth of it. His body stood directly behind hers, so solid, so reassuring. It would be easy just to yield, sink back into him. Why didn't she?

'Aoife.' It was Mrs Prendergast.

At the sound of the older woman's voice, Aoife stiffened again and swung around to face her, twisting Seth's hands off her shoulders. At last. A worthy target for her rage. 'How could you do that?'

'I take it you've seen the sign.'

'It's hard to miss.'

'I understand that you're upset, but I never misled you.'

'Not with your words, but with your actions you did.'

'What are you talking about?'

'Getting so involved in the garden. Encouraging us. Your bloody roses. Have you thought about that? Your precious roses. They'll all be ripped up.'

'We'll find good homes for all the plants, Aoife.' Seth laid a steadying hand on her arm but she shook it off, angry with the whole world.

'Of course I've thought about it,' said Mrs Prendergast,

her tone and expression cold. 'What I actually came over to ask you both was if you'd like to come to the house for dinner tonight. I've already asked your father, Seth, and he can make it.'

'I'd love to, thanks,' said Seth, sounding remarkably gracious.

'Aoife?'

'I'm afraid I'm washing my hair,' said Aoife, sounding remarkably ungracious.

'There's no need to be like that, my dear. I'm planning to make a special dinner, using mainly produce from the garden.'

'You're going to use *my* vegetables to make your – your last supper. Unbelievable!'

'I'd just like a chance to explain . . .'

'What's the point? Will you be sitting there counting your money? Go to hell, Mrs Prendergast.' She walked out of the garden, not wanting either of them to see the tears that were crowding at the corners of her eyes. She'd had so much work planned for today. But now it all seemed pointless.

A couple of hours later, she was curled up on the couch feeling sorry for herself. She had given up the pretence of marking papers and was flicking from one channel to the next. The doorbell rang. 'Oh, go away,' she murmured, making no attempt to answer it.

After a spell, it rang again.

'Piss off.' She covered her face with a big furry cushion and willed whoever it was to give up.

The doorbell rang a third time.

'Oh, for fuck's sake.' Flinging the cushion aside, she jumped off the couch and marched out to the hall. It had better not be someone trying to sell her something. She flung open the front door.

Seth. Leaning up against the wall, his arms and ankles crossed, his expression sardonic. 'For a second there I thought you weren't going to answer.'

'What do you want?'

'You'll have to work on your Irish welcome, now that you're back on the oul' sod.'

'Sod off.'

She turned and went back into the sitting room. Seth closed the door behind him and followed her.

Aoife was immediately conscious of several things. Her appearance: had her face calmed down yet after her prolonged bout of sobbing? Were her eyes still swollen and was her nose still red? Then there was the matter of the used tissues on the coffee-table. She bent down and shoved the bulk of them into her pocket, just as Seth came into the room. As for the tasteless décor she had inherited from the previous inhabitants of the house, she'd had no time to do anything about that. He'd just have to suffer it.

It occurred to her that Seth had never been to her house before. 'How did you know where I lived?'

'I didn't realize it was a state secret.'

'It's not.'

She sank down on the couch and folded her legs under her. Seth sat in the armchair opposite. It unsettled her to have him in her home.

'Nice wallpaper.'

'Have you come here to mock me?'

'No. I've come here to stop you making such a fecking eejit out of yourself.'

'I'm not!'

184

'Yes, you are. The old bag's trying to apologize and you're throwing it back in her face.'

'What does she expect?'

'Did she ever tell you she wasn't going to sell the garden?'

'No.'

'Well, then.'

'I just didn't think she'd actually go through with it. I see that now. After all the work we've put into it. After all the work *she*'s put into it, for God's sake. I don't understand.'

'Maybe she needs the money.'

'Her! You're joking. The woman's minted.'

'You don't know that.'

'Yes, I do. Have you never seen her clothes? All her stuff? It's the best of everything.'

'Well, why don't you come along anyway and see what she has to say for herself? Maybe it'll help you understand.'

'I don't think I could stomach it.'

'She probably wants to thank you too.'

'She needn't bother.'

'And you could always give her another piece of your mind.'

'I could, couldn't I?'

So that was how Liam and Aoife ended up at Mrs Prendergast's at half past seven that evening. Aoife marched up to the front door and knocked aggressively. She was damned if she was going to use the tradesman's entrance tonight.

'Why don't we just go through the gate, Mummy?'

'I forgot my key.'

And she couldn't bring herself to walk through the garden on such a rare and beautiful balmy summer's evening, when she knew it would be at its glorious best. Aoife closed her eyes and tried not to imagine – to imagine it there and imagine it gone. As far as she was concerned, her garden, and everything in it, was about to be murdered.

The door opened and there stood the murderer.

'Aoife. So glad you could make it. And Liam. Come on in. Kathy's already here.'

Aoife tried to hide the hostility in her eyes but it was impossible. It was as much as she could do to keep her mouth shut. Mrs Prendergast's eyes were hooded and wary. Aoife thought she detected ironic amusement too. She looked away. She couldn't afford to become more annoyed than she already was.

'We brought you some wine.' Liam was jumping up and down on the spot, as he did when he was excited. He smiled openly at the woman who had become to him a kind of surrogate grandmother. How on earth was Aoife going to explain to him that they wouldn't be seeing her any more? The little boy had had too many loved ones taken away from him during the course of his short life, but she honestly didn't see how they could go on seeing Mrs Prendergast in the circumstances.

Aoife handed her the bottle of wine.

'Oh, how very kind. Wolf Blass. One of my favourites.'

Mrs Prendergast's manners were impeccable. She had to give her that. Then again, so were Hannibal Lecter's.

Aoife and Liam walked into Mrs Prendergast's hall, for only the third time since they'd known her. Aoife recalled the first time vividly. Who could have predicted all that had happened since then?

The older woman led them to a small reception room at the back of the house. It felt unlived-in. But it opened out into a spectacular sunroom. Aoife had heard Mrs Prendergast refer to it many times but she'd never been inside it. It was a conservatory, really, of the curvaceous, domed variety. The

186

furniture was wicker and the plants numerous. The colour scheme was all reds, oranges and yellows – sun colours. A cushioned window-seat ran around the sides and a long oak table dominated the centre. It was set with crystal goblets, silver cutlery, delicate china and linen napkins. At least ten tea lights were scattered on the surface in pretty glass holders, and the centrepiece was a crystal bowl filled with water in which five bosomy, blossomy, blowsy, yellow roses floated. But by far the most beautiful thing about that beautiful room was the view of the garden through the open wooden door. Which tonight did nothing but add insult to injury.

Uri and Seth were seated at the table. Kathy was sitting on the floor, tying a sun bonnet on Harriet's head. Liam ran over and knelt beside them. Uri was his usual impeccable self: he stood up when Aoife entered the room and inclined his head to her. 'You look lovely,' he said.

'Thank you.' She loved his old-world manners.

Seth stood up too, more awkwardly than his father. 'You look very nice.'

'Thanks.'

She had actually dressed up. She was wearing a red dress with sparkly bits that she'd bought in Monsoon. It might have been the first time that any of them had seen her in anything other than jeans and wellies. Seth had dressed up too. She'd never seen him so clean. He was wearing chinos and a spotless white linen shirt. He scrubbed up well. She felt the full force of it.

It was strange to be with the people she saw week in, week out in unfamiliar clothes. And to be in the same location but in an unfamiliar room with an unfamiliar view of the garden. A different perspective of everyone and everything. It made Aoife feel shy suddenly and at a loss for anything to say.

'Wine?'

'White, please.'

Uri poured her a glass and a goblet of sparkling water. She sipped them both, grateful to have something to do with her hands. Grateful also that Mrs Prendergast chose that moment to bring out the starter.

'Onion tarts with goat's cheese,' she announced. 'The onions and the tarragon are from the garden.'

'Mummy, I don't like them.'

'Don't worry, Liam. I have fishfingers and chips for you and Kathy.'

'Yippee.' Liam returned to the floor and to the ongoing torment of Harriet.

'Oh, my God, these are exquisite.' Aoife hadn't meant to be so effusive in her compliments to Mrs Prendergast that evening, but she couldn't help it. The tarts were divine. 'I didn't know you could cook like this.'

Mrs Prendergast shrugged, but real pleasure showed on her face. 'I seldom get the chance to cook for anyone nowadays.'

Aoife quizzed her as to the recipe, but only half listened to the response. She was thinking how glad she was that they had the food to talk about. Normally, they mostly talked about gardening but that topic seemed redundant. She ate too fast in her nervousness and washed down the food with too many gulps of wine. She could already feel her head becoming light and the familiar heaviness in her thighs. She was glad. Being slightly drunk was the only way she could envisage getting through this evening.

She had to admit that Mrs Prendergast was being extremely nice to her, given her behaviour earlier on. She hadn't even apologized for being so rude. It was too early for her to say she was sorry, though. She didn't feel it yet. Some day she would and she'd say it then. Perhaps Mrs Prendergast's attack of niceness had been brought on by guilt. Or maybe she was thinking about her lovely pile of dosh. Aoife swallowed down her recurrent anger with another gulp of wine.

Mrs Prendergast brought out the children's food next and they all watched them slather everything with tomato ketchup and listened to them chattering. Harriet sat under the table hopefully, ears pricked, anticipating falling debris. Seth was quiet, she noticed, but not Uri and Mrs Prendergast, who both seemed remarkably cheerful and relaxed. Didn't they care? More anger. More wine. The warning voice inside her head was ignored. If she didn't know better, she'd think Uri and old Hatchet Head were flirting with one another. Mrs Prendergast wasn't so much laughing at whatever Uri was saying to her as giggling. Which, in Aoife's opinion, she should have grown out of a good fifty years ago.

The children's plates were cleared away and the main course presented.

'Broccoli and chicken lasagne, baby potatoes and salad. All the vegetables, herbs, spuds and salad are from the garden.'

'Good for you,' Aoife muttered, under her breath. If anyone heard her, they chose to ignore her.

There was no denying that the food looked and smelled superb. Mrs Prendergast had even decorated the salad with pansies. The taste almost made Aoife forgive her. Dessert was white chocolate and raspberry cheesecake ('Raspberries courtesy of Uri'). Afterwards they sat there, officially stuffed, sipping Earl Grey tea.

'I'd like to propose a toast,' said Uri. 'To Mrs Prendergast, for making us this magnificent feast.'

'Mrs Prendergast.' They raised their glasses and clinked with one another.

'And to Aoife, for growing most of the ingredients.'

'Not any more,' said Aoife, failing to clink. She was sick of it now – Uri's cheeriness, Mrs Prendergast's girlish giddiness. 'How can you both act this way? As if this is some sort of celebration? We have nothing to celebrate. Nothing! You'd be better off having a funeral mass.'

'Don't you think that's a little over-dramatic, my dear?' Mrs Prendergast smiled at her. To Aoife she looked incredibly smug.

'No, I do not. I don't know how you have the gall to sit there smiling when you're destroying everything we've done, everything we've worked towards. And for what? For money! Money you don't even need. You can't eat money. Don't you know that what you already have is far more precious by far? Priceless, even. It's an act of desecration to dig up those apple trees – they're even older than you are.'

'Aoife, that's enough now.'

But she couldn't be stopped. 'The roses. Emily's garden that she poured her heart and soul into. What about the insects, the bees, the butterflies? The robins! Where are they going to nest next year? You're just going to let them pour concrete over the whole lot. Destroy it all. Well, it's nothing short of sacrilege.'

Aoife's heart was beating wildly now as she stared down Mrs Prendergast. She knew she was quite drunk but she didn't care. She was glad, in fact. Glad that the wine had given her the Dutch courage to say what she felt she had to say. They were all looking at her. Except Mrs Prendergast, who took a demure sip from her teacup and placed it daintily back in its saucer. 'You know, my dear, I couldn't agree more.' She looked across the table at Aoife, her expression imperious. 'That's why I've sold it to Uri.'

There were a few seconds of silence.

'Did you just say you sold it to Uri?'

'That's exactly what I said.'

'Dad. Is this true?'

'Yes, it is.'

Aoife covered her face with her hands.

'Yes!' Seth leaped to his feet and punched the air. Then he grabbed his father, who was sitting beside him, and hugged him. 'Nice one, Dad.'

Uri laughed.

'And Mrs P.' Seth held out his arms to her in an expansive gesture. He advanced slowly around the table, not taking his eyes off her. Mrs Prendergast shrank back into her chair as he went down on one knee beside her.

'Mrs P,' he said again. Then he hugged her so tightly that Aoife was afraid he might break one of her ribs. He planted a big, noisy kiss on her right cheek. 'Mrs P, you're a legend.'

'Oh, good Lord,' said Mrs Prendergast, her face pink.

'I can't believe it. This is fantastic,' said Aoife. 'Oh, Mrs Prendergast, I'm so, so sorry. I've said some awful things. Please can you forgive me?'

Mrs Prendergast raised her eyebrows. 'I'll think about it.'

But Aoife knew she was already forgiven.

'Why didn't you tell us before?' asked Seth.

'We wanted to surprise you.'

'Well, it worked.'

A terrible thought occurred to Aoife. 'You're not going to . . . I mean . . . you wouldn't consider building on it, would you?'

'Absolutely not,' said Uri. 'It's going to stay a garden for as long as I have breath in my body. And hopefully a long time after that.' He looked at Seth, on whom the possibility that the garden would one day be his, at least in part, was just beginning to dawn.

'I'd like to propose another toast,' said Mrs Prendergast. She raised her glass. 'To the garden.'

They all held up their glasses. 'The garden.'

There was a knock on the front door, loud, angry, insistent. As if the knocker had been unheard for quite some time. It was possible, given the commotion in the sunroom.

'I'd better go and answer that,' said Mrs Prendergast, throwing down her napkin, her face flushed, eyes bright, as she left the room.

'Are you sure you can afford it, Dad?' said Seth, when she'd gone.

'Yes. I see it as an investment for the future.'

'But it's only an investment if you plan to sell it some time down the line.'

'I don't mean an investment for my future. I mean an investment for everyone's future.'

They heard voices at the front door. Mrs Prendergast's and a man's. They were too far away to make out what was being said. Then snippets of conversation floated in to them, although at first it wasn't clear if this was because the voices were getting louder or closer. After a while, it became evident that it was both.

'How much? Jesus Christ, you're joking.'

'Lance, please. I have guests for dinner.'

He entered the room and took in the scene. 'I should have bloody well known.'

His white shirtsleeves were rolled up and his formal tie was skew-whiff. His dark hair was sticking up as though he'd raked a hand through it repeatedly. He looked as if he'd been drinking. The atmosphere in the room changed instantly.

'Who the fuck do you think you are, ripping my mother off like that?' Lance glared at Uri.

'Lance!'

Uri remained calm and still, as if he'd faced a lot worse

in his time. 'I offered your mother considerably more but she refused to take it.' His voice was quiet but it carried. His dignified, almost regal, manner was totally at variance with that of Lance, who turned angrily to Mrs Prendergast.

'Is this true?'

'Mr Rosenberg paid the full market value.'

'You could have got double that, you stupid bitch.'

There was a sharp intake of breath all round.

'Don't speak to your mother like that,' said Uri, his face thunderous.

'What's it to you, you sly Jewish bastard?'

There was a moment's silence, then all hell broke loose. Seth was on his feet so fast that his chair fell backwards on to the floor. His face was contorted with anger and it was clear that he intended to launch himself at Lance.

'Seth, no!' Uri was on his feet, too, grabbing Seth's arm. Aoife got up, intending to head him off.

'Come over here and say that,' roared Seth, his face puce.

'Daddy, what's wrong?' Kathy and Liam were standing at the door to the sunroom, eyes like saucers. They'd been inside watching a DVD. They must have heard the raised voices and come to see what was going on.

The sight of his daughter seemed to bring Seth to his senses. His rigid body visibly relaxed and the red in his face reduced to an acceptable pink. 'Nothing's wrong, sweetheart. Go back inside.'

'Daddy, why is your chair on the floor?'

'I knocked it over by accident, Kathy. Come on back inside with me and we'll watch the rest of the film.'

'It's over, Daddy.'

'Then we'll watch another.'

Seth herded the two children out of the room, not even looking at Lance as he walked past him. The four remaining adults stood staring at one another, the tension almost sickening.

'You won't get away with this,' Lance snarled at Uri, his voice quieter now yet somehow more menacing. Then he looked at his mother. 'This transaction isn't going through. I won't allow it.'

Then he was gone, as if he'd never been there, except that everything in the room was altered. No one spoke, moved even, until they heard the front door slam. Mrs Prendergast emitted a peculiar high-pitched sound and sank into the nearest chair. Uri was at her side instantly. Aoife noted with alarm that the other woman was trembling. She wasn't surprised. If Liam grew up and spoke to her like that . . . It didn't bear thinking about.

'Here. Drink this.' Uri poured some brandy out of a bottle that was standing in the middle of the table. He held the glass to Mrs Prendergast's lips. She took it in a shaking hand and sipped. Aoife began to lift dirty plates from the table.

'Leave that, Aoife,' said Uri.

'But hadn't somebody better clear up?'

'I'll take care of it. You and Seth take the children home. I don't want them seeing her like this.'

'You sure?'

'Quite sure.'

Aoife put down the plates and went to find the others. She followed the squeals of the Disney DVD. The children were transfixed, their faces lit by the swirling colours on the screen. Seth was sitting on the edge of an armchair, his elbows on his knees, his head in his hands.

'Seth.' Aoife's voice was soft. He didn't hear her so she walked over to him and touched his hand. He jumped and looked up. As if by instinct, he took her hand and held it to his cheek, brushing her palm with his lips. Aoife pulled away. 'Come on, kids. Time to go.'

'I don't want to.'

'But, Mummy, it's only just started.'

'Come on. You can watch the rest tomorrow.'

She ignored their squeals of protest as she ejected the DVD and put it back in its case.

'Kathy, it's way past your bedtime.'

They bundled the children out into the night air. It was ten o'clock and still bright. 'How are you getting home?' asked Seth.

'On foot.'

'We'll walk you there.'

'There's no need.'

'I insist.'

'Okay.'

They walked in silence for a while, at least the two adults did. Kathy and Liam skipped ahead, hand in hand, singing nonsense songs.

Eventually Aoife said, 'Do you get that kind of thing a lot?'

'What?'

'Anti-Jewish stuff.'

'Not really. But it does rear its ugly head every now and then. Some prick like that.'

'Poor Mrs Prendergast,' Aoife mused.

'I know.'

They watched the children for a while. Then Seth said: 'I like your dress.'

'Thanks.'

'The colour suits you.'

'Thank you.' Aoife felt pleased and embarrassed at the same time.

'I was beginning to think you didn't have legs.'

She smiled. 'They've been there the whole time.'

'So I see. They're quite long, aren't they?'

'Yes, they go all the way to the ground. Here we are.'

They stopped outside her front door.

'How are you getting home?'

'I have the jeep. It's parked opposite Mrs P's.'

'Are you okay to drive?'

'I only had one glass.'

Aoife nodded. She'd been so busy knocking it back that she hadn't noticed what anyone else was doing. 'Good night, then. Thanks for walking us home.'

'But, Mummy, I want to show Kathy my new excavator.'

'You can show her the next time.'

'But I said I'd show her now. Please, Mummy.'

'Please, Aoife.'

'Okay. Hurry up, though. You both need to get to bed.'

Aoife opened the door and the children ran inside, talking and laughing. She felt awkward now. 'Do you want to come inside and wait?'

'No, it's all right. It's nice out here.'

It was a lovely night but Aoife didn't like the way Seth was looking at her. It was making her feel flustered. He took a few steps forward and she fixed her eyes hard on the pavement. What happened next was what she wanted but at the same time didn't want. He put his arms around her waist and pulled her close. He stroked her lower back with the tips of his fingers. 'Aoife. Look at me.'

With huge difficulty, she met his eyes. They seemed to go on for ever. Oh, God, one more second and he'd kiss her. She broke away and stepped inside her front door. 'Kathy! Liam! Come on now.'

Sounding like a buffalo stampede rather than two small children, Kathy and Liam ran back into the hall.

'Ready, Kathy?'

'Yes.' She went outside and joined her father.

Aoife started to close the door. 'Thanks again for walking us home.' She didn't look at him.

'Aoife.'

'What?'

'You can't punish yourself for ever, you know.'

'Good night, Seth.' She shut the door.

'Mummy, what's punish?'

'It's what'll happen to you if you don't get into bed now. Come on. Up the stairs.'

The man didn't know what he was talking about.

29

The sunlight poured in through the gap in the curtains, bathing Emily's eyelids. This was her favourite way to wake up – from one dreamlike state to another. She lay there for some time, semi-conscious, believing herself back in her bedsit. And then she heard the tiniest whimper. Her eyes flew open. She sat up in the bed she'd slept in since she was a girl, in the room that had sheltered her childhood dreams: ponies and gymkhanas, her teenage fantasies of Westlife and Gary O'Connor. All of that gave way now to adult reality. (She must get rid of that ridiculous poster.)

Rose had settled herself back to sleep, although her restlessness indicated imminent wakefulness. Emily knew it would be wise to go downstairs and prepare a bottle, but she couldn't drag herself away. Her reality now was so unreal. So magical.

'Wow,' she said to her sleeping daughter.

'Wow,' she said to herself, countless times a day. Because she loved it all. Every second of it. Even when Rose bawled her head off. Even when she did it in the middle of the night. That gave Emily the excuse to take her into her bed and hold her close, breathe her in.

Now Rose slumbered in the cot her mother had slept in, as had all the other Harte babies. There was a baby-shaped indentation in the mattress, and Rose fitted snugly into it. There was a gentle rap on the bedroom door. 'Come in.'

The door opened to reveal her father. He was dressed

in his outdoor clothes and had the air of someone who'd been up for hours. He'd probably sorted the cows already. 'Is Madam awake?' he said.

'Not yet. But she will be soon.'

'Will I bring you up a bottle?'

'That'd be great, Dad.'

He nodded and disappeared. She listened to his footfall descending the stairs and marvelled anew at this miraculous turn of events.

The day she'd brought Rose home had been a seminal day in the Harte household. Her mother had been wonderful – coddling her, forgiving her instantly. If anything, she blamed herself for not being there for her daughter, although what she thought she could have done when she hadn't known a thing about it . . .

One by one the Hartes had come home. Reactions varied from shock to joy to indifference. Until the only one left was Emily's father, Thomas. Home from the fields. Innocent of all that had occurred in his absence.

The house fell silent as the back door opened. They were gathered in the kitchen, all of the Hartes, including the newest arrival. They listened collectively as he took off his boots and removed his jacket, whistling tunelessly as was his habit. He entered the kitchen and drew back in surprise. His entire family was looking at him so strangely. Then he saw Emily and his face opened up in delight. 'Well, hello, stranger. What are you doing here?'

Emily gave her father a nervous half-smile.

He noticed Rose for the first time, currently nestling in his wife's arms. 'Where did the baby come from? Don't tell me someone else has roped you into babysitting. You're too much of a soft touch, woman. Would you ever tell them you've enough of your own to be getting on with? What's for tea? I'm starved.'

He looked at his wife expectantly, wondering why she wasn't responding to his words. Then his eyes swept over his family. He hadn't been imagining it. Something was definitely up. 'What is it?'

A couple of the younger siblings looked at Emily. The others looked at the ground. His eldest daughter cleared her throat but still her voice came out as a squeak. 'She's mine.'

What did she mean 'She's mine'? That she was minding her for someone else? But a part of his brain, the part that was reluctantly clicking into gear, knew that this wasn't true. The strange atmosphere in his kitchen told him so, if nothing else.

'What do you mean, girl?'

Emily swallowed visibly. 'She's my baby, Dad. I had her last September.'

Each second was a year. Many members of the family wished they weren't there. That wish was soon granted.

'Kids. Leave the room now, please.'

There was a scramble for the door. Emily longed to join in, but guessed she was no longer classified as one of the 'kids'.

Emily, her mother and father remained. And Rose, who was oblivious to all the fuss she was causing. Emily braced herself. Her father spoke. 'How could you, of all the girls in the world, be so bloody stupid?'

'I'm sorry, Daddy.' She felt her eyes fill with tears. This was it. The moment she'd been dreading ever since she'd peed on that plastic stick. Her father's rejection. The casting out from the warmth of the family fold.

Thomas advanced slowly and stopped in front of Bridget and Rose. He peered down at them for what seemed like an age. Then he scooped up the baby, with the practised ease of a father of six. He held her up in the air and appeared to examine her. Rose's limbs flailed, reminding Emily of an insect stuck on its back.

'Begod, she's a Harte through and through. Would you look at the cut of her?' He laughed out loud. 'Bridget, have you seen the nose?'

Emily almost swooned with relief. She closed her eyes and allowed herself a small smile, which her father caught. 'And don't think for one second, Miss, that this means you've got away with it.'

'No, Daddy.' Her voice was small, humble. She knew she'd got away with it. As did all the younger Hartes, who were listening on the far side of the kitchen door.

'And when any of your brothers and sisters ask, I gave you the bollocking of a lifetime. Is that clear?'

'Yes, Daddy.'

He laughed again and cradled baby Rose in the top right-hand corner of his chest. Rose rested her head in the crook of his neck. Then she vomited delicately down her grandfather's shoulder.

The next day was Sunday. Emily spent most of the morning in her room, feeding, dressing and luxuriating in Rose as the rest of the family got ready for mass in their noisy, haphazard, familiar way. Emily was confident she'd be excused from this Sunday-morning ritual. There was a knock on her door. 'Come in.'

Her father entered. 'Are you not even dressed yet?'

'I've been minding Rose. I thought —'

'It's nearly time for mass. Here. Hand me the baby while you get yourself ready.'

'But I thought —'

'This family always goes to mass together. Now, get a move on, girl.'

She should have known better. There was no point in putting up an argument as he was gone already. God. The thought of facing the neighbours. The people she'd grown up with. She pulled on the least crumpled clothes she could find. Pride, rather than vanity, dragged a comb across her head.

'Emily!'

They were all waiting for her in the kitchen. Then off they went to the church, two cars needed to transport the entire clan.

She felt her father sensing her misgivings at the entrance to the church. He bent low and whispered in her ear, 'Best to get it over with.'

They sat in their usual pew, a short distance from the top on the left. Emily saw all the familiar faces. Felt all the eyes on her and Rose. Knew she'd be the hot topic of gossip in the parish for the week. That little upstart got her comeuppance. Thought she was better than us. Look at her now.

Then the mass was over. Emily kept her head down, as they filed out. She was flanked by family on every side. But then something happened. Something wholly unexpected.

'Ah, would you look at her? Isn't she a dote? Is she yours, Emily?'

'She is. Yes.'

It was Mrs Brennan, whom Emily had known most of her life. Her daughter had been in the same class at school.

'How old?'

'Almost nine months.'

'Nine months. What a gorgeous age. Annie, come and have a look at this little one.'

Annie Dowling, a woman of similar vintage, came and stood with them. 'Ah, look. She's a stunner, all right. What's her name?'

'Rose.'

'Rose. Oh, it suits her. Can I have a little hold?'

'Of course.'

As Emily handed over her child, the heart that had been hammering in her chest slowed to a dull thud. Before long, she and Rose were encircled by the women of the parish, cooing, petting, loving.

Emily smiled a watery smile. It was their turn to shake hands with the priest, a gentle man she'd known since childhood. Her anxiety returned.

Her father went ahead of her. 'Father, how are you this fine morning?'

'Keeping well, Tommy. And yourself?'

'Father, I'd like to introduce you to my granddaughter, Rose.'

He nodded at Emily to come forward. Emily did so, holding up Rose for inspection.

'Well, would you look at her? Isn't she a beauty? The apple didn't fall too far from the tree. She's the picture of her mother.'

Emily smiled in acknowledgement and relief.

'We'll be off now, Father. Enjoy the sunshine.'

'I will surely, Tommy.'

'Father Curran, can I ask you something?'

All eyes were on Emily – that she would voluntarily prolong this encounter.

'Rose hasn't been baptized yet. I wonder if you'd be kind enough to do the honours.'

'I'd be delighted, Emily. Give me a ring in the morning and we'll work out a suitable date.'

Emily looked at her parents. They were smiling at each other. She thought her mother might cry. In this, at least, she could do the right thing by them.

And that had been three months ago. And not one of the Hartes could imagine their family without Rose. Emily could take no credit for it. It was all down to Rose and the spell she'd woven around them. And to her parents, whose love for her had overridden every principle they'd ever held. What a stupid girl she'd been, doubting them as she had. When she thought now of that first day in mass and the guts it must have taken, pillars of the church, both of them, proudly displaying, for their fellow pillars of the church to see, their fallen woman of a daughter, their illegitimate granddaughter. They must have been up half the night before, agonizing over it.

Rose was fully awake now, giving out to her mother for allowing her to go hungry for all of two seconds. Emily picked her up and held her close, relishing the way she snuggled into her, those sweet little snuffling noises. There was a knock on the door, closely followed by her father bearing a bottle. 'Here's Grandad,' said Emily, turning Rose around so she could see him.

'There's a phonecall for you. That girl Aoife. Will I feed Rose while you take it?'

'Okay. Thanks.'

Emily went down to the hall and picked up the phone. 'Hello?'

She listened while Aoife talked non-stop for two minutes flat, barely pausing for breath. At last it was her turn to speak. 'I think it's a great idea. But surely we can come up with a better name than the autumn party.'

30

She thought she was alone in the garden. It was early morning and it had been raining but it had stopped now and all the colours were magnified. Everything felt like a new beginning. Just Aoife and the birds. Liam was on a sleepover. She had come here to think. And where would be the perfect place to do that? The bower beneath the yellow trumpets of honeysuckle and the white stars of jasmine. She made her way there now, all green and leafy, dapple and shade. Blessed coolness. Balm on her soul. Peace of mind at long last.

But she wasn't alone. Someone else swung gently on the swing seat, wrapped in a plaid blanket, eyes closed. At first she was dismayed. To sit there had felt like her only hope. Then she felt glad for the other woman. She probably needed it more than Aoife did. Feeling her intrusion, she turned silently to go.

'Aoife.'

She had been spotted.

'Mrs Prendergast. I was just leaving.'

'Why not stay?'

How could she turn down this surprising invitation?

Mrs Prendergast moved along in the seat, making room for Aoife, who felt she had no choice but to sit down, although the intimacy of the situation made her somewhat fearful. There truly was nowhere to hide in a place like this. The only saving grace was that they didn't have to look at one another. Sitting side by side felt easier than face to face. Less confrontational. They swung gently together, backwards and forwards, lulling each other. Aoife began to relax. Just two women sitting in a garden together. For the first time she didn't feel the age difference between them. Together, they could still be alone with their own thoughts. Aoife was amazed at how easy and companionable the silence was. It was like a spell that spoken words would break. But, after a while, words became inevitable. Necessary.

'I'm sorry about the other night,' Mrs Prendergast said.

'Don't be. It was marvellous. The food was superb.'

'You know what I mean.'

Aoife paused, trying to find the right words. 'That was hardly your fault. If anybody should apologize, it's me. I was so rude to you. I'm sorry.'

'You were just sticking up for your garden.'

They swung for a minute, not saying anything.

'He has gambling debts, you know.'

'You mean . . . ?'

'Lance.'

'I see.'

'My brother told me. I rang him up the next day because I was still quite . . . upset. Lance had approached him for a loan and he'd got the truth out of him.'

'That would explain why he was so angry.'

'Yes. But it's no excuse for the way he spoke to me. To Uri.' She sniffed.

'I suppose not.'

Aoife stole a glance at Mrs Prendergast's profile. She wasn't crying but she wasn't far off it.

She sighed. 'I hope your son never speaks to you like that.'

Aoife agreed fervently. But she couldn't think of a way to say it that didn't sound rude or hurtful so she said nothing. Neither did Mrs Prendergast, but Aoife could feel the pain radiating from her. She wanted so much to convey her sympathy to her but she wasn't sure how. Had it been a woman of her own age or younger, she would have given her a hug. But Mrs Prendergast wasn't the hugging type. At least, Aoife felt it would be inappropriate. Instead, still staring straight ahead, she felt for her hand and gave it a squeeze, then released it. There was no visible response, but she sensed Mrs Prendergast relaxing beside her. So much so, apparently, that the older woman said: 'What happened to your husband?'

'He was killed in a car accident.'

'Ah. I'm sorry. When did he die?'

'Two years, three and a half months ago.'

A pause.

'Do you think you'll ever marry again?'

'Good God, I have no idea. It's too early to say.'

'You think almost two and a half years is too early?'

'It is for me.'

'I hope you don't always feel that way.'

'Why?' Aoife was beginning to feel slightly irritated.

'Well, for your own sake, but mainly because of Liam. It's better for a boy to grow up with a father. I sometimes think that if I'd married again, well, things may have worked out differently.'

Aoife resented the implication that she and her indomitable love were not enough for her son. At the same time, she felt a gnawing fear when she thought of his future.

'You know,' said Mrs Prendergast, her tone altered, 'there was a time when I hoped you and Lance . . . but I don't suppose you'd have any interest now. He hasn't exactly showed you his best side. He can be lovely. Really he can.'

'I don't know him, Mrs Prendergast, but I doubt we'd be on the same wavelength. I *am* flattered you thought of me in that way.'

'Don't be. His girlfriend is an abomination. Awful vulgar girl. Anybody would be better than her.'

Aoife smiled and shook her head. Good old Mrs Prendergast. She must be feeling better. So, no need to tread so carefully. 'Can I ask you a question?'

'What?'

'Why are you selling the land to Uri?'

Mrs Prendergast sighed. 'A number of reasons.'

'Care to elaborate?'

Mrs Prendergast sighed again. 'Well, he asked me, for one thing. At the start, I really just wanted to get rid of the land. It wasn't so much about the money – until Lance got wind of it. It reminded me too much of the past and it was weighing me down. And then, you know, I became fond of the garden again. And the roses. And finding the time capsule made me think of things in the past that weren't so bad. Then Lance was so rude to Uri. I suppose I wanted to make it up to him.'

'What's all that about? What does Lance have against Jews?'

'I think it goes back to his childhood. When Lance and I first had to fend for ourselves, times were hard. I'd sometimes have to take valuables down to the pawnbrokers. They were Jewish and Lance would come with me, of course, and, I don't know, I think it left a bad taste in his mouth. Which is ironic, because if it wasn't for that pawnbroker, I'd have had difficulty putting food on the table.'

Mrs Prendergast stood up quite abruptly. 'Anyway. Back to work. I'm off to plant some myrtle.'

'Where?'

'Don't worry. I'm staying within the confines of the rose garden.'

'I'm not worried. But why would you plant myrtle in the middle of a rose garden?'

Mrs Prendergast drew on a pair of gloves that had been hidden beneath the swing seat. At first, Aoife didn't think she was going to get an answer, which wouldn't have been out of character in a woman who was capable of unimpeachable politeness at one minute and mind-blowing rudeness at the next. Aoife stood up and stretched, already thinking about what she was going to do next.

'It's my name,' said Mrs Prendergast.

'Excuse me?'

'Myrtle. It's my name.'

'Really?'

'Really.'

'How . . . unusual. It's lovely.'

Mrs Prendergast snorted. 'Liar.'

Both smiled furtively. Aoife watched the older woman as she walked away from her, straightening her back. She called after her, 'Does this mean I can call you –'

'Mrs Prendergast.'

'Right.'

God, she loved it – everything about it. The low ceilings. The thick swirls of cigarette smoke that hung in the air, having nowhere to escape to. The hormones bouncing off the walls. The scent of Johnnie Walker on the breath of the men she danced with. Not as overpowering as it had once been, in the days when you were obliged to be squished against the man in the death grip of the slow waltz. She thanked God in heaven for whoever had invented the jive. It made everything seem much lighter – much freer.

It was 1957 and London was booming. Rationing was out, prosperity was in. Harold Macmillan told his people that they'd never had it so good and they believed him. It was on the night of 4 October 1957 that Myrtle met Martin Prendergast. An auspicious date – chosen by the Soviets to launch Sputnik, the first artificial satellite to be sent into space.

She'd noticed him from the very beginning. She'd heard his booming voice, watched him throw back his head and laugh voraciously. He had a natural lust for life that compelled her. And what he had, she wanted. She set her heart on it, fixed her gaze on it, made him notice her in her own quiet, determined way. She wasn't the prettiest girl there, she knew that, but she had something – she knew that too. And it was this certainty that drew Martin to her, of his own volition, he thought. She held his gaze – just long enough – then went back to being aloof, a role she inhabited well. She waited for him to make his inevitable move.

'Would you like to dance?' He held out his larger-than-life

hand. His eyes laughed at her, challenging her. She recognized his accent and her stomach lurched. Irish. Forbidden. As she stood up, she felt as if she were falling.

His hands were rough and she knew immediately that he worked with them. From his face, he spent a lot of time outdoors in all weathers. His eyes creased at the corners every time he smiled, which was often and always at her.

'I'm Martin,' he said, her blue felt skirt swishing against his legs.

'Marnie.'

'Marnie?' It was a struggle to hear over the music.

'That's right.'

'Is it short for something?'

'Just Marnie.'

'Hello, Just Marnie.'

She smiled demurely and looked away, anxious not to reveal the effect he was having on her.

In those days, she didn't call herself Myrtle. She had disowned her name and her restrictive background in the process. Marnie was her new persona, the person she aspired to be and believed she was when you peeled back the middle-class layers. Her parents, her upbringing, her education: everything had prepared her to be the person she now rejected. Martin was her passport out of herself. She recognized this instantly. Her parents would hate him. At least, her father would.

He was tall, stood head and shoulders above her. His hair was black and his eyes were blue. What she thought of as Irish blue, a vibrant, all-singing, all-dancing blue. Nothing like her own insipid slate-blue-greyness. Everything about him was so alive. He made *her* feel alive and it wasn't a sensation she was prepared to relinquish.

When the dance was over, they were reluctant to let go of each other.

'Can I buy you a drink?'

'That would be lovely, thank you.'

He smiled at her, as if he found what she said both delightful and amusing. Which was how he made her feel in general. As if he saw the self she had always known she could be, which had been clamouring its whole life to get out. How was she to know that he made every woman feel that way? And at that moment how was she to care?

They had their drink, talking intermittently and smiling continuously. And then chaos was unleashed, the room in uproar. A raid! The police in one door, Martin and Myrtle out of the other and into the night, laughing and running, hand in hand. Then, without saying anything, Martin held open the door of a coffee shop and she ducked inside. It was one of the new breed of Soho espresso bars, not the old, classic Italian style. The décor was loud and shiny and tasteless – the epitome of cool. The clientele were a blend of beatniks, teddy boys and art-college types. He ordered coffee while Tab Hunter's 'Young Love' played on the jukebox.

'Where are you from?'

'County Mayo.'

'Is that in Ireland?'

'It surely is.'

He smiled at her again. His voice was a rich, deep baritone. She wondered if he could sing. Surely someone with a speaking voice so lilting, so lyrical –

'Where are you from?'

'I'm from here. London.'

To Myrtle, this was embarrassingly boring. (To Martin,

it – she – was impossibly exotic.) Each was what the other aspired to be.

'A genuine London girl. Next you're going to tell me you were born within the sound of Bow bells.'

'Not exactly.'

Not exactly was right. Myrtle – named for her paternal grandmother – had grown up in the affluent suburb of Woodford, with her parents and one younger brother. It seemed crucial now to conceal this from Martin, whose background, she guessed correctly, was a million miles away from where he was right now.

'Tell me about County Mayo.'

'Nothing much to tell.'

'There must be something. What part of Ireland is it in? Is it near Dublin?'

'Miles away. On the west coast.'

An image appeared in her mind from her grammar-school geography book. 'Did you live in a thatched cottage?'

'I did.'

She raised her shoulders to her ears and her expression became gleeful. 'How romantic.'

His laugh was short and mirthless. 'You wouldn't think that if you had to live in one.'

'Why?'

He leaned back in his seat and put one foot up on the chair beside her, an action she found both intimate and cocky, although it seemed unconscious on his part.

'We had nothing growing up. Nothing. And the only people left living in the thatched cottages now are the old people. The whole west of Ireland is empty.'

'How do you mean, empty?'

'Emigration. I went home for my sister's wedding last summer and the priest said it was the first wedding in the parish for seven years. There are only two directions for the young to go in and that's west to America or east to England.'

She could tell he was trying to keep the bitterness out of his voice, but she could hear it still, biting at the edges of his words.

Martin went on to tell her how he had chosen the latter, lured by tales of work to be got and money to be made by building on the ruins of blitzed London. He'd started out labouring – backbreaking work that might have broken the heart of a lesser man. But not Martin. He kept his head down and worked, listened and learned. At night, he drank pints with the other Paddies on the Kilburn High Road. And it was those Paddies he recruited on to the first crew of Prendergast Construction. At first contracts were hard to come by, but he persevered and built up his reputation as a reliable, hard-working professional. The jobs started rolling his way, and, after a decade of hard graft, he was rolling in it.

What he didn't tell her was that he was ready to take a wife. A wife in keeping with his new station in life. A wife to aspire to. A life to aspire to. Myrtle. Or Marnie, as he knew her then. He was looking to join that which she was champing at the bit to escape: the Establishment. To him, she was an ethereal Grace Kelly figure. A class act. He wanted some of that for himself. He knew he had her, just as she knew she wanted to be had.

As Myrtle listened to Martin's account of all that had gone before, something struck her quite forcefully: how brave it was of him to reveal so much of himself to her. So much that might easily have sent a nice middle-class girl like herself running in the other direction. But his story had the opposite effect, as Martin had known instinctively it would. She admired his courage. She admired his grit and determination.

But, most of all, she admired the muscles that were straining under the material of his suit. Straining to get to her.

Someone selected 'All Shook Up' on the jukebox. They smiled at one another.

'Do you like Elvis?'

'I just love him.'

'Do you want to come and see *Jailhouse Rock* tomorrow night?'

'All right.'

Years later, when Myrtle heard the expression 'whirlwind romance', she thought of her early days with Martin, their courtship. Listening to Long John Baldry in the Soho coffee houses, jiving all over London to Buddy Holly and the Crickets, Andy Williams and Johnnie Ray. Their day trip on the Flying Scotsman, inadvertently taking in a lungful of acrid smoke as she stuck her head enthusiastically out of the window. Their picnic on Margate beach, chasing their windbreaker, laughing like loons as it was carried off on a strong breeze. Everything was fun and games, drinking and party-going. She knew he'd have to meet her family sooner or later – and later rather than sooner, if she had her way. But Martin was pushing for it. She wasn't sure why. Curiosity? The misguided belief that he'd be accepted into the fold? She tried to explain to him what her father was like.

'He can be quite – difficult.'

'How do you mean?'

She sighed. How to explain? 'He's very stern. Almost Victorian in his outlook. And he's Scots Presbyterian.'

'So?'

'So he's not too keen on Catholics.'

'Leave him to me. I'm good with parents.'

Myrtle felt a painful sensation in her chest. How many

girlfriends had there been before her? How many sets of parents had he charmed? And how many girlfriends were there to come? That wasn't all that troubled her. She doubted her father would be the pushover Martin anticipated. She guessed how he would rate him: flash, arrogant, an unreliable type.

'What's your mother like?'

'Pathetic. No mind of her own. Does everything he tells her to.'

She resented the way Martin looked at her then – with disapproval in his eyes, presumably for the disrespectful way in which she had spoken of her mother. He didn't know the extent to which she'd felt let down – rejected – so many times. All the times she had looked to her mother for support and it had never come, when she alone had had to stand up to the vagaries of her father's temper. She herself would never live like that, in fear of the man she was supposed to love.

'Mothers are my speciality,' was all Martin said.

She remained doubtful. Her younger brother, Roger, was the only member of the family likely to be impressed by Martin's worldliness.

An invitation to tea was procured that Saturday. They turned into the cul-de-sac where Myrtle had spent her formative years. 'Stop!' she shouted.

Martin slammed on the brakes of his new Humber Hawk. 'What?'

'I have to tell you something.'

'Jesus, Marnie. What is it?'

'Stop the car.'

'It is stopped.'

'I mean turn off the engine.'

He switched off the ignition and turned to look at her. 'You're not having second thoughts about me meeting your parents?'

'No. I mean, yes, I am. Second, third and fourth. But that's not it.'

'What, then?'

She sighed. 'You'll probably find that my family call me Myrtle.'

The corner of his mouth twitched. 'Why would they do that?'

Another sigh, deeper than the last. 'Because it's my name.'

'Then why did you tell me it was Marnie?'

'Myrtle! Wouldn't you lie if you had a name like that?'

He stared hard at her. Oh, God, what must he think? To lie about something so fundamental. Then he started to laugh, as if it was the funniest thing he'd ever heard. He threw back his head. He even brought his hand down so hard on the steering-wheel that the horn sounded.

'Careful!' She looked around, anxious that they didn't draw attention to themselves. She imagined all the twitching curtains.

When he'd composed himself, he took her face in his two hands and kissed her firmly on the mouth. 'You're something else.' Then he restarted the engine and drove slowly down the street to number forty-eight.

'These are for you.' He handed a bunch of peach-coloured gladioli to Myrtle's mother. Myrtle could tell she was impressed, but that was irrelevant.

They were shown into the front room, where her father and brother were watching *Hancock's Half Hour*. The older man's eyes never left the TV screen. Martin advanced confidently, his hand outstretched. 'Pleased to meet you, Mr Ferguson.'

For one terrible moment, Myrtle thought her father would refuse Martin's hand. He certainly thought about it, of that she was sure – she could almost hear him thinking it. But at the last second he shook it perfunctorily, glancing up briefly from the television at which he stared with fierce concentration. He didn't rise from his armchair. Myrtle knew this to be a slight. Her whole family did. If Martin recognized it as such, he didn't show it. Instead, he sat in the remaining free armchair, not waiting for an invitation to do so that would never come.

Myrtle perched uneasily on the arm of the sofa. She glanced anxiously at the rigid form of her father, then at Martin. The chair in which he sat sagged low in the middle. He looked ludicrously large in it, his knees looming up to his chin. Myrtle thought he seemed ridiculously out of place. Something about the two worlds in which she co-existed coming together and clashing discordantly.

'I love this programme,' said Martin, nodding at the TV screen, in which they could make out the figure of Tony Hancock through the snowy haze.

Roger grinned in agreement. Mr Ferguson remained silent as a stone.

'Do you like *Double Your Money*?' Martin asked Roger.

He had just opened his mouth to reply when his father interjected: 'We don't appreciate that kind of American rubbish in this house.'

The other occupants of the room shifted uncomfortably while Tony Hancock and his canned laughter filled the roaring silence.

'I see you drive a Simca, Mr Ferguson.' Martin had decided to change tack.

Myrtle recognized, with a sinking feeling, that he still thought he was in with a chance.

'And what do *you* drive?'

'A Humber Hawk.' The pride was evident in Martin's response.

Myrtle's father made an indefinable sound. It might have been a snort. But its meaning was clear. Don't think much of that.

Myrtle's unease grew. She knew they shouldn't have come.

'You're Irish.' It was an accusation.

'Yes, sir.'

Martin's easy confidence was deserting him. She could see it and it pained her, even though she had known it was inevitable.

'What's your full name?'

'Martin Prendergast.'

'What class of a name is that?'

At this point, Roger excused himself and left the room. Myrtle longed to follow him, dragging Martin by the arm as she went.

'I don't know what —'

'Are you a Catholic?'

'Yes.'

Mr Ferguson pursed his lips and took up the newspaper that had been lying on the table beside him. He opened it with a snap, obliterating his face as he did so. Martin and Myrtle looked at one another, Myrtle with real dismay, Martin with evident growing anger. 'I don't see what —'

'I suppose you work on a building site.'

'I have my own construction company.' He stood up. His efforts to get out of the chair would have been comical in any other circumstances.

'Marnie,' he said, his fury barely contained. 'I think it's time we left.' He held out his hand.

When Myrtle looked back on this moment, she saw it as a pivotal point in her history. Should she embrace Martin, embrace her future, become the Marnie she'd always longed to be? Or stay and be the Myrtle she'd always been, with her taciturn father, her submissive mother?

She took Martin's hand.

Martin sped out of Woodford in his Humber Hawk, skidding around the corners of Myrtle's estate.

'Slow down!' She held on to the dashboard in alarm.

Thankfully, he brought the car to a shrieking halt at an old bombsite, minutes away. It was an area upon which several houses used to stand. In summer, it was lush and pink with rosebay willowherb. Now, it was stubbly and grey. Martin got out and slammed the door. Myrtle watched him uncertainly as he kicked an innocent rock several times, then picked up a large branch and beat the rock until he'd got the rage out of his system. She was about to get out when he returned and sat beside her, his breath heavy and rasping. His normally perfect quiff was askew. She could smell the Brylcreem off him. From that day on, the scent would propel her back to that moment. She was afraid to speak. Afraid of what she'd just witnessed. But in an odd way she felt even more drawn to him. His actions spoke to her of real passion.

'Are you all right?' she said.

He drummed his fingers on the steering-wheel, not looking at her. 'I've been offered a big government contract.'

'Oh – that's wonderful, Martin.'

'It's in Dublin.'

'Oh.'

She felt the fear like ice water down her spine. Had she misjudged the situation back at the house? Was he leaving her? She closed her eyes, leaned back in her seat and felt an incredible rush of hatred for her father. Why did that man have to ruin everything for her?

'Did you hear what I said?'

'I heard.'

'What do you think?'

'I'm pleased for you.'

'Marnie, you're not hearing me. I want you to come with me.'

'You mean . . .'

'I want us to get married.'

And there, in the back of that Humber Hawk, their marriage was consummated before it had even begun.

Martin Prendergast and Myrtle Ferguson got married in Woodford Register Office on as cold and inhospitable a day as early January could muster. Myrtle stood nervously on the pavement in her ice-pink two-piece, clutching her bouquet to her breast. Martin stood beside her, his suit crisp and black, smoking a rare cigarette, which he ground out with his heel after he had peered impatiently down the street for the umpteenth time. A girl called Gladys, to whom Myrtle referred as her friend, accompanied them. The two often went dancing together, although they had seen less of each other since Martin had arrived on the scene.

Myrtle was aware that she didn't possess a talent for friendship. There was something about her that put other girls off. She liked to tell herself that they were jealous of her success with men, her ability to make the most of herself, but, deep in her core, she knew her lack of warmth put them off. From her father, she had inherited not just a pale blondeness but a glacial coolness. She didn't know how to be any other way, although she longed to open up. She hoped that Martin could perform this miracle for her.

So Gladys was the closest thing she had to a female friend, and today she was to be her witness and her bridesmaid. The two women got on tolerably well. Gladys was a bookish girl who wore thick, black-rimmed glasses. An intellectual, it never occurred to her to be jealous of Myrtle. She appreciated an intelligent person with whom she could have a decent conversation. And, besides, it was handy having someone to go dancing with. Once on the dance-floor, Gladys had no problem attracting men, thanks to her generous bosom and a surprisingly sensual dance technique. Today her bustline was hidden by a dark winter coat made of thick serge and buttoned up to her neck. Still she shivered.

Three heads whipped around to the sound of running footsteps. It was Myrtle's brother, Roger, adjusting his tie as he ran.

'Where have you been?' Myrtle snapped at him.

'Sorry. I had to run back home to put on my suit.'

'Are they . . . ?'

'Sorry, Myrtle. They're not coming.'

She took a deep breath and it appeared to the others that she shrank slightly. Roger looked anxiously at her. Newly eighteen, he felt a responsibility as the most senior Ferguson male present to say something, but words failed him.

'Right, then,' said Myrtle, brightly. 'Let's go in.'

And so they were married. Myrtle resented the silent assumption in the registrar's eyes that theirs was a shotgun wedding. On second thoughts, maybe it was.

They adjourned to a nearby pub to celebrate. It was hardly the wedding that Myrtle, with her flawless taste and eye for detail, had meticulously planned since girlhood. But, she told herself repeatedly, she was Martin's wife now and that was what really mattered.

All day long she ignored the sick feeling in the pit of her stomach.

Some might have called it a gut instinct.

That night they boarded the ferry to Dun Laoghaire. They

were to have a honeymoon of sorts in the west of Ireland, during which Myrtle was to be shown off to an assortment of Martin's relatives. She was under strict instructions to maintain the deception that they'd got married in a Catholic church. Myrtle didn't know what she'd say if someone asked her straight out if she was a Catholic.

It was a rough winter crossing and Myrtle was as sick as a dog. As she groaned in their cabin, Martin repaired to the bar where he commenced drinking with a motley crew of Irishmen who were returning to the Emerald Isle, the majority only on a temporary basis, to wives they scarcely knew any more and children who'd grown up so much since their last visit that they barely recognized them. The drinking was serious and heavy. Songs were sung, increasingly maudlin, as the night wore on.

Myrtle lay tossing disconsolately in the top bunk, retching her guts up into a tin bucket. Her discontent was added to considerably by Martin's long unexplained absence. Some wedding night this was turning out to be. Finally, the key turned clumsily and noisily in the lock and the groom materialized. Martin staggered into the cabin. At first Myrtle put down his unsteady gait to the rocking and rolling of the ship. She'd seen him with drink on him many times before and he was generally able to carry it well.

'Where the hell have you been?' She raised herself up on her elbow and addressed him angrily.

Martin stood looking at her, swaying slightly. He appeared to be having difficulty focusing. It was then that she realized he was very drunk. His lip curled into a kind of snarl. Nothing like Elvis's. 'Shut up, you stupid bitch.' He fell on to the lower bunk and began to snore almost instantly.

That was the day Sputnik fell to earth, having spent exactly three months in orbit.

32

There was something so precious about late summer. The knowledge that the flowers would soon be gone made their beauty all the more intense in the eyes of their beholders. The sensory garden that Emily had planted now came into its own. It was as if the butterflies were having a farewell party. Every time Harriet gambolled past the buddleia, a host of tortoiseshells and painted ladies rose into the air as if the petals themselves had come to life and taken flight. The bees were in overdrive too, collecting the last of the pollen for their winter pantry. As for developments among the garden's human inhabitants, they, too, proceeded at quite a pace.

Following the ill-fated dinner party, Aoife had convinced Mrs Prendergast to create a range of pies to sell in the Good Food Store – first, the older woman was such a sublime cook, but also she wanted to take her mind off her errant son. Emily's aunt jumped at the idea, as did the punters, who couldn't get enough of 'Mrs Prendergast's Gourmet Pies'. Their major selling point, apart from their succulence, was the guaranteed fresh, local produce that went into them. Spinach and goat's cheese was Aoife's favourite.

As for Aoife, she was going through a weird time. Changes were taking place at a faster rate than she could handle. Liam was starting 'big school' the following month and the prospect flooded her with a gamut of emotions – most of them negative. She'd made two attempts so far to purchase his uniform and each time had had to leave the store in tears. It pained her immeasurably that Michael wasn't there to see his son take his first real steps into boyhood. And because Katie was no longer coming up behind him, this might be the only time she'd experience such a monumental step, which added to its poignancy.

She was also in a quandary over Seth. Since the night she had rejected him on her doorstep, a polite but cool distance had opened between them. She didn't know how to bridge the gap or even if she wanted to. As for Seth, she couldn't work out if he had lost interest or was just biding his time. She hoped it was the latter but that might have been vanity speaking.

Plans were under way for the harvest festival. The idea was to open the garden gate and let the public flow in. They would be given guided tours and there'd be stalls selling fruit and veg and homemade soup. Aoife was in quite a flap about it. Mrs Prendergast watched her with some amusement. 'If you like,' she said, 'I could ask some of the women from the Mothers' Union to help out.'

'Really? Do you think they'd be useful?'

'Well, they're forever making jams and chutneys and doing unspeakable things with doilies. I'd imagine that this type of thing would be right up their street.'

'Do you think they'd mind?'

'Mind! You must be joking. That lot would sell their own children for a chance to get a look inside my house. I have to warn you, though, some of them are insufferably bossy. They'll probably give you a pain in the neck trying to take over.'

'I'd be delighted if somebody took over.'

So it was decided.

The sale of the garden to Uri proceeded without a hitch. Uri busied himself with building a house in the apple tree for the children and nailing up a bird box to house the robins through the winter months.

And then one day the bombshell. It didn't look like a

bombshell. Just a harmless piece of paper. It was the words that were written on it that were so incendiary.

'Can he do this?' Aoife spoke in hushed tones to Uri. They were both watching Mrs Prendergast, who was hunched over her kitchen table, her head in her hands, a pose that was utterly at odds with her usual composure.

'According to my solicitor, yes, he can. Doesn't mean he'll succeed, of course, but he can slow things down.'

'Bastard,' said Aoife, in even more hushed tones. It wasn't for her to call Lance names, what with his poor wounded mother sitting just a few feet away. Lance was accusing Uri of duress – of forcing Mrs Prendergast to sell the garden to him. It was almost laughable: the idea of anyone forcing Mrs Prendergast to do anything. But it must have felt to her like the ultimate betrayal. Lance had literally turned around and bitten the hand that had fed him since he was an infant. He must need the money very badly. Still . . .

Uri looked furious, in that particular way he had, his face concentrated and fiercely blank. He muttered something in a language Aoife didn't understand, then sat down beside Mrs Prendergast and put his arm around her shoulders, his face close to hers. Aoife left them to it.

She walked out into the garden straight into Seth. Typical.

'Have you heard?' she said. At least they had something constructive to discuss.

'Yes. What a bollocks.'

'As usual, Seth, your descriptive powers are spot on.'

She didn't like the way Seth was smiling at her. In her opinion, he wasn't trying hard enough to pretend that everything was normal between them. She was trying her hardest. 'I hope Mrs P can cope with this.' She spoke rapidly, not wanting to leave any gaps for him to fill with words she didn't want to hear.

'Of course she'll cope. She's a tough old bird.'

'You reckon?'

'Yeah. You can bet she's been through a lot worse than this in her life. You can see it in her. She's like one of those ladies the British Empire was founded upon.'

She smiled in spite of herself and hoped he was right.

'Have you seen my dad?'

'He's in there with her now. Which reminds me. Where exactly is he originally from?'

'You mean you've never asked him?'

'I've wanted to but I get the impression he doesn't like talking about his past.'

' He's German. Anyway, I'd better leave them alone if she's upset.'

'They're getting close, aren't they?'

'I suppose they are.'

'Are they "an item", do you think?'

'Couldn't tell you.'

'Would it bother you if they were?'

'Why should it?'

'You know, because he's your dad and she's not your mum.'

'If it makes him happy then I'm happy. A person can't mourn for ever.'

This was said very pointedly and it annoyed Aoife that she had walked straight into it. 'I've got to go,' she said, feeling his eyes bore into her back as she walked away.

It wasn't just his mother who was affected by Lance's legal action. The whole future of the garden was once again in jeopardy. Aoife and Uri had been in the middle of their autumn bulb selection. What now?

'It'll never work, what he's doing,' said Uri. 'No jury will believe it.'

But Aoife noticed that his enthusiasm for their proposed planting extravaganza had waned considerably. Maybe they'd all lost a bit of their zest.

But the plants didn't know what was going on so they did what they always did and kept on growing. There was a renewed poignancy to their loveliness. The grass was that little bit greener, the colours of the flowers magnified, their scent more intense. Surely this was a change in the perception of those who beheld them and not a trick of nature.

33

Myrtle found the west of Ireland rugged. It reminded her somehow of Martin's dark features and it seemed fitting that he'd been nurtured by this land.

They arrived in the town a little before eleven on a Thursday morning. The main street was surprisingly dense with people and cattle. 'Fair day,' said Martin. 'I forgot all about it.' He seemed pleased, though. They drove slowly behind a herd of cows, their bony haunches swinging from side to side, surprisingly high. City girl Myrtle had never seen an udder so close, so heavily veined, so pendulous. Although the car windows were shut tight, the stench of excrement was vile. Martin revved at the last of the herd to scare the beast out of the way.

'Stop!' she said.

'What?'

The town's women were out in force, bearing buckets of water and stiff brushes to scrub the dung off their walls. The few men who were left were scattered around in small groups. Conversations stopped and heads turned as the Humber Hawk advanced slowly along the street. Several men nodded in Martin's direction and he raised his fingers from the steering-wheel in salute.

The houses thinned out and the countryside deepened. The rain fell, slanting, and Martin was quiet.

'How far now?'

'Not far.'

He hadn't mentioned the incident on the boat. Neither

had she. She doubted he remembered. She wished she didn't.

The land was bad here, Martin had told her, the soil thin. The fields were small and uneven, bounded by low stone walls. Here and there the murky green was interrupted by the black and white of a cow. Apart from that, nothing much. Hedgerows and stones. A lowering grey sky.

'Bleak, isn't it?' Martin was looking at her, his eyes searching.

She chose her words carefully. 'I expect it's nice in the summertime.'

He looked straight ahead, his expression gloomy. 'I'm never coming back.'

Before long and without indicating, Martin turned abruptly down a narrow lane. The going got considerably bumpier as the car careered over numerous potholes. It wasn't much more than a dirt track with a rough line of grass growing up the centre. And then a long, low, whitewashed cottage loomed before them.

'Is this it?'

'Yes.'

'But it's not thatched.' She was amazed at how disappointed she was.

'I bought my mother a new slate roof two summers ago.' His pride was evident.

He stopped the car and they both got out and stretched. The rain felt like icy pinpricks on Myrtle's face and hands. As Martin got their bags out of the boot, the front door to the cottage – a half-door like the one in her geography book – opened inwards. An old woman came out. Myrtle, feeling suddenly shy, stayed by the car and let Martin greet her first. She was tiny, the top of her head only reaching Martin's chest. She had to raise her arms almost vertically to clasp his face in her hands. She must be Martin's mother, although it seemed improbable that she could ever have borne such a hulk of a man, never mind his five siblings. After a brief exchange, Martin beckoned to her. She walked slowly towards them.

'Mam,' he said, 'this is Marnie.'

It wasn't until much later that it dawned on her he'd introduced her as Marnie. That was his name for her. She was his now.

As Myrtle drew close she tried not to look shocked at the woman's ancient appearance. She couldn't have been more than a decade older than her own mother, but the difference in years between them looked more like thirty. The lines on her face were many and deep, and her smile showed that several of her teeth were missing. But it was warm and genuine and made Myrtle feel welcome. She was heartened and relieved as she entered the cottage, and realized how pathetically she wanted this woman to like her.

It wasn't much warmer inside than out, despite the peat fire. A couple of chairs were huddled around it.

'Sit yourself down, my dear. You're very welcome.'

Myrtle was offered the one and only armchair in the room.

'Let me take your coat.'

She would have loved to keep it on but, ever polite, she slipped it off and handed it to Martin's mother.

'You must be parched.'

' I beg your pardon?'

'I'm sure you'd like a cup of tea after your journey.'

'That would be lovely, thank you.'

Myrtle watched in fascination as Mrs Prendergast removed a teapot from a hook above the open fire and poured tea into a cup.

'Bread?'

'Please.'

She cut a thick, rough slice of sodabread and buttered it thickly, then handed it to Myrtle.

'Thank you. Did you make this yourself?'

The other woman gave her a strange look. 'I did, of course.'

Myrtle sipped the stewed tea, absorbing everything, while Martin and his mother conversed. The room was a fair size, with a high arched wooden ceiling. The furniture was sparse – a dresser with crockery, a rough kitchen table with chairs, the armchair she sat in and the rocking-chair in which Mrs Prendergast rocked, a black and white cat purring companionably on her lap. That was it. The floor was linoleum and the open fire appeared to be the only source of heating and cooking. Behind the rocking-chair there was an intriguing curtained alcove, which Myrtle later discovered was where Martin's mother slept.

Photographs were handed around. A head-and-shoulders shot of a man in a police uniform – Martin's brother Joe in Boston. Various American grandchildren – the offspring of Vincent and Kevin in New York. A picture taken last summer on the occasion of Martin's sister marrying the solicitor from Castlebar.

'Oh, wait till I show you.' Martin's mother got up from her seat in an excited manner, tipping the indignant cat on to the lino. Myrtle looked at Martin, who nodded, and she followed them out to the side of the house where a small, rough extension had been added. Martin's mother opened the door and stood aside. 'Look,' she said, her eyes shining.

Martin stuck his head in first. 'That's great, Mam.'

It was Myrtle's turn. She felt Mrs Prendergast's expectant eyes on her as she peered inside. What to say? 'It's lovely.'

The correct response apparently, as Mrs Prendergast

beamed before closing the door reverently and walking ahead of them back into the house.

Myrtle looked up at Martin. 'It's a lavatory,' she whispered, baffled.

'Think yourself lucky. Six months ago you'd have had to go in a hole in the ground.'

They were only back in the house a few minutes when the front door opened again. In walked a man in his thirties, wellingtons, donkey jacket, Aran jumper, cloth cap. A couple of hens ran in with him and he whooshed them out with his feet.

'Martin!' he said, taking off his cap and flinging it on to the table.

Martin got up and the two men shook hands warmly.

'Good to see you. How are you keeping?'

'I'm well. And you?'

'Mighty. Just sold a heifer down at the fair.'

'Did you get a good price for her?' said Mrs Prendergast.

'Begod, I did.'

The man looked over Martin's shoulder at Myrtle. Martin followed his gaze. 'Séan, this is my wife, Marnie. Marnie, this is my brother, Séan.'

He nodded at her. 'Pleased to meet you.'

So, this was the elder brother Séan. The one who'd got the farm. He was similar to Martin but a shadow of him, his looks not as striking, the jawline a little less defined, the eyes a little less blue. He was shorter than his younger brother too. Less powerful-looking. But he had the same outdoor, craggy look. Myrtle wondered how he'd got home from the fair and realized he must have walked all the way. At first she expected him to be intimidated by her, imagining she must seem quite the sophisticate. But Séan possessed a quiet confidence, and a certainty about who he was that made *her* feel gauche. He was a man completely comfortable in his own skin, a claim she had never been able to make about herself.

The two men went out to admire the car while Mrs Prendergast made preparations for dinner, Myrtle helping when she was let. She was allowed to dig up the carrots, onions and potatoes from the plot at the back of the house. It reminded her of the Victory Garden her mother had kept during the war. She brought back the vegetables and Martin's mother chopped them for the stew.

The day passed pleasantly and uneventfully. Myrtle was amazed at how relaxed she felt, staring into the flames of the peat fire as the short day darkened and closed in around them. She gazed at her husband, who sat at the opposite side of the fire, staring into his own private flames. She felt such an overwhelming surge of love for him that she thought her heart would burst. That night in bed, the bed that as a child he'd shared with his brother Joe, Martin reached for her, but only for reassurance: his mother was on the other side of the wall.

'You don't think any less of me, do you, Marnie?'

It was safer saying this into the pitch darkness.

'Why would I think less of you?'

'Now that you've seen where I come from.'

'If anything, I think more of you. I can see how far you've come.'

He pulled her closer to him and she knew she'd said the right thing.

They left early the next morning, after a hearty breakfast of sodabread and eggs. Martin's mother waved until they were out of sight.

'How long since your father died?'

'Six years.'

'What was he like?' The silent spectre of the man had hung over their entire visit.

'Let's just say he was handy with his fists.' Martin's face had closed, signifying that the subject was over.

After visiting Martin's sister in Castlebar, they spent a couple of days in Westport, then headed down to Killala Bay. It was a wild day. The waves hurled themselves at the rocks and the wind whipped up mini-sandstorms. Martin stared out to sea, his mood reflective, as it had been since the start of their honeymoon.

Together they explored the desolate beauty of Connemara, illuminated by the sun at rare intervals. The sight of two children with a donkey and a cart of peat almost made up for Myrtle's disappointment at the lack of a thatched roof on Martin's mother's cottage. Then it was on to Galway City, Yeats country in Sligo, and home to Dublin to start their new life together.

34

It was shocking, really, how alone she felt. The acuteness of her loneliness bit into her soul, removing massive chunks of the Myrtle she used to be – the Marnie she used to be . . . whoever it was she used to be. It left her uncertain of herself in an uncertain world where everything seemed a pale imitation of her life in London. She had Martin, of course. But Martin was never at home. And she had no need of a job, not now that she was a wife, comfortably looked after by her able husband. She was expected to be content with furnishing her new home on the outskirts of the pathetic little town that laughingly called itself a city. She threw herself into the task, bringing her considerable good taste to bear on what she had to admit was a most handsome Victorian red-brick house. Martin was delighted with the result and bought her a new-fangled Hotpoint washing-machine as a reward. She would have enjoyed it more if she'd had someone to show it to.

She had her prize, though: her man. Then why did she feel so hollow? She tried so hard to do everything that was expected of her. She checked her hair and makeup to ensure she looked perfect for Martin when he came home. She cooked his favourite meals, timing them with precision. The trouble was, she never knew when to expect him. He became impossible to predict. And all too often his meals would slowly congeal in the lower half of the oven. She tried not to be annoyed. She knew how hard he worked and she didn't want to waste what little time she had with him arguing, especially since he was often the only person she'd spoken to all day. But in spite of this, or perhaps because of it, she began to fray at the edges. It didn't help that he came in most nights reeking of whiskey. They couldn't *all* be business meetings.

The first time she confronted him she stood, pinny on, hands on hips, feeling like a fishwife out of a film. 'What time do you call this?'

He didn't answer, instead choosing to walk past her into the sitting room. A decanter of whiskey sat on a silver tray on a side table, flanked by two upside-down cut-glass tumblers. They hadn't been a wedding present. Almost everything in the house was hand-picked by Myrtle and paid for by Martin. There'd been a dearth of presents on her side. On his, anything decent could scarcely be stretched to.

Martin turned one of the glasses the right way up and sloshed a generous quantity into it. He downed it in one go. Was it normal for a man to drink so much? Myrtle had no idea. Her own father had been teetotal and she had no one else to compare him to. Martin had drunk a lot during their courtship, but she hadn't paid it much heed since they were out socializing all the time. Alcohol had been intrinsic to their lifestyle. And she'd always known that he loved going out. It was just that it had never occurred to her that, once they were married, he'd be going out without her. The party was over. Or, rather, she was no longer invited.

'Well?' She stood behind him now, hands still planted on hips, furious at being ignored.

'What's for dinner?' he said, still with his back to her.

'You mean what *was* for dinner. It *was* lamb chops but they've burned to a crisp so now there's nothing.'

He turned to her, having refilled his glass. He took a sip, appraising her thoughtfully. 'Well, you'd better make me something else, then.'

He walked away from her, leaving her stranded on the rug

in the sitting room. Once she'd got over her initial shock, she was in hot pursuit. 'How dare you walk away from me? I will *not* make you another dinner –'

The words were gasped out of her because he turned suddenly and grabbed her roughly by the chin. He brought his face down close to hers and hissed into it, 'No wife of mine speaks to me like that. Now get me some food.' His features were contorted. He released her chin, pushing her back as he did so. Myrtle was trembling with outrage and fear. How dare he? Never in all her born days . . . She'd never seen her father treat her mother like that – he'd never laid a hand on her. She had always dismissed her parents' marriage as passionless. Now . . . She touched the tender skin on her chin, then covered her mouth with her hand as she started to cry. Silent, free-flowing, gut-wrenching tears. Her first instinct was to run and tell someone – preferably her mother. But the only person she had to tell was waiting to be fed. So she went into the kitchen and started cooking.

In time, Myrtle began to meet a few women of her own age, mostly at her own dinner parties. Martin would announce that he had invited a few 'associates' over. If she was lucky, she'd get twenty-four hours' notice. More often than not, she'd have just a few hours to prepare.

The first time it happened, she rushed out to Eason's and bought *Mrs Beeton's Book of Household Management* and Fanny Cradock's latest. She spent the afternoon cooking up a storm. She thought it had gone well. Everyone had been in raptures over her sherry trifle. Still, you never knew with the Irish – they did tend to exaggerate. With an almost physical stab of longing, she wished she was back among her own people. Still, the women had been kind to her. At one stage, while the men were talking shop, one of them had whispered to her: 'Your husband is *so* handsome.'

She had felt herself expanding with pride. Yes, Martin was handsome. And he was hers. She was proud, too, of the way he held court over the dinner table, entertaining everyone with his highly embellished stories, taking care of every awkward pause and empty glass. And he must have been pleased with her because he winked at her when no one was looking. It was a good night, which continued in the bedroom later.

She didn't know what to make of it. Her new life. Her new role. Her new husband. It was all so hard to get her head around. What was normal, what was not. What was acceptable, what was not. If only she had a sounding board. Something or someone to judge it all against. But there was no one. This isolation was disconcerting. She'd always known who she was – it had never occurred to her to question it. But now, uprooted, she had to rediscover herself all over again. She wasn't sure she liked what she was finding, reflected as she was in the eyes of just one other. She was uncertain now. Of herself. Of him. Unease seeped into her soul. Had her father been right? The thought was summarily banished – because it wasn't fit to be admitted.

She saw that her husband had two sides: Public Martin and Private Martin. Public Martin was loud and gregarious – the *craic* all the way up to ninety. Private Martin was saturnine and introspective. He sat in a chair in the dark with a five o'clock shadow. The only thing the two men had in common was that they were both drink-fuelled. It frightened her, the prospect of living in a strange land with a total stranger. She tiptoed around this dark side, not wanting to get on the wrong side. This was what she had chosen. Her bed to lie in. Her man to understand. She tried.

Myrtle was lying in bed one morning, listening to Martin getting ready. She lay on her right side, facing away from him. Her stillness, the absence of rhythmic breathing, betrayed her wakefulness. He came around to her side and sat on the edge of the bed, looking down thoughtfully at her listless form as he buttoned the cuffs of the blue shirt that she and her iron knew intimately. She turned on to her back and looked up at him.

'What's wrong?' he said.

Don't you know?

'Nothing's wrong.'

Not when he looked at her like that, there wasn't. The gentle, tender Martin.

'You know what you need?' he said, his eyes warm.

'What?'

'A baby.'

'A baby!' Her voice was incredulous, although she didn't know why. Isn't that what married couples did? Breed?

'Yes, a baby. You know. Tiny little creatures. Squawk a lot.'

'I know what a baby is.'

'Think about it.' He bent down and kissed the tip of her nose.

She lay there for a long time after he'd gone. A baby. It wasn't that she hadn't thought about it. Part of her longed to have Martin's children. But the other part . . . She felt so empty. Of course, she wouldn't feel empty if she had a baby growing inside her. She rubbed her taut belly and tried to imagine. Maybe Martin would be home more often if they had a family. That thought sealed it. Her dream of what their life together would be had slipped away from her of late. But now it drew back into sharp focus. She with her swollen belly, wearing a charming maternity smock that she'd made herself, Martin's hand on the demure rise of the material. A laughing Martin bouncing a laughing baby boy on his lap. Because, for some reason, her fantasy conjured a boy, dark and dimpled and handsome like his father. She didn't know why this should be so because in her heart she'd always wanted a girl. Something about having no sisters and a distant relationship with her mother. She could give birth to her own sister. Or create the mother-daughter relationship that she'd always yearned for. But a boy was what she saw. Either sex would change them from a struggling couple into a family. Complete. And there might be other babies – lots of them. As the glee took hold of her, she stretched her body to the maximum, fingertips grazing the headboard, toes flexed. Then she curled up abruptly into the foetal position, hugging herself and rocking gently. Maybe if they had a baby Martin wouldn't drink so much.

The trouble with family planning is that it's not an exact science. This can work either way. In Myrtle's case, what happened was nothing. A whole lot of trying and a whole lot of nothing. And the more nothing happened, the more anxious she became. It wasn't something she discussed with anyone, least of all Martin. He just went about his business as usual and, for all she knew, had forgotten their conversation. She couldn't. It began to consume her, tensing her shoulders and creasing her brow. She'd be sitting there and, before she knew it, a thumbnail would be bitten to the quick. She also developed the habit of chewing her lower lip. Barely four months had passed. No time at all in the great scheme of things.

One night Martin came home extra late and extra drunk. She'd learned to read the signs at a glance. She placed the remains of his partially charred dinner before him. He chewed it slowly. His well-well-well-done steak. 'What's this crap?'

'I can make you an omelette if you like.'

'I don't want an omelette. I want a steak. A decent fucking steak.'

He stood abruptly, pushing back his chair with his calf muscles, causing it to screech against the kitchen floor. Myrtle winced. 'Stupid bloody woman. Can't do anything right. Can't cook. Can't even bloody well get pregnant.'

He pushed past her, out of the kitchen and into the sitting room. She knew better than to follow him. But she could see him as clearly as if she had, sloshing the whiskey into the tumbler and knocking it back. She felt her cheeks burn with shame. He was right. She *was* useless. She'd never thought it before but she thought it now. Who was she to contradict what was ultimately the truth? She was a failure as a wife – she felt it in every nerve and sinew. To her shame, he felt it too.

It took another two years. Two long years. In the words of Martin: 'You could have given birth twice by now.' But she was pregnant. That was the thing. The triumph. And no one was going to take it away from her, least of all Martin who, she could tell, was pleased.

She longed to tell her own parents. When the three-month danger period had elapsed, she wrote them a carefully crafted letter, informing them as to her condition and asking after their health. It contained no hint of recrimination. Neither did it contain an apology. She received no reply. And during the silent months that followed, something inside Myrtle withered and died.

But a new excitement coloured her days. A life that had been dull and empty was now vibrant and full of possibilities. She had a nursery to decorate, clothes to make for herself and the baby, blankets to crochet. It was down to her, just as she had always known it would be. She didn't mind. It was the way she preferred it, really. Myrtle had always been solitary in her pleasures. And, of course, now she was never alone. She took to talking to the embryo, the foetus, the baby.

'What will we call him?' Martin asked.

'How do you know it's going to be a him?'

'How could it not be?'

She smiled. She felt the same way.

'How about Martin?' he said.

'Wouldn't that be a little confusing?'

'It worked for my father and me.' He was defensive.

She didn't care. There was no way her son was having such a Catholic name. But she'd save that argument for another day.

They'd been getting on quite well since they'd found out she was pregnant, both anticipating the difference a baby would make to their lives. But everything changed once she started to show. He would stare at her belly, an odd, unfathomable expression on his face. He grew sullen and withdrawn, and stopped touching her. She began to feel isolated again. Fearful. Were the first years of marriage so difficult for everyone? She'd never have guessed it could be so hard. If she didn't know better, she would have said he resented the new life growing inside his wife, was jealous even, ridiculous as the notion sounded. How could he be jealous of someone who didn't even exist yet? His own flesh and blood, for God's sake.

The late nights away from her grew more frequent again. The heavy drinking, briefly suspended, began again in earnest. He would roll in spoiling for a fight and she, in her heightened emotional state, was increasingly willing to give him what he wanted. Ready, in fact, to goad him. She felt that her vulnerable condition gave her a superior edge, made her, ironically, invulnerable.

'Here he is,' she said one night, easing herself out of her chair, in the way peculiar to heavily pregnant women. 'Stinking of booze as usual. You should be ashamed of yourself, treating your wife this way. I am carrying your child, you know.'

She was indignant, self-righteous. Martin said nothing as he stood unsteadily in the hall, eyeing her warily.

'Is this how you're planning to behave when our child is born? A fine example you're going to be.' She came right up to him, standing close. And her eyes widened with incredulity.

'What's that smell?'

'What smell?' He looked a bit scared.

'You know what smell. It's perfume! It is, isn't it? You've been with a woman.'

'Don't be so bloody stupid.'

'Don't you call me stupid. You have, haven't you? You're reeking of it.'

Her voice rose several octaves, out of control, hysterical. 'How could you do that to me? I'm your wife. I'm having your baby.'

She drew back her hand and slapped him across the face, feeling as if her life had descended into some bad piece of melodrama. Without missing a beat, Martin slapped her back. Except his slap was in a different category. While he experienced a light sting, she was sent thundering into the wall. At first she didn't know what had happened. She'd never been struck before. She felt as if someone had tried to twist her head from her neck. For a few seconds, she remained where she was, dazed and stunned, then slid to the floor, her knees falling to the side, her eyes blinking repeatedly.

In an instant Martin was all over her. 'Oh, Jesus, Jesus, I'm sorry. Are you all right? Can you get up? Oh, Jesus. Here, I'll help you, you're all right, you're all right.'

She focused on his unnaturally white face as he scooped her up and carried her into the sitting room. He laid her tenderly on the couch and placed cushions behind her back and head. She continued to focus on his face, his jawline twitching. She couldn't fully comprehend what had happened. It was so far outside her usual frame of reference. Should she have seen it coming after the previous incident, which, she realized now, she had successfully put at the back of her mind?

'Oh, my darling, you're all right, you're all right,' Martin was muttering over and over, half to her and half to himself.

'The baby,' she said.

'What about it? Is something wrong?'

'I don't know, but . . .'

'Do you feel any different?'

'Well, no. But I think I should be checked by a doctor.'

'No! No reason to bother a doctor. None at all. You're fine. I'll look after you.' He left the room like a man on a mission. She lay on the couch, shivering slightly. Then her teeth started to chatter, which caused a shooting pain in the bottom left half of her face. She reached up with shaking fingers and touched her cheek. Her skin felt hot and she could feel it throbbing. Martin returned. He was carrying a frozen steak and the bedspread from upstairs. 'Here. Hold this against your face.'

She did as he had instructed and felt some soothing. He arranged the bedspread around her, tucking it up to her chin and around her feet, from which he gently removed her slippers.

'You hit me,' she said, eyes brimming, teeth still chattering.

'No, I didn't.'

'What do you mean, you –'

'I know I did, but it was only a slap. And you slapped me first.' He attempted a sickly smile.

'And that makes it all right?' She started to cry properly.

'Oh, God. I'm sorry, I'm sorry.' He cradled her, laying his cheek against her good side. 'I'll never do anything like that again. I swear to you, Marnie. I'll never hit you again. I'll change. It'll be all right. Everything's going to be all right, you and the baby.' He rocked her back and forth and she cried in his arms.

'The perfume,' she said.

'There's no other woman, Marnie. I swear to God. There's only you. No other woman but you. I was in a club, that's all. You know how you get crushed up against everybody.'

She wanted desperately to believe him, his tender words balm to her aching spirit. The throbbing in her cheek subsided to a dull ache and she ceased to shake. Martin sat with his arms around her for an hour or more, the room, the house growing dark around them. Until he felt she believed him.

In time the fingermarks faded and her cheek was no longer tender. Martin continued to be attentive and remorseful. No more late nights. He came home when he said he would. If there had been a woman, she was put on the back burner. The baby was all right: he stayed where he was until ten days before his due date. Martin wasn't present for the birth. He was relegated to the smoke-filled waiting room with all the other expectant fathers. But he came in as soon as he was let and allowed Myrtle to call their son Lance, either out of a sense of guilt or some upwardly mobile tendency within him.

Lance had his father's hair but not his eyes. His eyes were Myrtle's — slate-blue-grey eyes that saw the world for how it was and not how they wanted it to be. He was quite a sedate baby, which was just as well, because how would she have coped otherwise, what with everything else the situation had thrown at her? Martin's strange moods – one minute delighted with her and the new baby, the next sulky and petulant, as if he were the older sibling instead of the father, jealous and vying for her attention. Until this point she had only needed to be wary of his moods when he had drink taken. But now, as if aching nipples and eyes falling out of her head with tiredness weren't enough, she had his mercurial rantings to put up with.

'You're giving that child too much attention.'

'You're spoiling him. Let him cry.'

And: 'You care more about that baby than you do about me.'

Of course I bloody well do, Myrtle felt like screaming. What do you expect?

Because the love she'd had for Martin had almost run out. Like an egg-timer with the tiniest quantity of sand left to trickle through. He'd squeezed the life out of it with his big, rough hands.

And she'd loved him so much.

She wept for her lost love, so strongly held. She missed it and mourned it. And it could have been his for ever if only he'd known how to keep it. All that she had now was resentment. Another dull ache to put up with. Perhaps it would get better as Lance got older and she wasn't so tired all the time. Nowadays, if someone commented on how handsome or entertaining her husband was, she didn't feel proud. Instead she felt anger and a powerful urge to blurt out the truth. She did this once, when the urge to unburden herself became too great.

The woman was called Frances. She was the wife of a colleague of Martin's. She and Myrtle often found themselves thrown together at dinner parties. She'd had a baby girl around the same time that Myrtle had given birth to Lance, and the two women would visit each other's homes in a bid to stave off the madness that often besets the first-time mother, at home alone with her baffling baby.

Myrtle was really just trying to find out if her marriage was normal. That was how it started.

'How's Bill adjusting to fatherhood?'

'Oh, he loves it. He's wonderful with her. I'm sure Martin's the same.'

'Not really, no.' She was sick of lying, trotting out the accepted untruth just to please.

Frances looked a little taken aback, as well she might. Myrtle was not playing the game. 'Maybe he needs more time to get to know Lance.' Her words were designed to reassure herself as much as Myrtle. 'It doesn't come as easy to men as it does to us.'

She looked so smug and snug in her feminine role that Myrtle wanted to hit her. But she couldn't do that so she slapped her verbally instead. 'I sometimes think Martin's jealous of his own baby. Do you ever think that about Bill?'

Frances looked shocked. 'No, I don't.'

'He's jealous of all the attention I give Lance. He was even jealous of him when he was in the womb. He hit me once, you know, when I was pregnant.'

'I'm sure —'

'He did. Flattened me up against a wall. Did your husband ever do anything like that to you?'

'Jesus, Mary and Joseph, no.'

'So it's not normal, then?'

'Of course not. I'd better go.' Frances was gathering up her things. It was clear that she didn't want to know – feared getting involved.

After that Myrtle didn't see much of her. She didn't tell

anyone else. And the wound in her soul festered and turned into an oozing, weeping carbuncle.

It wasn't all bad. As Lance got older the less wholly dependent he became on Myrtle, and this suited Martin. He liked to play with the boy – rough-and-tumble games, throwing, tickling and flinging, that caused him to squeal with delight. Myrtle was glad for Lance that he had an alternative to her sedate reading-colouring-walking routine. It was true that children needed two parents – a mother and a father. Although Martin never talked of his own father. And, come to think of it, her brother Roger hated theirs. She hoped the cycle could be broken.

Her more pressing concern, though, was whether or not her son needed a sibling. She had never intended him to be an only child and, given the amount of time it had taken her to conceive him, perhaps they shouldn't delay too long. Her humming and haaing came to an end one day when Martin announced gruffly: 'Lance needs a little brother.'

That was decided, then.

It took six months this time, a lot less than before. Things were good. Martin was happy and so was Lance. Father and son patently adored one another. Myrtle felt happy about her growing family and newly optimistic about the future. But this happy phase in her life was to be short-lived. Because, again, the problems began when her pregnancy started to show. She wasn't sure why this should be so but it was. The constant reminder of her condition seemed too much for Martin. He became surly again, eyeing her belly suspiciously, as if it was an intruder in their home, as if it was none of his doing. The drinking began again. The staying out. She accepted it all with a sense of dread. Lance was the only recipient of Martin's smiles – that was when he saw him. More often than not, he'd been asleep for hours by the time Martin fell in the door. There was a new quality to his drinking. It was getting worse. *He* was getting worse. She wasn't sure if he was drinking more or just wasn't able to hold it as well as he once had. But it certainly seemed to have a hold on him.

She was four months pregnant. She liked to talk to the baby. To hold her hand on her stomach and feel its first flutterings. It had become her habit to go to bed early and feign sleep when Martin came in. The pregnancy gave her an excuse and, besides, she was exhausted anyway. Usually it worked and he left her alone. But not that night.

She tensed when she heard his footfall on the stairs – heavy, uneven, ominous. Normally he stayed downstairs and drank some more, falling into a drunken stupor on the couch. She kept her eyelids resolutely closed as he entered the room and sat heavily on the bed.

'Are you awake?'

She lay still as a stone.

'Marnie, wake up.' He shook her shoulder.

Still she didn't react.

'Wake up, you stupid cunt.' And, with one almighty shove, he pushed her out of the bed.

She struck her forehead on the bedside table and lay stunned for several seconds, vaguely aware that he was coming around to her side of the bed. She looked up at him in abject shock. 'What are you doing, Martin?'

'That'll teach you to ignore me, English bitch.' And he kicked her hard in the stomach.

It was a girl. Tiny, perfectly formed and dead. She would have called her Rose. She wouldn't be able to have any more children.

She stayed in the hospital for a week, staring at the wall as Martin sat on the bed and talked. He was the tender Martin she'd once known. Attentive. Above all, remorseful. While he unloaded his guilt, she weighed up her options. By the end of the week she concluded that she didn't have any. It was the 1960s. At that time, no one of Myrtle's acquaintance was separated, divorced or a single parent. She hadn't spoken to her parents since she'd got married. She loved her brother, Roger, but he was still young, feckless and broke. She was fond of Martin's mother and his family, but they would hardly take her in if she left their son and brother. What female friendships she had forged since landing on this godforsaken island were superficial. And Martin had said he'd stop drinking and that he'd never harm her again. She didn't believe him but it was all she had. On the seventh day, he brought Lance in to see her.

'When are you coming home, Mummy?'

'Now.' She got out of bed and started to dress. She met Martin's eye.

'Thank you,' he mouthed.

35

Aoife and Seth had spent the morning busily ignoring one another. Aoife, digging up potatoes as if her life depended on it. Seth, messing around by the pond and achieving very little. It was pretty uncomfortable. Aoife would have left a long time ago but she was waiting for the two women from the Mothers' Union. She had taken Mrs Prendergast up on her offer. She'd been in such a tizz at the prospect of organizing the harvest festival – or the autumn party, as Kathy and Liam insisted on calling it – that the idea of two experienced pairs of hands had been too tempting to turn down. She hoped that she hadn't been too hasty. She also hoped that Seth would clear off home. He wasn't even doing anything.

'You must be Aoife.'

She turned to see two women picking their way daintily through her vegetable patch. They tiptoed around the turnips and greeted her at the garlic.

'You must be . . .'

'Joyce and Pearl.' Joyce was the spokeswoman.

'Pearl, Joyce, delighted to meet you.'

They all shook hands rather formally and Aoife felt herself on familiar territory. She recognized these women, although she had never met them before in her life. They were the women of her childhood. The women who worked the stalls at church fêtes. The women who ran committees. And Joyce was a dead ringer for Aoife's first headmistress. Despite her Catholic upbringing, she had attended the local Church of England school for reasons of reputation and convenience.

And these women were unmistakably and indisputably Protestant. She couldn't quite pinpoint what it was about them – other than that they were in the Mothers' Union – but she knew she was right.

'I must say, Aoife, I've heard a lot about this garden but none of the descriptions did it justice. It's simply glorious. And the vegetable patch is magnificent. I can't remember the last time I saw such healthy chard.'

'Do you grow your own?'

'Oh, yes. Have done for years.'

Here was someone else who knew more about gardening than she did.

They all looked around at the crunching sound on the gravel path. It was Seth, grinning expectantly.

'Joyce. Pearl. This is Seth.'

'Ladies.' Seth proffered his hand and smiled his best smile.

'Joyce and Pearl are going to help with the autumn party.'

'Oh.' Pearl spoke for the first time. 'I thought it was a harvest festival.'

'Well, autumn party, harvest festival – it's the same thing, really.'

'Actually, no, it isn't.'

There was an embarrassing silence. Pearl might have been a quietly spoken woman but, Aoife noticed now, she had the mad look in her eye of a religious zealot.

'So,' said Joyce, to everyone's relief, 'tell us what you've got planned so far. Or perhaps we should discuss this inside the house.'

'Oh, I wouldn't want to disturb Mrs Prendergast. It's still quite early.'

'Nonsense. Myrtle's always been an early riser. I expect she's been up for hours.'

'Myrtle!' said Seth. 'You're joking me. No wonder she kept quiet about it.'

Aoife gave him a withering look. 'Ladies, why don't I show you around the garden?'

As they walked away from Seth and the vegetables, Joyce giggled in the high-pitched way peculiar to some women of a certain age. 'Oh dear. I hope we haven't let the cat out of the bag on poor Myrtle.'

'Not at all. I'm sure she won't mind.'

'Are you sure we shouldn't just look in on her first? I'd hate to appear rude.'

'You know, come to think of it, I don't think she's even at home. I saw her heading off about half an hour ago. Probably doing her weekly shop.'

'Oh, that's a pity.'

The two women looked so disappointed that Aoife almost felt sorry for them, but she was under strict instructions from Mrs Prendergast not to let them anywhere near the house. Her exact words had been 'If you let either of those nosy old bags within ten yards of my home, I'll set Harriet on them.'

'What's she going to do? Fart at them until they're both completely asphyxiated?'

'Don't be so cheeky, my girl. I mean it. If you let them anywhere near me I'll cancel the whole thing. Let me remind you that I'm still the owner of this garden.'

Mrs Prendergast had shaken a crooked finger at Aoife. There was a glint in her eye, but Aoife knew she was serious. She'd seen the telltale twitch of the bedroom curtain when the women had first arrived, and imagined their reedy voices floating to the uppermost reaches of the house, where Mrs Prendergast was waiting, watching, checking.

To Aoife's frustration, Seth had insisted on following them. She knew that he knew she had meant him to stay put.

Typical. She gave him a look and he grinned back.

The three women chatted as they walked. It came as no surprise to Aoife that Joyce and Pearl were retired teachers.

'What's going to happen on the day?' asked Joyce.

'Well, I thought we'd have a stall selling fruit and veg and that I could make some soup.'

'What kind of soup?'

'Parsnip. We've got a glut at the moment.'

'I've a wonderful recipe for honey-roasted parsnip soup I can give you.'

'I already have –'

'Now. Bread.'

'What about it?'

'You have to have some homemade bread to go with the soup. Would you like us to make it?'

'Um. Maybe. I'm not sure. Can I get back to you on that?'

'Fine. What else?'

'I hadn't really thought much further than that.'

'What about a cake stall?' This from Seth.

'Excellent idea!' Joyce beamed at him. 'We can use some of the fruit from the garden. Pies, flans, crumbles. That sort of thing.'

'And jams,' said Seth.

'Oh, yes. Jams, jellies, chutneys. I must say, you're full of wonderful ideas.'

'Oh, he's full of it, all right.'

If Aoife didn't know better, she'd have sworn Joyce was flirting with Seth.

'Now.' Joyce was striding with great purpose towards Emily's sensory garden. 'This lavender. I know it's past its best but it's hanging on in there. I'm sure we could put it to some use. Soaps. Lotions. Scent.'

'What about the roses?' said Seth. 'They're shedding their

petals right now. Could you make something out of them?'

Joyce clasped her hands as if in ecstasy. 'Yes! Your husband has such wonderful ideas,' she told Aoife.

'My what?' She could hear Seth snorting with laughter behind her.

'Oh, I do apologize. I assumed you two were married.'

'Um. No.'

'Where shall we put the vicar?' Pearl seemed quite oblivious to the conversation going on around her.

'What do you mean?'

'For the ceremony.'

'What ceremony?'

'For the harvest festival.'

'Right. I think we may have got our wires crossed. It's not going to be a religious event. At least, not a Christian one. We hope to have many people here from all sorts of different faiths. We wouldn't want to alienate anyone.'

Pearl looked most put out.

'I'm sorry if we've misled you,' Aoife continued, 'and of course the vicar is very welcome to come along. I'll understand if you don't want to participate in the circumstances.'

'Oh, don't be ridiculous,' said Joyce. 'Of course we do.'

Pearl didn't look so certain.

When their visit was over, Seth and Aoife went with the two women to the gate. Seth walked ahead with Pearl while Aoife dawdled with Joyce, who stopped every now and then to admire some plant, invariably calling it by its Latin name.

'Can I ask you something?' Aoife said abruptly.

'Of course you can, dear.'

'Why did you think Seth and I were married?'

Joyce giggled. 'Sorry about that. I don't know, really. Something about the way you are with each other. I think it was the mixture of familiarity and contempt.'

36

By now Prendergast Construction Ltd was considered one of the premier building companies in the capital, testament to Martin's hard work and charm. He'd just been awarded another government contract, which meant that Myrtle didn't see much of him. It suited her fine. She and Lance got on very well with their lives without him.

She had infinite time to spend with Lance, since Martin had insisted upon hiring a housekeeper and a gardener as befitted his new status of master builder. She drew the line at a nanny – although the housekeeper suited her well enough: Myrtle's talent had always been in picking out exquisite items, not in keeping them clean. The garden was a different issue. They'd done little to it since moving in, the project seeming too monumental. It was a sprawling acre surrounded by high brick walls and dominated by weeds. The only plants of any account in it were a few old apple trees.

So a gardener was appointed and things started to happen. Myrtle watched in daily fascination as order was created out of chaos. Four quadrants were created. A pond was constructed in the centre and gravel pathways enclosed each section. And then there was the planting, which was where the real fun started. The gardener, a generous man in his fifties, allowed Myrtle to participate. They pored over catalogues together and made their selections.

Martin was equally delighted with developments. On his rare days off, he would help with the digging and the carting around of topsoil. Myrtle guessed it reminded him of his childhood on the farm, but she didn't ask. She didn't care about him any more. It mattered only that he was sober and leaving her alone.

But it was winter now and there was not much work to be done. The garden lay sleeping, and, inside the house, Christmas decorations were going up. Martin was due back from a junket in Amsterdam. A few days after that, his mother and brother Séan were coming to spend their first Christmas in Dublin. There was a lot for Myrtle to do but she was as happy as she could be.

Lance flew into his father's arms the second he got home. 'What did you get me?'

There was chocolate, of course.

'And this.'

'What is it?'

'It's an angel for the top of the Christmas tree.'

It was small and ceramic, blue and white.

Martin and Lance looked at Myrtle.

'It's lovely,' she confirmed.

Martin lifted up Lance and he placed the angel at the top of their little fir tree. Then they turned on the lights and had the best Christmas ever.

For her birthday that spring, Martin bought Myrtle her very own camera because he was still trying hard to please her. And she was pleased.

'Come on. Let's test it outside.'

The three trooped out and found the gardener. 'Would you mind?' said Martin, showing him how to use the contraption. 'A family portrait, I think.'

They stood in front of the apple trees, the entire Prendergast family. The gardener clicked.

'Wonderful.'

The time capsule was Martin's idea, enthusiastically

hijacked by Lance. They buried it the following week, on the very day the first batch of photos was developed. They spent a magical afternoon in the garden, the entire Prendergast family, discussing what to include and where to bury it.

That night Martin had a glass of Johnnie Walker. Just a small one. He deserved it after being so good for so long.

It began again, the old familiar dance. First came the smell. He tried to hide it but her sensitivity was heightened. She didn't say anything. Then came the late nights. Then both factors increased with intensity. Still she didn't say anything. She didn't see the point. There was such a dull inevitability to it all. A cycle as natural as the seasons. As winter followed autumn, so drunkenness followed sobriety. He still came home some nights and played with his son. The two adored each other and, thus far, Lance had never seen his father drunk. Didn't even know what drunk was, thank goodness. Although he did comment once: 'What's that smell, Daddy?'

'Toothpaste.'

'No, there's something else too.'

Martin had rapidly excused himself.

Then the insults started, insidious at first, becoming more obvious. The names. The slaps, the kicks, the shoves. Nothing serious. Base-level stuff. Stuff that by now she felt she deserved. At least he was good to Lance. He never lifted a finger to him, and as long as that continued, she could put up with anything.

It became worse – the drinking, the violence. She wondered how he continued to get away with it in the outside world. But at the same time, she was aware that to the outside world he was charm personified. It added to her sense of isolation, her desperation, the understanding that she alone knew the truth and that if she tried to share it she wouldn't be believed.

One evening he came home early. The housekeeper was ill so Myrtle was seeing to the dinner. The gardener had brought in some vegetables for the stew she was making. They had chatted a while about some new planting schemes while Lance did a jigsaw on the kitchen floor. She hadn't been expecting Martin until much later. Her spirits drooped at the sound of his voice.

'Daddy, Daddy!' Lance ran to his father and clung to his leg. For once he was ignored.

What Myrtle saw on Martin's face filled her with fear. He glared at the gardener, who beat a hasty retreat.

'What was he doing here?' he spat. It was clear he was mouldy drunk and looking for a fight.

'Lance, darling, why don't you go upstairs and play with your trains?'

'I said, what the fuck was *he* doing here?' he roared, and slammed his hand down on the counter.

Out of the corner of her eye, Myrtle saw Lance jump out of his skin, then stare at his father in wonderment and fear. He'd never seen him like this before.

Myrtle struggled to keep the tremor out of her voice. Even she'd rarely seen him so bad. 'He was bringing me some vegetables. Mary's off sick and I'm making the dinner.'

'What were you talking about?'

'The garden. We –'

'You've always got your heads together. Are you fucking him?'

'Martin, please! Don't be so stupid – he's old enough to be my father.'

'Don't you dare call me stupid, you fucking whore!' he bellowed.

'Lance, go upstairs. Now!'

'Are you making a fool of me, woman?'

He had her by the throat now, squeezing hard, the back of her head rammed up against the fridge.

'Stop it, Daddy! Stop it!' Lance was screaming now and pummelling Martin's legs with his balled-up fists. Myrtle wanted to tell him to stop but she couldn't utter a sound. It was all she could do to breathe, with Martin's hands tightening by the second. She pulled at them to no avail. She stared back into his murderous eyes and registered with horror the manic spittle on his lips. If she ever got out of this . . .

'Mummy!' Lance was hysterical now, running at his father and ramming into him with his head.

'Stop it!' roared Martin. But he wouldn't until Martin let Myrtle go, whereupon she collapsed in a heap. Then Martin launched himself at Lance and slapped him so hard across the face that the boy was knocked back several feet. He descended on the child and started to shake him. 'You little shit!'

'Take your hands off him.'

And suddenly all was silent, all was still.

Myrtle held a kitchen knife to Martin's throat.

Neither of them doubted her capacity to use it.

37

The weeks drifted by and all was suspiciously quiet. Neither Uri's nor Mrs Prendergast's lawyers had heard a peep out of Lance. Enquiries were made and the reason became abundantly clear: Lance had checked himself into rehab.

How was Mrs Prendergast to react? With relief that Lance was getting help for his problems? Or shame that her son had sunk to such depths? Either way, it was a difficult and emotional issue for her. She had to go and see him, of course. How could she not? Although part of her would find it difficult to forgive him for the way he'd behaved, he was still her one and only son and she his only mother.

She'd never been to a rehabilitation centre before and it was nicer than she'd expected. She'd had a vision of peeling paint, terrible lavatories and junkies lining the corridors, needles sticking out of their arms. But it was calm. Dignified. It reminded her of an active retirement centre she'd visited once.

Lance was sitting at a table, his back to her. The shock was physical: he looked so much like his father from behind. She realized he was now older than Martin had been the last time she'd laid eyes on him. The identical hairline. The broad expanse of his shoulders.

She sat down quietly beside him. He looked at her and promptly burst into tears. She didn't know where to put herself. Mother and son had always been in the habit of hiding their weaknesses from one another. Stiff upper lip and all that. She hadn't seen him cry since he was a teenager and she didn't know how to react. She felt overwhelming sympathy and compassion but she wasn't sure how to express either. She settled for a swift pat on the arm. This seemed to make him worse, whether because her action was too much or not enough she couldn't say. But Lance was clearly at the point in his treatment that made him cry like a baby at the tiniest thing.

Eventually he was able to get a few words out. 'I'm sorry.' He sniffed.

For what? For blubbering all over her? Or for breaking her heart?

'I've been such a shit.'

While she had no intention of actively agreeing with him, she couldn't bring herself to deny it either.

'How can you even look at me? After everything I've done. Everything I've said.'

'Oh, Lance.' She put her hand on his. 'I'll always love you no matter what you do. I'm your mother. I can't help it.'

This at least made him laugh. They'd always shared the same sense of humour. Dark. Ironic. Gallows humour, Martin used to call it. She surprised herself by thinking of him for the second time that day. Normally she was quite successful at blocking out such thoughts. She'd certainly needed gallows humour living with *him*.

'I take it this means you'll be dropping that ridiculous lawsuit?'

He nodded sheepishly and rubbed his eyes with the balls of his thumbs. 'Sorry.'

'So you should be. I mean, if you needed money, Lance, you should have come and asked me for it, instead of going about everything in such an underhand way.'

'I know, I know. I was ashamed.'

'Of what exactly?'

'Of how I lost my money.'

'You mean by gambling?'

'How did you know?'

'Uncle Roger told me.'

'Oh.'

'Yes. Oh.'

'Did he tell you the rest?'

'You mean about the drinking and the cocaine?'

'Oh, Jesus.' Lance was mortified. And amazed. He looked at his mother in wonderment. 'How do you know about cocaine?'

'How could I not know? I didn't come down in the last rain shower. I read the papers. I watch the news. I saw *Trainspotting*. I know you think I live a sheltered life, but I've got eyes and ears.'

'And you're not – shocked?'

'Well, I am a little. You don't expect these things right on your doorstep. And from someone who's had the benefit of a private education. But . . .' She paused. How to say this the right way? 'I think a part of me always wondered if it would come out in you. Your father was an alcoholic and, from what I can gather, so was his father before him. You have an addictive personality, Lance. I'm sure if cocaine had been available in their day they would have been shooting it up too.'

'Snorting it, Mother.'

'Don't contradict me. You're in enough trouble as it is. Anyway, the point is, you didn't get it from my side. The strongest thing my parents ever drank was coffee. I don't have an addictive personality. Some would say I have no personality at all.'

'I wouldn't.'

They were both smiling now, each with a tremendous sensation of relief.

'So.' She sighed. 'Are you all right for money now?'

'Yes. Uncle Roger bailed me out. He's paying for this too. But you probably know that already.'

'He may have said something.'

'He's been unbelievably good to me.'

'Yes, well, he's always felt a certain amount of responsibility towards you. He thinks of himself as a kind of surrogate father figure.'

Roger had turned out to be a bit of a genius when it came to business, building up several successful companies and selling them on for enormous profits. He spent most of his time now in semi-retirement, in his townhouse in Maida Vale, with his third wife, Anthea, who was twenty-five years his junior.

'There's something I need to ask you,' said Lance, his face darkening. 'I had what they call a breakthrough in group therapy the other day.'

God, thought Myrtle. It all sounds so appallingly American. 'I'm listening,' she said.

'And ever since then I've been having these – I don't know what you call them. Memories. Flashbacks. Almost like dreams except I'm already awake.'

'Go on.' Part of her knew what was coming.

'Did . . .' He faltered. 'The day Dad left, did something happen?'

She sighed, her limbs suddenly leaden. 'What do you remember?'

'Did he hit me?'

She nodded.

'Jesus Christ. I must have been blocking it out all these years.'

He sat there shaking his head for a few moments. Then he looked up at her sharply. 'And you? Did he hit you too?'

'Yes.'

'Just that time or others?'

'There were others.'

'Christ. All these years and I never knew. Why did you stay with him as long as you did? It's not like you to take crap from anybody.'

'That's what we women did in those days. You put up and shut up. There wasn't much of a choice. If you were unfortunate enough to have married the wrong man, you just had to make the best of it.'

'So why that day? Why did you finally snap?'

'I was in fear of my life, Lance. I hadn't felt that way before. But mostly it was because he hit you too – for the first time. I never thought he would – he doted on you.'

'And to think that all this time I blamed you.'

'For what?'

'For driving him away.'

'How could I have done that?'

'Well.' Lance squirmed uncomfortably in his seat. 'You're not exactly the warmest person in the world.' He threw her an apologetic look. 'Sorry.'

'That's fair comment, I suppose. But I wasn't cold with your father. Not in the beginning at least. I adored him, you see.'

'Did you?'

'Yes.'

They were both quiet. Each absorbed in their own thoughts, which touched at certain points.

'Mum?'

'Yes.'

'There's something else I remember from that day.'

'What?'

He laughed somewhat nervously. 'But it can't be right.

It's so far-fetched – my memory must be playing tricks on me.'

'What is it?'

'I somehow seem to remember you holding a knife to his throat.'

'Yes, Lance. I did.'

38

Uri and Aoife worked easily together. Yet again he was helping her, his endless patience and generosity amazing her anew.

'You must get tired of my constant questions,' she said.

'Not really, no.'

'But I'm forever asking you things.'

'The knowledge isn't mine to keep. It's for passing on to the next generation. That's you. Then it will be your turn.'

She digested this for a while, wondering how far she could push her luck. There was an unspoken rule in the garden: the respecting-each-other's-privacy rule. But he seemed in the mood to be open . . . 'Seth tells me you're from Germany.'

He looked up at her briefly, something indefinable in his eyes, then turned his attention back to the sapling he was tending. 'That's right.'

'What part?'

'Just outside Berlin.'

'Do you ever go home?'

'Dublin is my home now.'

'But you must have some family over there.'

'Not any more.'

There was something definitive about the way he said it. She knew that their discussion – such as it was – was at an end.

He gradually wandered away from her then, the atmosphere now slightly strained. In any case he preferred to work alone. It meant that he could perform his tasks uninterrupted and that his daydreams remained undisturbed. Unfortunately there was the ever-present danger that his thoughts might wander into forbidden territory.

He touched his fantail fig lovingly, rubbing a fruit between his fingers – fruit that was soon to be transformed into something even more delectable by the women of the Mothers' Union. His own mother used to make something with figs. What was it again? He closed his eyes and tried to recall.

He had loved to sit and watch his mother bake. He and his sister would stand on chairs overlooking the counter on which she worked: rolling, kneading, mixing, creaming, chopping, peeling, filling, trimming. Sometimes she let them help. Always she let them lick the bowls. Well, he got the bowls because he was the biggest and Hannah got the spoons. If there was one thing better than watching her bake, it was eating the results afterwards: challah loaf, bagels, blintzes, honeycake, rugelach, kugel and tzimmes.

Sometimes Uri would bring these treats to school for his lunch. The other boys did so too, but Uri was sure that his mama's were the best.

Then, one day, his school was closed down. He didn't know why exactly, but it had something to do with the soldiers, although what they could have against him learning his letters and numbers and playing chase in the yard, he couldn't work out. It was exciting at first, like being on holiday. But after a while Uri missed the other boys and even learning things. Another funny thing happened around that time. He was no longer allowed in his favourite playground. His mama said that it had been closed down but he knew that wasn't true because he had seen other children playing there. He thought it might have something to do with the yellow star on his clothes because none of the children playing there had stars. He asked his mama if he could take it off so he could go and play. But she said he had to wear it. He thought this was very mean and sulked in his room for a while. So, no school and no playground. Life was boring. Uri liked to play with other boys on the street but sometimes children without stars would shout names and rude things at him. It wasn't very nice, but not so bad if he was with his mama or papa. Then he would just hold their hands tighter, look straight ahead and pretend he hadn't heard a thing.

All this meant that he spent a lot of time indoors and mostly the only one left to play with was Hannah – and she was useless. The only thing she was good at was messing up his games. So life was pretty dull. Then one day his parents said that they were moving. To somewhere called Ghetto. He'd never heard of it before but he hoped it had a playground.

They didn't seem pleased about moving, maybe because it happened so quickly that they didn't have time to bring everything. They had to leave the big things, like tables and beds. Uri got to bring most of his toys with him so he was happy about that. And his parents could always come back for the rest of their things later.

The new house wasn't what he was expecting. It was a lot smaller for a start. Before, they'd had a whole house and garden to themselves. Now they had to share a house with other families, and it didn't have a proper garden – just a yard. Uri didn't have his own room any more either. He had to share with his parents and sister, and not just for sleeping. They had to do everything in this room – cooking, eating, playing. In the beginning, he would ask his mother to bake him honeycake. She would say she couldn't, then look all nervous and worried and bite her lip. So he stopped asking.

But there were good things too. The best was that now there

were lots of boys to play with. There wasn't a playground, as Uri had hoped, but they made up games, and they could play on the street all the time because in Ghetto everyone had a star and there was nobody left to call them names.

Another good thing was that Uri's father was at home all the time. He used to have a job at the Palace Gardens. His was the most important job of all, and the other men who worked there had to do what he told them. He had taken Uri to work with him a few times, on the special seat on his bicycle. Uri liked having his father at home, mainly because he told such brilliant stories. Even though he was quiet and normally didn't say very much, his stories were fantastic. It was funny: his mother talked all the time but her stories weren't nearly as good. Most of Papa's stories had dragons in them, because they were Uri's favourites. Except when Hannah was listening too and then Papa had to include princesses and other stupid girls' stuff. But Papa would wink at him to let him know he was only putting in these bits to keep Hannah happy.

When he wasn't telling stories, Uri's father looked sad. He would stare out of the window. Uri thought he was probably worrying about his flowers and plants in the Palace Gardens. Normally he didn't like to leave them, even for a few days, so he must be wondering how they were getting on without him and hoping that somebody else would weed and water them until he got back. Uri would try to cheer him up when he looked like this, with little jokes and tickling games.

Then one day they had to leave their new house – even more quickly than the last time. He could only bring a few of his small toys. It wasn't a nice day. There were lots of soldiers with guns and they were shouting loudly and making people run to where they wanted them to go. They all ended up sitting in the town square – hundreds and hundreds, maybe even a thousand people. All wearing yellow stars. Then they started moving them in big groups. Uri and his family were in the second group. After a while, they could tell that they were going to the station.

39

Once they were on the train, Uri could hardly breathe. He stood awkwardly, pressed up against his mother, his cheek cradled by her hip bone. They had to stand because there was no room to sit down. His father held Hannah in his arms. She had fallen asleep some time ago, her body slumped heavily against Papa. As an old man, Uri could still see the haunted expression on his mother's face that day on the train. But every time he looked up at her, she smiled and touched his cheek or his hair. This would have embarrassed him normally. He *was* ten years old, after all. But things like that didn't seem to matter any more. A few hours earlier he had seen a boy from his school, a boy who was a lot bigger than Uri, crying like a baby. He wouldn't do that. He looked up at his mother again and returned her smile. She touched her fingers to her lips and pressed them to his. He hugged her hip, wishing he could reach up and hug her properly. He could just see through the slats that it was growing dark outside.

Elsewhere in the carriage, parents sang lullabies to their children. Prayers were muttered. Uri hadn't known that it was possible to fall asleep standing up. But that was what he did.

The train juddered to a halt and they all fell against one another. Uri's eyes felt gritty, as if he hadn't slept at all. He could hear men shouting outside the train. The doors were opened and the people spilled out, gasping at the fresh air. One man didn't get up at all. Uri and his family had to step over him. Uri wondered how he could stay sleeping with all the noise and activity that was going on around him.

The air outside was very cold. It bit into Uri's skin. His mother wrapped her arm around his neck like a scarf as they were herded quickly along. The guards shouted orders at them. By now he'd had plenty of experience of those guards. They always seemed angry about something or other. One was screaming at everybody to leave their bags on the train. Uri wished he would stop – it was hurting his ears. One old man wouldn't let go of his briefcase so three of the guards pulled him to the side. There was a lot of shouting, and then, a few seconds later, an even louder noise like a gun going off. Uri heard his mother gasp and she covered his ears. He didn't see the old man again.

When they got inside the camp, it was the men and boys on one side, the women and girls on the other. Uri's mother wouldn't let him go. She smothered his face with kisses and held him so tight against her coat that he could hardly breathe. Then a guard yelled at her and hit her on the side of the head with the butt of his rifle. The last time Uri saw his mother, she was scrambling to her feet, blood running down her face.

'Be a good boy,' she said. 'Do everything your papa tells you.' Then she picked up Hannah, who was crying and grabbing at her leg. As they walked away, Hannah held out her hands to Uri's father, like she did when she wanted him to pick her up. But he couldn't go to her. It wasn't allowed. He took Uri's hand and they joined their queue.

They made everyone take off their clothes. Uri couldn't understand why they did this when it was so cold. It wouldn't have been so bad if it was summer. In the summertime, Uri would go down to the river behind their house in Berlin. He'd strip off all his clothes and jump in. Sometimes there were other boys with him and they would take turns diving off the rocks and seeing who could make the biggest splash. Once a fish had nibbled at Uri's toes. It was kind of ticklish.

He was at the top of the queue now and two men sat behind a desk looking at him. They took down his name and age, then made him turn all around. Then one of them looked inside his mouth. It was a bit like being at the dentist and the doctor all in one. It wasn't too bad because he could see his father the whole time in the queue beside him. Next they gave Uri some new clothes to put on. They were blue and not the type of clothes you'd normally wear outdoors. Uri didn't think they'd keep him very warm. Then he copied what the boy in front of him had done and went into this big hut. He found it was best to do what everybody else did and not make a fuss. That meant you didn't get shouted at so much. The only time Uri got upset was when he thought about his mother. He tried to put her out of his mind, not think about the last time he'd seen her, with blood running down her face. Maybe somebody would bandage it for her later. As scary as her blood was to Uri, her tears were even scarier. He'd only seen her cry once before – when she'd had a baby and it had died. She'd had three babies who had died. One between him and Hannah – a girl called Esther. Then two boys after Hannah – Oskar and Jacob. They were both dead when they were born. Uri felt especially sad about them because he would have loved to have a brother to play with. They remembered them in their prayers every day.

When you got to the top of the queue in the hut, you sat in a big chair and a man shaved off all your hair. He was rough, not like Mr Rothschild in the barber's Uri went to at home. Mr Rothschild always chatted to you the whole time, asked you questions about school and what sports you liked, and when he had finished, he gave you a sweet. The man in the hut didn't say anything at all.

Next was the worst bit because all the boys had to go off together in a big group and he couldn't see his father any more. The guards made them run to another hut. There were loads of huts all over the place and they looked the same. This one was full of beds, except they weren't like real beds, more like long wooden boxes that you had to share and try to sleep in. Everyone was very quiet until the guards went away. Then Uri could hear a few whispers. But mostly he could hear other boys crying. Uri squeezed his eyes tightly shut and rolled up into the smallest ball ever.

That night, he dreamed he went fishing with his father and grandfather near his grandparents' home in Heidelberg. Uri caught a small blue fish that thrashed and glistened in the sunlight. Then, quick as a flash, a kingfisher swooped down, grabbed the fish in its beak and carried it away. Uri could still see the vivid colours when he first woke up. The dream made him feel warm inside, even though he was so cold. The strangest thing was that his grandfather had died two years before. But in the dream he was alive and smiling and exactly as Uri remembered him.

All the boys in Uri's hut were his age or older. There were no little ones. Uri couldn't work out what had happened to all the little ones. They must have been keeping them in a different part of the camp. Over the next few days, Uri kept an eye open for his mother, father and sister, but then the boys were moved to a different camp. Uri was upset because he wanted to stay where his family were, even if he couldn't see them. Unless, of course, they were all being moved. There was no way of knowing. He looked out for them the whole time they were marched to the train and while they were getting on board, but there was no sign. All he saw, as the train was pulling away, was that the sky above part of the camp was orange. A terrible stench filled his nostrils, something he'd been smelling on and off since he'd got there. Years later, when he walked the streets of Dublin as a young man, he sometimes thought he could smell it still.

The first day in the new camp they set them to work breaking up stones. They might have been to put between the railway sleepers. That was what they looked like to Uri. Hard and grey. There were lots of men working there too, not just boys. Uri was overjoyed to see his father among them. For a moment, he thought he was going to cry. He and his father saw each other at exactly the same time. They stopped what they were doing and smiled. But not for long because there were guards all around. But now and then they would glance up and smile when the guards weren't looking. What Uri really wanted to do was to run over to his father and hug him and to be hugged back. Which was strange, really, because he'd never done that before. His father was kind but distant. It was to his mother that Uri had gone for hugs. But everything was different now.

The work was hard but Uri was strong and quick. Which was just as well because the guards whipped you if you were too slow. Some of the boys were finding the work more difficult than Uri, but they didn't have a father to smile at them every now and then. They didn't have the happiness of knowing where their papas were and having them near.

Uri didn't see any women or girls in the camp.

Later on, when they were giving out the bread, he was able to talk to his father for a minute.

'Have you seen your mother and sister?'

'No.'

His father gave Uri half of his own bread, which wasn't fair because he must have been starving too. But he made Uri take it. And Uri ate it because he was so, so hungry. He'd never been so hungry in his whole life.

That night, he dreamed he was at home and his mama was cooking him dinner. It must have been a special occasion because she was making all his favourites: matzoh-ball soup, gefilte fish, blintzes.

He ate until he was so stuffed he could hardly move. His mother didn't look as she had the last time he'd seen her. She was smiling and happy and laughed a lot. The dream felt very real, and when he woke up, it was as if she was with him still. He was to have this dream several times. It was his favourite.

There was a man in the new camp, another prisoner, called Viktor, although some people called him Dr Frankl. He was friendly with Uri's father. He wasn't an ordinary doctor, although he did know a lot of stuff and he could help you if you were sick or hurt. Many of the boys had sores on their bodies. Uri had one on his head. Dr Frankl looked at it for him one day. Uri felt the man liked him because of his father.

'Hold still,' he said, smiling at Uri as he examined him. He was from Austria but you wouldn't have known it because he spoke German so well.

'Have you had many dreams since you came to the camp, Uri?'

That was the kind of doctor he was. He was more interested in what was going on inside your head than on the outside. The question took Uri by surprise and he wondered if he'd been talking in his sleep and one of the boys had said something. 'Why are you asking me that?'

'Because many of the men have been having very vivid dreams since they got here and I wondered if it was the same for the boys.'

Uri told Dr Frankl about his dreams.

'Did you dream much before you came?'

'Not as much. And the dreams – didn't have as many colours in them.'

Dr Frankl nodded. 'Hold your dreams tightly to you, Uri. Don't let them go. And don't let go of your dreams for the future. They're important too. You're a strong boy. You have your father with you and he's a good man.'

'Dr Frankl?'

'Yes?'

'Do you think my mother really comes to me at night?'

Dr Frankl looked at him for a long time. 'Yes, I think she does. I think your mother is always with you and always loving you, even when you can't see her. Her love is real, Uri. There's nothing more real.'

This thought helped Uri through the long, cold winter months. Because it was very hard. Sometimes a boy didn't get up when he was called and they couldn't wake him. They'd all be sent out to work, and when they came back, the boy would be gone and they would never see him again. At least working kept you warm.

Uri was worried about his father. He had a bad cough that wouldn't go away. It made him work more slowly and sometimes he got whipped. Seeing this made Uri very sad and angry. He arranged it so that he could work alongside his father sometimes and help him when he couldn't keep up. And he would make him eat all his own bread. Because of this Uri was extra tired at night but that was all right, because it meant he fell asleep straight away.

One night, he dreamed his brothers were with him. Even though they were dead when they were born, they were alive now and quite grown-up. They were still a little smaller than Uri but not much – big enough to play with. His two brothers were quite different from one another. Jacob was quiet and shy. Oskar was noisy and laughed a lot. Uri taught them both to jump off the big rock into the river behind their house – it was their home too, and their river. The boys had never lived in Ghetto. Sometimes he thought they were lucky to be dead but he didn't let himself think that too often.

Surely the winter would be over soon. There weren't many boys left now. Most of the ones around his age had already gone.

Uri's father's goal was constant: to reunite his family. For the four of them to be together once more. And for that he would beat his cough. For that he would beat the Nazis.

Then one evening, the day's backbreaking work at an end, a guard came into his hut and called his number. He was taken outside, his limbs shaking slightly. Was this it? What was to become of his boy? The guard who had singled him out wasn't the worst of them, although they all followed the same set of vile orders.

'This way,' he said.

'Where are we going?'

'The commandant wishes to speak with you.'

For what possible reason could the commandant want to talk to him? Many possibilities buzzed around his head, none of them good.

He was led, not to an office, but to a house at the far end of camp. He'd never been there before. The unfamiliarity made him even more nervous. It was like any house you might see in an affluent suburb of a German town. Windows with curtains. Samuel would never have thought that ordinary windows could seem so extraordinary. The house looked incongruous at the edge of camp. Like a jewel in a cess pit.

The guard knocked at a side entrance. They were allowed inside and escorted to an inner door. The guard knocked once more.

'Enter.'

The guard ushered Samuel into the room. A thick-set middle-aged man sat behind an enormous desk.

'You are a gardener. Is that correct?'

'Yes, sir.' Samuel stared straight ahead at a spot on the wall. He didn't risk looking the commandant in the eye for fear of appearing insolent.

'And you were in charge of the gardens at the Palace in Berlin?'

'Yes, sir.'

'Excellent. You will look after the garden of this house. You will start today. You will be shown a shed at the back of the house where you will find all the tools you need. Any seeds and so forth that you require, you are to inform my household staff and arrangements will be made. Is that clear?'

'Yes, sir.'

'Go now.'

Samuel felt opportunity bubbling in his throat. 'I beg your pardon, sir, but may I have permission to speak?'

The commandant regarded him with a mixture of surprise and annoyance. Out of the corner of his eye Samuel could see the guard getting ready to strike him, should it be necessary. He felt the blood rushing in his ears as he braced himself for the guard's blow and the commandant's refusal. But he said gruffly: 'What is it?'

'The garden is large. Usually for a space of that size I would have at least one assistant. My son, who is also in the camp, is my apprentice. We could make greater progress if there were two of us.'

He could feel the commandant staring at him. 'Why not?' he said at last.

'Thank you, sir.'

'Get him out of here,' he told the guard, then returned his attention to the papers on his desk.

'*Heil Hitler.*'
'*Heil Hitler.*'

Samuel kept his head down to hide his jubilation. Smiles weren't easily tolerated among the prisoners, not to mention seldom seen. Now he'd be able to spend hours at a time with his son, talking to him, protecting him, teaching him. And he could hold him. His heart swelled and ached at the thought of his boy. He was so proud of how Uri had conducted himself, working alongside him, taking up any slack, doing more work than many a man twice his size. Like Samuel, Uri was small but stocky. In a sense, he was a man now. How his mother would –

But it pained him to see how thin Uri had become. Viktor had expressed concern for the boy only recently. Samuel feared he would go the way of so many other boys in his group, that one night he would go to bed and never wake up. Samuel quickened his pace behind the guard. But that wouldn't happen to Uri now because everybody knew that the personal servants had access to better food. And he could easily grow extra vegetables and smuggle them back to the camp. For the first time in months, a ray of light shone into Samuel's grey world. They came to a shed, whereupon the guard stopped abruptly. 'You will stay here,' he instructed.

'And my son?'

'Will be brought here shortly.'

Uri felt the familiar sense of foreboding when his number was called. He ran to the guard and saluted briskly.

'This way.'

He'd never been to this part of the camp before. His head never stopped turning, looking out for his mother. He knew she was out there somewhere, loving him. They brought him to this strange house, except the house itself wasn't all that strange. It was just that it was so unexpected. He was brought to the back through a spacious garden. By now, he was more curious than afraid. Then he saw his father and didn't know *what* to make of it. And his father's face was happy and relaxed. Not smiling, but the expression he wore sometimes that let Uri know he was smiling inside.

'You will be working here from now on,' the guard said, as he walked a few paces away and lit a cigarette.

'Is this true?' said Uri.

'Yes, it is.'

'Together?'

'Yes.'

The guard turned away as father and son embraced each other hungrily.

Harvest

*To forget how to dig the earth and to tend the
soil is to forget ourselves.*

Mohandas K. Gandhi

40

Summer deepened into autumn. The garden hardly noticed at first. But little by little, the edges of the leaves burned to an orange crisp. The grass slowed its hectic growth. Everything had bloomed. Now it was time for harvest.

It was also time for big school, for Liam and Kathy. In Aoife's mind, the terrible day had dawned. The great letting go. She fixed a bright smile on her face as she helped him into his brand new uniform. He stood in front of her, fully dressed and beaming. 'You look very handsome.' She tried not to cry. Privately, she thought he looked as if he was playing at being grown-up. Unnatural. Ludicrously beautiful. She had to roll the sleeves of his jumper up several times to find his hands.

Liam was too excited to eat his Weetabix. He was ready to go, branded to within an inch of his life with his *Thomas the Tank Engine* rucksack and his *Bob the Builder* lunchbox with his breaktime snack. She held his hand as they left the house and made the short journey to school. She wondered how much longer he'd permit her to hold it in public.

The school gates were busy after two months of abandonment, with throngs of mothers and maroon-jumpered children. It was a beautiful morning, which promised to turn into a scorching afternoon – traditional for the start of the school year. At least they'd be off at lunchtime. Aoife planned to spoil Liam rotten that afternoon. Provided, of course, he didn't have too much homework. The thought appalled her. Surely five was far too young to start school – too early to institutionalize their precious little minds.

So that morning, as they neared the school gates, swinging their hands between them, Aoife's heart was heavy but her smile was bright. It dimmed, however, when she saw who was coming in the opposite direction. Kathy was resplendent in her new gear, flanked by Seth on the right and a woman, presumably her mother, Megan, on her left. She was holding hands with both of them, smiling up at each in turn. They looked like the quintessential happy family. Aoife felt the most extraordinary pang of what she was honest enough to name as jealousy. She knew this was ridiculous. Not only was Megan Seth's ex. She was also a lesbian. Which meant that it was hardly likely they were going to get back together any time soon. Unless Megan changed her mind again. Shit. They were all going to reach the gate at exactly the same time.

'There's Liam and Aoife,' Kathy squealed and, disengaging herself from both of her parents, ran to Liam and started jumping up and down on the pavement. They giggled, too excited for words. Their parents were a little more restrained.

'Hello.'

'Hello.'

'Aoife, this is Megan. Megan, Aoife.'

'Yes of course. Delighted to meet Liam's mammy at last. I've heard a lot about you.'

Did she mean from Kathy or from Seth?

The two women smiled and looked each other up and down a little. Megan was slim, petite and pretty. Exactly the kind of woman who made Aoife feel clumsy and whale-like. 'Lovely to meet you too.' What a liar she was.

They walked into the school together, the children chattering one hundred to the dozen. The high-pitched noise of all these little people speaking at once made Aoife feel as if she was trapped inside a beehive.

Liam and Kathy all but ran into their classroom and descended on a pile of Lego in a corner. Liam immediately struck up a conversation with a boy Aoife recognized from his crèche.

'It's best to go quickly if your children are happy,' the teacher told the gaggle of anxious parents standing at the doorway, her voice kind but firm.

Oh, God. So soon. Aoife went over to Liam and crouched beside him. 'I'm going now, Liamy. I'll be back to pick you up in a little while.'

'Okay, Mummy.'

'Have a nice time and be a good boy. Remember to say please and thank you.'

'I will.' He allowed her to plant a kiss on his cheek.

''Bye, then.'

'Bye-bye.' His attention was diverted by the Lego tower that the boy beside him was building. She got up and left, seeing that Seth and Megan were talking earnestly to the teacher. Perhaps they were explaining Kathy's unconventional living arrangements.

Was that it? She walked back down the corridor, feeling as though she'd just been disembowelled. She couldn't stop thinking of how today should have been, with Michael by her side, Katie's hand in hers. She felt her lone-parent status keenly. It had been so difficult, agonizing over which school to send Liam to. No Michael to give his ever-practical, ever-logical opinion. She hoped she'd made the right choice. Prayed she had. Do you approve, Michael?

She quickened her steps out of the school grounds, her vision blurring, wanting to get a safe distance away before the flood came. How embarrassing. Liam was fine. He was

289

happy. It was good that he'd reached this milestone – a cause for celebration. Then why did she feel so wretched? She was thinking of herself and not of her son, which was wrong. So intent was she on curbing her tears, that she didn't hear the footsteps behind her.

'Aoife.'

She swung around and almost collided with Seth. 'By God, woman, you're a fast walker.' He looked at her face. 'Are you okay?'

She nodded, the first tears escaping.

'Is it Liam?'

She nodded again, furiously this time.

'Come here.' He put his arms around her and pulled her close. Her body stayed rigid at first.

'This isn't very English of you. Not very stiff-upper-lip.'

She laughed and her body relaxed. Then the deluge came. Seth held on tight as she shook and the shoulder of his T-shirt became soaking wet. A good five minutes they stood there, passers-by walking curiously around them, long after, in fact, Aoife had stopped crying. She was afraid to lift her head. What now?

'Aoife.'

She burrowed into his shoulder.

'Aoife.' His voice was soft as he disentangled himself and placed his fingers under her chin, making her look up at him. She was embarrassed by how red and blubbery her tear-stained face must be. She badly needed to blow her nose.

'It's okay. Everything's going to be okay.' Then he kissed her. And not only did she let him. She kissed him back. But only for a few seconds before she broke away.

'I can't.'

'Why can't you? What have you got to lose?'

'Everything. If something were to happen to you . . .'

'So you're going to live your whole life avoiding getting close to anyone in case they get taken away from you?'

'Sounds like a plan to me.'

'Sooner or later you'll have to put your heart on the line. Why not do it sooner? With me.'

When she didn't answer, he said: 'You could do a lot worse, you know.'

'You think so.' She couldn't help smiling.

'Aoife, I'm offering myself on a plate here. Please don't let me go cold.' He held his arms in the air and looked up to the clouds, as if appealing to the heavens. Then he put his hands on his hips. 'I won't be on the market for ever, you know. There are plenty of hot lesbians out there dying to get their hands on a man like me.'

This time she laughed outright. Then she swiped at her wet face with her sleeves, and blew her nose noisily and unselfconsciously. 'Okay. You can walk me home.'

'Really? You mean all the way down the street? In broad daylight? Are you sure?'

'Do you want to or not?'

'All right. Hand, please.'

She put her hand in his and they strolled along, both feeling a little shy, but both smiling. They reached her front door. She opened it as he leaned expectantly against the wall.

'Are you coming in for coffee?'

'I don't want coffee.'

'I don't have any.'

'Then I'm coming in.'

41

Life was suddenly better for Uri. Yes, he was still in the camp. And, yes, his bones were still sticking out of his skin like sharp sticks. But he was with his father.

The worst of the winter was behind them now and Samuel's cough was much better. It was still cold but the housekeeper would bring them out cups of hot soup when the house was quiet. Years later, Uri was to speculate that she and her soup may have saved his life.

As Uri watched his father work on the garden, it was as if he was seeing him come back to life. His cheeks had a little colour in them, and when he smiled at Uri, his smile sometimes reached his eyes. Uri was relieved to get away from the unremitting greyness of the rocks they'd had to break. They still had to do that sometimes, when it became obvious that there wasn't much for them to do in the garden, but they did so much digging and made so many ambitious plans for new beds and borders, that they were very successful in making extra work for themselves, and had to go back to the rocks less and less often. The commandant would come out from time to time to see what they were doing and ask Samuel lots of questions. Samuel and Uri would stop what they were doing and stare straight ahead of them. The commandant nodded and looked quite pleased as he walked away. Uri felt like telling him he should be pleased, and did he know how lucky he was to have one of the best gardeners in all Germany working for him?

Every so often Uri would wonder who had looked after

the garden before and what had become of them. He was going to ask the housekeeper but thought better of it. As he held the tools, he thought of those who had held them before him and silently blessed them.

He was newly impressed by his father. He had always respected him but had never realized the breadth of his knowledge. A new bond was forged between father and son as Samuel painstakingly taught Uri the secrets of plants. Uri had to admit that he hadn't been all that interested before but now – now he could see that there was something to it.

At sunset, they would go back to their huts. Uri felt guilty when he saw the other boys passed out from hunger and exhaustion. He knew what they had gone through and that their day had been infinitely worse than his. But he also felt lucky. Maybe he felt a little too lucky.

Uri was starving all the time. Of course, he had been permanently hungry ever since he'd arrived at the camp, but there was a new quality to his hunger now. It was insatiable. His father said it was because he was growing that his body needed more food. Uri could see for himself that he had grown a good two inches since his arrival because his trouser hems now floated somewhere above his ankles. At night, he got strange pains in his legs, not the usual ones. Dr Frankl told him they were growing pains. Then Dr Frankl was transferred to another camp and they didn't see him any more. At least, they hoped that was what had happened to him.

The delectable smells that floated out to the garden from the commandant's kitchen window mocked Uri daily. There were times when he felt he'd go crazy with food lust. One day, when he was pushing his wheelbarrow past the window, he happened to look inside. Sitting on the kitchen counter, completely unattended, was a tray of dumplings. Uri was filled with an uncontrollable craving. He walked on with his wheelbarrow and tried to immerse himself in his work. He got a spade and dug and dug and dug. After a while, he took up his wheelbarrow and walked past the house again. There was no harm in looking. They were still there. Still unattended. A trickle of steam rising from them. He glanced down to the other end of the garden. His father was thinning onions, oblivious to all else. The house was as quiet as a tomb. His head turning constantly, Uri set down his wheelbarrow and walked as rapidly as he could down the path. His heart hammered wildly as he inched open the back door, which was, as usual, unlocked. Nothing. Nobody. He went into the kitchen, the tray now looming ahead of him, just a few sweet feet away. One last look around and he was on it. There were so many of them that no one would notice. He crammed one into his mouth and closed his eyes. It was better than he'd imagined. The softness, the warmth, the sweet spicy apple flavour. He thrust another into his pocket and turned to leave. He stood stock still. Framed in the doorway was the commandant's wife. At first she was silent and they stared at one another. The seconds ticked slowly by – one, two, three – then she was screaming at him.

'What are you doing here? Dirty Jewish boy in the kitchen. Stealing my food. Get out! Get out!'

She grabbed a broom and struck him with it. Uri crouched on the floor, adopting a submissive position, his hands shielding his head. He heard footsteps – running – getting closer. Now he could see the black boots.

'What is it?'

'This boy. This Jewish rat. He's been touching my food. Stealing from me.'

A guard yanked him to his feet and dragged him out of the house. He threw Uri on to the lawn where he lay cowering.

Then he tore off his shirt and started to whip him. Once. And again. And again. Uri was vaguely aware of his father's voice. Shouting. Running footsteps. Then the whipping stopped. Uri lay there for a few seconds, anticipating the next strike. When it didn't come he looked up. The guard was on the ground and Samuel was sitting on top of him, his hands around his throat. The guard's face was red, Samuel's hands were tightening. A shot rang out. The crows on the roof of the commandant's house rose in black unison, cawing and croaking their cacophony. Samuel's hands loosened and he fell to the side, a gaping red hole in his left temple.

'No!' Uri fell on his father, shaking him first, then cradling his head. The guard rolled away, coughing and clasping his neck. The soldier who had fired the pistol came running over and crouched beside him.

'What is the meaning of this?'

The commandant strode across the lawn. He stood over Uri and his father. 'Who did this?'

The second guard stood up and saluted.

The commandant slapped his face. 'This was the best gardener I ever had. What has occurred here?'

'Sir.' The first soldier spoke through his coughs. 'I caught this boy stealing food from your kitchen.'

'Stand up, boy,' said the commandant.

Uri stood up, swaying slightly, his face awash with tears, his mind with grief. Through his tears he could see the face of the commandant's wife, screwed up and hard, pressed against the window. Then he heard the click of the gun that her husband was pointing at him.

Uri closed his eyes and awaited oblivion. Nothing happened. The gun clicked again and he opened his eyes.

'Better not,' said the commandant. 'I've already lost one gardener today.' Then he raised his gun and struck Uri across the face with it. Uri fell to the ground, not caring. Someone with big boots kicked him in the back.

He lay on the ground, bleeding profusely, until long after he was able to get up. His father's body was gone. He walked unsteadily to the onions that Samuel had been working on and knelt on the ground. Then he finished the job his father had started, his blood mingling with the earth.

Back in his hut, the men he lived with waited for Samuel's return. Until it got too late. Some of them mourned. For others it was too late.

42

Uri didn't know if he could fill his father's shoes. Had Samuel taught him enough for Uri to pass himself off as a gardener? Increasingly, Uri didn't care. And then came the day when it really didn't matter any more.

It was April, tulips bobbing their pretty red heads in the breeze. But there was no other sign of activity in the garden or the house. There was an almost unearthly silence. Where were the guards? It seemed that they had vanished overnight. Even the watchtower was empty. Prisoners emerged from their huts to stand around in straggly groups, whispering and shaking their heads, as if they were afraid it was all some elaborate trick and that, at any moment, the guards would jump out with their guns and their whips, their vicious dogs barking.

The silence was broken by strange sounds emanating from the other side of the camp. The sounds were strange because they weren't of a type that the prisoners were accustomed to hearing. Shouting, singing – jubilation. They looked at each other and started moving towards the sounds, slowly at first, getting faster.

Uri couldn't believe what he was seeing. Seven giants surrounded by prisoners, who were whooping and hugging and kissing them. The giants were dressed as soldiers but they were not German. As Uri drew close, he recognized the uniforms as American. They were young men, older than him but not much more than seventeen or eighteen. It seemed they had cut through the wire. They were there to liberate them.

Uri joined in with the general mayhem and jumping around. But part of him felt that it was happening outside himself. Liberation. What did it mean? What would happen to him next?

There were lots more Americans outside the camp. They set up tents for the sick, which was just about everybody, but the sickest went first. Uri watched them stretchering out the half-dead. It took three people to lift each one. The first took the head, another the body and the third the legs. They had to go slowly so the skin wouldn't tear. He wandered out after them, stepping for the first time beyond the boundaries of the camp. He didn't feel so different. Part of him wondered if he'd ever feel anything again.

One of the American soldiers handed him a package. Uri sat on the ground and opened it. It contained a tin of meat. The soldier crouched beside him and held the tin in front of Uri's face. 'Spam,' he said. Then he made a gesture, bringing his fingers to his lips. 'Eat. It's good.' The American tried to smile at him but he didn't quite make it. He was looking at Uri with the oddest expression.

There was chocolate in the package too, and some milk powder. Uri ripped open the wrapper on the chocolate and rammed it into his mouth.

'No!' Somebody wrenched the rest of the bar out of his hand. Uri cowered instinctively and covered his head with his hands. Another man hunkered down beside him. He was older and spoke gently to Uri in a language he didn't understand. When he got no response, he switched to German. 'I'm sorry,' he said, 'but you mustn't eat that. Your stomach is unused to such food and it will make you sick. Please spit it out.'

Reluctantly, Uri spat it on to the grass and wiped his mouth with the back of his hand. The man spoke sternly to the soldier in the language Uri didn't understand. Then he held out his hand and helped Uri to his feet. 'Come with me,' he said in German.

Uri followed him into one of the tents. The man spoke rapidly to a woman in uniform. Then he turned to Uri. 'This lady is a nurse. She will look after you.'

The nurse bade Uri to sit on the makeshift bed. Then she gestured for him to take his top off. Uri did so. He continued to sit there for a long time, waiting for her to do something. But she just stood there staring at him. She made a funny noise in her throat but she didn't say anything. At last she moved towards him. She prepared a needle and indicated to Uri that she was going to stick it into his shoulder. He let her do it. It only stung a little. Then she walked around the back of Uri and gasped. He knew she must have seen the red weals and felt ashamed. He watched her as she picked up a tube of cream. She held it up to him and pointed at his back. Uri nodded. The cream was cold at first and he winced, but soon it started to feel good, soothing. The nurse's head was above his. He felt her hot tears landing on his scalp but she made no sound. It reminded him of his mother and now he was crying too, silently, but his shoulders shook. The nurse wrapped her arms around him – gently so as not to hurt him – and he tucked his head under her chin and cried some more. They stayed like that for a very long time. Long enough for some of the humanity to seep back into him.

Later, the man from before came back into the tent. By now, Uri had worked out that he was a doctor. He told Uri he was going to examine him.

'Can I have something to eat first?'

'You can have a cup of tea.'

'But I'm so hungry.'

'I know, Uri, but we have to take it slowly.'

Tea! Were these people trying to starve him too?

The doctor and nurse exchanged a glance and the doctor looked at Uri. Right in the eye. 'I know,' he said. 'Who could do this to a child?'

Uri felt like telling him that he hadn't been a child for a very long time. That he never would be again.

After two hours, they let him have some weak, milky mixture. He signalled to the nurse that he wanted some more but she smiled sympathetically and shook her head. Uri lay on the bed, hungry and frustrated, and pulled the covers over himself. He didn't think he'd sleep with all the activity going on around him, but he did. He didn't dream, though. For the rest of his life, he never had another dream.

When he woke up, he was allowed a kind of broth, then every couple of hours, a little more. The food got better and more solid. The next day, some potatoes. The day after that, meat. The doctors and nurses stared as he gobbled everything they put in front of him, then looked for more.

It took them four days to fill him. The doctor smiled as he watched him hoover up the last of his stew. 'Is there anything else I can get you, Uri?'

'Yes. My mother and my sister.'

43

Seth and Aoife collected the children together, on their first day of school. They were lucky to make it on time. Liam and Kathy accepted their joint appearance as totally natural, which of course it was. They babbled about the morning's goings-on.

'We did colouring and then we played with Marla.'

'You mean Plasticine.'

'It's called Marla.'

'No, it's not, it's –'

'Hey, hey. Never mind that. What else did you do?'

'We went out to the playground and we ran around,' said Kathy.

'Super fast,' said Liam.

'Daddy?'

'Yes.'

'Why is your T-shirt on inside out?'

'It's not.'

'It is. Look at all the knobbly bits sticking out. And there's the label at the back.'

'I must have put it on like that this morning.'

'No, you didn't. It wasn't like that when we came to school.'

'I know what it was. I was doing some work outside and I took my T-shirt off because it was so hot. I must have put it back on inside out.'

'Oh.' She lost interest.

Seth squeezed Aoife's hand. 'Okay, kids. What do you want

to do this afternoon? We all have the day off so we can do anything you like.'

'I want to play in the garden.'

'Me too.'

'Are you sure? You can go anywhere you like.'

'The garden!' they chorused, then ran ahead hand in hand, laughing and chattering.

They stopped off at the Good Food Store to buy themselves a picnic lunch – luxurious, celebratory, no holds barred. 'Would you ever tell Mrs Prendergast to bring over some more of her gourmet pies? They're flying off the shelves.'

'Will do, Mrs Harte.'

As they walked along the hot city streets towards the garden, Aoife felt a peculiar lightness. A long-forgotten, once-familiar sensation. And she realized she was happy. It crossed her mind for a second that she should feel guilty and she thought of Michael. But at that moment she knew with absolute certainty that he'd be happy for her. She smiled up at the flawless sky and, for the first time, felt forgiven – by Michael and, more importantly, by herself.

When they arrived Uri was working alone. Despite the sweltering heat, he was formally clad as usual, in his shirtsleeves – although he had undone his top button.

'Grandad, Grandad!' The two children ran to him and he hoisted them both up in a massive bear-hug.

'How was school?'

They chattered to him like a cage of budgies newly released. Then: 'Grandad. Will you tell us a story?'

'Yes, with lots of dragons in it.'

'After lunch, kids. Here, Dad. Take this drink while it's still cool. You look like you need it.'

They set out the food, laughing and talking – the atmosphere pure carnival.

'Where's Mrs P?'

'She's gone to collect Lance. They're letting him out of rehab today. They'll be back soon.'

'What do you mean "they"?'

'He'll be staying here.'

'So she can keep an eye on him?'

'No. Because his house has been repossessed.'

'That's serious. So we'll have to suffer him for a while.'

'He *is* her son, Seth,' said Uri.

Seth kept quiet.

The sun beamed down hotter than ever. The children took their shirts off and protested vociferously as Aoife slathered them with sunblock. They wriggled like little wet fish in her grasp. Seth lay back on the grass and shielded his eyes.

'Daddy, why don't you take your T-shirt off if you're hot?'

'You know, I think I will.'

'Don't forget to put it back on the right way around this time.'

'I won't.'

'Mummy, why don't you take your top off too?'

'It's okay, Liam. I'm not that hot.'

'Can I take my vest off?'

'You can if you like, but you'll have to have more lotion.'

'No, thank you. Why don't you take off yours, Uri?'

'I'm too old. I might frighten you with my hairy chest. You might think I'm a bear. Grrrrr!' He held up his hands like claws and made a gruesome face. The children screamed and giggled.

Seth peeled off his top and Aoife got to see his tattoos for the second time that day.

'What are those pictures on your skin?'

'They're called tattoos, Liam.'

'Where did you get them?'

'A man gave them to me, using needles.'

'Did it hurt?'

'Only a little bit.'

'My daddy has my mammy's name tattooed on his arm. Look.' Kathy held up Seth's arm for everyone to see.

'I'm having it removed,' he whispered to Aoife.

'What's that star on your other arm?' said Liam.

'It's called a Star of David.'

'But your name isn't David.'

'I know it isn't.'

'What have you got it for, then?'

'To show that I'm proud of who I am and where I come from.'

'Stoneybatter?'

They all laughed, except Liam who was evidently confused.

'Grandad, why don't you show Liam *your* tattoo?'

There was a change in the atmosphere. Barely discernible, but it was there. Uri sat perfectly still. Then he unbuttoned his cuff and rolled up his pure white left sleeve to the elbow. Aoife froze. It was something she'd suspected, but to see the evidence up close – that was another matter.

'It's just numbers.' Liam was distinctly underwhelmed. 'Why did you want numbers on your arm?'

'I didn't.'

Liam wrinkled his nose. 'Then why do you have them?'

'Some bad men gave them to me.'

'Like baddies?'

'Yes, like baddies.'

'Where are they now?' Liam raised his eyebrows and looked slightly alarmed.

'They lived far, far away a very long time ago.'

'So they're gone now?'

'Yes.'

'Come on, Kathy. Let's play football.'

'Okay.'

They ran off in pursuit of the ball and Harriet ran after them in her own arthritic way.

The day was just the same. The sun was still as high in the sky and the sky was just as cloudless. But everything was different. The party was over and Aoife felt sick. 'I didn't know,' she said to Uri. 'I'm so sorry.'

Uri nodded and rolled down his sleeve.

'You must have been a child.'

'I was ten.'

She closed her eyes and swallowed.

'Back to work,' said Uri. He got up and walked away without looking back.

Aoife watched him go and turned to Seth. He was sitting up, his chest still bare, his elbows resting on his knees. His brow was furrowed. 'He doesn't like talking about it?' she asked.

'No.'

'What happened to his family? His parents?'

'All killed in the camps.'

'Oh, God. Where?'

'Do you mind if I tell you about it another day? I don't want him to think we're talking about him.'

'Okay. Yes. You're right.'

'Now come here.'

'Someone might see.'

'I don't care.'

It was an hour later when Lance and Mrs Prendergast came out to the garden. Lance's air was nonchalant, but in a way that was almost too studied. He examined the plants intently, looking at everything there was to look at – at everything except the people. They – Uri, Seth and Aoife – were standing in a small circle, chatting. The talk died away when they spotted Lance.

He and his mother drew close. Greetings were exchanged. Lance seemed well, Aoife thought. He'd put on a little weight and his cheeks had filled out. He'd lost that gaunt, waxen look. He seemed more relaxed too. Less twitchy and no longer brimming with nervous energy. Although he was somewhat nervous. He met Uri's eyes with difficulty. Then he held out his hand. The others held their breath as they waited to see what Uri would do.

Uri took Lance's hand and shook it.

'I'm sorry,' said Lance. 'What I said to you before. It was wrong. Unforgivable. It'll never happen again.'

Uri nodded. 'Apology accepted.'

Lance's face relaxed into a relieved smile. 'Thank you,' he said. 'Thank you so very much. That means a lot.' He turned to his mother. 'I'll be up in my room if you need me.' He put his hands into his pockets and walked back to the house.

'Thank you, Uri,' said Mrs Prendergast.

Uri smiled.

'I think he's going to be all right,' she added.

44

Along with thousands like him, Uri was sent to a displaced-persons camp in Germany. The conditions were better than they had been in the concentration camp but only just. Crucially, he was no longer in fear of his life or anticipating a beating. But there was never enough food and it was too cramped.

He scanned every female face, every girl child. Sometimes he would get excited by the back of a head and run around to the front, but he was always disappointed. He did this for weeks. And the weeks stretched into months. His hope was fading. Then, one day, he had an idea. What if his mother and sister had gone back to their home in Berlin and were waiting for him there? There was only one way to find out. Without saying anything to anyone, he saved up three or four days' rations, packed a knapsack with what few belongings he had, and set off to find his family. It was easy to sneak out. Nobody took much notice of an eleven-year-old boy. He knew he wasn't far from Berlin – he had made some seemingly innocent enquiries – and the thought that his mother might be waiting for him, just a short distance away, was too much of a temptation to resist.

It took him a week. It was summer so there was no problem with sleeping outdoors. If it was a bit chilly, he'd find a nice snug barn and fall asleep to the sound of animals breathing. He would wash in a stream in the morning, laughing as he splashed his face with icy drops. He was good at finding his way. He'd been on many camping trips with his father and grandfather before the war and they had taught him more than he had realized. He felt at home in the fields and the woods.

But it shouldn't have taken him a whole week. He must have gone wrong somewhere. But make it he did, although he didn't know it at first. Because all was changed. The house was no longer standing. It was nothing but a pile of rubble – as were their neighbours' houses. There was no one around. Birdsong filled the air. Uri sat on a piece of the old kitchen wall and cried his heart out. Until then he hadn't known how strongly he'd been clinging to the hope that the house would be standing, his mother cooking in the kitchen, his sister playing in the garden. Throughout it all. Through everything that had happened to him. He'd never felt so alone. He had to face the possibility that he'd never see his family again, and it was almost too much for his little-boy heart to bear.

When he was all cried out, Uri got up and looked around the rubble, remembering where everything used to be, imagining it as it once was. Some of his parents' furniture was amazingly intact. There was the kitchen table, and his parents' bed seemed to have fallen through the roof and landed where the dining room used to be. A thousand memories of his family all together. He cried again when he found the shredded remains of a poster that used to be on his bedroom wall. He looked for signs that his mother and sister had been there before him – perhaps looking for him. But there were none. He did find a teddy that Hannah had left during their hasty move to Ghetto. He remembered her crying for it one night. There was nothing his parents could do. They weren't allowed to go back. Uri hadn't understood that at the time. He saw now how they had tried to shelter him from everything. Now, less than a year later, there was so much he knew. So much he wished he didn't.

He picked up the teddy and stuffed it into his knapsack. Then he wandered down to the river behind the house. It was still there, remarkably unchanged. The same water, the same rocks. Just as he'd seen it in his dreams. He stripped off and dived in. He imagined he was a fish, quicksilver and light. Fish didn't have to worry about being Jewish. They were just fish. Or he could be an otter. He rolled, he splashed, he played. He felt nine years old again. But once he was out of the water, the familiar heaviness descended upon him and he was eleven-year-old Uri once more, with everything that he knew.

He lay on a rock until the sun had dried him off. Then he dressed and walked back to the house. His stomach was starting its eternal rumbling and he'd had an idea. He went to where his father's kitchen garden used to be. There was a small chance . . . yes! Just as he had hoped. The raspberry canes were laden with fruit and there was no one to eat it. No one but Uri and the birds. He gorged himself, then moved on to the gooseberries. He'd never have considered them before the war, but now . . . When he'd eaten his fill, he stuffed as many berries as he could into his knapsack. Then he headed back to the camp. He had nowhere else to go.

The return journey took him four days. His raids on abandoned kitchen gardens sustained him as he went. He thought a lot as he walked, mostly about his family. By the time he reached the camp, he'd come to a decision. The next day, he approached one of the teachers at the camp's makeshift school.

'What is it, Uri?'

'My father has family in Ireland. Will you help me get a letter to them?'

* * *

It took weeks to get an address for Samuel's cousin. They finally tracked him down through one of the Jewish agencies. Then the letter was sent. Uri wrote it but the teacher helped him and made sure the return address was legible. Uri felt as if he was sending out a letter in a bottle.

For two whole months he waited, each day checking the post, each day more anxious. He'd never met this man or his people. Would they even care about his existence? Be willing to take in a boy they'd never met?

At last a reply, with a return address in Dublin. Uri went off on his own to read it – his entire future in his hands. He opened the letter and this was what he read:

My dearest Uri,
I am overjoyed to hear of your survival. I can only assume from your letter that your father and the rest of your family were not so fortunate. Nothing would make me happier than for you to come and live with us. Of course you must come. I will set things in motion immediately. In the meantime, please write often.
G-d be with you,
Jacob Rosenberg

Uri clutched the letter to his chest and closed his eyes. He was no longer alone in the world.

But the plan was to take another three years to come to fruition. Not until 1948 did Ireland agree to take in a hundred and fifty refugee Jewish children. The government didn't want to, but its leader, de Valera, made them.

Uri arrived at the port at North Wall, a tired, undernourished fourteen-year-old. His new family were there to meet him on dry land. He recognized them from photos they had sent.

They embraced him as if they had known him for ever and brought him back to their home – the first proper home he'd known in years. It was a heady experience. At first, it overwhelmed him and he didn't know what to do or say. But they were so welcoming, so kind, so full of unconditional love for this boy whom they had never met that they saved him.

There was his uncle Jacob – because that was what he was instructed to call him – his aunt Martha and his two young cousins, ten-year-old David and eight-year-old Sarah. They astounded him, these happy, robust, pink-cheeked people. He wasn't used to seeing such well-fed Jews. And the children played so happily, as if they'd never had to endure hardship or witness a bad thing in all their lives. Which, of course, they hadn't. Uri vaguely recalled having been like that once.

At first, he didn't believe in them, his faith in humankind smashed almost to nothing. But, little by little, they won his trust and later his love.

Jacob was a tailor, and the following year, Uri began his apprenticeship in that trade. He was hard-working, quick, dextrous and, most of all, grateful for being given a second chance. He learned quickly and advanced rapidly. It seemed as if his luck had turned. He wondered sometimes if it was possible for a person to use up all of their bad-luck quota for a lifetime. If it was, he had certainly used up – exceeded – his. But he wasn't optimistic enough to believe that.

Jacob's business partner – a Mr Stern – had a daughter. Her name was Deborah. She would come to the shop sometimes. She had glossy curls, which bounced every time she laughed, which was often. And her dimples. Uri could have watched them for hours. She was the most beautiful thing he had ever seen. Now he knew that perfection existed in this imperfect world.

'Close your mouth, Uri, you're catching flies.' The other men had laughed at him. Which embarrassed him because he wasn't normally so transparent in his emotions. Uri was a reserved, serious and well-mannered young man, prone to dark moods but also to great kindness. Had his destiny been different, he might have been different. But that was something neither he nor anyone else would ever know for sure.

Miraculously, she liked him too. Her light was drawn to his darkness. He pulled her in. It was lucky that she was a forward and loquacious girl, because he might never have had the courage to approach her.

She would come up to him in the workshop and engage him in conversation. This wasn't always easy: Uri's innate reticence, combined with the dumbstruck nature of his regard for her, rendered him monosyllabic, but she must have sensed that there was something there, something beyond words, in the same way that Uri saw something beneath the girlish dimples. Depth. A woman deep enough and strong enough to take him on. She might even be his *bashert*. His soul-mate.

So it was that he found himself knocking on Mr Stern's office door one afternoon.

'Come in.'

The fear that Uri felt surprised him. He hadn't felt such fear for a long time – because nothing had meant so much to him for a long time. Once he had thought that there was nothing – no one – left for anyone to take away from him. But now there was.

Mr Stern's face opened out into a smile. 'Uri. What can I do for you?' The older man leaned back in his chair, glad of the distraction, and placed his hands behind his head.

Uri closed the door behind him and, cap in hand, approached the desk. 'Mr Stern.'

'Yes?'

'It's about your daughter.'

'Ah.'

'I would like your permission to ask Deborah to go dancing with me this Saturday night.'

Uri waited and waited, as Mr Stern regarded him solemnly for what seemed like an age. Finally, he spoke: 'You have my permission.'

Uri allowed himself to breathe. 'I do?'

Mr Stern laughed. A deep, raspy chuckle. 'Why the surprise?'

'Because I have nothing.'

That shocked them both and hung in the air between the two men, waiting for a response. It was a long time coming, as Reuben Stern thought back on the years he'd known this boy – now a man – how from the very first day he'd observed his capacity for hard work, his respect for his elders, his loyalty, his integrity. His gratitude.

'I think you have everything my daughter needs,' he said quietly.

'Thank you, sir.' Uri inclined his head and backed towards the door.

'And besides,' said Mr Stern, as Uri was about to leave, 'you're Jewish, aren't you?'

That Saturday night, Uri's heart caught in his throat every time he looked at Deborah and when his arm encircled her waist, her hand resting gently on his shoulder. Many years later, the widowed Uri could still remember the feel of her in his arms. He didn't even have to close his eyes: Deborah was as real to him as if she were still living and breathing beside him.

They were betrothed a year later, but it was another full year before the wedding ceremony took place. A year in which Uri worked outlandish hours to earn enough to set up home with his bride.

The week before the ceremony, in which the bride and groom were not permitted to see each other, nearly killed Uri, but it made his first glimpse of Deborah on their wedding day, her eyes sparkling with unshed tears beneath her veil, all the more mesmerizing. As they stood under the *chuppah*, the seven blessings recited, Uri had the strangest feeling that something was being returned to him – the feminine element of his life, which had been missing since that first day in the camp. And in the riotous celebration that followed, he laughed as he hadn't done since he was ten years old.

He marvelled at the forces that had brought him to this point in his life. An orphan, but with a family. In a strange land, but with a home. And now setting up his own home and about to start his own family.

On their wedding night, Uri told Deborah what had happened to him and his family during the war. Even the part about his father being shot and his own hand in it. He hadn't told another soul. But she was his wife now, and part of him. She listened to the grim reality of a life she had only half guessed at and they cried in each other's arms. Deborah promised Uri that it would be her life's work to heal his pain with her love. She was as good as her word.

They waited a long time for the children to arrive, so long that they'd begun to think they wouldn't come at all. Part of Uri was content with this – a part he tried to keep hidden from Deborah. Did he really want to bring his children into a world in which so many terrible things could happen? He didn't know that he could survive another loss. But the children arrived in their own good time. Deborah thought them a miracle.

They had two sons – Seth and Aaron. The day Seth was born, Uri finally knew how much his father had loved him. He'd always thought he'd known, but now he knew it in his soul. And when he saw Deborah with their child, he understood how much his mother had loved him.

The boys grew, as boys do. They gave him unimaginable joy and unimaginable sadness – first, because they would never know their grandparents and, second, because their grandparents would never know them. He wondered what kind of aunt Hannah would have been. What type of woman would that precocious child have become?

There were times when Seth looked so like his grandfather, Samuel, that Uri felt as if God was ripping out his heart with his bare hands. Such piercing, bittersweet pain. And when Seth exhibited a flair for gardening, Uri knew for sure that his father lived on. He taught Seth everything he knew, everything his own father had taught him, and he watched that talent grow and blossom.

But a part of him could never fully connect with his children, the same part that couldn't talk about the past. They felt it and he felt it too. It was at its worst when they were teenagers, their moodiness colliding with his own. They were all so lucky in having Deborah to coddle, correct and act as a warm, cuddly buffer between them.

By the time Deborah died, they had reached an accommodation, Uri and his sons. They gathered around each other and held each other up, urging each other to go on in their own individual ways. Privately, Uri didn't know if he could. Deborah had sustained him for so long that there were days when he felt he could no longer go on living. He survived for his sons, and in memory of those who hadn't had any choice as to whether they lived or died.

Then one day, about a year after Deborah's death, Uri saw a notice in a local food store. Or was it a sign?

Could it be that, for a second time, a garden would save his life?

45

Pearl, the quiet but intense Protestant lady, had set Aoife thinking. Even if she didn't want the gathering to be religious in the strictest sense of the word, perhaps they could inject a little meaning into it to make it something more than a mere autumn party.

The name itself was something they discussed endlessly. The children were vociferously unanimous in favour of the Autumn Party. Emily, who was now on the phone almost daily with her constant ideas and enthusiasms, wanted to call it Cornucopia, in reference to the ancient symbol of food and abundance, otherwise known as the horn of plenty.

'I have one of those,' said Seth.

'Stop!' Aoife hissed – Mrs Prendergast was within earshot.

'I don't know what all the fuss is about,' the older lady said. 'Why can't we just call it a harvest festival and have done with it?'

'That's too traditional,' said Aoife.

'What's wrong with tradition?'

'Nothing. But it might give people the wrong impression. Make people think it's something it's not. Like what happened with your friend Pearl.'

'She's no friend of mine, dear.'

'Okay. But you know what I mean.'

Mrs Prendergast was silent, which indicated that she did know what Aoife meant but wasn't going to admit it.

Then Aoife suggested, 'Fall Harvest.'

'No,' said Uri, very firmly, surprising Aoife as he normally offered no opinion on the matter, instead listening to their endless discussions with tolerant amusement. Seth seemed uncomfortable too. It wasn't until she got home and looked up 'Fall Harvest' on the Internet that she discovered why. Her face burned, even though she was alone in her own house: it was a term the Nazis had used to describe a particular phase of Jewish murders.

Mrs Prendergast had got Aoife thinking about tradition. She remembered the corn dollies of her childhood and realized that she had no clue as to their significance. So she looked them up too. She learned that the practice of plaiting wheat stalks to create a straw figure came from the belief that the corn spirit lived in the wheat and, as it was harvested, fled to the wheat that remained. By making the dolly, people believed they were keeping the spirit alive for the following year and the new crop. The next spring, the dolly would be ploughed back into the earth.

Aoife had a word with Liam's teacher, purchased several wheatsheaves at the local agricultural show and had the boys and girls of that year's junior infants busily making a veritable army of corn dollies.

Another memory from the harvest festivals of her youth was the bread. From the Church of England primary school she had attended, she had a clear recollection of a large loaf of bread in the shape of a wheatsheaf. She consulted Mrs Prendergast.

'Yes, that's right. It's to symbolize thanksgiving for the harvest. They usually surround the bread with lots of fruit and vegetables.'

'Like a display. What a great idea. We could do that. Surround a loaf with produce from the garden. Let the people see what we've been doing. Do you think the Mothers' Union would bake the loaf for us?'

'Well, I could help you with it if you like.'

'Really?'

'Yes. I did it a few times when Lance was a child.'

'That would be terrific. In fact . . .'

'What is it now?'

Aoife's mind was joyfully ticking overtime. She had a dim recollection of an essay one of her students had written. It concerned the Celtic celebration of the harvest, the feast of Lammas, or the celebration of bread, when all the women of a village would come together to prepare the bread, this being seen as a sacred ritual in itself.

'We need lots of bread to serve with the soup. Why don't we all get together for a great big baking session?'

'Who's "we"?'

'You, me, Emily, Emily's mother, Kathy . . . Well, that's it, really.'

Emily was coming up a few days early to help. She was bringing Rose and her mother with her. They were staying with Mrs Prendergast – her first house guests, Aoife reckoned, for a very long time.

'So just women, then?'

'I think so. That'd be more fun, wouldn't it?'

'You can use my kitchen if you like.'

'Thank you!'

'Or had you made that assumption already?'

'Kind of.'

Mrs Prendergast tried to look grumpy and failed miserably. The matter was settled. Aoife began organizing the ingredients that very afternoon.

The news Aoife received the following day caused her to feel both happy and anxious: her mother was coming for the party. While she was looking forward to having her there, and happy that Liam would get to see his nana, she couldn't help but worry. She supposed this had mostly to do with Seth. Her mother had known Michael and that seemed to matter. Furthermore, he had been her beloved son-in-law, the father of her grandchildren. Of course, she didn't *have* to tell her about Seth. It wasn't as if they were living together, and nobody else knew about it yet.

They had decided to keep it secret – mainly for Liam and Kathy's sake in case it all went pear-shaped. So that was it. She wouldn't tell her. Nothing to worry about.

The Autumn Party was the title decided upon, greeted with much whooping and jumping by the children. They put flyers all over the neighbourhood:

> Come join us for our Autumn Party,
> Music sweet and food so hearty,
> Homemade soup and bread for all,
> Come celebrate the harvest haul.

'What music?' said Emily. Aoife had just read the flyer down the phone to her.

'Hold on. I haven't read the rest of it. "Bring your musical instruments, dancing shoes, story-telling hats and hours of sunshine." '

'Oh.'

'Well. What do you think?'

'Um. It's very good. Only . . .'

'What?'

'Do you mean we're just relying on people bringing their own instruments and making their own music?'

'That's right.'

'Isn't that a bit risky?'

'How so?'

'What if they don't, and everyone's standing around waiting to be entertained?'

'It'll be fine. They'll make their own entertainment.'

'If you're sure.'

'I am.'

Then Aoife's mother arrived. They went out to Howth, a mutual, almost unspoken decision – they'd both loved it in their separate childhoods. It was to be beside the sea as much as anything else, on the beautiful, golden, windswept autumn day, Liam running ahead in a state of high excitement. The seals were in the harbour – five of them, so close that you could hear them breathing, watch their nostrils opening and closing, see their sleek, glistening bellies as they rolled over and dived. A dog stood on the quayside, barking dementedly at them. Aoife bought a bag of fish scraps from the fishmonger across the way and Liam fed the seals, laughing joyously as they caught the fragments in their mouths.

They bought late-season ice creams – ninety-nines with red syrup – and devoured them on the way to the lighthouse, waves crashing against the walls and roaring in their ears. Then they doubled back on themselves and walked up the hill to Howth Head, keeping the sea on their left.

Aoife hadn't been to Howth since she'd settled in Ireland permanently. It was on the other side of the city now, and she hadn't wanted to come on her own. She noticed and her mother commented on how Liam's legs wouldn't have been sturdy enough to make this climb just a year before.

'He looks good,' she said. 'You both do. My God, Aoife. I was so worried about you moving to Ireland. It seemed like such a rash decision to make at the time. But now I can see you were right to follow your instincts. The move has done you the world of good. Both of you. I haven't seen you looking so happy since . . . well, since Michael.'

'I still miss him.'

'Of course you do. You always will. That's normal.'

'And I'll never let Liam forget him.'

'And neither should you. But that doesn't mean you can't move on. Both of you. The last thing Michael would want is for you to stay stuck in your grief for ever.'

That afternoon, Aoife took her mother to visit the garden. She was fishing around for her key in the bag when she saw that the gate was standing wide open. That was unusual. Unprecedented, even. She walked cautiously inside. At first it looked as if no one was about. Then Uri emerged from the foliage like a woodland creature. He grinned broadly at Aoife.

'What's going on?' she asked.

'It's gone through.'

'What has?'

'The sale. You're looking at the proud owner of . . .' he swept his hand in an expansive gesture '. . . this.'

'Oh, Uri.' She kissed him on both cheeks. 'That's wonderful. Congratulations. Oh, where are my manners? This is my mother, Moya.'

Uri kissed Aoife's mother firmly and enthusiastically. He looked as if he was in the mood for kissing everyone.

'Does this mean you're going to keep the gates open all the time?'

'Yes. Every day from sunrise to sunset. From now on, it will be a true community garden.'

'What does Mrs Prendergast make of all this?'

'I don't know. I haven't told her yet.' He was too polite to point out that it was no longer any of Mrs Prendergast's business.

Next to arrive were Emily, Rose, and Emily's mother, Bridget. Rose was crawling now and pulling herself up on anything that was available to her, be it stable or otherwise. Mrs Prendergast, having forgotten what babies were like, had left her home exactly as it was, much to Emily's fright. She spent the first half of her visit removing breakables from all the lower surfaces.

She seemed every inch the proper mammy now. It was as if Rose had always been a part of her. In a way, she always had. Big pea, little pea. So alike.

Upon arrival, Emily released Rose into the hungry arms of Uri and Mrs Prendergast and went directly to inspect her sensory garden. Aoife found her on the swing seat, beneath the entangled stems of the jasmine and honeysuckle, both past their prime, but beautiful in their autumnal state. 'Do you mind if I sit with you?'

'Please do.' Emily patted the seat beside her and smiled. She sighed as Aoife sat down. 'It's good to be back.'

'Are you staying?'

'Yes. Mum'll be here for a week to settle us into our new flat. I have Rose enrolled into the crèche in college. Only two years left to go. Then I'll hopefully be able to get a job and support her properly.'

'Sounds like you've got it all sorted.'

Emily laughed. 'Hardly. My God, it's hard work, all this baby stuff. Why didn't you tell me?'

'I didn't want to put you off.'

'I can see that now. But . . . she's lovely, Aoife.'

'She is.'

'I can't believe she's mine. I'm so happy.'

'Good! Good for you.'

'Mum's been brilliant.'

'And your dad?'

'Great.' She laughed. 'I can't believe it, really, how well it's turned out.' A cloud passed over her face. 'All I put myself through. And Rose. It was all for nothing.' Her sigh seemed to come from a deep well inside her.

'Come on, Emily. Enough of the maternal guilt. The important thing is how well it's all worked out. Remember how terrified you were of your dad's reaction?'

'Yes. I guess Rose just won him over. You should see him with her when he thinks no one's looking.' She laughed. 'I think he still feels he has to come across as stern and disapproving in case my little sisters think it's okay to arrive home with their own bundles of joy.'

They swung together for a while, lost in the motion, Aoife entranced by the way the delicate tendrils of jasmine and honeysuckle twirled and wrapped themselves around each other.

'How are things with you?'

'Great.'

'And Seth?'

'He's fine too.'

'You know what I mean.'

'No, I don't.'

'Fair enough.'

46

'I keep finding bowls of goo everywhere. Places you wouldn't believe – the airing cupboard, for pity's sake,' Mrs Prendergast complained in a whisper. But Aoife knew from her expression that part of her was enjoying the unpredictability of sharing her house with other human beings. Not only did she have Lance at home for the first time in years, she also had Emily, her mother and baby Rose staying with her.

'What do you mean "bowls of goo"?'

'Some experiment to do with the breadmaking.'

'Oh, I know what that is. She's making sourdough bread. She'll be trying to capture particles of yeast from the atmosphere.'

'For goodness' sake. Can she not buy it in packets in the supermarket like everyone else?'

Each woman had been assigned a different type of bread: Emily, the aforementioned sourdough, and her mother, Bridget, sodabread because she made it every morning of her life and was an acknowledged world expert. Aoife's mother, Moya, was on poppy-seed detail. Aoife and Mrs Prendergast, as well as being in charge of the wheatsheaf loaf, were attempting a variety of flavoured breads such as sun-dried tomato, cheese and onion, and raisin. Kathy's job was to squelch down the newly risen dough with the palms of her freshly washed hands. She was also the official licker of bowls and utensils. They felt that, between them, they had all bases covered. Aoife just hoped they weren't being overly ambitious.

On the night before the party they gathered together. Five and a half women in Mrs Prendergast's fabled kitchen. Seth called them 'the coven' and Aoife privately thought he had a point. There was something about a group of women together, a unique dynamic, fascinating to feel and watch. It was in the way they sat so comfortably, kicked off their shoes, threw their heads back and laughed with abandon. Aoife perceived that the women she had come to love most in all the world were in this group. The thought made her smile as she watched Mrs Prendergast boss everyone about. She hoped this wouldn't cause a clash with Bridget, who was quite a domineering presence herself and used to being in charge of a kitchen. She seemed quite relaxed so far, though.

There were a few bottles of wine knocking around. Aoife wondered if she should suggest opening one. On the other hand, she didn't want them all so pissed that they messed up the bread. She'd bide her time and choose the moment of inebriation carefully.

They all wore pinnies. Aoife's was patterned with flowers and kittens. She felt as if she were in home-economics class, Mrs Prendergast the strict and bossy teacher.

'Now, girls,' she was saying, relishing her role as the one in charge, 'it's probably best if we keep to our own sections of kitchen at all times.'

They were designated a piece of counter each. Everybody had brought their own bowls and bits and pieces, which they laid out now. When this was done, Aoife announced: 'Okay, ladies. Let the great bake-off commence.' She saw Mrs Prendergast's sour face and understood that the older woman had been planning on making such a declaration herself. Oh, well. Too late now.

So, off they went. Weighing, measuring, sifting, mixing, kneading, rolling, chattering. So much chattering that a passerby might have been forgiven for mistaking the noise for that of a gaggle of excited schoolgirls released on a school trip.

There were quiet times too, every woman intent on her work. Aoife and Emily looked up during one such interlude at the same time. They smiled at each other, then went back to their dough. Aoife felt as if she was participating in some ancient ritual. There was something about making bread – the staff of life. Perhaps it was the knowledge that generations of her female ancestors before her had done the same. It was a soothing notion that filled her with a sense of contentment. Aoife hadn't made bread in years, but she had helped her mother sometimes when she was a girl. She was amazed at how quickly it came back to her, as if the knowledge had been locked away inside her the whole time. A secret memory. Coded, in fact, in her very DNA.

They came to the point when most of them had to stop and wait for their bread to rise. Not Bridget's sodabread, which was the first to enter the oven and fill the air with its delectable aroma. They cleared up as best they could, and then the clinking began – of chilled wine bottles and glasses. A party atmosphere invaded the kitchen. Mrs Prendergast produced a tray of nibbles she'd secretly prepared earlier. They descended on them greedily, in the manner of women who know that no men are present. No pretence of delicacy here. 'I thought we might need these to stop us munching the bread,' she said. 'Looks like I was right.'

'Well, smelling all that delicious bread baking is making me feel starving,' said Moya. 'Especially since I know I'm not allowed to eat any of it.'

'Not necessarily,' said Emily. 'I mean, we're making so much bread that it'd probably be okay to nibble just a little bit.'

'But if we start we might never stop,' said Bridget.

'Do you think we've made too much?' Aoife was suddenly filled with fear. 'What if nobody shows up?'

'They will.'

'But what if they don't? What'll we do with all the bread?'

'We can bring it home and eat it ourselves.'

'Or give it to the ducks.'

'Don't worry, Aoife. It'll be fine.'

'I wonder how the Mothers' Union are getting on with the soup.'

Joyce, Pearl and some other members had volunteered to make the honey-roasted parsnip soup. Aoife had brought them around a massive crate of parsnips that afternoon.

'Oh, I'm sure they're on their second gallon already,' said Mrs Prendergast. 'Honestly. That woman. You should have heard her yesterday. "All the honey is sourced locally." I mean, what did she do? Take down the names and addresses of the bees?'

Aoife giggled as she imagined the scene and the ruthless efficiency that Joyce would apply to it. But she was grateful. Those women had come up trumps for her.

The atmosphere mellowed as the women sipped their wine. It was during this time that Lance came home and unwittingly walked into the kitchen. He blinked a couple of times, as if caught in headlights. 'Oh, I'm sorry. I didn't know you were all here.' This was clear. He wouldn't have come anywhere near them if he had known. The group of women knew their power to intimidate a lone male. They felt their strength in numbers. 'Something smells good.'

'Are you hungry, Lance? Shall I make you a sandwich?'

'That'd be great.'

'Go through to the sitting room. I'll bring it in to you.'

He nodded his thanks and beat a hasty retreat.

'Poor guy,' said Emily.

'How's he getting on?' Aoife asked Mrs Prendergast, when she came back.

'Very well.' She smiled a smile of genuine happiness. 'Although he thinks he isn't because that trollop of a girlfriend of his has broken up with him. Lost interest when she found out there was no more money in the pot. He'll work out soon enough that he's had a lucky escape. Which,' she said, suddenly switching her focus on to Aoife, 'means that he's free, for anybody who might consider him.'

'I – I –' Aoife was mortified.

'Oh, I forgot. You're otherwise engaged with Seth.' She smiled again, wickedly this time.

Aoife turned the colour of beetroot. Everybody laughed.

'Who else knows?' she asked, in a strangled tone.

'Aoife,' said Emily, 'the dogs on the street know. Even Harriet here knows.' She reached out a stockinged foot and rubbed the supine, overweight Harriet, who was passed out under the table, having satisfied herself with lickings of flour and rogue pumpkin seeds. Harriet snorted in her sleep and emitted a silent but violent fart, which rose up and mingled with the scent of the sodabread, somewhere around ceiling level.

Aoife took a glug of her wine, mind ticking furiously, craving the quick fix of revenge. She felt her mother's eyes on her but didn't look up. 'You and Uri seem to be getting on very well lately, Mrs Prendergast.'

'Yes, we are.'

'I'd almost say that you're inseparable.'

Emily's mother interjected, 'I'd imagine that when you get to your time in life, Mrs Prendergast, it's more a question of companionship.'

Mrs Prendergast faced them. 'Actually, no. It's all about the sex.'

There was a moment's silence – then the room exploded into uproar and laughter.

'Uh-oh. Little pitchers have big ears,' said Moya, when the general hilarity had died down, inclining her head in the direction of Kathy, who was sitting in the corner, goggle-eyed. She was in a privileged position: a child in the company of adults who had forgotten about her.

'Kathy,' said Emily, in a bid to distract, 'it's time for you to push your hand into the dough. Remember I told you it would be your special job? It should be ready by now.'

The distraction appeared to work. They peered into their tea-towel-covered bowls. As if by magic, the dough had risen. To Kathy's disgust, they made her wash her hands again. 'I already washed them.'

'But you've been licking your fingers.'

'No, I haven't.'

'Yes, you have.' A chorus.

'Oh!'

But she did it and the first bowl was set in front of her.

'Ready?' said Aoife.

'Ready!' shouted Kathy.

'One, two, three – go!'

Kathy splatted her hand into the dough and laughed as the air escaped and the mixture flattened. 'That felt funny. I want to do it again.'

She did it to the remaining mixtures, punching the last two with her little fist. 'Pow!'

The women finished their loaves and dispatched them to the waiting oven.

'I hope someone's sober enough to set the timer,' said Aoife.

They finished their wine as they waited.

It was after eleven by the time all the loaves were baked,

including the *pièce de résistance* – the one in the shape of a wheatsheaf.

'Come on, Miss,' said Aoife to Kathy. 'Your eyes are nearly falling out of your head. Let's get you home to bed. You have a big day tomorrow.'

They all had. Hopefully they wouldn't be too hung-over to do the necessary.

'Plenty of water before you go to sleep tonight, ladies,' she called, as they were leaving.

'Who's minding Liam?' Emily walked them to the door.

'Seth.'

'Really? That's cosy. Will he be staying over?'

'He will not. He'll be bringing Kathy straight home.'

'Goodnight, then. See you first thing.' Emily kissed Aoife's cheek.

'Goodnight – cheeky pup.' She smiled.

They stepped outside and pulled their coats tightly around them, Aoife, Kathy and Moya. Aoife knew that her mother was dying to ask her about Seth so she chattered animatedly and aimlessly, not allowing her to get a word in. She was grateful, too, for Kathy's presence. It meant Moya couldn't ask her detailed questions.

They were almost home by the time Moya managed to interrupt her daughter: 'Aoife. Stop talking for one second, will you? I couldn't be happier for you. I think it's wonderful news. I really like him.'

Aoife relaxed. 'Really?'

'Yes, really.'

They were home. Seth let them in.

'How are things?' said Aoife.

'Great.'

'Did Liam behave?'

'Yes. Asleep only half an hour after his official bedtime.'

'Not bad. That's better than I normally do.'

'Did you have a good time?'

Kathy jumped up and down. 'I splatted my hand in the dough!'

'You did?'

'Yes. It was fun.'

'That's great. Now, leave your coat on. We're going straight home to bed.'

'Goodnight, Seth. I'm going up myself.'

'Night, Mrs Madigan.'

She surprised him by embracing him warmly, as one might a future son-in-law.

Seth and Aoife smiled at each other.

'Night, then,' he said. 'See you in the morning.'

'Thanks for babysitting Liam.'

'No problem.'

'Daddy, you can give her a kiss, you know. I won't mind.'

Seth looked at his daughter in surprise, then at Aoife. She shrugged. He gave her a peck on the cheek. Then, to Aoife's delight, Kathy did the same, and hugged her ferociously.

Aoife stood in the doorway, watching them as they got into the jeep. She heard Kathy's voice ringing out in the crisp night air. 'Daddy?'

'Yes, Kathy?'

'What's sex?'

47

The morning was sacred, as was everything in it. Wreaths of mist rose from the earth. To some, it might have looked like smoke. The landscape was otherworldly. Ethereal. The garden . . . but somehow not the garden. The apple trees reared out of the mist like giant arthritic hands, the earth beneath them sweetened with windfalls. The mist cleared a patch over the lawn, revealing a fairy ring that had appeared overnight. Aoife laughed. The sound was uncommon.

She was the first. In a while, other figures would emerge through the mist. One by one. Seth. Uri. Emily. Mrs Prendergast. Custodians of the garden all. To dress and decorate her on this her special day.

Seth and Uri were the first to arrive, erecting a hut with wooden walls and a living roof – evergreen boughs that wouldn't shed.

'What is it?'

'A *sukkah*. It's part of the tradition of the Jewish harvest festival. In ancient times, the Jewish farmers would walk out of the village each day to tend their crops. At harvest, they built shelters in the fields to avoid wasting time walking backwards and forwards. That's where it comes from. Families put them up in their gardens during the festival and eat their meals in them. I thought we could set up a table and chairs and people can have their refreshments in it.'

'What a great idea.'

One by one the women came. Tables were carried out and covered with cloths – yellow, orange, brown and gold – all the colours of the harvest. Pretty soon they were laden, the first with the wheatsheaf loaf. The shape was a little uneven. Aoife thought she noticed a few of the Mothers' Union women eyeing it critically, but that might have been her own insecurity. Then they surrounded the loaf with the choicest produce they could find, sunbursts of colour, like a living work of art. It would, thought Aoife, make you feel quite proud. Then there was a table selling surplus vegetables and another for fruit. A big sign was erected above: 'All profits to be ploughed back into the garden'. Certain parties found this funny.

Then there was the table for non-edibles.

'Look what they've done with my lavender!' Emily said, beside herself with excitement, and rushed off to grab Rose again. This time she had crawled under the vegetable table and was pulling at the cloth from underneath in a manner designed to bring everything tumbling on top of her.

Lavender toilet water, lavender room spray, dried lavender bags for underwear drawers and liquid lavender soap.

'We tried to make bars of soap but we couldn't get them to set.' Joyce sounded apologetic.

'You don't have to explain yourself to me, Joyce. As far as I'm concerned, you've worked miracles. And the packaging is divine. What lovely little bottles!'

Joyce smiled like the sun coming out. 'It was no trouble at all.'

'Well, I'd say you went to a huge amount of trouble.'

'I enjoyed it. We all did. And we're just so delighted to be involved.'

The Mothers' Union had made the same range of products in rose. Aoife was starting to feel seriously excited. She could have kissed every one of those women. Perhaps she would before the day was out.

The corn dollies, courtesy of the Low Babies of St Mary's, came in a startling array of shapes and sizes. Some had one leg longer than the other. Others were bona fide amputees. One even appeared to have no head. But each was cherished and proudly displayed in Mrs Prendergast's kitchen, in her sunroom, above the stalls and from the roof of the *sukkoh* – on either side of a big, colourful sign with the words '*Bruchim Habaim*' and underneath, 'Welcome'. The less edible-looking apples also served to decorate its roof, along with artfully placed fig leaves.

But the table that Aoife kept returning to, the table that nobody could keep their eyes off, was the one with all the cakes. It looked fit to topple over, under the weight of so much confectionery: fresh fig filo tart, Greek yogurt and fig cake, rhubarb pie, rhubarb crumble, pomegranate cheesecake, berry brûlée tart, blueberry muffins, blackcurrant bread and butter pudding, alpine strawberry and rose petal shortcakes, fresh berry pavlova, plum and marzipan pastries, cherry and hazelnut strudel, plum tart, plum crumble, pear and polenta cake, Dutch apple cake, French apple tart, chocolate, pear and pecan pie, filo-topped apple pie and spiced apple crumble.

Aoife wanted everyone to leave so she could dive in and scoff the lot. Again, the ladies of the Mothers' Union had excelled themselves. And that was before you got to the jam table: damson jam, strawberry jam, bramble jam, bramble and apple jam, bramble jelly, quince jelly, redcurrant jelly, crabapple jelly, damson chutney, pickled peach and chilli chutney, and fig and date chutney.

What with all the goodies on display, it was amazing that the garden wasn't stripped bare. But it was as if nothing had been picked: it gave the impression that you could go on picking fruit and vegetables for ever and never run out. A sense of unlimited abundance.

The gate opened at twelve, which meant it was almost time to organize the teas and coffees and bring out the soup and breads. This was the moment the Mothers' Union had been waiting for – the moment they got to set foot inside Mrs Prendergast's kitchen. They gripped each other's arms and giggled like schoolgirls. Mrs Prendergast had been up half the night scrubbing the place. She regarded them sternly. 'I'll thank you to remember,' she said, 'that the rest of the house is out of bounds. If you need to use the toilet, there's a perfectly adequate Portaloo at the far end of the garden.'

'Oh, chill out, Myrtle.'

'I beg your pardon?'

'That's what my grandson says to me. Now, let's get this show on the road.'

Get the show on the road they did. By five to twelve, everything was set up. The soup was hot, the ladle gleamed. The sun had burned off the last of the morning mist. The gate was open. They were ready.

48

The people trickled in at first. Then they formed a steady stream. Before long, a river of bodies was flowing along the pathways of the garden. Aoife hardly had time to register pleasure at the turnout, so engrossed was she in selling leeks, handing out teas and trying to keep track of her son.

'Has anyone seen Liam?'

'He's over there.'

'Liam!'

He obliged his mother by running over, his face lit up with happiness from within. 'Yes, Mammy?'

'Did you just call me "Mammy"?'

'No.'

'It's okay if you did.'

'Is it?'

'Of course it is.'

'It's just that the other boys in my class call their mummies Mammy.'

'That's fine, Liam. You can call me Mammy if you like.'

'Maybe I'll call you Mummy at home and Mammy when we're out. Okay?' He grinned and ran off to play.

'Stay where I can see you.'

A young man with a guitar slung across his shoulder approached her. She thought she recognized him from the college. He cleared his throat and stared at a pyramid of onions as he spoke to her. 'I was looking for the band.'

She beamed at him. 'You *are* the band!'

'What?'

Before he could run away, she was over to his side of the table with her arm around his shoulder. 'Now, I keep seeing people wandering around with various instruments. It's about time we got you all together.'

'What do you mean, I'm the band?'

'Well, we were hoping it would kind of spring up organically. Look, there's a man over there with a fiddle. Come with me.'

Aoife gathered up the bemused musicians and found some chairs, which they arranged in a semi-circle on the lawn. They had two guitarists, a traditional flautist, a guy with a set of uillean pipes, a fiddle-player and a Finnish woman with a bodhrán. Once the band members had got over their initial shock, they entered into the spirit of things. The music began, hesitantly at first, as Aoife walked back to the stalls, a very definite swing in her step. She'd secretly brought her tin whistle along. She was itching to play it but didn't want to come across as the plastic Paddy. Still, they had a Finn with a bodhrán. Maybe later. Right now, she was too busy.

She was back at the soup station, currently manned by Joyce and Emily. Joyce was in her element. 'The soup's going down a treat,' she said.

'I'm not surprised. I tasted some and it's beautiful. You were right to roast the parsnips first. Gives a much better flavour.'

Joyce tried to look modest. 'Oh, you don't get to my age without learning a trick or two, my dear.'

Aoife turned to Emily. 'It worked out.'

'What did?'

'The musicians.'

'Oh. Yes.'

'What's wrong?'

'Nothing.'

'Then why the glum face?'

'It's silly, really. It's just that nobody's eating my sourdough bread.'

Aoife looked down into the bread baskets. There did seem to be a higher proportion of sourdough left. Admittedly, it was quite forlorn and lumpen. 'It's only because sourdough doesn't rise as much as the other breads and they don't know what it is. They probably think it's normal bread gone wrong. It just needs some advertising.'

She wrote a sign in Magic Marker: 'Get the last of the sourdough bread.'

'Write that it's made with genuine rain water,' said Emily.

'What?'

'Aoife.'

She swivelled at the sound of her name. It was Seth. She smiled in relief.

'I haven't seen you in ages.'

'No. It's going well, isn't it?'

'Brilliant.'

'Hello, Aoife.' Megan stepped out from behind Seth. 'Good to see you again. You know, Kathy never stops talking about you and Liam. We'll have to make time for a proper chat one of these days.'

'I'd like that.' What she didn't like was the knowing way that Megan was looking at her.

'This is Siobhan, by the way.'

Aha. The other woman.

A voluptuous brunette emerged from Megan's shadow. She nodded at Aoife.

'Anyway,' said Megan, 'we won't keep you. It's clear you're up to your eyes. Come on, Kathleen.'

Aoife started at the name. She was surprised to see Kathy, whom she hadn't noticed before, running to her mother's side and taking her hand. 'Kathy's name is Kathleen?' she said.

'Yes.' Megan gave her an odd look.

'You know, all this time I assumed it was Katherine. I don't know why.'

'I suppose Katherine is more usual. No. I named her Kathleen after my grandmother.'

'I see.'

'Anyway, talk to you soon, I hope.' Megan threw a furtive look behind her to see where Seth and Siobhan were. They were standing a few yards away, Siobhan listening intently while Seth pointed at the herbaceous border. She leaned into Aoife. 'You've got a good man there, you know. Hang on to him. Unfortunately, he had one too many penises for me. Come on, Kathy! Let's take a look at this little hut.'

And off they went. Aoife's eyes followed them up the path towards the *sukkoh*. It was packed out, all the chairs occupied, people talking and laughing and eating – clearly taking the welcome sign at face value. Her eyes wandered across to the lawn where the musicians were in full flight. A woman she'd never seen before was leading the children in a session of Irish dancing. Liam was the only child doing his one-two-threes backwards. She allowed herself a smile and a moment to relax. If somebody told her this was heaven, she wouldn't be disappointed.

'Aoife.'

'Yes.'

'The Portaloo's blocked again.'

Mrs Prendergast was enjoying herself. Of course, she had no intention of admitting this to anyone. She was in the kitchen, wiping breadcrumbs off the counter.

Lance came in. 'Can I do anything to help?'

'No, thanks. It's all in hand.'

340

'Can I get you some soup? It's nearly all gone, you know.'

'No. It's all right, darling. I'm not hungry yet.'

'It's going well, isn't it?'

'Yes, it is.'

'I'm glad you didn't sell the garden to developers, Mum. You did the right thing.'

She stopped what she was doing and looked up at her son. 'Thank you for saying that, Lance.'

They smiled at each other. Then he came to her, put one long arm about her shoulders and hugged her to him. 'See you outside.'

''Bye, Lance.'

Alone again, she was surprised by the prickling sensation at the back of her eyes. 'Stupid old woman,' she said to herself, and resumed her cleaning.

When the kitchen was spotless, she went out to the hall. Imagine her surprise to find Pearl, Mothers' Unionist, floating down the stairs, her head turning this way and that, oblivious to Mrs Prendergast's presence.

'What do you think you're doing?'

Pearl nearly stumbled down the last few steps. 'Oh, Lord. I didn't see you there, Myrtle.'

'Clearly not.'

'I was just looking for a toilet.'

'Something wrong with the Portaloo?'

'Yes, actually. It's blocked.'

'Oh. Well, there's one at the end of the hall. Downstairs,' she said, with emphasis.

'Oh, thank you so much.'

Mrs Prendergast watched her, making sure she was going directly to the loo and making no detours. Honestly. Bunch of nosy, incontinent old biddies. She must have been mad agreeing to all this.

But then she went outside and her heart lifted. She could never have imagined such a thing. In *her* garden. Well, it wasn't technically her garden any more. But *her* garden. *Her* home. And she was part of it. Part of something really good. She felt the prickle at the back of her eyes again. She'd have to get that checked out. Probably glaucoma.

She stepped into the sun and into the milling throng. It was good to feel anonymous. She meandered along the path, humming slightly, her hands behind her back.

'Hello, Marnie.'

She stopped. She wanted to believe she was hearing things but she knew she wasn't. She turned and looked up at him. 'Hello, Martin.'

'Long time no see.'

'Indeed.'

'You're looking well.'

She didn't reply. She was too busy taking him in. Same frame. Less meaty now. Same features – craggier than before. Same blue eyes, a little faded but still Martin. He still had most of his own hair and teeth by the look of it.

'It must be . . .'

'Forty years.'

'Is it that long?'

'I've been keeping count.'

He smiled and she was back in the jazz cellar in Soho, barely twenty years old, her blue felt skirt swirling around her, about to be swept off her feet.

Her sum knowledge of Martin up to now had been that he was still alive. Lance saw him from time to time but she didn't ask questions as she didn't want to know. The memories kept popping up, one after another, like a slide show. Her eyes grew cold.

*   *   *

Myrtle held the blade to Martin's throat. Nobody moved. It was like some gruesome still life, her standing above him dramatically, him down on one knee, his neck twisted awkwardly. The clock ticked on the wall. A dog barked in a neighbouring garden.

'Now don't do anything stupid, Marnie.' Martin's voice was calm and cajoling.

'I've already done something stupid,' she said. 'I married you.' Then she grabbed a handful of hair on the top of his head. 'And don't. Tell me. What to do.' She tugged his hair roughly, several times, to emphasize her words. The blade dug deeper into his throat each time. A drop of blood trickled down his neck and fell on to the collar of the white shirt she'd ironed for him the night before. He felt the wetness.

'Oh, Jesus, Marnie. Please don't. I'm sorry. Truly I am.'

She was amazed at how calm she felt. How strong. She, Myrtle. Holding a man twice her size and breadth at her mercy. She knew it was partly luck she had him in such a position that, at the smallest move he made, she could slit his throat wide open. Like a horrible great gaping red grin.

She felt as if she were outside her own body, looking down on herself. Amazed at the bloodthirsty thoughts of the woman below her and the level of hatred she felt for her own husband. But not appalled. Never appalled. It was just. This was justice. She looked at Lance. He was hiding under the table, his head in his hands. He couldn't see. Just as well.

'Now, you listen to me and you listen to me carefully, Martin Prendergast. Give me one good reason why I shouldn't slit your throat right now.'

'Because I'm your husband.'

'Hah! Not good enough.' She tugged his hair another three times. Martin whimpered as the blade bit deep. She could

343

have laughed. What a coward. All this time and she'd never known.

'Please don't, Marnie.'

'I may decide to spare your life but I have my conditions.'

'What? What are they? Anything.'

'Anything?'

'That's what I said.'

'You're to leave this house immediately. You're to go directly to your solicitor and tell him you're transferring this entire property, including the garden, into my sole name. Then you tell him you're giving me a divorce on the grounds of *your* unreasonable behaviour. If my terms are unacceptable to you, I have some fresh bruises that the police might be interested in. Not to mention a very sympathetic doctor who will be more than happy to give me a detailed medical report going back years. Now. Do I make myself clear?'

'Yes.'

'Is everything all right?' It was the gardener. He was standing at the back door, a turnip in each hand, his face incredulous.

'Yes, thank you, Paddy. Mr Prendergast was just leaving.'

She released him. He sprang to his feet and faced her, backing away, rubbing his neck.

'Mad bitch,' he murmured.

She crossed her arms in a fishwife position. 'Leave your keys on the counter, please. You won't be needing them any more. And I'll have you know that the locks will be changed this evening so don't get any funny ideas.'

Like a man who'd seen a ghost, Martin dropped his keys on the kitchen counter and backed towards the door. When he reached it, he looked at the gardener, one last time at Myrtle, then turned and left. Only when he was out of view did Myrtle collapse on the floor, the knife clanging on the tiles beside her. She began to shake.

'Jesus Christ. I'm calling the police,' said Paddy.

'No, don't. Please. He won't be back. Lance, come here, my darling.'

Lance didn't move. Myrtle crawled under the table. 'Lance, it's all right. It's over. He's gone.'

Lance lifted his head and looked around. Then he threw himself into his mother's arms and they rocked together until they'd both calmed down.

'You're not going to throw me off your property, are you?'

'I couldn't if I wanted to. It's not my property any more.'

'You've sold the house?'

'No, just the garden.'

He nodded. 'This is a great set-up. I'm delighted to see it being put to such good use.'

'Is that so?'

He looked sharply at her. 'Yes, it is. You remember how fond I was of this garden.'

'Yes, I remember. Fonder of *it* than you were of me.'

'Now that's not fair.'

'Don't you turn up here after all this time, Martin Prendergast, and tell me what's fair.'

'You're right. I apologize.'

She inclined her head.

They started to walk along together.

'It's been under lock and key, you know, for the last forty years.'

'What? The garden?'

'Yes.'

'Why would you do something like that?'

'So I wouldn't be reminded of you, of course.'

345

'Of course.'

'How did you know about the party?'

'I saw one of the flyers. I moved house a while back. I'm living quite close now.'

'I know. Lance told me, in case I had the misfortune of bumping into you. You'll forgive me if I don't invite you over for dinner.'

He laughed. So familiar. 'You haven't changed a bit, Marnie.'

'Oh, yes, I have.'

'You know, I have too.'

'A leopard doesn't change his spots.'

'No. But people do.'

'I seriously doubt it. Not where you're concerned.'

'Look.' He stopped walking and they turned to face each other. 'Did Lance tell you I had a heart-attack?'

'He might have mentioned it.' What did he want from her? Sympathy?

'When something like that happens, it makes you think. I know it sounds clichéd, but it reminds you of what's important in life.'

He was staring into the middle distance and she took the opportunity to examine his features for any signs of the ravages of ill health.

'There were two reasons for me coming here today,' he said. 'The first was – well – I couldn't resist taking the opportunity to see this place again. I'm glad I did. And I'm glad I saw you too, Marnie.'

'Nobody calls me that any more.'

'I'm sorry. Myrtle. Because my second reason for coming today was to say sorry.'

She remained silent.

'For everything I've ever done to you. Every hardship I've

put you through. The hitting.' He bowed his head. 'Our baby. All the babies you never had. I'm so sorry, Marnie – Myrtle. It's not possible for me to make you understand how guilty I feel. Do you think you'd have it in you to forgive an old man?'

She gazed at him for a while.

And she thought of all those times.

All the bruises.

The hurts.

The scars that still bore witness on her body. The wound across her soul, which at times felt mortal.

Over the years, Myrtle had anticipated such a meeting. Rehearsed her speech. How she would make him pay for all that he had done to her. Pierce him with her barbed words. But as she looked at him now, the hulking frame diminished, the eyes full of sincerity, all the anger she'd counted on, the anger she'd planned and thought she wanted, it all fell away. As if she was shedding a skin – as if she were a giant, upright snake standing right there on the garden path. The old Myrtle slipped away from her and she felt lighter than she had done in years.

'Soup?' she said.

'What?'

'Would you like some soup?'

He frowned. 'All right, then.'

'This way.'

They moved through the crowds to the soup station.

'Joyce. Any left?'

'You're just in time. We're down to the last couple of bowls.'

'That's all we need.'

'Actually, I always think it's the best part myself. All the nice chunky bits sink to the bottom. Here you go.' She handed a bowl to Martin and another to Myrtle. 'I don't believe we've met.' She eyed Martin speculatively.

'Oh, how rude of me. Do let me introduce you. Joyce, this is my ex-husband – Martin Prendergast.'

Joyce's eyes popped and her mouth gaped. The ladle fell out of her hand and on to the ground. Everyone in the vicinity stopped what they were doing and stared. Mrs Prendergast clinked her soup bowl with Martin's. 'Cheers,' she said.

The rumour that Mrs Prendergast's husband had been resurrected and was at large in the garden spread like wildfire. But he was already gone before it was fully ignited. His ex-wife looked very smug. Aoife could tell she was enjoying herself.

'Well. You certainly shocked the Union today. You shocked me too.'

'Did I?'

'You know you did.'

'Oh, well. That's what you get when you listen to scurrilous rumours. Although I must admit I'm going to miss my status as the local black widow. Now I'm going to have to find some other way of frightening people off.'

'Where has he been all this time?'

'Spain mostly. Building collapsible apartments. That's where he went after I sent him packing.'

'And why did you send him packing?'

'Because he was a violent drunk.'

'Oh! I'm sorry.' Aoife was genuinely shocked. She'd never had Mrs Prendergast down as a battered wife. Really, the woman never failed to amaze. 'You seem quite friendly with him now. That *was* him, wasn't it? The tall, distinguished-looking man you were with?'

'Distinguished.' She laughed. 'I suppose he is. Yes. That was Martin.'

'You've forgiven him, then.'

She seemed to consider this for a while. 'It was a long time ago. He's gone through two other wives since me. He's had treatment. I don't think he drinks any more and I know he regrets what he did. So, yes, I suppose I have forgiven him. After all, if it wasn't for him, I wouldn't have Lance.'

'He looks so like him.'

'Yes, he does. And if it wasn't for Martin, I wouldn't be living in this house, with this garden. We wouldn't be having this day, with all the people enjoying themselves.' She smiled. 'In a sense, we have Martin to thank for all this. He was the start of it all.'

'That's one way of looking at it.'

'I've learned recently that it's the only way of looking at it. You know, I heard this saying and it's so true, that not forgiving someone is like drinking poison and expecting the other person to die. I've decided I don't want to drink poison any more.'

'So you forgive Pearl for using your toilet?'

'You must be joking. Come on, Harriet. You're getting far too excited.'

Aoife watched Mrs Prendergast as she retrieved her retriever. She felt she'd just caught a glimpse of the real woman. It only happened once in a while before the barriers went up again. But it was something worth waiting for. Something special.

49

The soup and bread had been devoured and all the cakes and produce sold. The band was unstoppable. Aoife, Seth, Uri, Emily and Mrs Prendergast came together for the first time that day. None of them could stop smiling. The Autumn Party had exceeded all of their expectations.

'Is it time for . . . ?'

'I think so. I'll go and get it.'

'Oh, hold on. We have one more thing to do first. Lance!'

'Yes?'

'Can you take the photograph now?'

'Sure.'

'Over by the apple tree?'

'Perfect.'

They collected Liam and Kathy on their way. Then the seven of them arranged themselves in front of the tree. Emily sat on the ground flanked by the children.

'You have to have Rose too.'

Emily's mother handed her the baby, who sat benignly on her mother's lap, still for perhaps the first time that day. Uri and Mrs Prendergast stood behind them to their left. Uri had his arm around her shoulders.

'Oh, we must have Harriet too. Harriet!'

Harriet settled noisily on Emily's feet, a few of the flowers that the children had twisted into her collar still there. Standing behind them to the right were Seth and Aoife, Seth standing directly behind Aoife, his arms wrapped tightly around her waist, his head resting against hers.

'Okay. Ready?' said Lance. 'Everybody say "vegetables".'

'Vegetables!'

He took a few shots, just to make sure.

'Right. I'll go straight to the chemist and get this printed. I see they have a new self-service machine.' He looked at his watch. 'I should just make it before they close.'

'Oh, Lance, get a newspaper while you're at it.'

Ever since they'd dug up the time capsule, Liam had been pleading with his mother to bury another. What better time? A crowd gathered around Seth as he dug the hole.

'Right. Who's going first?'

'Me, me!' Kathy danced on the spot.

'Okay. What have you got?'

'My Little Pony. I'm too big to play with her now so maybe some other little girl can play with her in the future.'

'Very good. How about you, Liam?'

'My yellow digger.'

'Are you sure?' said Aoife. 'It's one of your favourites.'

'I want to put it in.' Liam pursed his lips.

'Okay, then.'

'Emily?'

'My contribution is this Babygro belonging to Rose that she's grown out of. And my copy of *Beowulf*. I spent almost my entire first year of college reading this book and I never want to see the damn thing again. In fact, burying is probably too good for it but here you go anyway.'

'Thank you, Emily. While we're at it, I'm putting in this pair of secateurs. They were the first tool I bought when I set up my gardening business. I found them the other day when I was clearing out my shed. They're not much use for gardening any more, but I thought they might be ... symbolic or something.'

Those gathered around murmured their assent.

'Right. Who's next? Mrs P.'

'I've decided to put this back.' Mrs Prendergast handed Seth the blue and white ceramic angel that had been unearthed in the first time capsule. 'On the basis that it appears to work.'

'Okay. Aoife?'

Aoife took a deep breath and handed Seth a small ornate pillbox. 'This is a lock of my daughter Katie's hair.'

There were a few seconds in which no one said anything.

'Are you sure?' said Emily. 'It's a very precious thing to bury.'

'Don't worry. I have about a dozen locks of her hair at home. And I like the idea of someone finding a little piece of her in years to come.'

'Can I see?'

Aoife nodded and Seth handed Emily the box. She opened it and exclaimed at the sight of the red-gold curl, secured at one end by a tiny pink ribbon. 'What a beautiful colour. I bet she was gorgeous.'

'She was.'

'May I?' said Mrs Prendergast.

The box was handed around and Aoife felt proud and emotional as everyone admired her daughter's hair. Finally, the box was handed back to Seth. 'Dad, you're the only one left. What have you got for us?'

Uri handed Seth a small threadbare teddy bear.

'Dad, are you . . .'

Uri nodded. 'This bear belonged to my little sister Hannah. I found it in the wreckage of our home after the war. For years I kept it with me in the hope that I might be able to return it to her. Today I lay that hope to rest.'

It was a little while before Seth could speak. 'Thank you, Dad. Now if you could just hand me the newspaper and the photo, Lance. Thank you. I think we're just about done.'

Seth packed all the objects neatly into the box and closed the lid. Then he placed it reverently in the earth and covered it with soil.

Liam burst into noisy sobs.

'What is it?'

'My yellow digger.'

'Hold on, Seth.'

The box was exhumed and the digger resurrected. Liam replaced the digger with a lesser Dinky car he had in his pocket. Then the time capsule was reburied once and for all.

Now it was time for the procession.

Uri was Master of Ceremonies. He narrated the movement of the children as they progressed in an undulating line from the gate to the *sukkoh*.

'These are the children of St Mary's. We're very grateful for all their help with the Autumn Party. You will see that some of them are carrying lanterns. They have made these themselves.' The lanterns were jam jars of various shapes and sizes, with little bits of coloured tissue paper stuck on each in an *ad hoc* fashion. Every lantern housed a night light, which glowed colourfully in the gathering twilight.

'The other children are holding an *etrog* fruit in one hand.' These looked like large lemons. Uri had been carefully cultivating them in the far reaches of the garden. Now Aoife knew why. 'In their other hands, the children are holding bunches of leaves known as *lulav*. These are made up of palm, for uprightness, willow, for humility, and myrtle, for faithfulness. Together they symbolize brotherhood and peace. This procession is part of the tradition of the Jewish harvest festival. It serves as a reminder of the beauty of life. Speaking of beauty, the girl wearing the crown is my granddaughter Kathy. This is known in Germany as the

353

"harvest crown" or "*Erntekrone*". It's made of ears of grain, flowers and fruit.'

One by one, the children reached the *sukkoh*. Those with *lulav* placed it on the roof. Those with lanterns hung them from the eaves. Kathy kept her crown on. This might or might not have been part of the plan but, from the expression on her face, it would have to be prised off her.

There was silence while the children returned to their places in the crowd, alongside friends and parents.

'Now we have a presentation to make,' said Uri.

This was news to Aoife. She wondered what it could be.

The crowds parted to allow through Seth and Lance. Between them, they carried a bench. It was clearly homemade, rustic-looking. The seat was a log sawn in half – a large one at that. The remainder was constructed of branches bound together with split roots. On it there was a metal plaque with writing. Aoife couldn't make it out from where she was standing.

'Aoife? Where's Aoife? Can you come up here, please?'

Aoife stiffened. Those around her pushed her gently forward. As she entered the clearing, everyone started to clap. How mortifying. She stood beside Uri and he put his arm around her shoulders and turned her to face everyone.

'You're looking here at the woman who made this possible. This garden. This wonderful day. Through her vision. Her hard work. Her bossiness.'

There was an appreciative laugh from the audience.

'For this, my dear Aoife, we thank you from the bottom of our hearts. And, as a token of our appreciation, we hereby present you with this bench – to be located at a site of your choosing.'

Everyone clapped again.

'It was made by Seth,' continued Uri, 'so it really is a labour

354

of love.' He squeezed her shoulder. 'Could you read out the inscription, please, Aoife?'

She cleared her throat: '"For those we have loved and lost, that they might linger here". It's beautiful,' she said. 'Thank you all so much.' She nodded at everyone, not trusting herself to say more.

'The idea,' said Uri, 'is that we all have a special place to go to think about our loved ones who are no longer with us. Now.' He gave her shoulder another squeeze. 'Where do you want it?'

She pointed. 'Over there beside the pond.'

'Gentlemen?'

Lance and Seth carried the bench to the designated spot and Aoife was released – whereupon she ducked back into the crowd and hid herself as best she could.

But Uri hadn't finished. 'If I might have your attention for a few more moments.' He bowed his head and was quiet for so long that people began to glance at one another and fidget. Then he lifted his face and spoke. 'My friends. This day fills me with great joy. It is the culmination of nine months of hard labour. You could say that today signifies the birth of this garden. This creation. Because, really, she is still only in her infancy. She has many years of growth yet to come. And it is up to us to make sure she fulfils her potential. This generation. And generations to come. May we cherish and sustain her, just as she sustains us.' He bowed his head again, for some time. People weren't sure if he had finished or not. An uncertain round of applause broke out, then died rapidly as his voice rang out again.

'Gardens have always been an important part of my life. This comes from my father and his father before him and who knows how many generations back? Men – and women – who worked the land and participated in her bounty. And now when I see my son working, he's so like my own father that it hurts me,' he put his hand up to his heart, 'here. How proud he would have been. And of Kathy. Working on her own little flowerbed.' Uri smiled, on the verge of tears. 'What I'm trying to say is that gardens, nature, this garden have given me so much. They probably saved my life. My prayer is that you allow ours to save yours too.'

He walked away, so that everyone knew this time that he'd finished. The crowd clapped once more then merged in upon itself.

After that a lot of people went home, but many stayed on – reluctant to let go of such a magical day.

Seth found Uri sitting quietly on the bench. 'Do you mind?'

'Not at all.'

'Nice speech.'

'Thank you.'

There were a few moments' silence.

'Are you okay?'

'Never better. In fact, there was something I wanted to ask you.'

'What is it?'

'Would you come to Germany with me? You and your brother?'

This wasn't what Seth had been expecting.

'Well – yes. Of course I will. And Aaron too, I'm sure. But what brought this on? You've never wanted to go back before.'

'I know. Perhaps you'll understand when you get to my age. The need to say goodbye.'

'Don't talk like that, Dad. You've got years in you yet.'

'Maybe so. But who knows? I'd like to show you and

Aaron where I grew up. The river I used to fish and swim in. Perhaps visit my grandparents' house down south.'

'I'd love that.'

'And I'd like to visit the camps. The one where your grandfather was shot. And the one where your grandmother and aunt were murdered.'

'I didn't think you'd found that out for sure.'

'It's the only possible explanation. There's no record of them. They must have been brought straight to the gas chambers the day we arrived. Those people weren't registered.'

Seth nodded and didn't say anything.

'If you think it's too morbid, you don't have to come.'

'No. Not at all. It's important to you. To all of us. So I can show Kathy when she's older.'

'Yes.'

They were quiet for a while.

'You never know,' said Uri, 'we might find some long-lost relatives. I couldn't trace any of them after the war, but so many were displaced at the time. It's worth looking into, I think.'

'It's a great idea. I'll start researching flights tomorrow.'

'Thank you, Seth. Now I'd like to sample some of your poteen.'

'Only if I can have a glass of your elderberry wine.'

'Deal.'

The alcohol was produced. Under its influence, the playing of the band took on a new, more frenzied dimension. And with most of the children gone home for tea, the adults began to dance, heavily improvised versions of 'The Siege of Ennis' and 'The Walls of Limerick'. Then a young man crossed two brooms on the ground and danced gloriously around them, his hands hanging loose at his sides, his thigh muscles admired collectively by all the women present. A very old man got two kitchen chairs and held on to the backs of them, one on his left and one on his right. Between them, he performed the best jig anyone had ever seen. It even inspired Aoife to take out her tin whistle and tootle for a while.

Many songs were sung that night. Emigrant songs by people who had never left the oul' sod in the first place. Rebel songs by those without a rebellious bone in their bodies. Love songs.

'This was a brilliant idea,' said Emily. 'We should have a party to celebrate the change of every season.'

'You can organize it next time,' said Aoife.

'We could do the winter solstice. And May Day – we could have a maypole!'

'Where are you going to get the morris dancers?'

'We could do it.'

'They're meant to be men.'

'We could be the Morrisettes!'

'Hey, Mrs P, tell me something,' said Seth.

'For pity's sake, will you stop calling me that. Call me Myrtle if you must. Anything's better than Mrs P.'

'Myrtle! If you didn't murder your husband and bury him in the garden, how come you never let us dig in that little patch at the back?'

'Because – you fool – Harriet's mother is buried there.'

'Thanks, Myrtle. That's all I wanted to know.'

The party went on until the early hours. None of the neighbours complained – because all of them were there.

Afterword

Liam sleeps in his own bed now.

I sleep with Seth, the contours of his body following my own. Of course, every now and then, Liam has a bad dream and comes in to us. As does Kathy. On those occasions, we adults hang off the respective edges of our bed, childish knees and elbows digging into our spines.

Just like that, my family has doubled. At first it made me uneasy. I felt I didn't deserve it, this miraculous second chance. But over time I learned to be grateful. And it is this gratitude that has blossomed and transformed my life.

Acknowledgements

I have many people to thank:

My editor at Penguin, Patricia Deevy. Thank you for taking me on in the first place. I've enjoyed your insights, your direct approach, your love of words and your unstinting dedication to all things grammatical.

Much gratitude also goes to Michael McLoughlin, Brian Walker, Cliona Lewis and Patricia McVeigh at Penguin Ireland. And to all the people, Penguins and otherwise, whom I have yet to meet, who will contribute to this book. Particularly Keith Taylor and Ellie Smith in the London office.

My agent Faith O'Grady. I have many things for which to thank you. First, your role in helping me to conceive of the idea for the book in the first place, and for the pep talk that spurred me into writing it. If it wasn't for you, the walled garden would have been a scruffy corner plot and the deli would have been a dingy corner shop. And thanks for getting me this book deal.

Hazel Orme. Copy-editor extraordinaire. Your attention to detail is astounding.

Many moons ago, Lenny Abrahamson was kind enough to meet up with me and share valuable insight into what it means to grow up Jewish in Dublin. At last, I was able to put that knowledge to good use. Thank you.

Heartfelt thanks to Emma Delahunt, for filling me in on what 'the young people' wear, drink, smoke and do nowadays. Emos and Dubes. Who knew?

I am also very grateful to Emer O'Carroll, who, a long time ago, gave me valuable information about the nature of adoption in Ireland.

And thank you very much Eithne Hegarty BL for your expert legal advice.

To John and Dorothy Allen, who set me straight on Eucharistic ministers, to Neal McCormack, who told me about Tin Pan Alley, to Kay in Thomastown Library, who sourced the books on the 1950s, to the people in the Lisa Richards Agency who came up with a suitable book for Emily to read, and to the motley crew who racked their brains to help me come up with a title for this book – I thank you one and all.

To those family members, friends and neighbours who make up my inner circle, thank you for being in my world. I'd particularly like to thank both of my parents for sharing their stories about growing up in Ireland in the 1950s.

To Leo and Marianne, I love you both, you little squirts.

And to Rory, my first reader and editor. Thank you for your enthusiasm, encouragement and patience.

Finally, I would like to pay tribute to three beautiful gardens, all of which inspired me: the walled garden at Woodstock, Inistiogue, the Water Garden in Thomastown and the walled garden at Mount Juliet, Thomastown, all in South County Kilkenny. To those of you who designed, planted and care for them, I thank you all. Especially Paddy Daly of Mount Juliet.

He just wanted a decent book to read ...

Not too much to ask, is it? It was in 1935 when Allen Lane, Managing Director of Bodley Head Publishers, stood on a platform at Exeter railway station looking for something good to read on his journey back to London. His choice was limited to popular magazines and poor-quality paperbacks – the same choice faced every day by the vast majority of readers, few of whom could afford hardbacks. Lane's disappointment and subsequent anger at the range of books generally available led him to found a company – and change the world.

'We believed in the existence in this country of a vast reading public for intelligent books at a low price, and staked everything on it'
Sir Allen Lane, 1902–1970, founder of Penguin Books

The quality paperback had arrived – and not just in bookshops. Lane was adamant that his Penguins should appear in chain stores and tobacconists, and should cost no more than a packet of cigarettes.

Reading habits (and cigarette prices) have changed since 1935, but Penguin still believes in publishing the best books for everybody to enjoy. We still believe that good design costs no more than bad design, and we still believe that quality books published passionately and responsibly make the world a better place.

So wherever you see the little bird – whether it's on a piece of prize-winning literary fiction or a celebrity autobiography, political tour de force or historical masterpiece, a serial-killer thriller, reference book, world classic or a piece of pure escapism – you can bet that it represents the very best that the genre has to offer.

Whatever you like to read – trust Penguin.